"Reading *Ernie's Bleachers* is like time-traveling back to 1940s Chicago and becoming the precocious protagonist in a compelling coming-of-age story that's full of heart, hope, fear and wonder. It's well worth the trip."

— Steve Parolini, author of *Stolen Things*

"A deep dive into an era, a storied neighborhood, and events that deserve a second look. *Ernie's Bleachers* bleeds with atmosphere. It takes the nation's pulse during a seminal moment in the history of baseball and all of sports, with the shadowy beginnings of the Chicago Outfit, the brutal politics of Chicago, and the final chapter of World War Two as its backdrop. This story of an Italian-American family trying to make it in the City of Big Shoulders during a dangerous time has it all."

— Michael Just, author of *The Dirt*

"Reading this book brought me down memory lane when life was simple. There was no TV or air conditioning. The neighbors were friendly, and everybody knew everybody. We lived so close to Wrigley Field we knew when the Cubs hit a home run or when they lost."

— Florence (Pareti) DeBellis

ERNIE'S BLEACHERS

Tim Pareti

Ernie's Bleachers

ISBNs:
979-8-218-00301-2 (paperback)
979-8-218-00302-9 (eBook)

Erniesbleachers.com

Baseball? It's just a game as simple as a ball and a bat, yet as complex as the American spirit it symbolizes.

—Ernie Harwell

PROLOGUE

A late autumn wind swept away smoke trailing from a Lucky Strike cigarette that dangled on the lips of Eddy Pareti. He had dropped off his mother, brother, and sister in front of Murphy's Bleachers, and parked his brother's Cadillac in a lot across from the tavern where the Sinclair gas station had once been. He and neighborhood kids threw snowballs at its green dinosaur logo so many years ago.

Eddy couldn't smoke in the tavern, so he stood outside and shivered in the cold. There was a time a guy could smoke anywhere except in a church or at school. He hunched his shoulders and took another drag and exhaled. It had been years since he'd been back to the old neighborhood. He had once known every nook and cranny, every shortcut through the gangways and alleys where he and his friends would play kick the can with an old Hills Brother's coffee can or hit a sixteen-inch softball in a game of line out until dark. He could feel the rattle in his bones every time an El train would rumble blocks away like distant thunder.

His eyes shifted to the tavern that his father had built. It was once a place where everyone from mobsters to cops, from bookies to ball players, from politicians to war widows, rubbed elbows. Bets were wagered, and World War II was won. Suitors proposed. Gals wrote Dear John letters with gauzy tears at the back booth. Lifelong friendships were forged. Gin filled the emptiness of sons and husbands lost at Anzio or Guadalcanal. Eddy had seen it all as a kid, the pain and happiness like the sweet sting of a Negroni cocktail.

Those were different times.

He walked around to the side of the tavern with the spryness of a manager popping out from the dugout to argue a call at home plate. At seventy, Eddy spent most of his time on the golf course. He was scratch golfer, and earned walk-around money on bets against well-heeled Floridians who acted as if they played on the Senior Tour.

He glanced around. It was the middle of the day on a Saturday and not a kid in sight. They were probably inside pecking away on their computers, he thought.

Eddy shook his head and puffed on his smoldering square. He blew a smoke ring as he studied the bleacher's entrance of Wrigley Field across the street. A skinny kid could probably squeeze through that gate like he had done a thousand times. He squinted up at the back of the Cubs scoreboard that loomed behind center field, and above the intersection of Waveland and Sheffield. He smiled. At least, that was still the same after all these years. And so are the Cubs, in the cellar of the National League again.

The last time the Cubs made it to the October classic was the year he thought he was ready to take on the world.

TOP OF THE FIRST

Eddy Pareti sat on his bed with a baseball bat resting on his lap. He tossed a rubber ball in the air and caught it with his right hand. He kept an eye on the rusty El track a few feet from his window, waiting for the train to make his escape.

The radio blared from the front room on the other side of the third-floor flat. It was a Zenith Stratosphere, a fifty-inch-tall console with three speakers. *If the Wrigley Field loudspeakers ever broke the Stratosphere would be a good replacement*, Eddy thought.

The radio announcer, Arthur Godfrey, soaked the apartment with his smooth and avuncular voice that seeped through the plastered walls and closed oak door of Eddy's bedroom.

"Between the innocence of boyhood and the dignity of manhood, we find a delightful creature called a boy. Boys come in assorted sizes, weights, and colors, but all boys have the same creed: to enjoy every second of every minute of every hour of every day and to protest with noise..."

"Ernie, turn down that radio! We're not hard of hearing—you are," yelled Eddy's mother, Margaret. Her shrill voice sounded to Eddy like a cat screaming in the throes of death.

"Leave me alone, Marge. Let me read my paper in peace."

"It's too loud, Ernie. I can't hear myself think."

"Mothers love them, little girls ignore them, older sisters and brothers tolerate them, adults ignore them and heaven protects them. A boy is truth with dirt on his face..."

High heels clicked across the hardwood floor, charging down the long hallway. The rushed rhythm of the steps echoed with the urgency of a prison guard.

The radio's volume lowered. "Ernie! It's early in the morning. Eddy is still sleeping. The neighbors can hear it."

A newspaper rustled, and muffled feet thumped on a thick rug.

"Son of a pup! Marge, don't touch the radio."

Godfrey's voice blasted the flat again.

The volume lowered, and a few seconds later, it rose to earsplitting decibels.

"Oh, for Pete's sake, Ernie, I can't take this anymore. I'm leaving you."

"He is not much for Sunday school, company, school, books without pictures, music lessons, neckties, barbers, girls, overcoats, adults, or bedtime..."

"Did you hear me, Ernie? I'm leaving you and taking the kids with me. I know you can hear me."

"Go ahead, Marge. Maybe I can get some peace and quiet around here for once."

"A boy is a magical creature. You can lock him out of your kitchen, but you can't lock him out of your heart. You can get him out of your study but not out of your mind..."

"You are impossible!" Margaret screamed.

Heavy footsteps stomped to the front door; its hinges groaned as it opened. The door slammed so hard it sounded like a car had backfired in the front room. The walls shook and dishes clattered in the cupboard.

"When you come home at night with only the shattered pieces of your hopes and dreams, he can mend them all like new with the two magic words: 'Hi, Dad.'"

Eddy lobbed the ball in the air again. He caught it and cocked his head sideways to listen. A grinding rumble like pealing thunder grew louder as if a storm were speeding closer. The windows rattled and trophies vibrated on his dresser.

Eddy jumped off his bed and stepped over clothes that had been flung on the floor. He shoved the ball in his pocket, positioned the bat handle under his right arm, and cracked open his bedroom door. He peeked down the hallway. The coast was clear. He stepped into the kitchen like a runner creeping off first base and tiptoed across the linoleum floor. Godfrey had ended his monologue. Swing music boomed out of the Stratosphere and pulsated against the walls of the flat.

Eddy opened the back door and flew down the porch, two steps at a time, each step echoing in the cramped stairway. He held the bat close to his body, making sure it didn't clang against the wall or stairs. The bat was a Rogers Hornsby Louisville Slugger, a gift from his parents last year on his twelfth birthday.

The train roared past, giving Eddy cover for his escape. Living across from the El had its advantages; his parents couldn't hear him sneak out of the house, especially his dad, whose hearing was so poor he couldn't hear the crack of a home run ball if he was standing behind home plate. The Stratosphere helped too.

He'd be in trouble for sneaking out, but all he could see was the light at the bottom of the stairs, and it was pulling him toward it.

He charged out of the stairway and into the chilly April morning air that smelled of soot and car fumes. A damp Lake Michigan breeze blew through his jet-black hair, cowlicks sprouting in every direction like wild weeds. He raced through the parking lot, gravel and glass crunching under his gym shoes, and stopped at the end of the alley on Waveland Avenue.

Cigarette butts, paper cups, and hot dog wrappers littered the street. A trail of glass shards that looked like sparkling flakes of ice were scattered across the sidewalk. Someone had busted a beer bottle; the jagged edges of its neck took the shape of a knife.

Eddy drew cold air into his warm lungs and exhaled. Breath vapors swirled in odd shapes, disappearing into the battleship gray sky, the same color of back porches in his neighborhood.

Two men in navy uniforms wobbled past as if they were walking on a swaying boat deck. They didn't notice Eddy, his fingers fumbling around in his jacket.

Eddy pulled out matches and a pack of Lucky Strike cigarettes he'd stolen from his dad's tavern, Ernie's Bleachers. He clinched the bat between his knees, hunched his shoulders, and lit a match. He cupped his hands around the flame and held it to the cigarette, sucking life into it. The tip flared an orange ember. He shook the match and flicked it in the street.

A stream of smoke escaped Eddy's mouth and curled into the air. His eyes locked on the navy men who were stumbling away. Were they fighting the Japs or the Nazis? His head swiveled the other direction. He squinted as he took a slow puff at his cigarette and studied the bleacher's entrance of Wrigley Field, a wild pitch away from his Greystone three-flat and his family's tavern.

He exhaled and gazed up at the scoreboard, a monumental shrine plopped down into the middle of his neighborhood, soaring above all other buildings. Its rectangular sign read, Chicago Cubs, in white letters emblazoned on a navy-blue pennant inside a lead gray background. He wondered why the letters of Cubs were capitalized. Sister Mary Edmunds would rap his knuckles with a ruler if he capitalized every letter in a sentence. He knew to capitalize names and places and the first word in a sentence even though he was the worst reader in class and failed most spelling tests. In fourth grade, Sister Lucy Roberts read aloud in class a letter he wrote about his dog, Fuzzy. The nun noted how Eddy wrote *bog* instead of dog. He was embarrassed.

He had lived across the bleacher's entrance all his life and never gave the Cubs sign any thought. *Ya gotta lot to learn, kid*, he could hear his dad's booming voice lecture him about life after he finished yelling at Eddy about his backward spelling.

Eddy puffed away on his cigarette. His body shifted from foot to foot, and his brown eyes darted around like a gambler searching for some action.

His eyes landed on his dad's tavern. It was opening day. Within hours, thirsty and hungry fans would pack inside Ernie's Bleachers ordering hamburgers, hot dogs, French fries. And it was Eddy's job to cook the food. Maybe that's all he'd ever be good for, armpit jobs, he thought. He knew he'd never make it to college like his older brother and sister would. Bobby and Florence were in high school earning straight A's and endless praise from his parents, relatives, neighbors and teachers.

Should he go inside and work? What's the worst thing his parents would do if he skipped out on opening day? Yell at him? Big deal. He was used to it. Take away his allowance? He didn't need it. He had other ways of making money. His parents worked the tavern on busy days without his help. *They can do it today*, a voice in his head said. *You can't let your friends down. They're waitin' on you.*

A gray catbird meowed in a sugar maple tree next to Eddy. He glanced up expecting to see a cat but instead a songbird hopped and sidled on a branch, mewing like a cat. *It must be one of those birds that migrate north in the summer except this one came early*, Eddy thought. The bird flicked its rusty-colored wings and meowed once more. It launched into the air, its wings to its side, and, like a bullet, flew over the right field wall and dive-bombed into Wrigley Field.

Eddy took another drag but didn't inhale. His mouth formed an *O*, and with a slight cough, he tried to blow a smoke ring. What came out was a wavy wisp of smoke in the shape of a half circle. The smoke expanded, rose, and vanished into a formless cloud, swept away by the cold wind. It was an improvement.

Across the street, the train closed its doors at the Addison stop and screeched northward, snaking its way between buildings of brick, concrete, stone, steel, and glass. A car horn beeped, startling Eddy. He spun around and ran east on Waveland, cigarette dangling from the corner of his mouth.

Eddy ran everywhere. He ran to the corner store, to the newspaper stand, to his friends' house, to Cubs Park, and to his uncle's gas station that wasn't a gas station but a hangout to scalp tickets and gamble. His pace was that of a home run trot around the bases, cocky, confident, and purposeful.

As he passed under the El tracks, a black blur scurried across the sidewalk in front of him. Eddy jumped back, his eyes sweeping the shadows under the El, searching for the rodent.

Flecks of faint light filtered through the gaps in the tracks, splashing dull rectangular specks below. Shade from the El blanketed the alley and backyards of brick bungalows that soon would be packed with parked cars. Rusted rows of rivets raced up steel girders that shed flakes of peeling white paint. Corroded trash barrels and pigeon droppings dotted the gritty landscape.

Life under the El was a creepy dark underworld, a rough and rugged region where sidewalk people didn't go. A no-man's-land where men fought for dibs to park cars, drunk Cub fans pissed behind steel beams, or bums dug through trash looking for God knew what. It was also a refuge for rats. Lots of them.

There it was. A rat the size of a small cat, sniffing around a trash barrel. Its scaly tail stretching the length of a foot-long hot dog. It was the biggest rat he'd ever seen, and he'd seen plenty of rats, especially when taking out the garbage. It was a chore he hated most and couldn't wiggle out of it no matter how hard he begged his parents. He'd kick the trash can and with a stick lift the lid. Rats would screech and scratch at the bottom of the can. But sometimes there were so many packed inside that dozens would jump out two feet in the air and scurry in every direction like gamblers scrambling out of a house during a police raid. They'd let out a high-pitched squeak—*skreek, skreek*—as they climbed up the brick wall of his apartment, claws scraping on mortar. Some would fall and whizz past his feet. His brother, Bobby, said their teeth never stop growing, and they could chew through metal, concrete, and brick. They could even swim through sewer pipes and pop up in the toilet.

Eddy picked up a rock the size of a baseball and whipped it at the rat. The rock ricocheted off the trash can with a ping. The rat scampered under a rotted wooden fence and escaped into the backyard of a bookie joint.

Eddy went on his way, crossing Wilton Street without breaking stride. He waved to the owner of the corner store who was sweeping the front stoop. "Hi, Mr. Giampietro."

"Hey, Eddy, what's the hurry? Who ya runnin' from?"

"Gotta hot date," Eddy said as he sprinted by.

"Oh, is she Italian?"

"No, she's an impasta," Eddy shouted in jest.

Three blocks later, Eddy spotted his friends playing fast-pitch at the LeMoyne schoolyard. He strutted to them at a fast clip with a bounce in his step.

"What's buzzin', cousin?" Phil Gerace hollered as he lowered his bat and leaned on it. Wind twisted his moppy hair into tangles as he snorted with fake derision. "Skipped out on the old man? Ain't you got balls."

Gerace's eyes bugged out as if his fingers were stuck in an electric socket. He was a Catholic boy, and a paisano like Eddy. They were the same height, but Eddy was stronger and more athletic. With the exception of his bulging eyes, he and Eddy could pass as twins.

Eddy dropped his cigarette butt and stomped it out with the toe of his shoe. He yanked the rubber ball from his pocket and tossed it in the air. "Speaking of balls, who's gonna bat against me?"

"I'm pitching today," Hootie Hale said, his upper lip curled. He wore a gray sleeveless sweatshirt and concrete-colored corduroys. Veins bulged in his muscular arms as he held out his right hand and squeezed a dirty rubber ball.

The kids in the neighborhood didn't razz Hootie. Though usually friendly, he also had a temper. Rub him the wrong way and he was ready for a fight. But Eddy was tough too, and out of mutual fear and respect, the two never came to blows.

"Hootie's on fire today. Nobody can hit him," Gerace said, his arm wrapped around the muscle-bound hothead. "The ace is strikin' everybody out."

"Eddy can hit him," said Chuckie Warman. "Right, Eddy?"

Thick tangled blond curls flopped over Warman's jutting forehead that hid obsidian eyes the size of pebbles. He was eleven years old, the youngest in the group, but he was as big as most kids in high school. His flabby thighs were the size of tree trunks, and when he moved, his belly jiggled. Some of the older kids in the neighborhood called him Baby Huey, but not his friends.

"That's right. Nobody's gonna strike *me* out," said Eddy. A spirited and confident smile spread across his face.

Warman plonked his mitt-sized paws on Eddy's shoulder. "My money's on Eddy."

Hootie grinned. "Pareti, I'll bet you a nickel that I'll fan you in three pitches with *my* ball."

Eddy exhaled with a pfft sound. He snatched the bat out of Gerace's hands and sauntered to a two-by-three-foot square carved in chalk on the brick school building. He twirled the bat with his right hand like a baton and then swung it around his back to his left hand, striking the handle of the bat on the ground. He let go at the same time. The bat popped up in the air. Eddy caught it with his forefinger, balanced it for several seconds and flung it straight up. He snagged the bat on the way down, gripping the handle. In one motion, Eddy swung the bat, let it go, and grabbed the handle with both hands after it made one rotation as if he were swinging through. "Let's raise that bet to a dime."

Hootie turned in the direction of Gerace and Warman behind him and sneered. "Hey, guys, siddown. This hot dog ain't gonna hit nothin' but cold air."

Hootie bent forward, his right hand behind his back, rotating the ball with his fingers. "This one's coming straight for your head."

He reared back as if he was going to throw the hardest pitch he could, but he lobbed it with a high arc. Eddy stepped into the pitch, figuring it would come in fast. The lob threw him off balance, and he didn't swing. The ball landed in the middle of the square for strike one.

"He threw an Eephus pitch!" Gerace screamed, his head bent back in laughter.

"What's an Eephus pitch?" Warman said.

"It's like a softball toss, but he throws it overhand," Gerace said. "Rip Sewell of the Pirates throws it."

Eddy twirled his bat. "What are we playing here, softball?" he cried out. "You throw like a broad."

"That's funny. You can't hit a broad's pitch. You're not even good enough to be the batboy for the Rockford Rowdies," Hootie answered with a gritted smile.

On the next pitch, Eddy whiffed on a curve that hit the lower right corner of the square.

"One more strike, Pareti, and you owe me a dime," Hootie said. "Hey, Chuckie, you said your money's on Eddy so ya wanna bet me a nickel he strikes out? I'll give you five-to-one odds."

Warman shifted side to side. He didn't have a nickel, but the odds were tempting.

"It's a sure bet, Chuckie," Eddy said. "I've got his number."

Warman shook his head.

"Smart kid," Hootie snickered.

Eddy crowded the square that was home plate. He took practice swings. The playfulness left his face.

Hootie, his jaws clenched on his wide face, wound up, and with a high leg kick, fired a fastball. Eddy swung and fouled the ball against the wall. He dropped his bat, which hit the pavement with a clank, and held out his hand. "Pay up, Hootie."

Hootie crossed his arms. "No. You didn't win the bet."

"You said you'd strike me out in three pitches, and you didn't."

"A foul ball's a strike, and I got three strikes on you."

"But you didn't strike me out."

The two stood face-to-face, staring at each other.

— — —

Ernie Pareti bent down, his knees locked, and lifted a case of Fox Deluxe beer, his thick arms hugging the cardboard box. He lugged it from the back door of his tavern to a small passageway under the bar counter he called "the cubbyhole." He adjusted his grip, ducked under the counter, and stepped down into the basement of his three-flat like a ball player walking into the dugout for the millionth time. He set the case down on the basement floor and climbed back up, lowering his head as he entered his tavern.

Ernie's Bleachers was a one-story brick building shaped like a cigar box that didn't have a basement. Ernie had saved enough money from a hot dog stand he operated on the same lot to build the tavern in 1940. But he came up short during construction and had to cut corners.

He used his connections as the neighborhood precinct captain to bypass building inspectors and canopied the tavern against the family's three-flat. He cut a hole on the north wall of the three-flat basement, connecting it to the tavern. He paid the alderman a pretty penny under the table to do it, and no one ever complained.

Ernie mopped his brow and ran his hand across his bald head. His underarms dripped with sweat, soaking his white short-sleeved shirt. He removed his owlish black-framed glasses from his fleshy nose and cleaned them using the ends of his untucked shirt. His round brown eyes glanced around the tavern, the ends of his mouth pointing north.

There was no sign of Eddy. Bobby was working the grill next to the customer window.

"Where's your brother?" Ernie shouted.

Bobby sliced open a hot dog bun and, without looking up, said, "He's probably at the schoolyard."

Ernie banged his fist on the bar, and the ends of his mouth sank. "Son of a pup! We need him."

Ernie expected a huge crowd. The war in Germany was ending, and a big influx of thirsty soldiers were flooding back to the States, their pockets loaded with money. The government had eased ration restrictions on food and other goods, and people were eager to splurge. After surveying workers at nearby war plants, the Cubs front office had decided to change the game time to 1:30 p.m. from 3:30 p.m. A 1:30 p.m. game time fit the night shift plant worker's schedules.

Ernie had to prepare for a rush that was coming earlier than usual. It had been a long winter with steady business, but Ernie's Bleachers was going to get a whole lot busier, starting about noon.

"Go get him, Bobby. He's not getting out of this," Ernie said.

A portly man, sitting on a stool at the bar, cleared his throat and interrupted. "Go easy on the boy."

Ernie flashed a smile. "There's a time to have fun and a time to work, Walter. Today, it's time to work."

Walter was a regular and Ernie's self-described bodyguard. If there was a fight or an unruly drunk, Walter would handle the problem. His thick bushy eyebrows sprouted around a small pair of round-rimmed wire glasses that hung on his pig-nosed snout, stuffed with thickets of hair. The corners of his wide mouth sank as if he were a sad clown. He seemed more hideous than intimidating.

"Come on, he's just a kid," said Walter, half pleading, half kidding. "Let him have some fun."

The man sitting next to Walter spoke up. "I don't mean to butt in, Ern, but I agree with Walter. Eddy's a good kid. Let him be."

Ernie gripped the edge of the bar, the smile still on his face. "Let him be? Sailor, he's been goofing off too long."

"Aw, come on. They grow up fast, and before you know it, they're out of the house and you start missing them real bad," said Sailor, another regular.

Everyone called him Sailor because he owned a sailboat at Belmont Harbor, and his son was in the navy. He wore a wine-colored long-sleeved shirt, a dark-blue tie, a V-neck gray vest, navy pants, and a wool tweed sports coat with two flap pockets large enough to hold his tobacco pipe. His laced two-toned Oxford shoes gleamed in the tavern's dim light, and the tip of his brown fedora tilted down over the bridge of his arched nose, shaped like an eagle's beak. From head to toe, he was dressed like a professor at a preppy boarding school. But he worked the night shift as an assemblyman for Signode, a factory that manufactured electrical equipment. After the Japs attacked Pearl Harbor, Sailor had quit his well-paying job as an insurance salesman and landed the factory job. He told everyone it was done out of patriotic duty.

Ernie leaned on the bar and asked in a hushed tone, "How's your boy?"

"He's doing good. Wrote me a letter last week. Still in the Pacific fightin' the Japs but hasn't seen any action," Sailor said.

"You tell him, when he gets back, I'll pull some strings and get him a good job with the city."

"Thanks, Ern, but last time I sent someone to you, you whacked their head with a shoe."

"He was one inch too short to qualify for the fire department. Remember? So, I gave him a one-inch bump on his head. He got in, didn't he?"

"I guess. My son is six feet, so I don't think height requirements are gonna be a problem," Sailor said.

Ernie turned to Bobby. "Why are you still here? Get your brother. Now!"

"Dad, ya know he's gonna fight me on the way back. He always does. So, don't blame me if he comes back with a black eye."

"Just go get him." Ernie shooed his older son away.

Eddy never came back easily. Although Bobby was almost three years older and about a half foot taller, Eddy was more muscular. He was big enough to take on Bobby, and he could blow a fuse if someone told him what to do. Bobby whistled for Boots, a neighborhood dog that slept in the tavern at night, and strolled down Waveland.

He passed the corner store and stopped. Giampietro was sweeping the front stoop.

"Hi, Mr. Giampietro. You didn't happen to see Eddy, did ya?"

Giampietro laughed, pointing east. "He ran that way. What did he do this time, Bobby?"

"He snuck out again."

Giampietro smiled and shook his head. "Whaddya gonna do? Huh?"

"What can ya do with Eddy? He's gotta always do things his way. Never listens. See ya around," Bobby said, waving.

Eddy and Hootie stood nose to nose in a shoving match when Bobby arrived. He jumped in between the two and pushed them away from each other.

"Break it up, you two. Eddy, we have work to do."

Eddy ignored his brother. "Tell ya what, Hootie. Let's call the bet a wash and go again."

Before Hootie could answer, Bobby said, "Do you want the old man to come get you?"

Eddy picked up his bat and shuffled across the concrete lot as if he were going to lead the way home. He didn't want to walk next to his brother. Eddy stopped and wheeled around. "Hey, guys, come by later, and I'll get ya free hot dogs and pop."

Eddy knew a full day of work was ahead of him. He had to help prep the bar for the rush, park cars, and finish his paper route. Maybe he could find a way to get out of it all.

Bobby trailed Eddy out of the schoolyard. They walked west on Waveland with Eddy about two paces ahead. Neither said a word until they passed an apartment building on Fontana.

"Did I tell ya, Eddy, I made a killin' in this building selling war bonds? A bunch of factory workers live there, and they have kids in the war," Bobby said, ending his words with a sucking sound.

"Why do ya gotta do that?" Eddy said in a gruff tone. He stopped walking.

"Do what?" Bobby said, his arms outstretched, feigning confusion.

"That noise you always make after you say something. It's annoying."

"Why did you stop? Keep walkin'."

"No." Eddy's eyes widened, and he dashed around Bobby in the direction of the schoolyard.

Bobby lunged and grabbed Eddy's collar. "You ain't going nowhere."

Eddy dropped his bat as he was dragged backward. His arms flailing and body twisting, he tried to unhook Bobby's grip. "Get off of me," Eddy shouted. Boots circled and barked.

"You're coming with me whether you like it or not."

Eddy fell and ended his resistance. Bobby let go. "Get up and walk with me. No more funny business."

"Okay. Don't touch me."

Eddy grabbed his bat and slow-walked into the tavern with Bobby behind him, ready in case his little brother made another break for it. Idle chatter washed over the bar like the lazy murmur of a crowd during a lull in a ball game.

Margaret stopped slicing bread when she spotted Eddy. Her mercurial hazel eyes set wide apart on her thin face burned behind small, round, wire-rimmed glasses set tightly on her button nose. Strands of black hair hung down her narrow cheeks, and her lips twisted in a fit of anger.

"You're something else, kiddo," Margaret shrieked, her voice ringing over the bar chatter. It amazed Eddy how an earsplitting voice could come from such a petite frame. "Did you think we wouldn't notice you sneaking out of the house?"

Eddy studied the hardwood floor he was about to sweep and mop. It was pockmarked with cigarette burns and scuffed by the soles of countless customers. He straggled toward the jukebox, waiting for a tongue lashing from his dad who was shrouded behind a mix of cigarette and stale cigar smoke that drifted and eddied across the tavern like an early morning fog rolling in from Lake Michigan. Eddy licked his lips. He could use a cigarette right about now.

Ernie closed the beer tap in the middle of a pour and glared at Eddy. He shook his head and belted out an order like a drill sergeant. "Make yourself useful. Get that broom and sweep. Move!"

Eddy puttered to the corner of the bar near the washroom. He rested his bat against the wall and grabbed the broom. Sailor leaned over and handed Eddy a nickel. "Here. Play a song on that jukebox."

Margaret marched over and snapped, "He doesn't deserve a song he wants to hear, Sailor. He's done enough already."

Ernie set a drink on the bar. "Come on, Marge. Don't talk to the regulars like that." He locked eyes with Eddy. "Whaddya say?"

Eddy whispered, "Thanks, Sailor."

"Play whatever you want," Sailor said.

"Is that the lesson we want to teach him, Ernie?" Margaret growled, her greasy hands on her hips.

"Aw, Marge, let it alone. Will ya? We got a business to run," Ernie said. He popped open the cash register to make change for a customer.

Eddy moped to the jukebox and planted the broom against the wall. He dropped the nickel in the slot. It tinkled into the bowels of the juke and clicked. He pressed B7. The juke whirred and seconds later, Bing Cosby and the Andrew Sisters crooned his favorite song, "Don't Fence Me In."

Eddy grabbed the broom and swept the floor with long strides while mumbling the lyrics to the song.

"Let me be by myself in the evening breeze and listen to the murmur of the cottonwood trees, send me off forever but I ask you please don't fence me in…"

Heated words between his dad, Sailor and Walter interrupted his half-hearted crooning.

"I'm tellin ya, Mickey Livingston is a bum," Walter boomed, his words slow and slurred. "He has no arm, and he can't see for nothin'. How can he catch a fastball and throw a runner out at second if he has no arm and is blind?" The big man took another swig of beer.

"His company fought in the Battle of the Bulge, and only three hundred of them out of five thousand survived. But he wasn't there 'cuz the army kicked him out," Sailor said. "The man's lucky and grateful to be here. That's enough motivation to beat anyone's expectations."

"If I can tend bar with all the noise and do it with bad hearing, Livingston can throw runners out at second with bad eyesight," Ernie said, his elbows rubbing the bar and his head tilted to the side to hear. He stroked his chin. "How far is home to second anyway?"

Sailor and Walter shifted on their stools. Walter scratched the creases on his forehead. "I know that home plate to the pitcher's mound is sixty feet and six inches."

"You didn't answer Ernie's question," Sailor said. "How far is home plate to second base?"

"I know that home to first is ninety feet. So, I'm not sure but ninety plus sixty is one hundred and fifty. That's the answer. I think," Walter said, his chubby hands twiddling his beer mug.

"That doesn't sound right," Sailor said. He cupped his elbow with his right hand, and tapped his lips with the other hand. "We know the pitcher's mound is halfway between home and second. So, the answer must be sixty feet and six inches plus another sixty feet and six inches. That's one hundred and twenty-one feet."

Ernie straightened, and waved his hands. "Sorry I asked. None of us know."

"Hey guys, I know," Bobby yelled from the end of the bar. He strutted over to the men and grabbed Walter's napkin. He plucked the pencil from his dad's shirt pocket and wrote on the napkin. He drew a triangle, wrote numbers and letters, and mumbled formulas as he calculated. He circled a number and held up the napkin.

Bobby's chin rose and his shoulders rolled back. "Here's your answer. It's one hundred and twenty-seven point three feet."

"How do ya figure that?" Walter said.

"I used the Pythagorean theorem," Bobby said. "The bases are all right angles. We know home to first is ninety feet and first to second is ninety feet. We have to find how far home to second is and that's called the hypotenuse."

Bobby pointed to the triangle he drew on the napkin. "You add ninety square plus ninety square and that gives you 16,200. Then you find the square root of that number and you get the answer. The formula is A square plus B square equals C square."

The men sat in stunned silence, gawking at the math wizard. "Ernie, this boy has brains. You got a diamond there," Sailor said.

Eddy swept closer to the bar and twirled the broom over his head and around his back. He peeked over his shoulders with a playful grin, certain the men would be impressed.

"If you're done sweeping, Eddy, go and clean the washroom," Ernie said with an expressionless face.

Eddy dragged the broom across the floor, his shoulders drooped and his cheeks a sheepish shade of red. He slogged into the washroom, slammed the door, and locked it. He stood in front of the mirror, stuck the broom handle under his mouth and sang "Don't Fence Me In" in the lowest voice he could manage. *Not bad*, he thought, but he wasn't no Sinatra. He set the broom against the wall, leaned in closer to the mirror, and pointed both forefingers with the thumbs extended, making a finger gun. His lips formed a crooked smile, and he fired off his best impression of Edward G. Robinson.

"Now look here, see. You're gonna give me the keys to the safe, see. And if ya don't, see, it's coitans for you, see."

Someone banged on the door. "What's takin' so long. I gotta go."

Eddy opened the door and winced after catching a whiff of Walter's beer-soaked breath. The burly bodyguard brushed past Eddy and headed straight for the toilet.

"I just paid for this beer," Walter said, fumbling with his belt, his legs shaking with urgency. "Now it's time to pay the water bill. They get ya comin' and goin'."

Eddy smirked and stepped out of the washroom, closing the door behind him. Bobby was still schmoozing it up with his dad and Sailor at the bar.

Do they expect me to work while they clown around? Eddy thought.

His dad wrapped his arms around Bobby. "Outta of everybody in this family, you're gonna make it through college. Maybe become a lawyer or a doctor."

Waves of red-hot pricks burned through Eddy's body. It was a kick in the gut, watching his dad make Bobby into some kind of saint.

He snagged his bat and snuck out the back door.

BOTTOM OF THE FIRST

Eddy cranked the handle of a pencil sharpener inside the cloak closet, studying his classmates work on a math test.

Heads in neat rows of dark-stained wooden desks bowed toward Sister Mary Edmund's desk in front. Even the slats of the oak floors lined up in her direction. To the left of the nun's desk stood a three-foot plaster of Jesus, his arms raised and unblinking eyes following everyone in the room.

Eddy spun the handle, stopped, and glanced around the classroom. Feet shuffled on the hardwood floors, and pencil erasers rubbed violently on paper, peppered with occasional sighs. He had been standing at the sharpener for almost five minutes, grinding away. Pencil shavings sprinkled on the floor in small piles.

Eddy locked eyes on Gerace. He danced in the closet, hoping to get his friend's attention. Gerace sat in the back row, counting on his fingers, his lips moving and his eyes fixed on the ceiling. His eyes drifted toward the cloak closet, and his face woke from a trance when he spotted Eddy, hips swiveling and arms swinging. Eddy stuck a pencil in his ear and twirled the sharpener as his eyes rolled up and his mouth formed an O.

Gerace buried his head in his arms to smother his laugh. Eddy waved and pointed at Maria who sat across the aisle from Gerace. She hunched over her test; her dark-wavy hair draped across her thin face. She was a top student in the class. Her friends couldn't understand why she was attracted to a goof-off like Eddy, but he made her laugh. The neighborhood kids married her and Eddy when they were five years old. Gerace's older brother officiated while the other kids hummed "Here Comes the Bride." Eddy tied a twig around Maria's ring finger, closed his eyes, leaned in, and pecked her on the lips. It was their first kiss.

Gerace tore a small strip from scratch paper, crumpled it, and tossed it underhand. It landed on Maria's test. Her pencil froze. She whirled around to see who'd thrown it. Gerace smiled and pointed. Maria's crystal-clear blue eyes swung to the cloak closet.

Eddy bowed his legs, slouched his shoulders, curled his hands, and extended his lower jaw, showing the bottom row of his teeth and waddled back and forth. Maria clamped her hand over her mouth, her eyes rotating to Sister Edmunds's desk. The old nun sat motionless, correcting papers.

Muffled laughter broke the silence.

Sister Edmunds furrowed her brow, raised her beady eyes, and glowered at the classroom, her round wrinkled face squeezed out of the black habit and white apron wrapped around her head. She pressed her shaky and gnarled hands on her desk to support her weight and lifted herself out of her wooden chair. She stood upright, her body as stiff as a new catcher's mitt. She gripped a ruler in her right hand.

"Eddy Pareti!" The words rang out. "Come here and wipe that smirk off your face."

Eddy sauntered out of the cloak closet. The classroom erupted in laughter.

"Quiet," Sister Edmunds barked.

Eddy shuffled to the front of the nun's desk. He studied the lines on the hardwood floors. Was she going to smack him with the ruler again? He braced for the nun's wrath.

In third grade, Sister Edna Lorraine had grabbed Eddy's throwing arm, dragged him to the cloak closet and hung him on a hook. She closed the door and left him there for the rest of the class period. She lifted him off the hook and asked in a stern tone if he had learned his lesson. He said no, and she stepped on his toes. So he stepped on her toes. All that trouble and the only thing he did was leave his desk.

"You have so much potential, Eddy," Sister Edmunds said. Her eyes, like two burning coals, scowled down at him in disappointment. "Your brother and sister are excellent students. What happened to you?"

"It's my birthday," Eddy mumbled.

"What did you say?"

Eddy didn't answer.

"If you don't stop clowning around, you will flunk seventh grade, Mr. Pareti. Do you understand?" said Sister Edmunds, pressing her lips into a thin line. "Your behavior will not be tolerated in my classroom, young man."

Eddy nodded. His head faced the nun, but his eyes shifted toward Maria, sneaking a sidelong glance like a pitcher watching a runner leading off first base. Maria covered her mouth to mask a smile, but laugh lines surrounded her eyes.

Sister Mary Edmunds folded her sagging arms and snarled, "Go to the principal's office. Now!"

Eddy winked at Maria, loosened his tie, and strolled into the hallway and down the marble stairs. He reached the bottom and stopped. To his right was the principal's office. To his left were the front doors.

Voices rose from the first-grade classroom across the hall, their words too muffled behind an oak door. Eddy shook his head and smiled, remembering how he loved first grade. He cried all the way home after his first day of school. He didn't want it to end. Now, every morning when he got ready for school, he wanted to scream at the top of his lungs like an angry fan yelling at an umpire for a bad call.

Eddy surveyed the hallway in both directions. The marble halls were empty. He could scram out the front door. There was an hour left in the school day. What did it matter if he skipped out? He was already in trouble, and he was a failure; it came straight from the nun's mealy mouth.

Eddy pivoted left and flew out of Saint Mary of the Lake School, free as a bird.

He ran south on Sheridan Avenue and screeched to stop in front of Pepe's Ice Cream Parlor. He opened the screen door, strolled in and mounted a stool like the patrons in his dad's bar. He slapped a nickel on the counter. 'How ya doin', Armando? Gimme a chocolate shake with lots of whipped cream. It's my birthday."

Armando crossed his arms and asked suspiciously, "Say, Eddy, ain't you s'posed t'be in school?"

"They gave me the day off cuz it's my birthday. Like I said."

"A day off, huh," Armando said in a tone of disbelief. He leaned over the counter. "Seen Uncle Jimmy around?"

Eddy earned a little walking around money, running horse racing bets for Uncle Jimmy, a local bookie. His parents would kill him if they knew. But what's the big deal? *Dad lets Uncle Jimmy run bets in the bar, and everybody gambles*, Eddy thought. "Not lately. Things cooled down."

Armando slapped the counter and turned around to make the shake. He scooped chocolate ice cream into a metal cup, poured milk into it, placed it under the beater, and turned on the blender.

The blender's grinding reminded Eddy of the sharpener in the cloak closet. Dread gurgled up from his gut, and waves of guilt burned through his rebellious body. He ditched school.

So what? he thought. *It's just one day.* His parents knew he wasn't a bookworm like his brother and sister. They didn't expect anything different. They were happy with Bobby and Florence. So what did they care if he screwed up in school?

Who doesn't deserve a treat on their birthday? he said to himself.

Armando plopped the metal cup with the shake and an empty glass mug on the counter. "There ya go, birthday boy. Enjoy."

Eddy poured the shake into the mug. He placed his lips around the paper straw and sucked it down in one gulp. Only sissies fear a brain freeze. Satisfied, he went "Ahhh" and waited for the burp. He wiped his mouth with his sleeve and jumped off the stool.

The screen door squeaked and then slammed with a bang as Eddy dashed out of the ice cream parlor and ran south on Sheridan. He turned west on Grace and then back south on Clark Street.

He stopped in front of the Screwball Club, a local pool hall. He could hustle some money playing pool, he thought. He cupped his hands over his eyes and peered into the window for a better look. Walter's mammoth frame was bent over a pool table, his round belly hung over his belt and flesh bulged from his collar. Sailor was propped against the wall, waiting his turn to shoot. There was no way he could go inside. They'd tell his dad.

Eddy hustled south on Clark, and stopped on Waveland Avenue, his feet running in place. Wrigley Field's left field gate was open. Eddy ran to it.

A lanky man wearing suspenders and a short-sleeved white shirt stepped in front of the gate to close it. He had a receding hairline, a grizzled gray beard, and bandied legs skinny as baseball bats.

"Whaddya say, Barney?" Eddy said in a high-pitched voice he used with customers.

Barney turned and beamed a snaggletooth smile. "Eddy. What's tickin' chicken?"

"Nothing much. Just roamin' the neighborhood."

"No school today, huh?"

"They let me out because it's my birthday."

"Uh-huh. Birthday. Look at ya, getting' so big. Why it was just yesterday youse was a little pipsqueak runnin' around getting' in trouble," Barney said. He closed the gate. He scratched his head and laughed. "Remember when ya head got stuck under this gate? You was tryin' to impress the bigger kids by crawlin' under it and sneak into the ballpark. Whew, your mother was mad as a junkyard dog. She blamed me."

Eddy gave a lopsided grin. The only thing he remembered was his mother cussing and screaming at someone manning the gate. It might have been Barney or someone else. Eddy didn't want to talk about it.

"You still runnin' bets for Uncle Jimmy?" Barney asked.

Eddy nodded and glanced around, hoping no one heard. "The action is dead right now, you know."

Barney's eyes lowered. "Yeah, I know. The damndest thing they ever did was ban horse racin'. Makin' bets is patriotic as buyin' war bonds, if ya ask me. When they open back up come see me I gotta a lot of bets I wanna make."

Eddy rubbed his nose. Uncle Jimmy had ordered him not to take anymore bets from Barney. He was a mooch who didn't pay his debts. "You got it." He tilted his head and asked, "Do you mind if I go inside and watch the players practice?"

Barney scratched his balding head. "I dunno, Eddy. I ain't s'pose to let anyone in."

"Come on. What's the big deal? You've let me in a million times. It's my birthday."

"Ah, I guess. Just don't bother the players. Stay outta their way." Barney opened the gate.

"I won't. I will. Thanks. I owe ya one," Eddy said. He ran through the gate and hotfoot it down the third baseline, passing several Cubs players throwing.

Eddy slowed his pace once he came near the dugout. Most of the players were standing around, talking and laughing. He waltzed past them, leaned against the brick wall behind home plate, and watched Cubs Manager Charlie Grimm and another coach he didn't recognize hit golf balls from home plate.

Grimm was tall and stout with a square jaw and broad choppers. His muscular arms reared back and swung hard. The golf ball sailed high straight away and landed in the deep center field bleachers. "I hit the hell out of that one."

"Yeah, but you didn't hit the scoreboard. Not even close," said the coach, who sported a beer-barreled chest. His torso was shaped like a keg of beer with two pale logs sticking out of each end. "Let me give it a try," he said, taking the club from Grimm's stubby hands.

Grimm saw Eddy leaning against the wall. He stared several seconds.

"Why, Eddy. What are you doing here?" Grimm asked. "Shouldn't you be in school?"

Eddy walked closer to the men. "We got out early today."

The coach let out a guttural hiss and swung at the golf ball. It sliced and landed midway into right field. "Damn it to hell," he bawled.

Grimm squinted and cupped his left hand over his eyes. "Looks like that dropped in for a base hit."

"Aye, you don't know nothin'," the coach grumbled.

"Eddy, meet our new assistant coach, Red Smith." Eddy waved. Smith grunted when he bent over and set a golf ball on the tee.

"Eddy lives across the street next to his dad's bar, Ernie's Bleachers. You might like that place, Smorgy, they have some good card games over there."

"Where did he coach last year?" Eddy asked.

"The Green Bay Packers," Grimm said, his eyes flashing a sunburned smile. Eddy's face froze in a blank stare, wondering why a football coach of the Bear's main rival is shanking golf balls during the Cubs batting practice.

Grimm must have seen the confusion on Eddy's face. "He coached the Packers and then the Milwaukee Brewers last year."

Smith swung, and with a thwack, the ball sliced far right and landed in the box seats near the opposing team's bullpen. "Damn it to hell."

"He played two professional sports," Grimm said. "It looks like that won't become three."

"Why do you call him Smorgy?" Eddy asked.

"It's short for *smorgasbord*. The man eats like a horse."

Smith whipped his club in a fit of rage. It banged against the brick wall and bounced into the dugout.

"Hey what gives?" said third baseman Stan Hack who leaped over the flying club. "I guess that means batting practice is starting."

Eddy's muscles tightened and his feet felt like stakes in the grass. He gawked at the star third basemen with the wide-eyed gaze of a wonderstruck fan. Hack's thick eyebrows arched, and the corners of his wide mouth upturned into a permanent smile. No wonder the papers called him Smiling Stan.

A hand blanketed Eddy's shoulder. "Eddy, why don't you go into the outfield and shag some flies for us," Grimm said.

A smile cracked across Eddy's face, and the excitement spilled out of him like sunshine spreading across a warm day at Wrigley Field. He sprinted full speed into center field without a mitt. He would have asked to borrow one, but he didn't want to be a bother.

On the first pitch, Hack sliced a hard liner to left field. The ball skipped into the corner and careened against the left field wall. It bounced around like a pin ball. Eddy dashed toward it, caught it on a bounce, and hurled it. The ball landed in short left field and rolled into third base.

For the next two hours, Eddy chased balls and threw them back into the infield. He caught a few easy bloopers with bare hands. If only his friends could see him. He was playing ball with major leaguers!

Grimm whistled from third base and waved Eddy back in. Eddy raced the length of center field and cut across the infield, passing shortstop Boots Merullo. He stopped in front of Grimm and gazed up at the giant man. The manager placed his tree trunk arms around Eddy's shoulder. "That was some slick fielding. You know when I was about your age I worked as a peanut vendor in the old Cardinals' Park. That's where I really got started, shagging flies for the ballplayers before the games. You're welcome to stick around and watch the team do some drills."

Eddy nodded, rubbing his hands. They hurt, but he didn't want to say anything. Grimm pointed to the dugout and told him to get some lunch that was in an ice chest. Eddy ran to the dugout and flew down the steps. He paraded past the team trainer, Andy Lotshaw, massaging the left arm of pitcher, Ray Prim, and flopped on the bench.

"Hey, kid, fill this bottle with more lotion. Will ya? It's in the locker room by the laundry basket," Lotshaw said, handing Eddy a metal cylinder.

Eddy hustled down the tunnel steps. He stepped into the locker room and choked on a rank smell of dirty clothes that almost knocked him off his feet. He put his arm over his face and crept deeper into the dim and dank locker room. There was enough light from the entrance to see a half empty Coke bottle perched on a metal table. Next to it was a laundry basket crammed with discarded uniforms, socks, underwear, pants, some of it spilling onto the floor. Maybe the lotion was hidden under the clothes. He pinched a dirty jersey and lifted it, holding it at arm's length. No lotion. He hurried back to the dugout opening and gasped for a breath of fresh air. When he turned to go back inside, he saw a sign in neat handwriting on the wall. It read:

"Talent isn't enough. You need common sense and good advice. If anyone tries to tell you different, tell them the story of Hack Wilson. Kids in and out of baseball who think, because they have talent, they have the world by the tail. It isn't so. Kids, don't be too big to accept advice. Don't let what happened to me happen to you."

Eddy jumped when someone patted his back. It was Grimm. He bent down and leaned in close. The manager's smile formed lines in his craggy face that brightened like sunshine on a slab of cracked cement. He smelled of sweat and after shave, and his breath reeked of tobacco.

"Hack Wilson said that," Grimm whispered. "Words of wisdom. I wrote it down and hung it up for anyone who thinks they know everything. Hack Wilson. What a ball player. Ya know he's shorter than your dad, Eddy. He hit fifty-six homes runs and 156 RBIs, both records, in 1929. We were a great team that year, and Hack led us to the World Series. You saw me trying to hit the scoreboard with a golf ball. Well, Hack hit it in that World Series."

"What happened to him?" Eddy said.

Grimm bowed his head. "He didn't listen to anyone. He did whatever he wanted. Drank too much and fought anyone on a drop of a hat." There was a sadness in his voice. "He would have been as popular and rich as Babe Ruth had he just listened and not brawl with players, coaches, and fans. Now, he's washed up, broke, and beaten down."

Grimm smiled and squeezed Eddy's shoulder just like his dad would. "Did Andy send you in here for more lotion?"

"Yeah, but I can't find it."

Grimm laughed and pointed to a bottle of Coke on the table. "Just pour that Coke into the bottle you're holding. It's his secret potion. The players don't know it, but they seem to like it."

Eddy filled the bottle with Coke and ran back to the dugout. He handed the cylinder to Lotshaw, who poured some of it on Prim's left shoulder.

Grimm stepped into the dugout and grinned. "How's that left arm feelin', Pops?" Grimm asked, his voice soft and playful.

"Like a million bucks. Whatever you're using works, and it smells so sweet. Keep it a comin', Andy. You're a miracle worker," Prim said in a Southern drawl. He earned the nickname Pops because he was the oldest player on the team, nearing forty. Streaks of gray coursed through his dark hair that gave him a distinguished look as if he were born in the British royal family. But he had been raised on a farm in Arkansas. "Hey, Coach, why are left-handers called southpaws? Dogs have paws, and we ain't dogs."

The Cubs manager frowned. "Which direction is east or northeast from home plate?"

Prim scowled at the manager with suspicion. "I don't know, that way," he said pointing toward first base.

Grimm planted his hands on his hips as if he was about to contest an umpire's call and, in a raised voice, said, "You've been pitching for the Cubs almost two seasons, and you don't know which way is east?"

"Aw, you're a long drink of water," Prim said, his hand waving off his manager's ribbing.

"Eddy, which way's east?" Grimm said.

Eddy pointed toward the center field wall.

"That's right. Which way is south, Pops?"

The lefty scratched his head. "I ask about southpaws, and you give me a geography lesson."

Grimm pointed toward first base, "It's that way. When a lefty stands on the mound, his throwing arm faces south. That's where ya get southpaw."

"Aw, hell, coach, never mind. I don't care." Prim stood up and stormed out of the dugout and walked to the mound.

"Every now and then, he gets some wood on the ball and says something smart," Lotshaw said. "But most of the time, he's as screwy as the screwball he throws."

Grimm planted two fingers into his mouth and whistled, indicating a pitching change.

The manager's ears piercing whistle rang through the dugout that left Eddy momentarily deaf. He rubbed his ears. "How did ya whistle like that?"

Grimm pressed his thumb and forefinger together. "You make an okay sign. Curl your lips back like an old man without teeth." When Grimm did that, he crossed his eyes.

"Put your fingers underneath your tongue and bend it back, like this." Grimm's head bent back as he opened his mouth, placing his thick fingers under his tongue. The inside of the manager's kisser was filled with black spots and visible gaps where teeth should've been.

"Take a deep breath and close your mouth as tight as you can and blow. You try."

Eddy stuck his fingers in his mouth and blew, but he only made a wind sound.

"It might take time. Keep tryin'."

Stan Hack stepped down into the dugout, his metal cleats click-clacking on the cement. Eddy sat on the bench near the door, his fingers in his mouth and his eyes fixed on the third baseman like a fan about to beg for an autograph.

"What is our new batboy trying to do?" Hack said.

Grimm folded his arms. "I'm teaching him how to whistle. And he's not our batboy. He's a neighborhood kid."

"Gotta name, kid?" Hack said, smiling as wide as the outstretched arms of a catcher giving the four-fingered salute.

"Eddy Pareti."

"*That's* a name you can't forget," Hack said.

Grimm reached into a bag perched on a shelf near the bat rack, and pulled out a pocket-sized mirror. He handed it to Eddy. "Look at yourself when you try to whistle. It might help."

When Eddy held up the mirror and looked at himself trying to whistle, Grimm said with a mischievous toothy grin, "Eddy, smile in the mirror and then turn it over."

Eddy did. On the other side was a photo of Stan Hack and underneath were the words *Smile with Stan*.

"You're really smilin' with Stan, Eddy," Grimm said and then let out a laugh that sounded like the screech of a screen door.

Surprise tugged at the ends of Eddy's wet-licked lips as if two clowns were pulling them apart. Eddy whipped around and pointed the mirror at Hack.

"Where did you get that?" Hack asked, half joking and half accusatory as if it was stolen.

"I found it buried in my desk drawer," Grimm said. "You remember these mirrors. They were a giveaway, and the fans would point them in to reflect sun in the eyes of those damn Red Birds and blind 'em. What a game. I had to beg to umps not to forfeit."

"Yeah, I remember," Hack said, his voice subdued in a reminiscent tone. Hack grabbed his mitt, and headed for the dugout steps when he stopped. "We had great team that year. Just couldn't get past those damn Yankees. Could've used those mirrors then."

Hack bounced up the spike-scuffed steps and jogged to third base.

For another two hours, Eddy sat on the dugout bench and watched practice, sipping on a bottle of Coke and munching on a ham sandwich. After practice, the players and coaches shuffled into the locker room. Grimm and Smith trailed behind and were about to enter the tunnel when Smith saw Eddy. "What about him?" he said.

"What about him? He's a big boy. He knows his way home," Grimm said as he winked. The manager stopped. "Say, Eddy, how would you like to work some games as a batboy?"

Eddy's face beamed like a shiny dime. "You bet!"

"Now I can't promise you anything for the Cubs because that's something management handles, but there are other games scheduled here where I have some pull."

Grimm bent his large frame into the doorway of the locker room and shouted, "Anyone know when that Negro game is scheduled here?"

A voice inside hollered back, "June something."

Another voice cried, "It's June seventeenth."

"Okay, I'll set you up. All you have to do is come here in the morning of June seventeenth. We'll be out of town but tell someone working the game I sent ya. Sound like a deal?" Grimm held out his right hand.

"It's a deal." Eddy clutched the coach's huge paws that wrapped around his hand; it looked as if he were wearing a mitt.

"You won't get paid, but you might come away with some balls and broken bats."

"Thanks, Mr. Grimm. I'll tell my dad you said hello."

Eddy sprinted down the third baseline and whizzed past Barney at the gate. He turned on Waveland, toward home, his eyes dancing with excitement. He got a souvenir and a job as a batboy—the best birthday present ever.

Eddy stormed up the back steps, two at a time, and blasted through the door and into the kitchen. It smelled of freshly baked bread, garlic, and his mother's homemade meat sauce. He dipped his finger into a pot of sauce and licked it. His stomach growled. Soft murmurs mixed with sighs droned from the dining room. He listened for anger in the voices but there were none.

Eddy jammed the mirror into his pocket and gumshoed down the hallway. His dad sat at the head of the dining room table, across from his mother. His brother, sister, and grandparents were seated on opposite sides.

"There's the birthday boy. Ma made your favorite dish," his sister, Florence, said. She held the hot bowl of Bolognese spaghetti, and Eddy sniffed it. "Smells good." He scooted around the side of the table and sat next to his nonna. "Sorry, I'm late."

No one spoke. Silverware clanged against the blue willow china. Would he get bawled out for being late on his birthday? Eddy ran his fingers across the lace crocheted white tablecloth, smoothing the rough edges of its pinwheel design, handmade by his Nonna. He was about to compliment it when his mother spoke.

"Where have you been?" Margaret yelled. "It's almost six o'clock, and we've been waiting for you. How can you be late for supper on your birthday?"

"Sorry, Ma. I lost track of time."

Margaret's right hand balled into a fist, and she pounded the table. "There's one thing I will not tolerate is being late for dinner. Do you understand?"

Eddy nodded, his head downcast.

Margaret sighed and rubbed her forehead. "Who's going to say the prayer?"

"I will, Ma," Eddy said. He clasped his hands and lowered his head. "Thank you for this meat. Good God, let's eat." It was a line he had heard from one of the older players in his softball league.

Nonno's head snapped back, and he howled with laughter. Nonna leaned over and kissed Eddy on the cheek. "Isn't he a sweet boy?" she said in a thick Italian accent.

"That isn't an appropriate grace, you smart aleck," Florence said.

"Says who?" Eddy fired back. His playful smile disappeared when he spotted a blank expression on his parent's faces. He filled his plate with spaghetti and, in a serious tone, said, "Why don't you say grace, big sis?"

"Your principal called today," Margaret interrupted, her voice sharp and angry. "She said you were sent to the principal's office, but you never showed up. What do you have to say for yourself?"

Eddy shifted, and his shoulders slouched. He glanced over at Bobby, who was looking down at his plate. He had hoped Bobby would bail him out. There was a long silence at the table.

Margaret leaned forward and sniffed. "Have you been smoking again?"

"No, Ma."

"What's the matter with you?" Ernie said, his tone gruff. "Why did you walk out of school, and where did you go?"

Eddy stared hard at his spaghetti. The smell of his favorite dish distracted him. All he wanted to do was eat.

"I just walked around. That's all. There was only an hour left in school. I'm sorry. I won't do it again."

"Be nice," Nonna said. "He's thirteen now, a teenager. We were teenagers."

"Tomorrow, I'm taking you to the principal's office myself, and you're going to apologize. Do you hear me?" Ernie shouted.

Eddy bowed his head like he had done a million times before at the dinner table, in church, school. It was a miracle he didn't have a permanent crick in his neck.

"Your brother and sister are doing good in school. What happened to you?"

The room was silent.

"You're going to help out around here. No more goofing off," Ernie continued. "You better shape up. We're gonna make a man out of you yet."

"We're paying all this money to that school, and you're failing seventh grade?" Margaret shrieked. "You're going to hit the books, mister."

Another long silence.

"Did you read about Mussolini in the paper today, Nonno?" Bobby asked, finally bailing out his brother. *A little too late*, Eddy thought. "Those crazy dagos hung him upside down in the town square."

Nonno shook his head. "Good. May he rot in hell," he said over the sounds of cutting, chewing, and swallowing.

"Did ya know Italians could get arrested just for swearing in public. Can you believe that?" Bobby said, ending his words with a sucking sound.

"Buonanatte, Mussolini, fottuto bastardo," Nonno said and then belted out a hearty laugh.

Nonna playfully slapped her husband on the shoulder. "That's not nice, Ben."

"What did he say?" Florence asked.

"He swore," Bobby said, the sound of spaghetti smacking in his mouth. "By the way, I got into argument with Brother Thomas today at school. He sez to everybody the Pope is infallible, that he can't make errors when teaching about morals or faith. I stood up in class and said, 'That's impossible. No human is perfect.' Should've seen the look on his face. I challenged him in front of everybody."

"What did he say to that?" Ernie said.

Bobby chewed faster and swallowed, his forefinger pointed at the ceiling. "Something about the Holy Spirit guiding the Pope and that only his teachings on faith and morals are infallible. Then I sez, 'Was the last Pope infallible when he said fascism was a gift from God?' Should've seen the look on his face."

"Oh, Bobby, you didn't," Margaret said. "We're paying all that money to that school, and you're causing trouble. Not you too. I'm going to pray for you."

Eddy slurped down his spaghetti, his lips smacked, red sauce caked around the corners of his mouth.

"Slow down, Eddy. There's plenty more," Margaret said in a softer tone.

"I wonder what the current Pope thinks now. Mussolini and the fascists are done, and now the Nazis are trying to negotiate peace," Bobby said. "I think the war is over in Europe. What do you think, Dad?"

"There's a rumor Hitler is dead," Ernie said. "The Russians are in Berlin. They probably got him."

"My goodness, we find out Mussolini is dead and maybe Hitler too, and it all happened on your birthday," Margaret said. Her tight-lipped smile told Eddy her mood had shifted with the good news.

"Eddy, the day you were born a Cubs player hit a home run, and the ball bounced on Sheffield and into my hot dog stand. It landed right inside a pickle jar," Ernie said.

"Oh, come on, Dad. I don't believe that."

"You don't remember?" Ernie joked.

"Then who hit the home run?" Eddy said.

"It was Jolly Cholly."

"Charlie Grimm?" Eddy shouted in disbelief. It would have been nice if he had known this earlier in the day. "Do you have the ball, Dad?"

"I had to give it back," Ernie said with an impish grin. "In those days, you couldn't keep a ball that went into the stands or outside the park."

"Oh, cut it out, Ernie. You're full of baloney, and you know it," Margaret said. "I was there too, you know. That ball really didn't even hit the counter. It landed right on the sidewalk in front of our house. Just a few more inches, and it would have been inside the place."

Margaret paused in reminiscence. She reclined and smiled at Eddy. "I was ready to go, you know, and, oh, there was a big ball game, a doubleheader. It was such a big ball game that I couldn't even get a cab to take me to the hospital. And your dad couldn't leave the business, you know, because we had the hot dog stand then. Somebody helped him to get a cab, and the cab could not pick me up in front. I had to go in the alley to get into the cab to go to the hospital. Well, your dad came with me, and then he kept the cab waiting and went right back because it was so busy. Boy, what a day that was, aye yie yie. To think I had to go to the hospital and I couldn't even get there. I almost had you at home."

"Who watched the hot dog stand when you two went to the hospital?" Bobby said.

"I did. I own the bar and this building you eat and sleep in," Nonno said in a loud boastful tone.

Margaret shot daggers at Nonno.

"Cut it out, Dad. We know you're Daddy Warbucks," Ernie said. "We're paying you on time, aren't we?"

Nonno shrugged and waved off his son, avoiding another argument about money.

"This is the funny part of it," Margaret said. "I finally get there, and the nun taking me up in the wheel chair she says, 'You know, Mrs. Pareti, we gotta tell you that Dr. Regardio is very sick'—that's my doctor—'and he won't be able to take care of you, but there is someone to do it, so don't you worry now. Don't be surprised when it'll be a different doctor. And that's the reason because he's sick.' I was so sick anyway that I didn't give a rip who took care of me. I wanted to have the baby and get it over with."

"If the doctor wasn't there, how do we know your baby wasn't switched with another one?" Ernie said.

"You're about as funny as a cry for help. And it's *our* baby, Ernie, in case you didn't know," Margaret snarled.

"How do ya know, Ma?" Maybe I'm not a Pareti?" Eddy said.

"Oh, stop it, Eddy. Not you too," Margaret said. She sat upright and straightened her blouse. "You were fine, a nice baby. Anyway, it turned out I was never getting the bill from the doctor. And I called up and says, 'Gee-whiz, I wish you'd send me the bill so I can send it in.' I didn't know if it was more or less. I finally got a letter from the doctor's office that the doctor wanted my bill to be gratis. So you didn't cost a dime."

"You're paying for him now, Ma," Bobby said.

Ernie gave Bobby a good-natured slap on the back of Bobby's noggin.

"Are we going to ever sing Happy Birthday?" Eddy said.

Nonno stirred his spoon in his hot tea, reached over and planted it on Eddy's forearm.

"Ow, Nonno! Why you always do that?"

Nonno laughed and placed the spoon on Eddy's ear.

"Stop it. Will ya?"

Ernie tapped his wine glass with a fork and sang solo. "Happy birthday to you. You belong in a zoo. You look like a monkey, and you act like one too."

"Let's light the candles, first, Dad," Florence said. She plopped thirteen candles into the chocolate cake, lit them, and turned off the light.

The family sang Happy Birthday. "Make a wish, Eddy," Ernie said.

"I wish that the Cubs win the World Series," Eddy said. He leaned over the table, took a deep breath, and blew out all thirteen candles.

Florence turned on the lights and said, "You're not supposed to tell us your wish."

After they ate cake, Eddy opened his presents: shirts, pants, a pair of gym shoes, and a Cubs cap from his parents. "Go ahead put it on," Ernie said.

Eddy snapped the hat across his head, a snug fit.

"He's got a big head, all right," Bobby said.

"You can wear it when we go see the Cubs play in the World Series," Ernie said.

Eddy smiled. "Thanks, Dad. Everyone."

Eddy had forgotten about the trouble he was in with his parents and his principal. Tomorrow was not on his mind, only the joyful moments of gifts, cake, and a belly full of his mother's homemade spaghetti sauce.

TOP OF THE SECOND

It was a cloudy and cool early May morning. A brisk breeze blew from the east. Stores, schools, factories, the butchers, and restaurants were closed. A shadowy excitement blanketed the air like a heavy fog. Soon, Chicago, the stormy, husky, brawling city of big shoulders, would pop like a champagne cork.

The war in Europe was over.

Eddy sprawled on the front stoop of his three-flat, folding newspapers. He snapped a rubber band around the last one and shoved it into his canvas bag. He stood up, flung the bag over his shoulder, and skipped down the front stairs to the sidewalk below. He hopped on his Schwinn Autocycle and trundled across the street to Ray's Gas Station to fill his tires with air.

Nearing the air hose, he spotted a few customers, the mechanics, and the attendants crowding around a radio. Something important was happening. He parked his bike and jogged across the pump island. He skirted around a puddle of motor oil and rainwater that formed a swirling rainbow sheen, pink, yellow, and green. He opened the door and stepped inside, the cumbersome canvas bag strapped over his shoulder. A customer placed a forefinger over her lips and shot Eddy an intense glare like an angry nun. President Harry Truman was speaking:

"For this victory, we join in offering our thanks to the Providence which has guided and sustained us through the dark days of adversity.

Our rejoicing is sobered and subdued by a supreme consciousness of the terrible price we have paid to rid the world of Hitler and his evil band. Let us not forget, my fellow Americans, the sorrow and the heartache, which today abide in the homes of so many of our neighbors – neighbors whose priceless possession has been rendered as a sacrifice to redeem our liberty."

A woman wearing a mink coat and black gloves turned to one of the mechanics. "Did you know it's the president's birthday? My, what wonderful way to celebrate a birthday. Don't ya think?"

Everyone shushed her.

"Our victory is but half won. The West is free, but the East is still in bondage to the treacherous tyranny of the Japanese. When the last Japanese division has surrendered unconditionally, then only will our fighting be done."

Truman's speech lasted a few more long minutes. The commander in chief proclaimed Sunday, May 13, 1945 as a National Day of Prayer and called on Americans to work hard to finish the war with Japan.

Eddy strolled to his bike, and walked it to the air hose that was tangled in knots next to a bay door. He pulled and twirled the hose to remove the kinks and filled both tires. He reached into his bag for a newspaper and slid the rubber band off. He straddled his bike and opened the newspaper.

The words "VE Day Today!" splashed across the front page of the *Chicago Daily News*. When he turned to page two, a giant shadow cast over him.

"Any good news, Ace," said Clarence, the station's head mechanic. He played poker Saturday nights with Ernie and other gamblers in the tavern or the back porch of his flat. He was tall and spoke in a booming baritone voice. On game days, he would wave in cars wearing a brown trench coat and a black cowboy hat. All he needed was holster and a pair of guns, and he could be mistaken for a Wild West gunslinger.

"Hitler killed himself on my birthday. Bet you didn't know that," Eddy said.

"He was probably mad you didn't invite him over for dinner on your birthday. Everybody love's your mother's cookin'."

Eddy was five years old when he first laid eyes on Clarence. He snuck out of bed, wandered to the back porch, and watched his dad, Clarence and other men play poker. He pointed at Clarence and said, "Why don't that man wash his hands?" Eddy's mother lifted him into her arms and whisked the boy back to bed. As she tucked him in, Eddy asked, "Why does Daddy let him play cards when his hands are so dirty?"

"Some people have different color skin," Margaret said.

"Oh right. His face is the same color as his hands."

Eddy gazed up at the giant gunslinger and smiled. "I've got some bad news for ya. The Cubs lost a doubleheader against the Cardinals. They dropped down to third place."

"I'm a south sider, a White Sox fan. I thought you knew that."

Eddy turned the paper to the sports section. "Look at that, Clarence, the Sox beat Cleveland in a doubleheader. They're in first place."

"Well now ya talkin' my language. The Sox is gonna win the World Series."

"Don't get your hopes up. It's only May."

Clarence rubbed his hands. "I got some good news, Ace. Horse racin' back on, startin' today. It's in that paper you're readin'.'"

Eddy shuffled the page. "No kidding. It sez right here. 'All Bets On.' Chicago set to reopen track this week." Eddy struggled reading the news report. "With reports yesterday that hos…tilities in Europe vir…tually had ceased the Office of War Mo..bili…zation and Re…conversion announced the opening of horse racing that was banned in January."

"You still runnin' for Uncle Jimmy?" Clarence asked in a hushed tone of voice.

"Yeah, you gonna make a bet?"

Clarence took a glance round and dug out a pencil from his shirt pocket. "Hand me your cigarette pack." Eddy did. Clarence scribbled on the pack. He shoveled a buck out of the pocket of his oil-stained pants and handed it to Eddy along with the pack. He cupped his hands over his mouth, and whispered, "Busher. That's the winnin' ticket."

Eddy grinned and stuck the pack and dollar bill in his pocket. "I got an idea. Why don't you do my paper route? All you have to do is throw the newspaper and deliver all the good news. What a job, huh?"

Clarence's head bent backward and belted out a hearty laugh. "Don't you try to put one over on me, Eddy." Clarence raised his forefinger. "But if your dad keeps winning at poker, I might have to gets another job."

"How come you're working today? It's VE Day," Eddy said. "I thought everybody had the day off."

"We got to make money, Ace. Earn a livin' to pay the rent."

Eddy folded the paper he was reading and handed it to Clarence. "You can read it. I've got to go and earn my living. Not even paper boys get the day off."

"That's the right thing to do, Ace," Clarence said. "Stay busy and keep your hands in the books, not on the girls."

Eddy nodded and smiled as if that were ever going to happen. He slid a cigarette from behind his ear and popped it into his mouth. He drew a book of matches from his pocket, struck the match and lit the cigarette. He flicked the burnt match on the ground, and pedaled as fast as he could. He imagined riding a horse on the Great Plains like Gene Autry. He sang, the cigarette dangled in rhythm: "Oh, give me land, lots of land under starry skies above. Don't fence me in. Let me ride through the wide-open country that I love. Don't fence me in."

The route extended from Clark, to Grace, to Sheridan, and then to Addison. It was like its own country he had to defend. Eddy rode on the sidewalk, steering the bike with his left hand and flinging the papers onto the front porches with his throwing arm. He aimed for the front foyer door and, most of the time, made the throw dead on. Other paper boys would walk the route and climb the stairs of each flat, laying the newspaper at the doorstep. That took too much time, and the pay wasn't worth it.

Eddy reached the Lockerbie's flat, the last house on the route. He stopped his bike and stared at the gold star centered in the service flag that hung neatly in the front window of the first-floor apartment where Walter Lockerbie Jr. lived. The star had been blue for two years, but now it was gold.

Was this a bad joke? He collected payment from Walter's mother two weeks ago. They still lived there.

Eddy's eyes fixated on the gold star that only meant one thing: Walter Lockerbie had been killed in the war.

Lockerbie Jr. was six years older than Eddy. He was tall and lanky and walked with a long stride. Eddy had to run to keep up with him. Their friendship blossomed on the softball diamond at LeMoyne.

Eddy was the batboy for Lockerbie's softball team, and earned the nickname, "Fast Eddy," on the account he ran to home plate to pick up bats and sprinted back to the dugout.

A strong bond formed between the two one day after Eddy grounded out with the bases loaded and two outs in the bottom of the ninth to lose a charity championship game. Eddy sat on the bench and sobbed. Lockerbie wrapped his long arms around him and said, "You gotta learn how to lose before you can learn how to win."

Eddy sniffled and wiped his eyes, his shoulders slumped and head lowered. He let out a low whimper.

Lockerbie reached into his back pocket and yanked out his wallet. He opened it. "Look at this. I've got two dollars. How can we spend all this money? I know. Let's you and me go to Riverview."

In an instant, Eddy forgot about the game.

It took forever to get to the amusement park. They hopped off the bus and raced to the main gate that resembled the entrance of a medieval castle. Lockerbie bought tickets for forty rides.

They ran straight to the the Bobs and rode it ten times in a row. On the first ride, Lockerbie raised his arms and screamed at the top of his lungs, "Oh Nellie!" as the wooden roller coaster shook, dipped, twisted, and turned.

"You've got to raise your arms and scream, Eddy. Let it all out."

The next ride, Eddy raised his arms and screamed, "Oh, mama Maria!"

After they tired of the Bobs, Lockerbie led Eddy to the Flying Scooters.

Eddy froze in fear. "You go. I'll watch."

"If you can ride the Bobs, you can ride this. It's not that high, Eddy. It's like flying in a car."

The Bobs was manageable; the roller coaster was grounded on tracks. But the Flying Scooter lifted straight up into the air with nothing under it. Eddy wanted to say yes, but he was overcome by his fear of heights. He shook his head.

"All right, I'll go. Wait here. Let me know if you change your mind."

Lockerbie stepped into a rickety tub with a rudder in the middle. The tub, suspended by cables, lifted, and spun around, flying outward like a hang glider.

When the ride ended, Lockerbie stayed in the tub and handed the carny two tickets. He raised his eyebrows at Eddy and patted the empty seat next to him. Eddy shrugged and jumped in.

The tub lifted and spun clockwise. Lockerbie rocked it. "Help me snap the cables, Eddy. It makes the ride a lot more fun."

Eddy sat motionless, his eyes shut and his hands glued to the side of the tub.

They rode the Silver Flash, the Rotor, and the Jetstream. They saw the world's only four-legged woman inside Aladdin's Castle. Eddy's throw was on target in the African Dip, dunking Negroes sitting on wooden slats inside cages.

One yelled at Eddy, "This cutie pie throws like a girl. Come over here, honey, and give me a big smooch."

Eddy winged the bean bag that struck the center of the disc, collapsing the seat and dropping the man into a chest high tank of water. He wondered what Clarence would think of the game. It didn't seem right. He'd rather see a nun in the cage.

The Catholic Nun Dip, now that's an idea, he thought.

They strolled around the amusement park eating cotton candy.

"Who's Maria?" Lockerbie asked.

"She's my gal," Eddy said.

"You're in fourth grade, and you already have a girlfriend?" Lockerbie said. "Fast Eddy fits you like a glove. Say, we should double-date sometime. I bet my girlfriend would get along fine with Maria."

The double date never happened. The last time Eddy saw Lockerbie was at a softball tournament. Lockerbie bragged about his newly born baby brother but that he wasn't going to be around to see him learn how to walk and talk. He had to ship out for basic training the following week. "You take care of yourself, Fast Eddy," he said, handing him a quarter. "Don't spend it all in one place, kid."

Eddy laid his bike down and walked up the stairs to the front porch. He leaned closer to the window. Yup, the star was gold, all right.

A boy inside planted his lips and palms on the cold window, just under the service flag. The boy pulled back and pawed at the fog he'd made on the window. He smiled and waved. Eddy waved back.

"Did you know Walter, young man?" said a voice that came from the porch next door. Eddy turned. An elderly man wearing square wire-framed glasses leaned on the stoop next door, several feet from the Lockerbie's porch. Eddy nodded.

The old man looked down as if he dropped something and said, "He was a good young man, always ran errands for me. He flew in one of those flying fortresses, B-17s, I think they call it. His plane crashed in some lake in Canada. Everyone was killed on board. Took them a long time to find the wreckage. To think he was so gung ho to go off to war and he never saw combat." The old man paused. "I can't imagine. So many mothers and fathers fear that knock on the door. Every now and then, you might hear a woman scream somewhere. That's the sound of grief."

Eddy nodded again. He had heard screams and wailing down the block.

"The Lockerbies are moving to Indiana," the old man said. "Can't blame them. Maybe a change of scenery will help. I don't know."

The old man forced a laugh. "I'm blabbering. You got an extra newspaper there, young man?"

Eddy reached into his bag and tossed one.

The old man caught it with two hands and read the banner headline. "The war may have ended in Europe, but it will never be over for a lot of people."

The old man thanked him and sat down to read the news. Eddy dropped a paper on the Lockerbie's doorstep and glanced at the window as he walked down the stairs. Walter's little brother was gone, but the star was still gold.

Eddy rode home, his pace slow, his legs weak, his breathing uneven. He passed the Screwball Club, Pepe's Ice Cream Parlor, and the fire station but saw nothing. He needed a cigarette.

He snuck in the tavern from the back. Steal the cigarettes and get out before his dad barked out an order to sweep the floor, clean the table, wash the dishes, or take out the trash, a chore Eddy hated most.

Mindless chatter filled the bar. The usual customers drank and smoked and talked about the war, the Cubs, their factory jobs and whatever. None of it mattered. Ernie was leaning over the bar near the grill chatting with a redhead. She wore a blue blouse and black skirt. Next to her was a redheaded boy, looking bored. Thick-framed specs hung heavy on his ski-sloped nose. Freckles dotted his pallid and sickly face. He must have been her son.

Eddy stepped behind the bar and crept toward the cigarettes stacked in a drawer under the cash register. His eyes were locked on target. He reached over to open the drawer.

"Eddy, come over here!" Ernie yelled. Eddy's hand flung back. "Say hello to Louise and her son, Elmore. They just moved here from Michigan. They live on Sheffield a few doors down."

"Did he register you to vote," Eddy said. He forced a laugh, but his voice was flat.

"Oh, now you're the funny guy," Ernie said. "I want you to take Elmore and show him around the neighborhood. And don't be late for supper."

"Come on, Dad. I just got home."

"Then you can sweep the floor. There's the broom." Ernie pointed to the corner of the bar.

Eddy nudged the redhead. "Let's go," he said and charged out the front door. He ran east on Waveland toward the schoolyard.

Eddy heard a faint cry and turned around.

"Wait up," Elmore said. He was a half block behind, gasping for air. Eddy thought about ditching the redhead, but he would never hear the end of it from his dad.

Eddy ran to him and waited.

Elmore was slumped over. "I'm not much of a runner." His voice raspy and weak. "See, I had open heart surgery last year, and the doctors said I shouldn't run very much." He lifted his plaid shirt. A red scar crawled up the middle of his chest. The old stitch line looked like the seams of a baseball.

Eddy's impatient eyes scoured the neighborhood. Softball or fast-pitch with this kid was out of the question. *He's from Michigan. What the hell is he doing here?* "Which way is east?"

Elmore pointed in the direction of Wrigley Field.

"No, that ain't east. Which way's the lake?"

Elmore's forefinger hung from his chin. He looked around in every direction but all he saw were brick apartment buildings and bungalows. He smiled and aimed his forefinger toward Wrigley Field. "It's a trick question. Ain't it?"

"The lake's that way," Eddy said, pointing in the opposite direction. "If you know where the lake is, then you know where east is. And if you know that, then you know the other directions. Remember: the lake's always east wherever you are."

Elmore rubbed his eyes. "I'm tired. I think I'm gonna go home. Sorry."

"Which way's home?" Eddy asked with a smart-alecky grin.

Elmore closed his eyes and laughed. "The way we came, two blocks behind us. Come home with me, and I'll show ya my card collection."

"I dunno," Eddy said, his eyes gazing in the direction of the schoolyard. Elmore's head drooped like the old man living next door to Lockerbie. The four-eyed gingerhead had a bad ticker and was a new kid in the neighborhood. He could use a pal, someone to show him around. "All right, but I gotta do a couple of things first. Follow me."

They walked one block west to Giampietro's, the corner store. Eddy raced up the steps and sauntered in, Elmore trailed behind like a puppy dog. Giampietro sat behind the counter, reading a magazine. Glasses hung low on his wide nose. "Eddy, how are you? What'll it be today?"

"You tell me. I'm sure ya heard. Bets are back on. I'm makin' a run. Got anything for me?"

Giampietro nodded, his eyes fixed on Elmore. "Who's this?"

"Elmore. He's with me. He's good."

Giampietro plucked a pencil from behind his ear, wrote some numbers on a slip of butcher paper, and handed it to Eddy along with a fin.

Eddy thanked the man, stuffed the bill and paper in his pocket, hustled out the store, and straight into a group of older teens. One of them grabbed Eddy's shirt. "Where you think you're goin', jagoff?" He was a half foot taller and heavier. Eddy had never seen him before and figured he was a junior or senior at Lakeview High School. His friends who were just as big, howled like a pack of coyotes.

"Let go, asshole!" Eddy yelled. He flailed around, trying to escape the grip.

"How much money you got, punk?" the older teen said. He fumbled through Eddy's pockets and yanked them out. It looked as if two handkerchiefs hung from Eddy's side. Slips of paper and money flew out, spreading across the sidewalk. The bully shoved Eddy aside and grabbed the money. He held up two bills. "Look at that, boys. I just found six bucks."

Another teen picked up Giampietro's betting slip. He read it, crumpled it, and tossed it. "Bruce, looks like this punk's runnin' horse bets."

"That money ain't mine. You better give it back, or you're gonna be sorry," Eddy said.

Bruce stuffed the money in his pocket and swaggered over to Eddy. He stood within inches, fists clenched. "Whaddya gonna do about it, jagoff?"

Giampietro opened the door and stepped outside. "Manache! What's goin on out here?"

One of the bigger kids yelled, "Let's scram," and the bullies ran north on Wilton.

"Eddy, you all right?"

"I'm okay," Eddy said. He picked up the crumpled slip Giampietro gave him. "See ya around, Mr. Giampietro." Eddy turned to a stunned Elmore and said, "Follow me. Got one more person to see."

Eddy strode south on Wilton. Elmore trailed behind; his breathing heavy.

Eddy stopped in front of a redbrick bungalow. "I gotta see this guy. You stay here. Don't worry. Those dopes won't come back."

Elmore nodded and gulped. Eddy hustled up the steps and knocked. The door inched open, and Eddy slipped inside.

Jimmy Ginnochio, who everybody, even the coppers, called Uncle Jimmy, was a small-time bookie who ran his game out of his house. He was one of thousands of people in Chicago who subscribed to a racing-news service and ran bets from their apartments, taverns, newsstands, auto shops, just about any place with a phone. There was even a horse racing racket set up at the US Post Office downtown. People would go in, get their mail, and place a bet. The cops and politicians got a piece of the action, so they just looked the other way.

It had been a while since Eddy visited Uncle Jimmy's place. Everything looked the same. Two rows of folding chairs were set up in the living room. The blackboard was still in front of the fireplace. Old racing forms spread across a large desk, the kind a big shot lawyer would have. Next to them were six telephones, a microphone, and a new box of chalk.

Uncle Jimmy sat on a rickety chair behind the desk. He wore a cream-colored gabardine jacket, tan slacks, and loafers, no socks. He set his hands on his bald head and said, "Whaddya got for me today?" He had a bulging brow, narrow cheeks and a wide anvil chin. His head looked like a giant peanut. A pencil-thin mustache underlined a red fleshy nose. His murky eyes were the color of mop water.

Eddy handed the bookie Giampietro's slip and the pack of cigarettes with Clarence's bet. "Where's the cheese?" Uncle Jimmy asked.

"I got jumped. Some kid named Bruce. They got six bucks. I don't know who they are, but I'll find out."

"You better find out. It's on you to get me dat money. Understand? You gotta make your bones around here." There was an edge in his tone as sharp and quick as a switchblade.

Eddy nodded. His heart sank. Running bets for Uncle Jimmy gave Eddy some clout and respect among his friends. The money was good, five percent of the winnings. Eddy figured if he got enough betting customers that someday he could run his own bookie joint or maybe partner with Uncle Jimmy, who was a suave and savvy big tipper.

Uncle Jimmy recruited Eddy and Bobby when they were working at the tavern. The bookie leaned over the bar one day and called them over. He glanced around to make sure no one was looking and whispered, "I gotta a job for youse twos if you're interested. But yas gotta keep it between us."

Bobby picked up a few betting customers selling war bonds. But Uncle Jimmy found him more useful manning the phones, figuring the odds, and writing the race results on the chalkboard. Bobby was good with numbers.

Uncle Jimmy gave Ernie a cut in the action in return for allowing the bookie to take bets and settle debts in the tavern when things got hot, and at times, they did.

"Tell your brudder, Bobby, I need him ta run da phones tomorrow."

"I can do that, Uncle Jimmy."

"You're not ready for dat yet," Uncle Jimmy said, letting out a short and husky laugh.

Eddy rolled his eyes and sulked out of the house. Uncle Jimmy yelled, "Get me dat money, or it comes outta yer pocket!"

Eddy bounced down the steps and said to Elmore, sitting on the front stoop, "Let's get outta here."

They headed to Elmore's apartment, a brown-brick three-flat. Elmore was quiet, he didn't ask questions about Uncle Jimmy or the betting slips. Maybe the redhead was blessed with street smarts after all. They climbed a flight of stairs to the first floor and entered. The air was damp and musty, and the living room was bare: it lacked a couch, an end table and a radio. A few opened boxes with clothes strewn about littered the floor. Two chairs with ripped cushions sat next to the front window, overlooking Sheffield Avenue and Wrigley Field. Paint peeled off of cracked plaster walls. The dining room had a small metal folding table with two matching chairs.

Elmore disappeared into a bedroom. Seconds later, he came out, holding what looked like baseball cards. He handed Eddy a card that had a graphic depiction of Hitler. Eddy turned the card over and read 'To know the horrors of war is to want peace.'

"Why you givin' me this?" Eddy asked.

"They're Horrors of War cards," Elmore said. "I collect them. My mom doesn't want me to have them because they're violent, so I hide them. You might like this one."

Elmore gave Eddy another card that showed children being shot outside a school. Eddy took a quick look and then handed both cards back to Elmore. He pulled up his loose pants as if he was ready to run somewhere.

"What do you want to be when you grow up?" Elmore said.

Eddy lifted his shoulder in a half shrug. "I don't know." He thought the question was stupid.

"I want to be a general in army like Dwight Eisenhower," Elmore said in a deadpan tone.

Eddy gazed out the front window. "You ever been to a Cubs game?"

"No, have you?"

Eddy studied Elmore's face, looking for clues that he was joking. "Of course, I have. I grew up here. I'll take you sometime."

"How much does it cost to get in?" Elmore asked.

Eddy shot Elmore a puzzled look. "I never pay. We sneak in or bribe the ushers. Tell you what. I'll get you in free of charge. Don't worry about money."

═ ═ ═

An American flag that hung over the middle of a crowded bar was the first thing Dean Steiner spotted when he entered Ernie's Bleachers. Like every American and each soldier during the war, he'd seen the flag everywhere, but this time, he sensed a wave of relief and joy he hadn't felt since coming back.

On the upper portion of the entire east wall of the bar was a dun-colored vinyl tile painting of a baseball field and bleachers. The painting, set on diamond shaped tiles, showed a wide and elongated ball field under a metal gray sky. Two flying fortresses glided over the field and bleachers. The painting reminded Steiner of a farm in rural France.

Steiner had stayed home during VE Day celebrations that broke out across Chicago. He'd been cooped up in his parents' apartment for months, holing up like a prisoner of war since returning. He couldn't remember the last time he'd had a good night sleep. Hours after he'd finally fall asleep, he'd awake in a sweat, sometimes screaming. The nightmares never ceased and it was showing. He had dark circles under his eyes as did many others who saw combat. Shrapnel sliced through his right eye during the Battle of the Bulge. The eye was a mass of milky flesh. It looked hideous like a bulging spider's egg sac, inside millions of tiny spiderlings ready to crawl out.

He didn't want to endure the stares and wasn't in the mood to talk about the war now that it was over in Europe.

His parents nagged him to get out, visit friends, go on dates. He wished at times he wasn't an only child because his parents were smothering him. Maybe it was time to step out. Ernie's Bleachers was a short walk across the street from his second-floor walkup.

Steiner wore the only suit he owned, a double-breasted light-gray wool suit and a dark-blue tie to match. His dad picked out the tie. He rubbed his hands as he walked into the bar. No one seemed to notice him. Couples sat in the four booths along the north wall of the bar. Boots sat next to a man in a booth near the front door. Some of the revelers wore clownish-looking paper ties and hats leftover from the VE celebration on State Street earlier in the day. His friends had invited him to go with them downtown and even enticed him with the idea of kissing women at random. He might meet someone, fall in love, get married, and have kids, they said. He thought they were making fun of him and that his mother put them up to asking him out.

The tavern scene turned out to be a bad idea, he thought, and he was about to head out the door when two uniformed soldiers at the bar started to fight.

About a dozen people circled around the men. Steiner moved closer to the commotion. A burly blonde, wearing a Nazi helmet and jacket, emblazoned with German military medals, was play fighting with a smaller-framed soldier, dressed in a US army jacket. Both men, laughing, had their fists cocked ready to punch.

"Hey, kraut, the war is over. You lost," said a middle-aged man. A fedora tilted at a slight angle on his head and a tobacco pipe cocked to the side of his mouth. A long paper necktie hung from his collar. Steiner recognized the face. Everybody called him Sailor, the father of Johnny, his best friend and teammate on the high school baseball team. He and Johnny had played second base and shortstop and turned twenty double plays sophomore year. They had been drafted the same day. Steiner joined the army, and Johnny signed up with the navy. Sailor crowned the smaller man with a paper VE Day hat. "Our Germans are better than their Germans."

Sailor turned and bumped into Steiner. The first thing he noticed was Steiner's eye. "Dean!" Sailor yelled above the din of the crowd. "You look good. How the hell are you?"

"I look good? Doin' okay," Steiner replied, rubbing a gold crucifix that was attached to his necklace. "I was just leaving. I gotta work in the morning."

"Are you saying a prayer?" Sailor asked, his face warm and friendly.

Steiner tilted his head and paused. "Oh yeah." He massaged the crucifix. "A chaplain gave me this in France. There ain't no atheists in foxholes, ya know."

"Come with me. I have someone you need to meet," Sailor said. He gently placed his arm around Steiner's back and led him through the crowd and to the bar. "Hey, Ernie. Ernie!" Sailor shouted at the top of his lungs, his arms swinging wildly like a third base coach waving a runner home. Ernie didn't hear.

"How this half-deaf guy can take drink orders in a noisy bar amazes me," Sailor said. "Maybe he can read lips."

Eddy was dunking dirty beer glasses in the bar sink when he spotted Sailor. He nudged his dad and pointed.

Ernie saw Sailor and hurried over. "What can I get you!" Ernie shouted at the top of his lungs.

"Remember that eye doctor you said owed you a big favor?" Sailor shouted. "You think he can help this young man? He's my son's good friend."

Ernie tried not to look at Steiner's gross disfigurement. He grabbed the pen out of his shirt pocket, wrote a name and address on a napkin, and handed it to Steiner. He leaned over and shouted, "You go to this address and tell him I sent you. He will set you up with a new eye, not a glass eye but an acrylic eye. Free of charge."

"What's the catch?" Steiner asked.

"All you have to do is help me register to vote all of these veterans coming back and make sure they vote my way," Ernie said. "You'll even earn a buck doing it."

Steiner hesitated. It seemed like a deal that was too good to be true. The military doctors told him he would have to wait years to get a glass eye because the material was produced only in Germany.

"What do you have to lose, Dean?" Sailor asked. "What are you waiting for? Say yes."

Steiner saw himself in the bar mirror, liquor bottles lined up in front of it.

"I'll take a Manhattan on the rocks and…you gotta deal."

Ernie reached his hand over the bar, and the pair shook hands.

BOTTOM OF THE SECOND

Uncle Jimmy jiggled ten dice in cupped hands. "Come on, sixes." He blew into his palms as if they were cold and released the cubes. The dice bounced and rattled on a wooden table. No sixes.

"These dice are loaded. I tell ya."

"Don't spread false rumors, Jimmy. It's bad for business," Kitty Davis said. She was a bar regular at Ernie's Bleachers who ran Twenty-Six Dice, a game that paid winners a drink coupon. It cost a quarter to play, and the odds favored the house.

To beat back the advance of age, Kitty lavishly caked her face with makeup and piled on the perfume. Her finely plucked and drawn eyebrows arched over sleepy sloe- eyes. With her short-cropped raven hair, pale skin, and tall, thin figure, she had the uncanny resemblance of movie star Kay Francis. She wore a tight navy-blue-and-white dress with a square neckline that showed off her hourglass figure. She flirted easily and expertly, and that was good for business as far as Ernie was concerned.

The Illinois Liquor Commission had banned the dice game, but police and politicians winked as long as bar owners paid them off. In her younger days, Kitty had been a Twenty-Six Dice girl at the Palmer House. With her bright smile and long legs, she would "persuade" overeager men to play the game, tally the score and roll the dice.

Kitty lured Uncle Jimmy, Walter, and Sailor to the table, and they were losing.

A gust of wind blew open the bar's screen door of Ernie's Bleachers. It banged against the wall. A whoosh of spring air whipped strands of dark hair around Kitty's face and rippled the shirts of her pigeons. Trains howled in the distance, and cars clattered on the streets in the chaotic din of city noise.

Margaret closed the door, walked behind the bar, and wiped the counters.

Kitty swept aside her hair and pinned it into a victory roll. She pouted her bright red lips and said with a smoky voice, "Roll again, Jimmy. Luck is on your side. I feel it." She took a sip of her brandy and chased it with a cola, her coquettish eyes locked on Uncle Jimmy.

"Why is it, Kitty, that you spend your time here operating this game when you could be working in a factory?" Sailor said. "The war is still on, and factories are screaming for women workers. Our boys are gambling their lives every day in the Pacific, and you're busy rolling the dice."

"I have my reasons," Kitty said, waving a hand in the air. "Why is it that you're playing, Sailor?"

"Why don't you lay off her?" Uncle Jimmy said.

Sailor took a long swig of his Fox De Luxe beer and slammed it on the table. He pinched a swab of tobacco from his pouch and mashed it into the pipe. He struck a match that made a sizzle sound and lit the pipe. He sucked on his pipe, smoke billowing out of the side of his mouth.

"Sailor's son is in the Pacific fighting the Japs," Walter said, trying to defuse a tense moment. "He worries. That's all."

Sailor blew smoke at Uncle Jimmy. "Why are you here, anyway? Don't you got a bookie joint to run?"

Uncle Jimmy jerked forward and spoke out of the corner of his mouth. "Since certain people got morals, we can't run wide open all da time. Two nights ago, da dicks come around and told me I gotta move a while. I wonder who called dem in." He picked up the dice and shook them. He chose the number six and in nine rolls the number had come up nineteen times. He needed seven sixes on his last roll to win. If he didn't get sixes twenty-six times, he would lose his quarter. With ten dice, the odds were against him but Uncle Jimmy was a betting man.

Sailor's eyes narrowed. "You're able bodied. Why aren't you working in a factory?"

"You a cop? Dat's none of your bidness, pal." Uncle Jimmy rolled the dice. "Seven sixes! Lucky in dice, lucky in love. Whaddya say, Kitty, you and me go paint da town red tonight."

Walter slapped the table. "I think he's asking you out, Kitty."

"Oh, he's a foul ball," Kitty said with a teasing smile.

"You can't strike out on a foul ball," Uncle Jimmy said.

"Yeah, but you can't get on base neither," Kitty replied.

The men howled in laughter.

Uncle Jimmy dug into his pocket and pulled out a wad of cash the size of a softball. "Hey, Margaret, bring dese fine gents tree more beers. I'm buyin."

"What about me? Aren't you going to buy a lady a drink?" Kitty asked, her eyes blinking rapidly in a flirtatious manner.

"I didn't know youse was drinkin, beer," Uncle Jimmy said. "You're sippin' on da hard stuff."

"As Dorothy Parker once said, 'I'd rather have a bottle in front of me than a frontal lobotomy,'" Kitty said.

"That's what you'd get if you go out with this fella," Sailor said, pointing to Uncle Jimmy.

"Well, I don't put all my eggs in one bastard," Kitty said. "Dorothy Parker said that too."

"I'm buyin' a round, and everyone's pickin' on me," Uncle Jimmy said with a wry smile. "Ya gotta hand it ta Kitty. She can dish it out better dan she gets it. Her intoxicatin' beauty is swell on the eyes. She can give me a civil service exam anytime."

Kitty gently tapped Uncle Jimmy's arm and said, "It's all in good fun. You wanna roll again, darlin'?"

Margaret brought four beers to the booth and picked up the empty bottles. She turned around and saw two men leaning at the bar near the front door. They were dressed in expensive gray chalk-striped suits and wore hats cocked to the side. Their trousers had razor sharp creases. It was if they had stepped off the set of a George Raft movie.

"Can I get you boys something to drink?" Margaret said in a pleasant voice.

"We wanna speak to the owner of this fine establishment," said a swarthy squat man in in a gravelly voice.

"What do you want?" Margaret said, her tone changed from friendly to annoyed.

"Whaddya doin' here?" the man said, his voice gruff.

"What do you mean, what am I doing here? I'm working," Margaret said.

A jewel-studded diamond ring glittered on the pinky of the shorter man. His fingers were as chubby as cigars, and his nose was crooked and flat. The other man was taller, his eyes sunk deep into his dark brow.

"I said we wanna speak to the owner. Now," the swarthy man demanded.

"He's upstairs napping. Let me go get him," Margaret said, her voice thin and distant.

Walter rose and asked if everything was okay. "Can you please go wake Ernie?" Margaret asked.

The well-dressed men waited while Walter went upstairs, never taking his eyes off the gentlemen callers. The only sound in the tavern came from the jukebox that was playing, "One of Those Things," sung by Frank Sinatra. Margaret washed glasses that were already clean.

The men turned around and leered at Sailor, Kitty, and Uncle Jimmy, who had stopped playing dice. "Is everything okay?" the swarthy man sneered sarcastically. He nudged his partner to follow and walked over to the booth, his eyes locked on the bookie.

They hovered over the table, the swarthy man grinning like he was holding a couple of aces up his sleeve. "Why, look, it's Jimmy Ginnochio. Haven't seen you in a while. How you been?"

Uncle Jimmy rotated a bar coaster around his fingers. A crooked smile formed on his face, but he didn't make eye contact at first. "Hello, Nicky. What brings you here?"

"Business. Speaking of which, have you decided on what we talked about?"

Uncle Jimmy looked up and said, "Still dinkin' about it."

The man's eyes scowled at Sailor and Kitty. "Why don't you twos take five while I talk to Jimmy, here."

Kitty and Sailor slid out of the booth and hurried to the other end of the tavern and sat on stools.

Nicky's grin changed into a menacing frown. "You look here. You better join our wire service now, cuz if you don't, when we get full control, we'll decide who stays and who goes. Those chumps who went with the other guy, we'll be runnin' them outta town. You're either with us, or you're not. Can't walk the fence on this one. Understand?"

"Yeah, got it. Look, dey just opened up horse racing again, and I've been busy, getting' back into da swing of dings."

"You better get back in the swing of things fast. We ain't waitin' around."

Uncle Jimmy nodded.

The men walked back to the bar and waited. Kitty and Sailor moved back to the booth. A few minutes later, Ernie entered the bar from the back. He was tucking in his shirt as he walked behind the bar and to the front. He was smiling, as if there would be a pleasant surprise waiting for him.

"Can I help you?" Ernie said. His face brightened and his palms rested on the bar.

Nicky leaned in close. "We represents Century Music. We're a new outfit that distributes jukeboxes. We partner with Jake Guzik, one of Tony's boys, if ya know what I mean." Guzik was Al Capone's former bookkeeper who later became the financial advisor for Chicago Outfit boss, Tony Accardo. The newspapers nicknamed him "Greasy Thumb" Guzik because his job was to deliver cash payments to corrupted politicians and coppers.

Nicky pointed to the jukebox. "We gotta good deal for ya. The music this thing is playin' ain't the right kind, see."

"Nobody's ever complained," Ernie said. "Everybody likes Sinatra."

Nicky shook his head. "It's not so much who's on it but how it sounds. Ole blue eyes, see, he'd sound better comin' from a different juke. Our juke. Understand?"

"What's the setup?" Ernie asked. His voice rose, louder than necessary.

The men looked at each other. Nicky turned to Ernie, his eyes wide and his body stiff. "Why you talkin' so loud?"

"He always talks like that. He's hard of hearing," Margaret said.

"We know what you get," Nicky said. He shot a half smile. "The setup is the same—you get half the cut. The only difference is you deal with us for now on."

Ernie straightened, his eyes shifted to the ceiling. "Let me think about it."

Nicky bared his teeth. "You're gonna get rid of this juke and take ours. Understand? And you better not say no, or you won't have this place. You got one week. If you don't, we'll be back, and we won't be very nice."

Ernie's lips went horizontal. He held out his hand, but the men snickered and stomped out the front door.

"Should we call the police?" Margaret said, peering through the takeout window. "Where's the corner cop when you need him? Oh, but he's always here when he wants a handout from us."

"They own the cops, Marge," Ernie said.

"Then what are we going to do?" Margaret's voice sounded like the shrill scream of an alarm clock.

"We're going to take their jukebox."

— — —

Eddy pressed his face against the streetcar window and craned his neck to get a better view of the white glow blocks away. The Thillens Stadium lights towered above the rows of one-story brick buildings. It was as if stars fell from the heavens and ignited the dark sky over the ball field.

The streetcar click-clacked down Devon Avenue, its air compressor humming, diga diga diga. The bus jerked to a stop, and the compressor wheezed and stalled. The conductor pulled a rope, and a bell clanged. He stepped off. Seconds later, he poked his head through the side door. "Hey, Mack, I'll give ya three guesses, and the first two don't count."

"The pole disengaged again," the motorman said.

"You got it," the conductor said. "Folks, pardon the inconvenience, but we're having technical difficulties. If ya don't mind stepping off for a moment while we get things back on track."

Passengers trudged down the aisle and tramped off the bus. Eddy, Elmore, Warman, and Gerace were last in line, shuffling over confetti of transfer punches that littered the aisle.

The conductor yanked on a rope attached to the streetcar pole, a springy metal rod located on the top of the bus that connected to an overhead electric cable line. The pole resembled a giant rat's tail. It swung and wobbled about a foot off center. The conductor pulled on the rope and guided it to his right as if he were drawing curtains.

"This'll take forever. It's only a couple of blocks. Let's get outta here," Eddy said. He ran, and his friends followed.

They jumped into a short line at the front gate. Eddy pulled Elmore aside and shoved a quarter in his hand. "Don't spend it all in one place, kid." At that moment, Eddy remembered those were Lockerbie's last words to him. A comforting wave of sadness swept over him.

"Thanks, Eddy," Elmore said. "I won't be able to pay you back right away."

"Quiet. I don't want anyone to get the wrong idea I run a charity. Don't worry about it."

The sweet smell of cotton candy, popcorn, and soda filled the air. Eddy elbowed his way through the crowd, like he had done countless times at Wrigley Field. A loudspeaker crackled, and an announcer said, "Welcome to Thillens Stadium. Tonight, Eddie Feigner and three players, known as the King and his Court, will challenge a nine-player team of Chicago softball all-stars. Please take your seats. Play will begin shortly." His voice sounded as if he were speaking into a tin can.

The grandstand seats were packed with fans, it was standing room only. Eddy stopped in an area halfway between right field and first base. "This is good right here."

"Are they playing sixteen-inch ball?" Gerace asked.

"If they do, this King guy and his three players are going to get murdered," Eddy said. He pointed to the pitcher's mound. "Look at that guy."

Eddie Feigner, a muscular man in a flat-top crew cut, loomed on the pitchers' mound, gripping a bright yellow twelve-inch softball, and looking like the fearless marine drill sergeant he had once been, ready to do battle. Three teammates huddled with him. They wore red, white, and blue uniforms.

A man wearing a top hat and a short-sleeved white shirt walked to the pitcher's mound and handed Feigner a microphone.

"Good evening, ladies and gentleman," Feigner said in a crusty whiskey-like voice. "The King and His Court welcome you and this very fine team that is out here to beat us tonight. We want you to keep rooting for them, anyway."

The crowd cheered. "People always wonder why we have four men instead of three or two," Feigner said. "That's so we'll have a hitter when we get the bases loaded."

Feigner turned to one of his teammates and spoke into the mic. "Isn't that the guy you were telling me about?" Feigner asked, pointing to one of the opposing players standing next to their dugout.

The teammate, holding a catcher's mask, hunched over the mic. "It sure is, Eddie."

"What were you telling me?" Feigner asked.

"Well, he's very well known here in Chicago, but is he cocky," the catcher said. "I'll tell ya how cocky he is, Eddie. He promised two people here tonight that he'd get a hit off of you."

"Are they here?" Feigner asked, glancing around the grandstands.

"Oh, you bet your life they're here. His lovely wife sits over there, and his girlfriend is over there."

The crowd exploded in laughter. The man in the top hat grabbed the microphone and jogged off the field. Moments later, the umpire screamed, "Play ball!"

Elmore tugged Eddy's sleeve. "There's a better spot on the other side by third base."

"Naw, this is good right here." The crowd roared again, and Eddy's eyes spun around to the pitcher's mound. Feigner went into a windmill windup, his right arm twisting in every direction as if he were making the sign of the cross. The man's body leaned to the right as the windmill pitch came down and a yellow blur shot out of his hand. The batter swung, and the ball slapped into the catcher's mitt. "Steeerike!" the umpire yelled.

"Did you see that?" Eddy said.

"I couldn't see the ball. It was like a bullet," Gerace said.

Feigner pumped fake a pitch and went into another wild windmill windup, but this time, the hurler delivered the ball from behind his back for another strike.

Eddy jumped, his hands clenched on his head. "Did you see that?" He imitated Feigner's windmill windup.

"Don't you want to stand near the Chicago players?" Elmore asked.

"No, what's wrong with you?" Eddy said.

Elmore glanced over Eddy's shoulder. Eddy turned and saw four high schoolers, joking around. One of them was loud, his lean arms thrashing around like a caged monkey. It was Bruce, the guy who'd mugged him in front of Giampietro's.

Eddy's face flushed with anger. This Bruce guy had mugged him in broad daylight in his own neighborhood. He'd lost Uncle Jimmy's respect, and the bookie was hounding him for payment. How was he going to get his money back?

"So, I got on the train and saw this old hag standing outside on the platform," Bruce said. "The train pulled away. I reached out the window and grabbed her purse. She started screaming and running after the train. I held out the purse and pulled it back when she tried to grab it from me."

Bruce's friends bawled like drunks with an open bar tab.

"I got thirty-six smackers," Bruce said. "Can you believe it?" One of his friends pointed. Bruce turned and spotted Eddy and Elmore. "Hey, boys, look what we got here. Remember these two jagoffs?"

They goose stepped toward Eddy. Bruce pushed Eddy away from the crowd. "You said I'd be sorry. Guess what, I'm not. How much you got in your pocket, flat nose?"

"That wasn't my money you stole. It belongs to a guy named Uncle Jimmy. Ever hear of him? He's lookin' for you."

"Eww, I'm so scared. Look at me. My knees are shaking. Empty your pockets or I will."

"Why don't you lay off, blockhead!" Elmore shouted. He kicked Bruce in the shin.

"Look at this pipsqueek. A real tough guy, huh."

Bruce put Elmore in a headlock and groped around his pockets. Elmore flailed and twisted but couldn't break free from his attacker's grip. The mugger dug out a quarter and held it up like a prized ticket. "Look what I've got here."

"Give me that. It's mine," Elmore said. He lunged for the coin. Bruce held it over his head.

"Jump for it, pipsqueek. Come on, boy." Elmore punched Bruce in the gut.

"That's all ya got?" Bruce snorted and, with a backhand fling of his left arm, knocked Elmore to the ground. The redhead's glasses flew off in the opposite direction of his fall.

"Cut it out. He's got a bad heart," Eddy yelled.

"Why don't you make me, flat nose?" Bruce said.

Eddy took a deep breath and rolled his shoulders. There's no way he'd win this fight. "Come on, take it easy, will ya? We just wanna watch the game."

Bruce clenched his fists and mashed his lips. Eddy knew he was about to get flattened. He could go down looking or swing away.

Eddy swung and missed.

Bruce charged and wrapped his arms around Eddy's armpits in a full nelson and squeezed.

Eddy kicked and squirmed. "Let me go. Let go!"

"Hey, Bruce, go easy on him. There's cops around here," said one of Bruce's friends.

Bruce lifted Eddy and slammed him back first onto the grass. He shoved his hands into Eddy's pockets and pulled out a dollar in change. "You're lucky this time, but if I see you or any of youse anywhere, I'll bounce ya around like a basketball." Bruce strutted over to Warman and threw a fake punch. Warman didn't flinch. "Hey, look at this jagoff. What a Baby Huey, you are. Big and dumb. What are you guys still doing here? Get lost."

Eddy jumped to his feet, picked up Elmore's glasses, and handed it to the redhead. "Are you okay?"

Elmore nodded. Eddy grabbed a soda bottle laying on the ground. "Hey, jagoff." Bruce turned, and Eddy whipped the bottle at him.

Bruce ducked, but the bottle grazed his head. Eddy spun around and ran.

"You're dead!" Bruce said.

Eddy cut into the crowd like a halfback running around tacklers. He glanced back and, in the glare of the stadium lights, saw Bruce slithering his way through the throngs of fans, eyes bulged and lips curled with a savage fever. Eddy bumped into a hot dog vendor, knocking him against the fence. "Sorry."

Footfalls slapped on concrete, and heavy panting grew louder. Eddy raced past the front gate and around the backstop toward the Chicago player's dugout. He slinked behind a group of navy men standing several feet off third base. Eddy crouched and scanned the stadium. Maybe Bruce ran out the front gate.

"There you are," Bruce said. The crowd roared. He grabbed Eddy's shirt, his fist cocked, ready to punch. Eddy dropped, twisted free, and bolted onto the field in the middle of the game.

Bruce chased him. "You're dead!"

Eddy dashed across the pitcher's mound. Bruce, inches away, lunged for him. Feigner lifted his right leg and tripped Bruce. The bully landed face first on dirt. The pitcher grabbed the back of Bruce's shirt and lifted him with one arm. "Where do you think you're going, punk?"

Two ushers and a cop ran to the melee and escorted Bruce off the field and shoved him into a cop car.

Eddy weaved his way around the stadium, searching for his friends. There they were, huddled at the front gate. He ran to them.

"That pitcher tripped him, Eddy. The cops took him away," Gerace said.

"No kidding? He deserved it," Eddy said. Out of the corner of his eyes, he spotted Bruce's friends snaking through the crowd with fierce eyes, out for blood. "Uh-oh, his friends are coming this way. Run!"

They raced out of the stadium and toward the streetcar, but before they got there, its doors banged shut. Eddy swung his head around and saw that Bruce's friends were after them. "We gotta get on that streetcar," Eddy yelled. Elmore lagged behind, gasping. "Come on, Elmore. Keep running. Don't stop."

The streetcar clanged east on Devon Avenue. Gerace caught up and grabbed the back railing, pulling himself up onto the platform. Warman jumped on next, then Eddy, who held out his hand for Elmore. They had in the past hitched rides on the back of streetcars, ducking below the back window, out of view of the conductor. This time, Gerace pounded on the window, yelling to stop the streetcar. Bruce's friends were gaining on Elmore.

Elmore was inches away from Eddy's hand when he stopped and collapsed to his knees. Eddy jumped off and crouched into a boxer's stance, his fists ready to fly.

Bruce's friends reached Elmore and Eddy. "Say your prayers," one of them said.

The streetcar stopped and a burly conductor popped his head out the back door. "What da hell's goin' on?"

Gerace held up his transfer pass. "We got our tickets."

Eddy and Warman held up theirs. Elmore, breathing heavily, stood up, fumbled around his pocket, and pulled out his pass.

The conductor eyed Bruce's friends. "And where yours?"

"Aw, the hell with it," one of them said. "See ya next time, boys." The gang turned and skulked back to the stadium.

Eddy wrapped his arm around Elmore's shoulder. "That was a close call. You hung in there like a champ."

"Yeah, Eddy was about to clock 'em good," Gerace said, his voice soaked with sarcasm.

They boarded the streetcar and sat in the back. The doors closed, and the streetcar rumbled east.

"The next time someone calls me Baby Huey, I'm going to kill them," Warman said.

"If it's that Bruce guy, make sure you check his pockets. That asshole owes me eight bucks," Eddy said.

They rode in silence the rest of the way. The hum of the air compressor hypnotized Eddy, who drifted off in a daydream. He stared out the window and imagined pitching like Feigner but with a sixteen-inch softball.

Bruce stood at the plate. "Come on jagoff, pitch the ball."

Eddy gripped the softball, jumped sideways a foot off the mound and spun his right arm into a windmill windup like Feigner did. The softball sailed straight up in the air. Bruce strained his neck searching for the ball. The ball dropped out of the sky like a rock plummeting back to earth. Bruce swung and missed. It wasn't even close. The fans at Thillens roared. Eddy's Dad and brother cheered. Eddy pranced on the mound, wildly waving the ball. The next two pitches were the same, and he struck out Bruce. Feigner begged for his autograph. Excited fans tossed quarters on the field, more than the eight bucks Bruce had stolen. Eddy taunted Bruce, "Who's the jagoff now? Huh? You gonna cry now, jagoff?"

Elmore nudged Eddy. "This is our stop."

Eddy, Elmore, Gerace, and Warman jumped off the streetcar, said their goodbyes, and headed home. Eddy ran down Waveland, through the alley, and climbed the back stairs. He opened the back door of the flat and walked into the kitchen. He had missed supper and knew another tongue lashing would come. He tiptoed down the hallway toward the dining room. His parents were in a heated discussion, but they stopped when Eddy walked in and sat next to his brother.

"Where have you been?" Margaret yelled.

"I'm sorry. I lost track of time," Eddy said, bowing his head as if he were in prayer.

"How many times do we gotta tell you to be home on time for supper? Help yourself to some cold lasagna," Margaret said in a gruff tone.

"Oh, don't yell at Eddy. He's such a nice boy," Nonna said.

"He's a rascal," Nonno said.

Margaret pounded her fist on the table. The plates and silverware jumped and clattered. "Ernie, you've got to do something about this."

Eddy folded his hands on the table and straightened his posture. He sensed his mother was about to bawl him out.

Ernie dismissed the question with a flick of his hand. "It's nothing, Marge. Eat your supper."

"What do you mean it's nothing," Margaret said. "It certainly is something. We shouldn't just bury our heads and act if everything's okay."

"Ma, I said I was sorry. It won't happen. Promise," Eddy said.

"That's how things work, Marge," Ernie said. "You got to take the good with the bad."

"So, you want us to do nothing. Think what will happen, Ernie, if we just sit back and let it happen, "Margaret shrieked. "We need to call the police."

"What! Why do you wanna call the police, Ma?" Eddy said. Did his parents know he was running bets for Uncle Jimmy? Eddy turned to Bobby who was leaning on the table, listening.

"It's nothing to worry about. Eat," Ernie said. He threw his napkin on the table, got up from his chair, and walked down the hall and into the kitchen. Margaret jumped out of her chair and followed, trying not to yell.

Eddy, Bobby, and Florence rushed out of their seats and leaned into the hallway to listen.

Ernie glanced down the hallway to see if anyone was listening. In an angry whisper, he said, "We're gonna take their jukebox, and that's the end of that."

"For Pete's sake, Ernie, you're a precinct captain. Can't you talk to the alderman? He's your friend, you know," Margaret hissed in a loud whisper. "If we give in to this, who knows what else they might do?"

"Marge, I keep telling you it's no skin off our back. It's the same deal," Ernie said. "We're not the only tavern hit by these guys. They're taking control of jukeboxes all over the neighborhood. They're knocking off all the operators who don't play along. Owners who say no risk a beating or worse. Some places got hit with a stench bomb. They even get the union guys to picket in front of bars to shut 'em down. They got every which way but Sunday to get you."

Bobby leaned into the hallway. "What's going on?" Eddy asked.

"I don't know. Something happened at the tavern," Bobby said.

"What happened in the tavern, Bobby? What?" Florence asked.

"Sssssh. I heard something about a jukebox," Bobby said.

"Jukebox?" Eddy said. It skipped every now and then after he'd accidentally bumped into it once catching a ball he threw in the air. Years ago, he'd spilled his Coke on it. "Why are they mad at me about the jukebox?"

Bobby turned to look at Eddy, his lips pursed and his head shaking back and forth. "You think this is about you?"

Bobby and Florence looked at each other and laughed.

"Sit down and finish eating," Nonna said.

"Nonno, what are they arguing about?" Florence asked.

Nonna turned to her husband and said, "I giovani oggi non rispettano i genitori."

"Hanno bisogno di un calcio ne culo," Nonno said.

"E perche si litigano?" Nonna asked.

"Quando non litigano e quando me preoccupo," Nonno said.

"What did they say?" Eddy asked.

"They want to give you a swift kick in the ass," Florence said.

"Shhhhh, I can't hear," Bobby said. He peeked down the hall.

Margaret sighed and rubbed her shoulder. "Gee-whiz, Ernie, why is the Mob doing this? What's the point? How much can they make from a jukebox. It's nickel-and-dime stuff."

"They launder money, Marge. It's all cash. No receipts, so they can put down any number they want. If they control thousands of jukes, it adds up."

Bobby took a few steps into the hallway and cocked his head sideways.

"Can you hear them?" Florence asked.

Bobby flicked his hand and shushed her.

"Those two goons gave Uncle Jimmy the business," Margaret whispered. "They were really mad. They told him he had better join their service or else. Ernie, what were they talking about?"

Ernie drummed his fingers on the kitchen counter. He took a deep breath through his nose, exhaled and said, "The Outfit is trying to take control of a racket called the Continental Wire Service. It makes a fortune giving bookies quick horse racing results. Without it, you can't run a bookie joint. They have their own wire service, but they're muscling in on Continental to get rid of the competition. These goons are going around threatening bookies if they don't sign up with their wire service everybody calls the Dago Wire Service. Uncle Jimmy isn't stupid. He'll switch."

"And if he doesn't?" Marge asked.

"They'll send him a message. Maybe rough up his runners or chase him out of town or fill him with lead like some others that gave 'em guff," Ernie said, a little too loud.

Bobby stepped back into the dining room and looked at Eddy. "It's something about Uncle Jimmy! I think the Outfit's goin' to rough up his runners!"

Eddy's stomach did a somersault and then a backflip. "Whaddya mean 'rough up his runners'?"

"Just like it sounds. Knock 'em out, break a leg or an arm. Scare 'em so they quit their bookie," Bobby said.

"Aw, you're nuts. You didn't hear that," Eddy said, his voice cracked. "Uncle Jimmy would've told us."

"Who's Uncle Jimmy?" Florence asked. She never went into the tavern and wasn't interested in knowing the regulars.

"Listen to your Nonna. Sit down at the table," Nonno barked.

"They're coming," Bobby said. They scrambled back to their seats.

Eddy's parents sat. Ernie poured wine into a glass. Margaret fidgeted with her dress, her head lowered. The tension between them seemed momentarily subdued.

There was a long pause at the dinner table. No one ate a bite. Bobby leaned forward and broke the silence. "I read in the paper that two masked men walked into a west-side bar and shotgunned some guy named Polack

Johnny. He was a juke operator who didn't play along. They shot him in front of customers who told police they didn't see nothin'."

Ernie smiled and took a swig of wine. Margaret sighed. "Why do gamblers, crooks and even bank robbers come into our place anyway?"

"Whaddya talking about, Marge?" Ernie asked, his tone of voice unmasking a secret he had with his wife, something they agreed not to talk about at the table.

"Did you already forget about John Dillinger when we had the hot dog stand?" Margaret said. "He came in and wouldn't let anyone else but me serve him. And I hated the guy for that. All he did was put his finger up like that," Margaret said, pointing her forefinger in the air. "And then point it at me. He wanted about four slices of ham on one little hamburger roll. He would throw the dollar on the counter. You know how windy it is there. You're wondering if it's gonna fly away. And I wanted to give him the change, and he didn't want it."

"That's a pretty nice tip, Ma," Florence said.

"Ah," Margaret said, waving her hand. "When a guy throws a dollar at ya and you're workin' for a livin', you say to yourself, 'I don't want your damn money. I could give ya the sandwich'. He always threw a dollar. Never a ten-dollar bill. Always a dollar, and the sandwich was twenty-five cents. I know the girls that were working for me says, 'You ought to be glad you're getting a seventy-five-cent tip.' I said, 'That's one tip I don't like.'"

"Ma, how do you know it was Dillinger?" Eddy said. "He had plastic surgery, and no one knew what he looked like."

"He always came in with his lawyer, Louis Piquet," Ernie said.

"That's right, Piquet," Margaret said. "The lawyer came in about a couple of weeks after Dillinger was killed to tell us what happened. That he was Dillinger. Well, believe me, the copper around the corner said, 'No kidding, and here I am helping the guy across the street. I lost ten thousand dollars,' because that was the reward for his capture. And so did we."

Margaret glared at Ernie. "And what'd you do? Nothing."

"How was I supposed to know he was as crooked as a corkscrew," Ernie said, shaking his head.

"Dillinger? Of course, he was crooked, Dad. He robbed banks," Eddy said.

"No, you dope. He was talking about Piquet, the lawyer," Bobby said.

"How far your friends fall, Ernie," Margaret said. "He was a city prosecutor. Now, Piquet's a jailbird who throws whiskey down some dive on skid row. Ha."

"Why would Dillinger risk going to a Cubs game when the cops were looking for him?" Florence asked. "Somebody could have spotted him. Just think: there could have been a shootout right in front of the hot dog stand."

"He's long gone, and it's a waste of time to worry about it," Ernie said. "So we're not going to talk about Dillinger at this table," and he cut his eyes at his wife, "or Piquet."

"That's your answer to everything. Isn't it? Don't worry about it," Margaret yelled. "Just let bookies make bets in our place. Don't worry about it. Let Kitty run her dice game. Don't worry about it. They attract trouble in the tavern. Don't worry about it!"

"Is Uncle Jimmy in trouble?" Eddy asked, imagining another world war if his mother found out her sons were running bets for the bookie.

"Don't worry about it. I don't care for that man. I don't want him in our place anymore," Margaret growled, showering her husband with an unblinking glare.

"He's just tryin' to earn a buck, Ma. What's wrong with that?" Eddy said.

"Listen, kiddo, there are two sides in this world. Honest people are on one side of the fence, and crooks are on the other," Margaret said.

"Ma, this is Chicago. There aren't any fences," Eddy said.

Bobby laughed. "My little brother's getting smarter."

"I know the score," Eddy said.

"Then why don't you know the time? You're always late for dinner, and tonight you missed it," Margaret said. Her angry words echoed in the flat, louder than the Stratosphere.

Eddy poked at his plate with a fork. They never yelled at Bobby or Florence. He could be killed fighting the Japs, his name buried in the newspaper along with so many others, and they wouldn't care. He'd be another neighborhood kid like Lockerbie not coming back, soon forgotten. Would his parents hang a gold star in the window? Big deal. They wouldn't miss him. They'd have their straight A kids, Bobby and Florence, future doctors or lawyers or politicians.

"Don't you forget, Eddy. You're going to summer school," his mother said as if she could read his mind.

“Yeah, Ma, I know,” Eddy mumbled. “I’m gonna learn how to become a big shot lawyer like Piquet. Maybe I’ll end up in jail and pour drinks for bums in some bar.”

“Don’t be cute,” Margaret said. “You had better get on the ball or else.”

TOP OF THE THIRD

Eddy sprinted south on Sheffield. His gym shoes slapped across the pavement under dappled shade from apartment buildings and oak and maple trees, comfort from the hot June sun. A one-winged sugar maple seed that kids in the neighborhood called whirlybirds twisted and twirled in front of him like a butterfly with a clipped wing. He jumped over a two-foot-high wrought iron fence that encircled a sapling, rutted grass and geraniums. The fence served as a boxing ring for Eddy and neighborhood kids during Cub games. They would wait for fans to crowd around, make bets and cheer on their chosen champ. Eddy won most matches, either with a right upper cut, a right cross, or he'd bull his opponent over the fence. There were no losers. Every kid who stepped into the makeshift ring earned good tips.

Eddy crossed Sheffield, stepping over discarded cigarette butts and flattened paper cups that littered the curb.

He stopped and swung his head toward his flat. Did his parents see him cut out? No doubt they were looking for him. He could miss morning Mass and go later. They'd yell at him and tell him how disappointed they were. So, what, he thought. They'd get over it as long as they didn't find out he'd been ditching summer school.

Barney stood guard at the "elephants" gate, built to let in elephants when the traveling circuses performed at Wrigley Field. "Eddy. What's tickin' chicken?"

"How ya doin', Barney? I'm today's batboy."

"Go down that way to the visitor's dugout," Barney said, pointing toward first base. "Wait. I gotta bet to make." Barney dug into his pocket and pulled out a slip of paper. "A coat tugger told me about a first starter."

Eddy scratched his arm, his eyes flitted to the brick wall of Wrigley Field. He owed the skinny gate man some favors. "I'm sorry, but I can't take bets from you anymore. Orders from Uncle Jimmy."

"Aw, come on, Eddy. You owe me one."

"Go to another bookie. There's plenty of 'em around."

"None of 'em won't take me. Eddy, this horse is a lock, and I need the money."

Eddy was in Uncle Jimmy's doghouse, and he didn't want trouble if he was gonna make it in the bookie racket. "I'm sorry, Barney. I just can't do it right now."

"Okay, think about it. This horse ain't goin nowhere."

"See ya around." Eddy dashed through the gate.

The cloudless sky opened up, a deep ocean blue, Cubbie blue. But the Cubs were out of town. The teams playing today would have different colors.

Eddy ran down the first baseline and stepped into the visitor's dugout. A balding white man with a receding chin and elephant ears sat at the edge of the dugout. Black-rimmed glasses with Coke-bottle lenses clung to his bulbous nose. He wore a light green suit, and a solid yellow tie hung loosely around an unbuttoned shirt. He scribbled in what looked to be a scorebook. A cigarette dangled from the right side of his mouth. The ashes curved upright about two inches, ready to drop. Eddy waited for the man to finish, but seconds passed, and the man continued writing as if he was taking a test and knew the answers.

"Excuse me," Eddy said.

The man didn't look up. "What do you want?" He talked from the side of his mouth, the cigarette still dangling. The ashes didn't drop. Eddy thought it must be some kind of trick.

"I'm your batboy," Eddy said.

"Buster, show the batboy around." The ashes dropped. The man cupped his left hand and caught them as the pencil in his right hand scurried across the page. He dumped the ashes into a wastebasket next to his feet at the same time he wrote.

A Negro player wearing a white wool jersey entered the dugout and waved Eddy over. Two red lines on each side of his uniform extended down to the waist. The word, Clowns, in blue letters draped across his chest.

"So, you're our batboy today," he said. "I'm Buster Haywood. Gotta name?"

"Eddy Pareti."

"*Eddy Pareti.*" Buster sang the name, his voice raised an octave in pitch, accentuating the vowels. "That's catchy. I like it. That's a name no one can forget."

Buster led Eddy into the locker room. "You ever been inside these locker rooms?"

"Yeah," Eddy said. "I've seen everything in this ballpark."

It was true. Eddy had over the years snuck into Wrigley Field, usually at night during the off-season, and explored every part of the ballpark from inside the green scoreboard to the press box and both locker rooms. He had dug through the ivy and found lost balls. The only place he never saw was the ballpark apartment where the field manager lived. The neighborhood boys called him New York because he spoke with a thick New York accent. He chased kids inside Wrigley Field at night, his flashlight gave away his location. "You kids get outta dis pawk. If I find ya I'll beat ya to a pawp." He never did catch anyone as far as Eddy knew.

"You a neighborhood kid?"

Eddy nodded.

Buster opened a yellow suitcase big enough to fit a body and pulled out a gray uniform with the words "Clowns" on the front and "batboy" on the back. "This should fit ya."

"Your team is called the Clowns?" Eddy said. "What kind of name is that for a team?"

"I don't know. We likes to clown around. What kinds of name is Cubs? Baby bears? I guess that beat puppies or kittens."

"Who are you playing, the Jokers?" Eddy said with a friendly grin.

"The Memphis Red Sox and we playin' two today." Buster handed Eddy the uniform and then pointed to a box. "After you put this on, take those bats there and lay them outside the dugout. The bat handles need to face out and put them in order of bat size. When the game starts, all you has to do is pick up the bat after a hitter and bring balls to the ump. Oh, and we the Clowns, so play along with our act."

"You mean I can clown around too?" Eddy said.

"It depends on what King Tut and Goose Tatum have in mind."

Eddy finished his tasks and sat next to Buster at the corner of the dugout, watching the Negro players shuffle out of the locker room. Fans filed into the stadium.

Buster stuck a cigarette in his mouth, his hands pawing his pants and shirt. "Anyone gotta light?"

Eddy reached into his front pocket and pulled out a match and a pack of Lucky Strikes he had stolen from his father's tavern. He tapped the pack on the bench and a cigarette slid out. He put it in his mouth, struck the match on cement and lit Buster's cigarette and then his.

Buster took a long drag, his eyes slanted. "Syd, what are you writing? A book?"

The white man in the green suit smiled and turned to Buster. "I'm writing a press release for our next game. Tell me what you think of this line. 'Their bats are loaded with dynamite, they are as speedy as a flock of gazelles, and they handle the ball with the dexterity of shell game manipulators.'"

"Why don't you write, 'with the dexterity of major leaguers?'" Buster said. A puff of smoke swirled out the side of his mouth.

"I like it," Syd said. His pencil scratched across the page. "This is good stuff."

"We just as good as major leaguers. Hell, we are major leaguers. They just don't know it," said a tall lanky player. His head touched the top of the dugout, and his hands dangled below his knees.

Buster bounced to his feet and saluted. "Well, if ain't ole Goose Tatum. When they let you out?"

Goose raised his broad chin. "Got out four days ago, honorably discharged as sergeant."

Buster saluted again.

"At ease, private," Goose said with a return salute.

"Did ya know while you were away the Boston Red Sox gave three Negro players a tryout?" Buster said in a serious tone but with a smile still painted across his face. "It was all for show. They never said nothin'."

Goose sighed and shook his head with a return smile. "Who try out?"

"Jackie Robinson, Marvin Williams, and Sam Jethroe," Buster said. "Jethroe led the league last year in hitting, ya know. He better than some of they players."

Goose's shoulders hunched and his mouth formed a lopsided grin. "Yeah. They let a man with one arm play outfield in the big leagues and a fifteen-year-old kid but not us," Goose said. He peered into the stands as if maybe the fans were listening. There was a deep soulful sadness in his voice. He slapped the metal dugout railing and let out a throaty laugh that lasted several seconds and ended in a guttural growl. His smile disappeared for a moment, but then it returned. "Hey, but we playin' the Red Sox today, 'cept they from Memphis."

Syd yelled for the players to take infield practice. Goose and other players sauntered into the field. Buster sat on the bench and put on his shin guards and chest protector, a cigarette slung from his mouth. He stood, took a long drag, raised his head, and blew out a series of smoke rings as if his long thin neck were a smokestack and his mouth the rim.

"How'd you do that?" Eddy said.

"See here, you take a long drag, get as much smoke in ya mouth as you can," Buster said. "Point ya tongue toward the bottom of ya jaw and then make an O with ya lips like this." Buster's lips formed a circle. "Say, 'Boot,' while ya click ya jaws together like ya bitin' on a thick piece of rope. Just let out a little smoke at a time."

Eddy took a drag. The flame of his cigarette flared. His lips formed an O, and he said, "Boot," clicked his jaws, and exhaled. A half circle came out.

"Keeps practicin'. You get it," Buster said. He dropped his cigarette, stubbed it out with his cleats, and walked to home plate.

A man wearing a top hat and tuxedo stormed into the dugout, lugging the yellow suitcase that contained the team uniforms. His face was worn, washed out like the bleachers at Wrigley Field, weathered in the scorched sun. Deep folds creased around the sides of his mouth. "Hey, Syd, where the batboy at?"

Syd pointed to Eddy. "Batboy, you do what King Tut tells ya."

King Tut's head arched, and his saggy jowls flapped as he laughed a happy high-pitched yelp. "You the batboy? Syd, I thoughts we stopped paintin' our faces white. You wanna be a clown today?"

“I clown around every day. Just ask my parents,” Eddy said with a smartass smirk. He took another stab at a smoke ring, eyeing the funny man in the tuxedo. A half circle escaped his mouth.

“All you gotta do is get in the suitcase. Then when you hear three taps you open it and get out. Then you play shadowball with the players. Got it?” King Tut said. He opened the suitcase and bowed, his open hand inviting Eddy to climb in.

Eddy squeezed inside, his lips tightened around a lit cigarette. King Tut closed the suitcase and ran onto the field. The suitcase swung back and forth like a seesaw to the muffled ripple of cheers and claps. The suitcase dropped with a thud. Eddy’s body shook and shifted in the tight space. The latch unfastened with a click.

“Behold! Inside this suitcase here is my secret weapon,” King Tut said.

There were three taps. Eddy pushed open the suitcase and jumped out with the lit cigarette flopping on his lips. He blew a half circle that soared like a wispy snake and dissipated.

Eddy picked up a bat at home plate and stepped into the batter’s box. He twirled the bat over his head and behind his back. The crowd roared. Buster, catching behind home plate, raised his arms, his eyes widened in amazement. King Tut danced around home plate, pointing at Eddy, his secret weapon.

The pitcher, Roosevelt Duro Davis, went into a windup and threw an invisible ball. Eddy swung and raced to first. The left fielder, Henry “Speed” Merchant, ran back to the wall and dug around the ivy. Eddy rounded second, turned the corner at third, and dashed for home. Merchant found the invisible ball and hurled it to the relay, Double Duty Ted Radcliffe, who in perfect timing threw to the catcher. Buster caught it. Eddy slid, cigarette in his mouth. The ump’s arm stretched out as if he were about to take flight and yelled, “Safe!”

Buster gripped a ball, held it up for the crowd to see, and feigned outrage. Eddy jumped to his feet and blew a smoke ring that hovered like a halo before it unfurled into the summer wind.

Eddy hustled back to the dugout. If only his friends could see him now. He hit an inside-the-park home run in the Negro League. Yeah, it was pretend, but they don’t have to know that part.

"Ace. Hey, Ace." Eddy turned to the box seats near the dugout.

Clarence, the gas station mechanic, jumped out of his seat, and leaned against the concrete ledge, wrinkles formed in the corner of his eyes, and his smiled showed pink gums. "I'm gonna tell your father you're clowning around out here."

"Then I'm gonna tell your boss you're skipping work," Eddy said.

Clarence's head bobbed, and he laughed as if he had heard a joke from Bob Hope.

"Batboy, get back in the dugout," Syd yelled. "Game's starting."

"Gotta go," Eddy said. "I'll get you a game ball."

"Get someone's autograph," Clarence said.

Eddy crouched on one knee at the far end of the dugout, ready to sprint to home plate to pick up bats each time a Clowns player got on base. But it wasn't often. The game was a pitcher's duel.

In the bottom of the seventh inning, the score tied 1–1, Goose bolted out of the dugout and set a plastic fire hydrant on home base. He waved to the Clowns dugout.

King Tut strolled onto the field with a Daschund in his arms and parked the dog next to the hydrant. In pantomime, he pointed to the dog and then to the fire hydrant. The dog froze.

King Tut scratched his head. He raised his leg over the fire hydrant and smiled in encouragement. The dog wagged its tail, its legs splayed on the grass. King Tut grabbed the dog's hind leg, raised it over the hydrant, and shook it. Nothing happened.

The crowd cheered. The Red Sox players lolled at their positions in the field, unamused. King Tut raised his right arm with the forefinger extended as if he had an aha moment. He pulled a bottle of water and a small paper cup from his pocket and held it up for everyone to see. He poured water into the cup and placed it in front of the dog. The dog sniffed the cup and the catcher's cleats. King Tut faced the crowd, shrugged, and ran his forefinger across his neck.

Goose ran onto the field, carrying a red box with a crank at one end. He opened the top of the box, and King Tut plunked the Dachshund inside. Goose twirled the crank. Hot dogs strung together oozed out of the other end of the box. The crowd roared in laughter.

Back in the Clowns dugout, the mood was more serious. The pitcher, Davis, paced. "Remember this, fellas: when I pitch, I run the show, especially tonight. Got me a new woman in the stands. Gonna take one run to get me to heaven. One run to heaven. Get me that run."

"Duro, you ever see you toilet seat up at home?" Double Duty said.

"I dunno. What it gots to do with anything?"

"Well, a raised toilet seat means you wife got a house visit from Jody, the man who comes in the back door when you goes out the front door. While you trying to get to heaven here, your wife back home already in heaven."

The players broke out in laughter. Eddy smiled, lit a cigarette, and blew smoke rings in the corner of the dugout. Working as a batboy for the Clowns was more fun than Mass—that was for sure.

Two more innings went by with no runs. All of the Clowns players stood at the edge of the dugout. It was their turn to bat.

"Come on, boys. You got to play with fire and hustle. Fire and hustle," Buster shouted.

Goose lined a single to right. The next two batters, Double Duty and the player-manager, Hoss Walker, singled. The bases were loaded when Clowns third baseman Sam Hairston hit a dribbler to the Red Sox pitcher, who tossed it to the third baseman, Jim Ford. As Tatum ran toward home, Radcliffe took off from second and touched third. Ford chased Tatum, but then turned and chased Radcliffe who ran back to second. The Red Sox second baseman tagged Radcliffe in the run-down but Tatum scored.

The third base umpire ruled Tatum had scored. Ford screamed at the umpire, his arms flailing. Eddy couldn't make out the words, but he was angry. Other Red Sox players joined the scrum, some holding bats. The umpire yelled back, and Ford slugged him square in the mouth.

Clown players rushed onto the field. Players and umpires shoved and screamed at each other. Goose disappeared in a sea of white-and-red uniforms and remerged, his arms wrapped around the pitcher, Davis. In the chaos and confusion, nine uniformed Chicago policemen flew out of the stands and broke up the action. They escorted Ford off the field. The crowd booed.

Players stood around, unsure if the game would continue.

"This is no good. It looks bad for our league," Syd said. "The president of the Negro League is sitting in the stands, watching this crap."

"Hell, he owns the league and the Red Sox. Bet he don't do nothing but give 'em small fines," Buster said. "We in this pickle cuz they don't know what a force-out play is, and they blame the ump. They ain't no reason to hit him."

Muted applause erupted in the crowd as Red Sox players took their positions in the field. The game was back on. Eddy kneeled in the grass, ready to pick up bats.

In the bottom of the ninth, the Red Sox manager accused Clowns pitcher Davis of throwing spitballs. Syd called for a pitching change and put in reliever, Big John Williams.

Davis skulked back to the dugout. "It was a sweatball. Ain't nothing illegal about sweating and then grabbing the ball. How you 'pose to wipe the sweat from you armpit and forehead?"

The next Red Sox batter tied the game with a home run to the left field bleachers. The game went into extra innings and in the top of the twelfth, Clowns outfielder, Raul Navarro, a Cuban player, blasted a home run into the left field bleachers to take the lead. In the bottom of the twelfth, Williams walked a Red Sox player, gave up a double and two singles. The Clowns failed to score and lost the game.

Cleats scuffed along the dugout floor. Williams plopped on the bench and rubbed his face with a towel Eddy gave him. Other players lumbered back into the locker room.

— — —

The second game of the doubleheader went fast. Red Sox ace, Verdel Mathis, shut out the Clowns.

Syd closed his scorebook and turned to the few players still lingering in the dugout. "Do you know how hard I tried to land Verdel?"

"Yeah, the Red Sox about baked cornbread to get him," Buster said.

"We'll get 'em next time," Syd said. He spotted Eddy in the corner of the dugout, smoking a cigarette. "Batboy, gather the towels and put them in the laundry basket. Then see Buster when you're done. You did good, kid."

Eddy stubbed out his cigarette and picked up all the towels in the dugout. He carried them into the locker room, which reeked of sweat and dirty socks, and dropped them into the laundry basket. He turned around and saw Buster tossing several cracked bats into a garbage can next to the locker room door. "Hey, Buster, can I have those?"

"We ain't gonna need them. Whaddya gonna do with broken bats?"

Eddy pulled three bats out of the garbage. "I'm gonna tape them and use them for softball."

Buster wrapped his arm around Eddy's shoulder and said with a sportive grin, "You're the best batboy the Clowns ever had. We can't pay ya, but we can give ya this." Buster handed Eddy a new baseball.

"Thanks. Can you autograph it? It's for a friend," Eddy said.

"Syd, throw me ya pen," Buster said.

Syd tossed his pen, and Buster caught it with his left hand. He lowered his chin and scribbled his name on the ball. He handed it to Eddy. "Next times we here, ya come by and be our batboy again."

Eddy stuck the ball in his pocket. "Thanks, Buster. See ya around." He hustled out of the locker room and dugout and sprinted down first base, the bats clanking in his arms. He saw his shadow on the grass. It followed him like an infielder following a batter trapped between the bases.

Eddy entered the back door of his three-flat and stepped down into the basement landing. He pushed open the door. The bats clanked. He froze and listened. Was his dad in the office? He waited. No sound.

Eddy tiptoed inside and closed the door. He found tape on his father's desk, knelt, and taped the cracked bats. Footsteps shuffled behind him.

"I thought I'd find you down here," Bobby said. "We couldn't find you this morning so we decided to go to five o'clock Mass. Come on. You need to go upstairs and get ready."

"All right, be up in a minute."

"I know you, Eddy. You're gonna scram the second I walk out this door."

Eddy jumped to his feet. "What are you gonna do, drag me upstairs? Try it and see what happens."

"I'm on your side, Eddy. There's no reason to get on Ma and Dad's bad side. You're always late for dinner, and sometimes you never show up. You have to go to summer school because you're flunking seventh grade. And don't think Dad doesn't know you're stealing cigarettes from the tavern."

"Don't worry about it. I'll go to church. All right? Leave me alone."

Bobby glimpsed the bats. "Think of going to church as going to a Cubs game. You sit in the pews or the bleachers, listening to organ music. You stand. You sing. You watch the players and the priest and altar boys who are all dressed up in uniforms. You praise the Cubs or Jesus. Right?"

"Oh, cut the crap, Bobby. Will ya? Do ya gamble in church? Huh? Cuz I know everyone gambles at Cub games. I just want to finish taping these bats. Okay?"

"I'm not supposed to tell ya, but Ma and Dad are thinking about sending you to military school."

Eddy smiled. "That will never happen. Got that? Never happen."

Bobby walked out the door and, as he climbed the stairs, said, "I wouldn't bet on it."

Eddy waited a minute. He grabbed a taped bat and ran out the back door. He headed east on Waveland to play ball at the schoolyard.

BOTTOM OF THE THIRD

"Eddy, is that you?" Elmore leaned into a dark gangway, his eyes squinted like a pitcher standing on a mound, straining to read his catcher's hand signals.

An orange ember glowed in the shadows. "Quiet," Eddy whispered. "Get in here."

Elmore stepped into the gangway, a narrow passage from the front to the back of a six-flat just a few houses south of Eddy's flat. He sat next to Eddy. "What are you doing in here?" His voice echoed.

"Lower your voice. I'm ditching school."

"You're still in school? It's summer."

"I'm in summer school, dummy."

"You have to go to summer school, and you're calling me a dummy?"

Eddy laughed and blew out a smoke ring.

Elmore held up his forefinger and let the ring pass through it. "How long do you plan on staying down here?"

"Till my class is over."

"Then what?"

"I don't know. Yeah, I do know. Me and you are going to a Cubs game," Eddy said, his voice brightened. "You've never been to a Cub game, have you?"

"No," Elmore said. "I don't have money."

"How many times do I have to tell you? We never pay to get in. We're gonna sneak in. All right?" Eddy stretched his legs, and took a drag.

"It's like a cave in here," Elmore said. "We're like bank robbers in Jesse James's gang, hiding out. What would you do if you had a thousand dollars?"

"I dunno. Start my own hot dog stand. What time is it?"

"About noon."

"Let's get outta here." Eddy said. He stubbed his cigarette on the concrete floor, grabbed his school books, and stepped into the sunlight. Elmore followed. Eddy dumped his books in the foyer of Elmore's flat next door. They sat on the front steps.

"Here's what we're gonna do," Eddy said. "We're gonna crash the gate. That means you gotta jump the turnstiles and run as fast as you can. Get lost in the crowd. Think you can do that?"

"How high are the turnstiles?" Elmore said.

"I don't know. Maybe three feet high? Let's practice." Eddy rose to his feet, took a running start, and vaulted over the brick wing wall, his heels clicked as he flew over. He landed on the sidewalk without falling on his hands. "Now you try."

Elmore adjusted his glasses and climbed on the ledge of the wall. He sat on it and dangled his feet over the edge. His eyes cast a dead stare, locked on the sidewalk as if it were a thousand-foot drop. He turned around on his stomach and slid down the wall.

"You got to jump over it," Eddy said. "Not get on it and slide off. Watch me."

Eddy cleared the wall again. Elmore took a deep breath and ran to the wall. He planted his left arm on the ledge and swung his legs over the wall. His butt skidded across the ledge, but there was enough momentum that Elmore went over and landed on all fours. His glasses flew off on the way down.

Eddy handed Elmore his glasses. "Needs some work but not bad. Let's go."

The boys walked over to right field gate entrance on Addison. A line of fans waited at the turnstiles, guarded by two female Andy Frain ushers. They were dressed in navy-blue skirts with gold stripes, blue blouses, and capes of blue and gold.

"Now remember: they won't chase you once you get in the crowd, but they have walkie talkies," Eddy said. "I'll go first. Once their attention is on me, you go. We'll meet around the corner at the men's washroom. Got it?"

Elmore nodded. They wandered away from the line and inched closer to the gate. Eddy sprinted toward the turnstiles. He hopped it in a single bound and shot into the crowd. One of the ushers chased him, and the other screamed into her walkie talkie.

Elmore scaled the turnstile and slid down the other side and in front of the usher with the walkie talkie. "Stop!" she screamed.

Elmore froze. She grabbed his shirt, but he twisted free and ran around her.

The usher yelled. "We've got runners at Gate D."

Elmore rushed past the men's washroom, an usher in pursuit. Eddy whistled. The usher stopped and locked eyes with Eddy. She said something in the walkie talkie and headed in Eddy's direction. Eddy sped up the ramp to the terrace section and halfway up the stairs that led to the Cubs press box and the Pink Poodle, a room for reporters, coaches, and suits to drink and rub elbows. He caught his breath and scanned the stadium. The coast was clear.

He strolled down the ramp, eyes darting in search of the four-eyed redhead. He bumped into a man in a trench coat and a black fedora tilted low over his eyes.

"Sorry," Eddy said.

The man smiled and hiked up the ramp in long smooth strides. There was no mistaking his hawk nose and buck teeth.

"You're Joe DiMaggio!" Eddy shouted.

The man turned, his forefinger over his mouth. "Shhhh."

"Are you signing with the Cubs?" DiMaggio shook his head and hurried up the ramp. Eddy followed him. The Yankee Clipper climbed the stairs and stepped into the Pink Poodle.

Eddy fast walked to the men's washroom and found Elmore. "Guess who I saw."

"Your summer school teacher."

"You're not gonna believe it. I saw Joe DiMaggio. He was walking up the ramp."

"Isn't he in the army?"

"Maybe he's on leave. I dunno. But I know it was him. No one's gonna believe me."

"Maybe he's gonna play for the Cubs."

"There's no way. He'll always be a Yankee. He's probably just passing through and wanted to see the Cubs play."

Elmore sang, "Joe, Joe DiMaggio," and Eddy joined the chorus, "We want you on our side."

A thunderous roar shook the stadium. The game was underway. Eddy and Elmore ran to the terrace entrance, a concrete tunnel with stairs that led to the box seats and lower deck section. Eddy scaled the stairs, two steps at a time.

Elmore tramped up the steps as if he were sleepwalking. A cool breeze swept through his red hair, tousled like a flickering flame. He reached the top and froze, his lips parted in wonder. The infield was the color of golden sand. The outfield grass, a radiant green, looked like felt on a brand-new billiard table, glowing in God's light.

An usher had abandoned her post. Eddy grabbed Elmore's sleeve and guided him down an aisle near the visiting team's dugout. Peanut shells crunched beneath their feet. They scooted past a man in a straw hat and sat in the middle of the row. Stale beer, boiled hot dogs, and cigar smoke wafted in the stadium air, filled with the lazy sound of a pipe organ.

A sweaty overweight vendor lumbered down their aisle. He banged a metal box with a bottle cap and screamed in a hoarse voice, "Red-hot, hot, hot, dogs. Get your red hots."

Eddy nudged Elmore and pointed to the vendor. "That's Gravel Gertie. He sells the most dogs."

Gertie stopped at Eddy's row and stared at the man in the straw hat. "What's the matter? You too cheap to buy your sons a hot dog?"

"They're not my sons. Give me a dog." The man handed Gertie a quarter.

Gertie gave the man a hot dog. "You're gonna let these two boys starve? Buy them a darn hot dog!"

The man glanced at Eddy and Elmore. "Put relish on mine," Eddy said.

The man's kisser was a like a manager's frown after a bad play. He slid up from his seat, dug in his pocket, and pulled out two quarters. "Here. You happy?"

"Don'tcha feel better now?" Gertie said. "Enjoy the game, boys."

"Hey, there's no ketchup on my hot dog," Elmore said.

"Ketchup? You're not from around here, are you?" Eddy said. "We don't put ketchup on hot dogs."

"Why? You put relish on yours."

"Relish is different. Ketchup is too sweet. Would you put chocolate syrup on your hot dog?"

Elmore shrugged and bit into his plain hot dog. They munched on their free food in the afternoon June sun. Wrigley was nearly full, but there were empty seats scattered about.

A Reds batter hit a lazy pop-up to short for the third out. The Cubs players jogged back to their dugout. "Why do they leave their mitts in the field?" Elmore said.

"I dunno, that's the way they do it."

"Yeah, but somebody could trip on a mitt."

"I've never seen it happen, and I've watched a lot of ball games."

"It doesn't make sense. Why can't they bring it with them to the dugout?"

"If they're left stranded on base, they don't have to run back to the dugout to get their mitts. They just go to their position."

"The batboy can run over and give them their mitt."

Eddy wolfed down the last of his dog, sighed, and said, "Maybe they don't want to lose their mitts in the dugout. Do you bring your books home from school?"

"Yeah."

"That figures. I leave them in my desk. You always know where your books are. That way you don't lose them."

"Then how do you do your homework?"

"You ask too many questions."

"You don't do your homework, do you? That's why you're in summer school. Not bringing your books home makes as much sense as…I dunno… trying to steal first base. Say, why do the players run around the bases counterclockwise? Ever thought of that?"

Eddy scooped out a match and cigarette from his pocket. He struck the match on the concrete ground and lit the cigarette. He raised his head and took a drag. "That's a good question. Maybe that's the direction the first batter ran when they invented baseball, and nobody changed it."

The man next to them leaned sideways. "Most batters are right handed. It's easier for righties to run to first base rather than wheel around and run to third. The guy who invented baseball must have been right handed. I guess right-handed batters have the advantage."

"Tell that to Babe Ruth and DiMaggio. Both bat left handed," Eddy said, sporting a smart-alecky smile. He took another drag and watched Stan Hack walk to the plate.

"Come on, Smilin' Stan, hit one out," Elmore screamed.

"That's what the newspapers call him, but he has another nickname," Eddy said.

"What is it?"

"Stanilaus."

"Why they call him that?" Elmore said.

"Instead of Santa Claus, it's Stanilaus. Get it?" Eddy said. "The Cubs manager gave it to him. He gave all the players a nickname."

Hack lined a single into right field. The crowd was on its feet.

"I know all the nicknames. Go ahead, test me," Eddy said.

"What's the shortstop's nickname?"

"Lennie Merullo," Eddy said. "Boots, on account that he made four errors in one game. Merullo liked it so much he named his son Boots. Can you believe it? Who names their kid Boots? That's a dogs' name."

"What about the batter? Who's up now?"

"That's Don Johnson. Pep."

Elmore whispered the name, his eyes glued on the batter. Johnson smashed the ball over the center fielder's head for a double. Elmore and Eddy jumped to their feet as Hack rounded third to score.

Heinz Becker plodded to the plate.

"This guy's nickname is funny," Eddy said. "It's Heinz-a-poodle. I think it's because he has really bad feet. He's delicate like a poodle. He was born in Germany. The newspapers said he volunteered to join the army, but he was rejected because of his feet. He's a good hitter, but he can't run and looks clumsy at first. Just watch. It's brutal."

Becker connected on the first pitch. It sounded like a hard-hit cue ball smashing against all fifteen balls on a break. The ball sailed over the left fielder's head and into the corner. Becker winced as he hobbled to second for a double.

Eddy screamed over the cheering crowd. "See, what'd I tell ya? He's a good hitter, but he can't run!"

Eddy pointed to the Cubs bullpen. "See number thirteen. That's Claude Passeau. He's a pitcher, and his nickname's Mr. Chips. He had bone chips removed from his elbow. Over there. Number thirty-three. That's Hank Wyse, a pitcher. He's Hankus Pankus. And there's Paul Erickson. He's pitching the next game. I think his nickname's the Milkman, because in the off-season, he's a milkman in Chicago. Somewhere south of here. There's outfielder Andy Pafko. His nickname is Prushka. Don't ask me why."

"What about that player who came from Chicago?"

"Very good, Elmore. You heard about Phil Cavaretta, but everybody knows him. The Cubs drafted him straight out of Lane Tech. He's Philibuck. The best hitter on the team. An all-star."

Eddy boasted his way through the nicknames on the rest of the roster. He went on to the rest of the National League. By the seventh inning, he'd gotten through the American League.

An usher walked down the aisle and stopped at their row. Eddy whispered, "Don't look at her." The man next to Eddy nudged him and pointed to the usher.

"May I see your tickets," she said. She was a slim brunette with Coke-colored eyes, about eighteen years old.

Eddy stood up and emptied his pockets. "I threw my tickets in the trash."

"You're supposed to keep your tickets," she said.

Eddy stretched out his arms and shrugged. "What can I say? I'm sorry. By the way, you really have a nice smile. Keep smiling."

She laughed. "Thank you, but you can't sit here if you don't have your ticket."

"It's our first Cubs game. Give us a break."

The usher shook her head.

"What's your name? Mine's Eddy."

The usher smiled. "If you don't have a ticket, Eddy, you can't sit here."

Eddy turned to Elmore and said loud enough for the entire row to hear, "Did you hear that? She said my name. I gotta know your name, or should I just call you sweetheart?"

"Isabella. Now you two need to leave your seats."

"Okay. But, Isabella, if you let us sit here, you can get all the free hot dogs and drinks at my family's tavern just across the street. You might have heard of it. Ernie's Bleachers?"

"I get free drinks and food here. But you're kinda cute. Enjoy the game." She walked up the aisle.

"I think I'm in love," Eddy said.

"Don't you have a girl? What's her name?"

"Isabella. Oh, you mean Maria. I gotta lot of girls, kid. Stick with me, and you'll learn some things."

"What would that be? Skip school? Blow smoke rings? Whistle real loud?"

"Oh, a wise guy," Eddy said. He playfully punched Elmore in the arm.

"Who's your favorite Cub of all time?" Elmore said.

Eddy raised his head. His eyes swam in the blue sky. "Augie Galan. We'd be in the bleachers during batting practice and throw our hats on the field. He'd run over and put an old ball in there and throw it back up. He's the only guy in the National League to ever hit a homer from both sides of the plate in one game." Eddy puffed on his cigarette and blew a smoke ring. "Did you know he has a deformed right arm? He broke it playing ball as a kid. He never went to a doctor, and it didn't heal right. But can he throw from the outfield. I don't know how he does it. He's with Brooklyn now."

"Did he have a nickname?"

"You're not gonna believe this," Eddy said. "It's Goo Goo. I read that Grimm gave him the name because he has big round eyes. I don't know if that's true. Can't believe everything you read."

Eddy jabbed Elmore's arm. "I gotta a nickname for you."

Elmore smiled. "What?"

"The big little general."

Elmore laughed and turned his attention to the game. A Reds batter struck out for the third out. The Cubs were coming up to bat in the bottom of the seventh. Fans stood up for the seventh inning stretch, but Eddy and Elmore stayed seated.

A smooth summer breeze rustled through the lush ivy that clung on and covered the outfield brick wall, its thick green leaves fluttering and gently swaying upward. Above the green scoreboard, the American flag, and under it, eight National League team flags hoisted on a nautical-style mast, freely flapped in the direction of Lake Michigan. Soft cotton candy clouds sailed east over the ball game. The wind was blowing out.

Eddy took a drag. His eyes raced around the stands and swung back to the batter's box. Cavaretta walked to the plate, a Louisville Slugger slumped over his shoulder as if it were a rifle or a bazooka.

Eddy nudged Elmore. "Have you noticed what Cavaretta does when he walks to the plate? Watch him."

Cavaretta stopped short of the batter's box and spit. He swung at the spit but missed. He spit again and swung, this time hitting the loogie on the meat of his bat. Philibuck then stepped into the batters' box, taking practice swings, his lips pushed out and slightly parted.

"Yuck. Why does he do that?" Elmore said, his face scrunched in disgust.

"I dunno. He does it every time he comes to the plate."

Cavaretta swung at the first pitch and grounded out. The next batter, Bill Nicholson, swaggered to the plate. His brow furrowed under his Cubs cap, set low over his sneering eyes, a chaw of tobacco bulged from his cheek as he crouched in the batter's box. The lefthander leveled his bat across the plate as if he were measuring the strike zone.

"Swish! Swish! Swish!" Eddy yelled, his hands cupped over his mouth. "That's his nickname. He's a great hitter. Last year the Giants walked him with the bases loaded. Can you believe that?"

Elmore nodded, his eyes fixed on the big ballplayer, built like a fullback.

Nicholson swung at the first pitch, knocking the ball in the gap in right center field for a double.

The next batter, Mickey Livingston, bunted Nicholson to third. The crowd rose to its feet as pinch hitter, Paul Gillespie, singled in Nicholson. The stadium erupted in cheers and applause. Merullo and Hack flied and out and the inning ended.

The Reds scored a run in the top of eighth. In the bottom of the same inning, Becker walked, and Pafko singled with two outs. Nicholson came to the plate.

"I bet you he gets a hit," Eddy said. He nudged Elmore and pointed to the scoreboard. "How about a game of poker?"

"How are we going to play poker without playing cards? And I don't have any money," Elmore said.

"We'll use the scoreboard and play for fun," Eddy said. "The best hand from the jersey numbers of the batter, strike, balls, and out wins. I'll go first. Nicholson is number forty-three. There's one strike, one ball and two outs. So right now, my best hand is a pair of ones. If there were no balls, I'd have a straight, zero, one, two, three, and four. Got it?"

"There are no ones or zeros in poker," Elmore said.

"We're not dealing with playing cards, just numbers. Why do ya gotta make this hard. Come on, play along."

Elmore nodded. The next pitch was a fastball, high. Nicholson connected, and the crack of the ball sounded like a shotgun blast a block away. The crowd roared. The ball sailed out of the park. It was a three-run homer. Eddy whistled, and Elmore raised his arms and yelled, "Go Cubs."

Livingston stood at the plate. "He's number eleven! I've got a pair right there," Elmore said.

The first pitch to Livingston was a ball, and the next was a strike. "Look at that. I've got four ones," Elmore said. Livingston hit the next pitch, a sinker that sailed too high over the left field bleachers for a home run. The crowd went wild. Gillespie grounded out, and the inning was over.

Starting pitcher Passeau shut down the Reds' next three batters in the ninth, and the Cubs won.

"That was a humdinger of a game!" Elmore shouted over the raucous crowd. His voice was hoarse like Gertie's.

"You sound thirsty. Let's get outta here and go get a drink," Eddy said.

Eddy weaved through the crowd. Elmore trailed behind, his fingers pinched the back of Eddy's shirt. They passed the Andy Frain usher at Gate D.

"See ya, next time, sweetheart," Eddy said.

They drifted north on Sheffield.

"Hey, Eddy. Eddy, come here." It was Barney guarding the elephant gate.

"Damn," Eddy mumbled.

"What's tickin' chicken," Barney said, his eyes shifting back and forth.

"Nothing, just taking in a game with my friend, Elmore."

“I really need to do that thing we talked about. It’s life and death, Eddy. Ya gotta gimme a break. You’re my last chance.”

“No dice, Barney. You’re busted, and I don’t wanna be on the hook for everything you owe.”

“You got the whim whams. I get it. But I’ll split my winnin’s with ya, fifty-fifty. Ya can buy a lot of smiles with that kind of money.”

Eddy shook his shoulders as if there was a bug crawling on his back. “I dunno. How much you bettin’?”

“A half buck, but this one’s a lock, Eddy. You can sleep on it.”

“Fifty dollars! That’s too much. I can’t cover that.”

“Ya don’t have to. I got the inside scoop on this one. It’s a sure bet, and you get half. And don’tcha worry, kid. Uncle Jimmy ain’t no shortstop.”

Eddy needed the money to cover his loss from Bruce’s muggings. He raked his fingers through his hair and nodded. A bad feeling shivered through his body. Barney slapped a betting slip in Eddy’s hand and turned away.

Eddy shoved the slip in his pocket and walked toward the tavern.

“What was that about?” Elmore said.

“You don’t wanna know.” Eddy spotted Uncle Jimmy, leaning against the corner wall of the tavern, smoking a cigar. “Elmore go in the bar and save me a seat. I’ll be there in a second.”

“All right,” Elmore said.

Eddy bounced over to Uncle Jimmy and flashed his best poker face. “I gotta something for ya,” He handed Uncle Jimmy Barney’s slip. Uncle Jimmy studied it and stuffed it into his shirt pocket.

“What did I tell ya, Eddy? Not ta take any more bets from him.” Uncle Jimmy spoke in muted tones. “He ain’t gotta cryin’ nickel to his name, and he’s in da hole for a lot more dan you can handle. You’re on da hook if he loses. By da way, do you have da seven bucks ya owe me?”

“I’m workin’ on it,” Eddy said, his shoulders sagging and his eyes downcast. “Sorry.”

“Go on, beat it. And get me my money.”

Eddy trudged into the tavern and stopped in front of the jukebox. It was smaller and its color a faded tan. He dropped a nickel into the slot. The coin rattled through the bowels of the machine, and there was an unfamiliar clicking sound when it reached the bottom. The whir of the spindle was louder and longer than the other juke. Eddy's favorite song, "Don't Fence Me In," wasn't in the song list. He chose "Joltin Joe DiMaggio" by Les Brown and his Orchestra. Why did his dad get a new juke?

Eddy hummed the song, breezed across the floor, and plopped on a bar stool next to Elmore.

"What'll it be, boys?" Ernie said.

Elmore ordered a Coke. Eddy asked for a glass of brandy but also got a Coke. "Dad, where did ya get that juke? I never heard half the songs on that list."

"It was a deal I couldn't pass up."

"Did you see the slot machine by the bathroom," Elmore said, pointing to it.

"A slot? Is that legal, Dad?"

Ernie's smile turned into a frown. He dunked a glass in the sink. "Yeah, it was a gift. We'll see how that goes."

"A gift from who?" Eddy said.

Ernie didn't answer. A man in a rumpled yellow suit burst into the tavern, slumped on a stool next to Eddy and, in loud whispers, cried, "Ernie, Ernie, I need to talk to you right now."

"Whaddya say, Ken? How's business?" Ken Margolis owned the Autograph Bar on Broadway and lived in an apartment across from Ernie's Bleachers.

"Not good. Yesterday, two men stuck a gat in my shnozz and robbed me. They locked me in the washroom, stole one hundred and fifty dollars from the till, and made off with twenty-five bottles of whiskey," Ken said. "If that's ain't bad enough, last week two thugs came in and demanded I get rid of a juke and take theirs, or it'd be curtains for me."

Ernie tilted his head to the side, his eyes fixed at the end of the bar. They moved away from Eddy and Elmore.

"Take it easy," Ernie said. "Those guys came in here and said the same thing. They hit all the gin mills from here to Ashland."

"Take it easy? Today, I got a notice from the OPA telling me I gotta go to court and face a hundred-dollar fine for selling beer over their price ceiling. If the criminals don't ruin my business, the government will. I complained to the police, the mayor, and our alderman, and none of 'em won't do nothin'. You're in the tavern business, and you're our precinct captain. Ya gotta do somethin'."

Ernie reached over the bar and patted Ken's back. "Have a seat. What you need is a glass of giggle water." Ernie poured a beer and slid the glass to Ken. "Tell ya what, I'll talk to our alderman and see if I can get that fine erased. See our jukebox over there? It came from those thugs at no cost to me. They'll give you the same setup. There's nothing you can do about it except to take their juke."

A boom like cannon fire rattled the bottles in front of the mirror. There was the distant sound of glass breaking.

"What the hell was that?" Ernie said.

"I dunno. It came from outside," Ken said.

Patrons rushed out of the bar. Sailor rushed behind the bar and poked his head through the takeout window. "Ernie, ya gotta see this. Something bad happened down the street.

"Eddy, watch the place. I locked the till." Ernie ran out the bar and followed the crowd south on Sheffield.

Eddy snuck behind the counter and grabbed a pack of cigarettes. "Elmore, stay here." He raced toward the commotion.

Neighbors piled out of their flats, and bystanders rushed to the Grandstand Grill, at the corner of Sheffield and Addison. A green-and-white Chicago Motor Coach Company bus had plowed into the bar, the back end sticking out onto the sidewalk. Glass, bricks, and remnants of metal frame lay scattered on the roof and littered the front sidewalk of the tavern.

There were screams from inside the bus. Startled customers covered in debris shouted obscenities as they slowly climbed through the jagged rubble.

A woman in a navy-blue blouse drenched in dust debris limped out of the bar, clutching a bottle of beer. She howled in pain. Walter wrapped his arm around her and guided her to the curb.

She sat and took a long swig. She wiped her mouth with her forearm. "Jesus, Mother Mary, and Joseph, I thought the Japs bombed us."

Sailor and several other men rushed into the tavern and searched the wreckage for other victims.

Eddy slinked inside the shattered bar behind them. His shoes crunched on broken glass. The bus had upended a cigar display case, a metal table, and several metal chairs near a side door. A portion of the roof had collapsed, and bent framing hung off the front of the bus, extending over the bar counter.

Debris covered most of the bus, but the words "Please wave, dime ready" painted in white letters on the side of the bus were visible.

Passengers shuffled off the bus and plodded through a gaping hole that was once a window. Eddy's eyes locked on the cash register, located behind the bar. He stepped closer to the counter and craned his neck to get a better look at the till. It was open and emptied. *I just can't get a break,* Eddy thought.

Eddy slogged to the cigar display, its window casing shattered. Cuban cigars were scattered on the floor around it. He glanced around. No one was looking. He bent down and scooped up a handful of cigars. He stuffed them in his pockets and waltzed out of the busted-up joint. He bumped into Uncle Jimmy on the way out.

"Ain't you got no morals, Eddy?" Uncle Jimmy said.

Eddy gave him a cigar. Uncle Jimmy clipped it, stuck it into the side of his mouth, and lit it. "You forgettin' somethin'?"

"The till was empty."

Uncle Jimmy puffed on his cigar and grunted. "While your old man over dere is playin' Boy Scout, your meat hooks should be raidin' his till. Go get me my money."

"I can't. He locked it."

Uncle Jimmy waved away Eddy. A cloud of cigar smoke shrouded his face. "Beat it, kid."

Eddy slunk away but jumped at the sound of an angry voice. Paul Spizak, the owner of the Grandstand Grill, was threatening the bus driver, a short man with glasses and a beer belly.

"Where did ya get your license, in a Cracker Jack box?" Spizak shouted. He was in his fifties, tall, lean with a five o'clock shadow. "I'm gonna give you a knuckle sandwich is what I'm gonna do."

Ernie and Ken held Spizak. "Cool down, Paul. Hitting him ain't gonna solve nothing," Ernie said.

"Look at dis place. It's a disaster," Spizak screamed. "I'm gonna sue this son of a bitch and the bus company right into hell."

"Shuddup, Paul. Help us with this guy," Ernie said. An ambulance wailed in the distance.

"Help him? Are you crazy!"

"Why don't you go talk to the beat cop," Ernie said. "Give him your statement. He's right over there."

"Good idea. Betcha he asks for a handout." Spizak hurried away.

The bus driver staggered around the side of the bus. Blood trickled from the side of his mouth, and his eyes were glazed.

"You need to sit down. Take it easy," Ernie told the driver. Ernie and Ken aided the dazed driver into a sitting position on the curb. They kneeled in front of him.

"What's your name?" Ernie asked.

The driver gave a blank expression. "I'm feeling dizzy."

Ernie moved his forefinger back and forth as if he were a hypnotist swinging a pocket watch. "Look at my finger. Can you follow it."

The driver closed his eyes.

"You need to go to the hospital," Ernie said. "Did the cops talk to you yet?"

The driver shook his head.

"You see, Ernie, here's another thing we have to worry about, private bus companies who hire unskilled drivers," Ken said. "How many bus companies are in Chicago anyway? Too many. Maybe it's time the city consolidates them. They keep talking about it but they never do nothin'."

Ernie nodded, his eyes fixed on the driver.

"Ah, this city's so corrupt," Ken said. "No one's gonna do nothin'. The crooks run the game, and we're the pigeons. Say, why don't you run for alderman? You know people."

Ernie swung his forefinger side to side in front of Ken's eyes. "Are you feeling dizzy too?"

"Why not, Ernie? You're an honest businessman. You hate the crime and corruption as much as the next guy. You'd be perfect. A thorn in their side."

Ernie stroked his round dimpled chin. "Yeah, it would be good for business."

— — —

Eddy set the table, the forks on the left side of the plates, the knives and spoons on the right and the glasses above the knives, the way mother taught him. He took a seat, his back straight and his hands rested on his lap.

"Gee-whiz, Eddy, you set the table without me asking, and you're on time?" Margaret said. "You're not acting so silly today."

"Ma, you can call me anything, but don't call me late for dinner," Eddy said. It was an expression his uncle Emil would say. Emil was his dad's younger brother. He lived next door. He joined the army at age thirty-five and was in Italy.

"Nonna, have you heard from Uncle Emil?" Eddy said.

Nonna sat down next to Eddy and tousled his uncombed head. "He's still in Milan. He is…come se dice? Doing A-okay. Grazie a Dio." She coughed and gasped for air.

"Are you all right, Nonna?" Eddy said.

She caught her breath. "I'm A-okay. Grazie."

Nonno rubbed his wife's back. "Che cosa ce di male?"

Nonna gave a dismissive wave of her hand. "I'm A-okay."

"Ernie, get over here and eat," Margaret yelled.

Ernie lounged on the couch. He rustled the newspaper and turned the page.

"Ernie, did you hear me?"

No answer.

"I made chicken risotto with Italian green beans like he likes it, and he don't move a muscle. Then you can cook next time."

"Ma, Dad can't even boil water," Florence said.

"He'd better go before me, or he'll starve," Margaret said.

Ernie rose and walked to the table in a solemn way. His shoulders drooped, and his lips twisted like corkscrews.

"Ernie, is something wrong?" Margaret said.

"No, nothing's wrong with me," Ernie said.

Nobody ate. No one ate until Ernie sat at the table, and Nonna said the prayer.

Nonna coughed and cleared her throat. "Cuore di Gesu, benedite questo cibo e provvedi a tutti coloro che non ne hanno. Amen."

Everyone dove in. Margaret could really cook.

"What did you learn in school today, Eddy?" Margaret asked over the rushed rhythm of dinner forks and knives and plates clinking.

Eddy stabbed his fork into the risotto. "Nothing."

"Nothing? You better learn something. You're on the ropes, kiddo," Margaret said.

"I saw Joe DiMaggio today," Eddy said in a cheerful tone.

"You did! Where?" Bobby said.

"At Wrigley. He was just walking up the ramp like anybody."

"Oh, come on. Why would DiMaggio walk around Wrigley Field? There'd be a mob surrounding him," Bobby said.

"He was in disguise, wise ass."

Nonno smacked him on the head for cursing.

"What were you doing at Wrigley Field? The game started at one fifteen, and your class doesn't get out until one thirty," Margaret said.

Eddy lifted his shoulder in a half shrug. "I got there after class, Ma."

Margaret rolled her eyes and turned to Ernie. "What do you have to say about all of this? Why are you so quiet?"

Ernie chewed his chicken and stared at his plate.

Nonno poked him with a fork. "Wake up."

"Cut it out, Dad," Ernie said.

"What's got into you, Ernie?" Margaret asked, her tone soft but annoyed.

"Nothing, Marge."

"Don't tell me it's nothing with all the problems we have." Margaret took a deep breath and let out a long sigh.

"Can't you two ever get along?" Eddy said.

"When you get married, you'll understand," Margaret said, her lips tightened. She took a sip of wine, set the wineglass on the table, and turned to Eddy. "Did you know that when your father first called me your aunt Theresa answered, and she talked to him, but he wanted to talk to me. She wanted to go with him, you know. I was surprised when I answered the phone and it was him. And he says, 'Gee-whiz,' we see each other on the train. How about I have a date with you?' And I said, 'No, I don't think so.' I let on that I was busy. I really didn't want to go with him. He called me so much I finally went out with him." Margaret smiled and turned to Ernie, "How did you get my phone number?"

"A little birdie told me."

Margaret picked up her glass and twirled it, the red wine whirling around in smooth arcs. "You know I met your uncle Laury before your dad. I would see both of them on the train, and Laury came over and sat next to me. I got to know him pretty well. Then your dad came over to talk to me. He was a gentleman, kind. Where Laury was rough. I didn't like the way he talked. Imagine if I went with Laury, aye yie yie."

Margaret gently touched Ernie's arm. "I made the right choice."

Ernie smiled and said, "I'm gonna run for alderman."

Margaret slammed her wineglass on the table. Wine sloshed over the rim, spilling onto the white table cloth. "The hell you are!"

"Ernie, you can't do this. You have a business to run and a familia to feed," Nonno said.

"Where are you going to get the money to run for alderman?" Margaret said.

"I'll get it," Ernie said.

"You have a sixth-grade education, and these people you will be running against are all lawyers," Margaret howled. "And who's going to help you run a campaign while you run the business? Huh?"

"Ed Kelly never finished grammar school, and he's the mayor of Chicago," Ernie said. "The kids can help with my campaign."

"Sure, Dad, I'll help," Bobby said.

"Not me. I got summer school," Eddy said.

"Why do you want to run against Frank?" Margaret said. "He's done so much for us. He has the city pick up the tavern garbage and clear the snow in front at no charge. He helped us sail through the permit process when we built the tavern, Ernie. He's our friend."

"Did you see all that blood in the bus crash today?" Ernie said. "These drivers are patronage jobs, and they're not trained right. Politicians and the Outfit have their hands in all of these bus companies and there are too many of them. The Outfit threatens us if we don't take their jukes and slots. Frank won't stand up to them. He's been alderman for as long as I can remember. It's time for a change."

"And just what are you going to do if you're an alderman, Ernie? Nothing. They either buy you off or knock you off. Either way, nothing changes."

"I'm not going to change my mind, Marge," Ernie said. "That's that." When he'd made up his mind about something, anything from betting on a bad hand to going to St. Mary of the Lake instead of Our Lady of Mount

Carmel, no one could never change it back again. It was a sure bet Eddy could make with his dad.

Margaret jumped out of her seat. Her eyes flared, and her face flushed a deep ruby red. She smashed a dinner plate on the floor. "You're nuts. Come on, kids. Get your clothes. We're going."

"Where are you taking them?" Ernie thundered.

"To my sisters.'"

Bobby and Florence rose. Ernie barked at them. "Sit down."

"No, you're coming with me," Margaret said.

"Sit down," Ernie said.

Bobby and Florence walked to the front door.

"Where are you two going?" Margaret yelled.

"Out, Ma. Just out," Bobby said.

Nonna let out a deep cough and listed toward the front door. "I'm not feeling so good. I'm going home." Nonno followed, his hand clasped his wife's arm.

Margaret planted her hands on her hips and glowered at her husband. "You ruined our dinner."

"This risotto is tasty," Ernie said. He winked at Eddy. "And here it comes."

Margaret stormed to the door. "You are impossible, Ernie." The door slammed shut. The walls shook and plates clattered.

Eddy popped out of his chair. "I'll be in my bedroom doing homework, Dad."

Ernie hung his head, his arms crossed on the table.

"What are ya thinkin' about, Dad?"

"How to get the mayor's endorsement. Got any ideas?"

"I dunno. Pay him off like everyone else does."

Ernie smiled and stared at his empty plate. "There's got to be another way."

"I'll be in my room." Eddy left his dad to steam in solitude. He coasted down the hallway and tiptoed out the back. He flew down the porch and bolted onto the parking lot. He ran east on Waveland toward the schoolyard.

TOP OF THE FOURTH

A river of sweat rolled down the sides of Eddy's face. Salty droplets burned his eyes. He removed his shirt and rubbed his eyes with it. He squirmed in the driver's seat of a 1940 Packard Clipper parked behind Ernie's Bleachers. His sticky body peeled off the leather seat as if he tore a bandage off his back.

Why did he agree to work the parking lot on a day the temperature was above a hundred degrees? He had to sit in the hot box and watch the cars in the back of the parking lot during the entire Cub game. He could scram, but the last time he did, someone stole a car. It was found the next day on Broadway and Sheridan with a couple of dents and a broken rearview mirror. His parents made him pay the repair cost. It was another bum rap.

Eddy rolled down the windows. A lazy wind blasted his face as if he had opened an oven. Heat shimmered off the car hood. Beads of condensation dripped from a paper cup that contained warm Coke. A smoky haze hung low in the stale summer air.

He turned on the radio and spun the dial to the Cubs game. The cheerful even-keeled voice of Cubs announcer Bert Wilson said, "It's such a beautiful cloudless day and frankly it's such a beautiful day I don't care who wins as long as it's the Cubs."

"Not so beautiful in this hellhole," Eddy mumbled. He turned up the volume to stay alert.

"Stepping to the plate is Cardinal shortstop Marty Marion," the announcer said. "He's oh-for-one today with a strikeout and a walk. Prim has pitched a good game so far. He's taking his time on the mound. It's a hot one today."

Wilson's long pauses punctuated by the sweltering heat lulled Eddy into a fog. His breathing slowed, his eyes heavy. He struggled to keep them open. They closed.

Bert Wilson's voice faded in and out. "Here's the situation. It's the top of the ninth in the seventh game of the World Series and the Cubs ahead by a run. Yankees have a man on first with two outs and Joe DiMaggio is at the plate. You couldn't ask for a more exciting moment in baseball. Prim delivers, and there's a shot to right field, Eddy Pareti going back to the wall. Wait, he's climbing the vines. He reaches up. Oh Lord, he caught it in the first row of the bleachers. What a catch! Cub players are storming down right field. The fans are going nuts. Cubs win the World Series. And now they're carrying Pareti to the infield. Augie Galan is there shaking Pareti's hand, tousling his hair. Wait, someone handed Pareti a mic. He's going to speak."

"Today, I'm the luckiest man on the face of the earth..."

"Eddy, Eddy, wake up my handsome prince."

Eddy opened one eye, his head drenched in sweat. Maria leaned inside the car window and stroked his hair.

"I must have died and gone to heaven," Eddy said. "Either you're an angel, or I'm the luckiest man on the face of the earth."

Maria tilted her head, her blues eyes gazing down like a mother fawning over her little boy. "Eddy, you're soaking wet. Why are you sitting in this hot as hell car?"

"I'm working. And don't you get any ideas of taking one of these cars, or I'll have to make a citizen's arrest." Eddy spotted Gerace, Elmore, Warman, and Hootie, straggling behind Maria. Hootie's mug was peeking inside a Pontiac Streamliner. "And that goes for youse. Don't get any funny ideas." It was Eddy's tough-guy act.

"What's buzzin', cousin?" Gerace said. "Come on, get out of that roaster and come with us, will ya? I'm sweatin' just lookin at ya."

Eddy gripped the steering wheel. His hands jerked back as if he had touched a hot stove. "Damn, that hurt like dog." He raked his hands through his head and leaned out the car. "What inning is it?"

"I dunno," Gerace said. "Who cares? You comin?"

"Naw. I'll take a rain check. I gotta stay here. I'll catch up with ya later."

"Don't be a fuddy-duddy," Gerace said. "Since when did you start following the rules?"

"Lay off, will ya?" Eddy said. "I gotta watch these cars. The keys are inside. Anyone can drive off."

Gerace's eyes widened. "Why don't we take one of these for a spin?"

"Not a chance. My brother is in the front of this parking lot, watching cars. He'll rat on me, and I'm in bad with the old man. Don't need the aggravation."

"Eddy is doll dizzy. He ain't thinking straight," Hootie said.

Maria shot a look at Hootie and then turned to Eddy. "Meet us later at schoolyard." She blew a kiss and headed toward Waveland. Eddy watched her hips sway as she walked away.

"Ah, you're all wet," Hootie said, shooing off Eddy.

"See you in the funny papers," Gerace said. Elmore and Warman waved goodbye.

Eddy bit his lip and wiped his forehead with the back of his hand. "What the hell." He slipped on his sweat-soaked shirt, opened the door, and stepped onto the parking lot gravel.

A short pudgy man in a plaid short-sleeve shirt too small for his bulging belly stumbled toward Eddy. "Hey, you, get my car." He pointed in the direction of a blue Ford Tudor parked behind a Hudson Commodore under the El.

"Sir, can I have your ticket?" Eddy said.

The man fumbled around in his pants pocket, his sweaty face scrunched in annoyance. He dug out his wallet and held it with shaky hands. He dropped it, and as he bent over to pick it up, he lost his balance and almost fell. He steadied himself and rummaged through his wallet. The man shook his head. "I don't have it."

"I can't let you have this car without a ticket."

"Nobody told me about any ticket," the man yelled, saliva sprayed Eddy's face. "That's my car, you dope."

"Who ya callin' a dope. You lost your ticket. How do I know that's your car?" Eddy fired back.

The man squinted as if he were trying to focus. "Don't snap your cap at me. How old are you, boy?"

"What's that gotta do with anything?"

"You're not old enough to drive. If you don't move this car now, I'm callin' the police."

"What's going on over there?" Bobby shouted. He raced to the back of the lot and stood between the man and Eddy.

"He doesn't have his ticket, and he says he gonna call the police on me," Eddy said.

Bobby asked the man which car was his. The man pointed to the Ford.

"I remember you," Bobby said. "I saw you put your ticket in your shirt pocket."

The man reached into his shirt pocket and pulled out the ticket.

"You gonna apologize?" Eddy said.

The man ignored Eddy and handed Bobby the ticket. Bobby told Eddy to move the car.

"No way. I'm not moving a car for him," Eddy said.

"Wait here. I'll handle this, like always I do." He jumped into the Commodore and parked it into a vacant spot. The man staggered to his car, slumped inside, and drove out of the alley, almost hitting another car.

Bobby stormed over to Eddy. "You can't yell at drunk customers. You were about to get your jaw kissed. You know that?"

Eddy shrugged and headed toward Waveland.

"Where you goin?" Bobby yelled.

"I'm leaving. You can handle it, like you always do."

"Someone has to watch the back," Bobby said. "Nonno ain't gonna pay you if you leave."

"He's not here," Eddy said. He spotted the gang across the street under the El and ran toward them.

Gerace shinnied up an iron column of the El track like a monkey. He gripped a steel girder at the top and poked his head through the ties above the southbound tracks.

"See anything?" Hootie said.

Gerace lowered his head. "No train."

Sweat oozed from Eddy's palm, and his heart hammered in his chest. His head swiveled in the direction of the parking lot and his abandoned post. He shouldn't have come. The game of chicken terrified him, and he knew Gerace, Hootie, and Warman would challenge him. He had developed a fear of heights after he'd fallen from a gutter he had climbed at Chicago Stadium during a Jake LaMotta fight. He clambered halfway up and looked down. That was a mistake. His head spun, and his hands shook. He lost his grip and fell twenty feet. He landed in a patch of grass and weeds with a heavy thud that knocked the wind out of him. A cop had called his mother and an ambulance. Eddy stood there, clutching his broken arm while his mother and the cop argued which hospital to send him to.

Not long after his arm healed, he scaled a wall and a fence near the front gate of Wrigley Field. He hung on the fence and froze. Bobby climbed down to help, but Eddy wouldn't budge, his white-knuckled fingers hooked into the fence like a cat clawed in curtains. A cop ordered them down, but Eddy clung to the fence. It took a fire truck ladder to rescue him.

"I hear it!" Gerace shouted. The train barreled down the track, sparks shooting off the wheels. Gerace stuck his head above the railroad ties like a nervous prairie dog popping up from the ground for a look around. He flipped off the conductor and ducked under the tracks just in time. He leaned out from the column, raised his fist, and let out a whoop as sparks showered the air under the El. The train roared above him.

"That was aces," Warman cried. "It's your turn, Eddy."

Eddy shook his head. "Let's get outtta here. I'm supposed to be working in the lot. They might see me here."

Gerace scurried down. He curled his arms and flapped them. "Eddy's the chicken. Buck, buck, buck."

"Cut it out, will ya? I'm not afraid."

"Then what ya waiting for? Go up," Hootie said, pointing to the El.

"You don't have to do it," Maria said. "You might be a chicken, but you're a handsome chicken. I mean, handsome boy." Eddy's friends broke out in laughter.

"Even your girl thinks you're a chicken," Gerace said.

Eddy smirked. He slow-walked to the column and wrapped his arms around it. He glanced at Maria, her smile a shot of courage. He raised his head as if in prayer and climbed as fast as he could. In seconds, he was at the top. He closed his eyes, took a deep breath, and mumbled, "Whatever you do, don't look down."

Eddy poked his head through the ties and peered down the track. It was as straight as the first baseline at Cubs Park. A train rumbled in the distance. He pulled himself higher to get a better look. No train. The sound grew louder. Voices shouted below. He couldn't make out the words, and he wasn't going to look down. The piercing screech of the train was earsplitting. "Where the hell is it!"

A haunting realization jolted his body. Eddy swiveled his head. He saw the rusted grill of a train barreling down on him. He dropped and lost his balance. A metal spike hooked the back of Eddy's shirt. He gripped the column, but his shirt, caught in the spike, hung over his head. To the others watching below, Eddy appeared headless.

Maria fell to her knees and screamed. Gerace cried out, "Oh my God!" Elmore buried his head in his hands.

Eddy closed his eyes and hugged the column. He tore his shirt off the spike. How could he make such a stupid mistake? He took a deep breath but refused to look down. His body trembled. Voices screamed. The train thundered above.

"Why did ya look the wrong way? You live next to the train track. You should know better, you dope," Hootie shouted.

"You win. Now, come down, Eddy," Gerace said.

Eddy rested his forehead on the column. How could it feel cool on a hot day, he wondered. He inched down, but after a few attempts, he froze. His friends begged him to continue his descent. Then they were silent.

"Well, if it ain't flat nose, stuck up there like a scared sissy," Bruce said. His friends joined the taunt.

"Are you gonna cry?" said one of them in a baby voice. "Should we call your mommy to come help you down?"

"I'll get him down," Bruce said. He picked up a rock the size of a golf ball and whipped it. The rock struck Eddy's left calf.

"Ow!" Eddy cried out. Bruce's friends joined the attack. Rocks careened off the column like a hail of bullets whizzing past Eddy's head. Eddy scooted around the column, but he was unable to avoid the barrage.

"Stop it!" Maria screamed. She grabbed Bruce's throwing arm. The brute swung his free arm around her neck and flung her to the ground.

Gerace chunked a rock that struck the bully's head with a heavy thud. Bruce turned, his face scrunched in anger. "You moon-eyed moron. You're dead."

Gerace ran. He tripped and hunched over, his head buried in his hands and arms as Bruce pummeled him with wild punches.

Elmore drove his foot into Bruce's shin. Bruce yelped and backhanded Elmore. The redhead's noggin whipped back, and his glasses flew off.

Hootie coldcocked Bruce square in the jaw. The thug's head snapped sideways, but the hit didn't rock him. He tackled Hootie, pinned him down, and whaled away.

Satisfied of the beating, Bruce sprung to his feet. "Who else is hungry for a knuckle sandwich?" He sprinted toward Warman. "How about you, Baby Huey? Did you pee in your pants? Are you wearing diapers?"

Warman stood stone faced, clenched hands and mashed lips. Bruce glared, his eyes wide and teeth bared. "Take a shot, jag off. I dare you. You get the first punch."

No reaction.

Bruce's head turned in the direction of his friends. "It looks like Baby Huey's got his foot in the bucket."

Warman swung, a wild roundhouse punch that grazed the back of Bruce's head. Bruce stumbled backward but stayed on his feet. He countered with a right hook that struck Warman on the chin as the gigantic eleven-year-old hurled forward, unfazed. Warman grasped Bruce's left arm, and he rotated in a circular motion like an Olympian in the hammer throw. He released his grip after two rotations. Bruce flew several feet and landed on his back. He rolled to his side to lift himself up. Warman stomped on his head, and the punk's face ate concrete with a thump and a crack. It sounded like a bat hitting a softball. Bruce gasped for air. Blood oozed out of his mouth and nose. He bawled, "You're dead!"

Warman's shaggy golden hair shook like a lion's mane as he repeatedly stomped on Bruce's head and body in a bloodlust rage. Bruce shielded the blows with his arms and tried to crawl away from the attack.

Bruce moaned. "I give up."

Warman kept stomping, his eyes wide and fixed. Veins popped in his neck, and a ruddy fire glowed in his face.

A badly beaten Bruce yelled for his friends to help. The shortest one in the group shouted in cracked voice, "He gives up. It's over. You win."

Warman stopped and glowered at them. Bruce jumped to his feet and raced across Waveland and through Ernie's Bleachers parking lot. Warman chased after him, and the others followed.

Eddy had seen the blow-by-blow from above. It was better than any Jake LaMotta fight. In the excitement, he shinnied down from the rusty metal pylon and joined the crowd of onlookers.

Bruce crashed through the front screen door of Ernie's Bleachers and fell. Warman stormed in the bar like an angry beast and towered over his prey, panting and eyeballing his spoils, ready to kill. Sailor and Walter jumped off their stools and hurried toward the commotion. The scene was odd, an older and taller high schooler lay bleeding on the floor, fearing an oversized innocent-looking baby-faced preteen.

"What in the world?" Sailor said.

"Break it up," Margaret yelled. "You're not gonna fight in this place."

Bruce crouched in a fetal position, blood pouring out of his nose and mouth. Eddy reached into Bruce's pocket and pulled out its contents.

"This should settle the score," Eddy said, holding up a fin and five singles.

"Eddy what are you doing? Give that back," Margaret ordered.

"No way, Ma. This punk mugged me two times. I'm getting even."

"That's right, Mrs. Pareti. He mugged me too," Elmore said.

Warman kicked Bruce in the stomach.

"That's enough, Chuckie," Margaret said. She looked down at Bruce and said, "You! Go on. Get outta here and don't you come back."

Bruce rose to his feet and flinched when Warman threw a fake punch. The bloodied bully bolted out the front door. His stunned friends trailed behind.

Margaret told Warman to wash up and shepherded Eddy, Elmore, Hootie, Gerace, and Maria to a booth at the end of the tavern.

"What are you doing here, Eddy?" Margaret asked. "Aren't you supposed to watch the parking lot?"

"Yeah, Ma, but this fight broke out."

"Why is the back of your shirt ripped? Did you get into a fight too, Eddy?"

Eddy shrugged.

Margaret turned to Sailor and Walter and said, "Why do men and boys always have to fight? You're always fighting. All of you. There would be no wars if women ran things."

The men exchanged glances.

"It figures Ernie is at the game. I'm supposed to run the show and handle men fighting and cursing and drinking and bleeding all over the joint while he enjoys a Cubs game. Well, I'm not going to put up with that. I'll tell you what." She stopped and then raised her voice, "And he wants to run for alderman! The hell he will."

Nobody said a word.

Margaret sighed and placed her hands on her hips. "I guess, with all that fighting, you must be hungry."

"I'll take a beef sandwich, Ma, and make it juicy," Eddy piped in.

"All right, but you're going back to work, mister. The game is almost over, and we're gonna get busy." She tousled Eddy's hair and smiled. "You're still my baby."

Eddy flinched from his mother's affection. "Come on, Ma." He didn't want his friends to think he was a momma's boy.

Margaret wiped her brow and then whistled for Boots, who was lying in a booth behind Eddy. She pointed to Wrigley Field and said, "Boots, go fetch Daddy."

During the day, Boots would wander the neighborhood and at night sleep in the tavern. But sometimes on game days, Boots would hang around the tavern for food.

Five minutes later, Ernie walked in with Boots tracking him from behind. Margaret rested her hand on her husband's shoulder. In that moment, everything had changed.

"Ernie, your mother is in the hospital. They think she had a stroke."

BOTTOM OF THE FOURTH

Two brass lamps bulged out of the funeral parlor wall and cast light over the open casket that contained Nonna. She wore a button-down gray dress with a square neckline and padded shoulders. Her right hand clutched a white orchid that rested peacefully across her chest.

About two dozen relatives and friends sat in folding metal chairs, facing the casket. Muffled cries peppered with soft whispers filled the floral scented room. A line had formed, and one by one, mourners shuffled past Nonna to pay their last respects.

"Go up there, Eddy, and kiss your nonna goodbye," Margaret whispered. She gave a gentle shove in the small of his back.

Eddy hunched his shoulders as if he was trying to shake off a net thrown over him. His mother pushed harder, and Eddy lost his balance. He regained his footing and headed for the front door. His mother grabbed his arm and squeezed, halting the escape.

"You are going up there, and you are going to kiss her goodbye. Do you hear me?"

Eddy glanced at his father in the front row, hoping he would intervene. Ernie wiped his eyes with a handkerchief, his head bowed, unaware of what was expected of Eddy.

"Ma, I can't do this. Please stop," Eddy pleaded.

"She doesn't have a disease, Eddy. Now stop being silly and do it. Now."

"She's dead, Ma. Who wants to kiss a dead person?" His voice rose above the whispers. A few seated mourners swiveled around.

Margaret sighed and turned toward Bobby for help.

"Come on, Eddy, what's the big deal? Everyone's doing it," Bobby said.

"Then you go and kiss her," Eddy shot back.

"All right, we'll go up there together," Bobby said.

Eddy rolled his eyes and took a deep breath. He held it for a few seconds and exhaled. "Okay, big shot, after you." He bowed and flourished his hands in the direction of the casket.

Bobby gripped the edge of the casket, bent over, and kissed his nonna on her cheek. He glanced at Eddy with a smirk as if to say, "Now, it's your turn."

Eddy peeked into the coffin. Nonna's face had color, and the corner of her mouth bent upward. It was if she had climbed into the casket and taken a nap. Any moment, she could rise up and pinch Eddy's cheek.

Five years ago, Nonna had kissed him sweetly on the cheeks and lips after his puppy, Fuzzy, had been run over by a taxi. The dog laid on the street bloodied and mangled. Eddy sat on the curb and wept, his head buried in the crook of his elbow. She rubbed his back and hugged him. "Don't you worry, Eddy. Fuzzy is in heaven, and one day, you will see him again." She handed Eddy a homemade popsicle, pinched his cheeks, and smiled.

"Come on, Eddy, do it," Bobby said, his tone more mocking than encouraging.

Eddy gently stroked the dead woman's cold and bony hand. He turned to leave. His mother clutched his arm and swung him around.

"Ma, I held her hand. Come on, give me a break," Eddy whispered.

Margaret crossed her arms and nodded in the direction of the casket. Eddy tilted his head and made puppy dog eyes at his mother.

Margaret pointed at the casket and mouthed the word "Now."

Eddy gazed at Nonna and blew a kiss. He gestured with open hands, hoping that would please his mother.

Margaret bent over, teeth gritted, and whispered in Eddy's ears, "Don't make me get your father to come up here."

Eddy ran his hand through his hair and rubbed his nose. There was no way out of this one. He took a quick look at Nonna and memorized the location of her cheeks. He closed his eyes, leaned down, and kissed her. He opened his eyes and, in horror, realized his lips were pressed against his dead grandmother's mouth. Eddy lunged back up as if a snake had just bit him. He wiped his mouth with his forearm and raced to the back of the room.

The hushed whispers in the parlor stopped when Bobby burst out laughing.

— — —

Eddy slumped in the pews, his head lolled side to side with heavy half-closed eyelids. Spittle dripped from the side of his mouth.

The priest droned on in prayer. His words echoed monotonously throughout the church. When it was time to stand and sing, Eddy's eyes shot open as if the priest had splashed holy water on his face. He wiped his mouth with his shirt sleeve and rose. He straightened his dark suit and loosened his tie. His dad's booming baritone voice drowned out his mother and sister's crooning chirps. Bobby's lips moved but no sound. Eddy nudged his brother, who turned and winked. Eddy cupped his ear and pointed. Bobby smiled and gazed dutifully at the altar, his lips flapping in silence. Eddy stood on his toes to look at the priest. He wasn't singing either. If the priest didn't sing, then why should he.

Eddy sat in unison with the others. He turned to his brother and whispered, "Are we doing communion?"

Bobby shook his head, his eyes glued to the front.

Receiving the communion wafer made Mass tolerable. The priest would raise the chalice, recite, "The body of Christ," and stick the communion wafer on the tip of Eddy's tongue. Instead of an obligatory amen, Eddy would joke, "God bless you," or "Thank you very much." He would roll the wafer around on the top of his palate until it melted in his mouth. The body of Christ tasted like a thin ice cream cone, a treat for enduring an hour of singing, sitting, kneeling, standing, praying, and dozing.

Eddy scanned the church. There were no ushers passing around collection baskets. What a racket that was. Pigeons would stuff the basket with cash as if they were trying to buy their way into heaven. His parents would drop a fin each time. Priests were no different than police and politicians—they all had their hands out.

After the funeral service, Eddy and his family piled into his uncle's Ford station wagon that followed behind the hearse carrying Nonna. They joined a procession of about a dozen cars filled with relatives, some of whom came from New York. Car horns beeped as they passed Nonna's flat and Ernie's Bleachers. Several tavern patrons outside waved.

"Are we going home?" Eddy asked.

"No, dummy. We're going to the cemetery," Bobby said.

"Dummy, huh. You think you're a big shot just because they picked you to be a pallbearer."

Bobby smiled and shrugged. "It's not my fault no one asked you."

"Big deal, who cares?" Eddy gazed out the car window.

The procession made its second trip around the block, heading north on Sheffield toward Calvary Catholic Cemetery. Eddy licked his lips. He could use a smoke about now. He spent the entire morning in a monkey suit, and he kissed his dead grandmother on the lips. What else did they want?

A few dozen people crowded around Nonna's gravesite, somewhere in the middle of the cemetery. The priest recited yet another prayer. Eddy mumbled a prayer of his own under his breath, "Please, God, let this day be over."

The priest asked if anyone had any final words. Teary-eyed Nonno stepped forward and rested his right hand on his wife's coffin. He paused for a long time. Mourners stood in silence, waiting. A soft wind blew in from the lake, just east of the cemetery. The distant sound of waves lapped the shoreline.

Nonno had spent a week at his wife's bedside in the hospital. Eddy and his family visited twice, and both times Nonno insisted everyone kneel and pray. The old man refused to leave the hospital room and continued to pray over Nonna's bed even after doctors pronounced her death. Eddy's parents ushered the grieving husband back home. The time for prayer was over. Nonno had say to goodbye to his wife of more than a half century.

Nonno cleared his throat and spoke. "God took back his angel. This goodbye is only for a while. One day, I hope to see you again. Ti amero per sempre in paradiso." He rubbed the top edge of the coffin and looked at the priest.

"Does anyone else have any final remarks," the priest asked.

"I do," Ernie said. "My brother, Emil, couldn't make it today. He asked me to read a note my mother wrote him for his high school graduation. He carries it everywhere he goes." Ernie held up the paper and read.

"Dear Emil, there is a place for you in my heart, but there is a place for us both in heaven where the true love never part."

Ernie hung his head, and there was more silence.

Laury, Ernie's older brother, raised his hand. "I got somethin' to say. My mother was a good mother. She was a saint. There ain't no doubt she's in heaven. That's all."

After another long pause, the priest raised his arms and sprinkled holy water on the coffin as it was lowered. "Show compassion to your people in their sorrow. Lift us from the darkness of this grief to the peace and light of your presence. Amen."

— — —

Eddy elbowed his way to the dining room table, reached over his Nonno and grabbed a slice of focaccia. "Excuse me."

Nonno grunted. Eddy expected him to stick a hot spoon on his arm or bellow out some silly joke. But the old geezer wasn't in a playful mood. Who could blame him? Nonna cooked and cleaned for him. They went everywhere together. She was his best friend. And now she was gone.

Nonno sat at the head of the table, his head lowered in somber silence, sipping tea. Sitting across him were aunts, uncles, and Eddy's parents. They nibbled on focaccia, olives, celery, cheese, and coffee cake.

Machine gun chatter and fake apologies filled the noisy apartment that was lined with white lilies, some crammed on top of the dining room hutch. Eddy had never seen so many flowers. *And they were all dead*, he thought.

Some New York cousin named Vinny jostled to the table and snagged a slice of Asiago cheese. He bent down and draped his arm around Nonno's shoulder. "I'm so sorry for your loss. Your wife was a wonderful woman, always nice to me. She'll be missed. If you need anything, you let me know."

Eddy rolled his eyes. This guy Vinny probably never spoke to Nonna. He could give a rip about her.

Eddy wolfed down the last of his focaccia and spied the front door. Now was his chance to sneak out and slip off his itchy suit. But his stomach growled in protest. He took an olive and plopped it into his mouth like popcorn.

"Get this. Emil said his commander asked him where he needed to go and Emil said Chicago," Ernie shouted, his voice booming over the chatter and laughter of the apartment. "The commander said, 'I'd rather shoot myself in the head than go there.' Emil told him he could use blanks for that."

The table roared in laughter, except Nonno. "My poor Emil. He's such a momma's boy, and he couldn't be here to say goodbye."

"Flora would understand," said Nonno's brother, Johnny, who lived in New York.

"Don't say her name," Nonno shouted. "Her soul will come back here."

"That's nuts," Johnny said. "I'm sure she's in heaven, laughing down at you for saying that. Some people believe a soul stays on earth as long as those who loved them live on. It's all superstition."

Nonno grumbled and pounded the table. His chair scraped on the hardwood floor. He rose and walked to his bedroom. "Dad, where are you going?" Ernie asked.

"Let him go. He'll be all right," Johnny said.

Ernie studied the crochet tablecloth his mother had hand sewn. He placed his forefinger over the hollow of his upper lip. "Ma would always tell me that when I was born an angel touched me right here, leaving a fingerprint. I believed her for a long time."

"She told me that too. But I knew it was an old wives' tale," Laury said, laughing in disbelief. "Remember when the union guys bombed the Addison gate at Wrigley? The blast was so powerful it blew out the windows of every flat for blocks, except our bedroom window. Ma told us the window didn't bust cuz an angel lived in our room." Laury's eyes dropped, and he shook his head.

"She was the only angel that ever came in our bedroom," Ernie said.

Eddy grabbed another focaccia.

"Eddy, save some for the rest of us," Laury said.

Eddy smiled as he stuffed his mouth with food.

"I hear you're in summer school. That'll make your head more useful other than just something that keeps your ears apart. You wanna drink?"

Eddy nodded. Laury poured a few drops of water in a glass and slid it toward Eddy.

Eddy slid it back and asked for more. Laury poured a few more drops in the glass. Eddy kept asking for more, and Laury continued pouring only a few drops.

"Oh, for Pete's sake, Laury, pour him a full glass, will ya," Margaret yelled.

Laury's eyes narrowed, and his lips rose in a half smile. "Margaret, do you have any kind words for your deceased mother-in-law?"

"Well, of course, I do." She turned to Ernie. "Do you remember when Eddy and Bobby had scarlet fever, and we were quarantined in our house for about month? Flora did our shopping, cooked for us, and helped with the hot dog stand. She never complained once. She was an absolute angel."

"We had to hang a red quarantine sign over the front door of our flat," Ernie said. "My mother would kneel in front of it every morning with her rosary and pray."

"Remember that red rash around Bobby's mouth? Ugh, that was a such terrible time. But we got through it," Margaret said.

"There was a girl Eddy's age that died from it. What was her name, Marge?"

"Oh gosh, Ernie. You don't remember? It was the Steinberg's daughter, Roberta. She was in Eddy's grade. She went to St. Mary's of the Lake. It was awful seeing that poor girl in the casket. It's not fair."

Nonno stormed into the dining room and stared at Margaret. "Where's my wife's wedding ring?"

"Why are you looking at me? I didn't take it."

"You cleaned my apartment."

"Yes, but I didn't take it, and I didn't see it," Margaret shouted.

"I saw you going through her things in the bedroom," Laury said.

Margaret stood up from the table. "Is this the thanks I get for cleaning and cooking for you? You think you're a big shot because you own these buildings and can treat us any way you want. You won't get my help anymore." She marched to the front door and slammed it on her way out.

A hush fell across the apartment. There was the sound of swooshing suits. Ernie rushed out of the apartment. Eddy followed him.

Ernie raced down the front steps and stopped on the sidewalk. "Marge, wait."

Margaret ignored him. She entered the foyer of her apartment and climbed the stairs.

Eddy stood next to his father. The same day his dad buried his mother he gets into another fight with his wife. Eddy didn't know what to say.

Ernie waved her off. "Aw, let her calm down. Let's see if the bartender needs help closing the bar." Ernie's Bleachers closed early that day on account of the funeral.

The pair entered through the back door. "Max, how are things goin'?" Ernie said a little louder than necessary.

The bartender jerked away from the sink. He had been washing glasses. "Whoa, you scared the beejesus out of me. I thoughts you was a robber or something."

Ernie glanced around the empty bar. Boots sprawled across a booth seat. The floors were swept and mopped, and the chairs placed upside down on the tables. "I guess you don't need me," Ernie said.

"Yeah, you go on back. I'm almost done. Sorry about your ma."

Max shifted nervously. His voice was a shaky, and his speech faster than usual. Ernie strolled to the sink. It was full of soapy water. He stuck his hand in it and felt around. His hand came out with a fistful of quarters. He drained the sink and saw a pile of coins.

"What is this?"

Max shrugged. "Customers bought me drinks. But I don't drink. So I kept the money."

"Oh, so you did, huh? Well, this is a new wrinkle."

Ernie rubbed the back of his head. Max lived a lonely life in a bachelor apartment over on Waveland. He'd been an Ernie's Bleachers regular who'd been down on his luck. So Ernie lent him a hand.

"Go on, get outta here and don't come back. You're fired!" Ernie screamed. The color of Max's face drained. He opened his mouth to say something, but no words came out. He hurried to the front door and left without closing it. Ernie slammed the door and locked it. He walked to the radio above the grill and turned it on at high volume. He poured a beer and sat in a booth next to Boots, who rested his head on Ernie's lap.

Eddy sat across from his dad. Ernie stroked Boot's furry back, his faraway eyes gazed at the radio. The Catholic Hour by Bishop Fulton Sheen was on.

"Are you perfectly happy?" the radio asked. "Or are you still looking for happiness? There can be no doubt that at one time or another in your life you attained that which you believed would make you happy. When you got what you wanted were you happy?"

Margaret walked into the tavern. "Gee-whiz, what are you two doing? It's late."

Ernie placed his forefinger to his mouth. She sat down in the booth next to him and listened. Eddy walked to the bar, his eyes darting around for cigarettes.

The voice on the radio continued. "Perhaps it was marriage you thought which would bring you perfect happiness. Even if it did bring a measure of happiness, you admit that you now take your companion's love for granted. One is never thirsty at the border of the well. Perhaps it was wealth you wanted. You got it, and now you are afraid of losing it. 'A golden bit does not make the better horse.' Maybe it was a desire to be well known that you craved. You did become well known only to find that reputation is like a ball, as soon as it starts rolling, men begin to kick it around. If you were married you said, "If I had another husband, or another wife, I would be happy. Or you said, If I had another job..."

"I remember when you built that little hot dog stand," Margaret said. "I called my mother and cried because I married a hot dog vendor. She told me in Italian, 'Stand by your man.' Stai vicino al tuo uomo."

Ernie nodded. He drummed his fingers on the wooden table.

The radio continued to speak. "You want life, not for two more years, but always: you want to know all truths, not the truths of economics alone, to the exclusion of history. You also want love without end. All the poetry of love is a cry, a moan, and a weeping. The more pure it is, the more it pleads, the more it is lifted above the earth, the more it laments..."

"You know I listened to my mother. I've always stood by you. When she died, you were holding my hand. Are you going to stand by me now?" Her voice was surprisingly tender. Ernie smiled but didn't say anything.

The voice on the radio continued. "It is God you are looking for. Your unhappiness is not due to your want of a fortune, or high position, or fame, or sufficient vitamins, it is due not to a want of something outside you, but to a want of something inside you. You cannot satisfy a soul with husks. If the sun could speak, it would say that it was happy when shining, If a pencil could speak it would say that it was happy when writing—for these were the purposes for which they were made. You were made for perfect happiness. That is your purpose..."

"When my dad was dying in the hospital a week before we were married, he said not to cancel the wedding. He said you were a good guy and so did my brothers. But, your dad and your brothers, they don't think much of me, Ernie, do they?" Ernie slugged down the last of his beer and wiped his mouth with his forearm.

The radio went on. "Look at your heart. It tells the whole story of why you were made. It is not perfect in shape and contour, like a Valentine heart. There seems to be a small piece missing out of the side of every human heart. That may be to symbolize a piece that was torn out of the heart of Christ which embraced all humanity on the cross. But I think the real meaning is that when God made your human heart, He found it so good and so lovable that He kept a small sample of it in heaven. He sent the rest of it into this world to enjoy His gifts, and to use them as stepping stones back to Him, but to be ever mindful that you can never love anything in this world with your whole heart because you have not a whole heart with which to love. In order to love anyone with your whole heart, in order to be really peaceful, in order to be really wholehearted, you must go back again to God to recover the piece He has been keeping for you from all eternity."

Bishop Sheen's speech ended, and a commercial for toothpaste blared from the radio. Ernie rose, walked behind the bar and turned it off. He strolled to the jukebox, dropped a nickel in it and punched a number. Seconds later, "Moonlight Serenade," played by Glenn Miller and His Orchestra, softly drenched the tavern air. Ernie held out his hand and asked his wife, "May I have this dance?"

"Oh, Ernie," Margaret grumbled as she rose from her seat and meandered over to her husband in a zigzag step, half frowning, half smiling. He took her hand in his. They danced around the tables.

Eddy leaned against the bar counter and smiled. It was a rare sight to see his parents showing affection for each other. He shook his head as he slipped a pack of cigarettes into his pocket. "I'm going to bed. Good night."

His mom and dad didn't seem to notice.

TOP OF THE FIFTH

The morning rain pelted the living room window so hard it drowned out the noise from the shuddering cars below. The downpour sounded like a thousand Cub fans clapping at once. The wind pinned back the branches of the maple tree out front, and a sea of mist swirled in the driving rain. Water cascaded down the window pane, blurring the view of Wrigley Field. Eddy lay on the couch in his softball uniform, his lips pinched in a frown. The drencher ruined his softball game.

Eddy yawned and curled to the side. The rain's pounding rhythm lulled him to sleep. In his dream, he flew above the Lake Michigan shoreline on a sunny day. Free and untethered, he glided over tiny people swarming Montrose Beach like a colony of ants crawling around a mound of sand. He sailed past Riverview and saw Lockerbie riding the Bobs and waving. A familiar soft voice called his name. "Eddy, sweetheart. Come here."

He followed the voice to a pier at Belmont Harbor. He spotted Nonna perched on the stern of a sailboat named *Chestnut*. Eddy climbed aboard. She smiled. "Eddy, be like your brother and make us proud. Follow the rules."

The sky grew dark. Heavy rain poured from the heavens. A strong wind sent the mast crashing into the raging water. Waves surged violently against the boat, splashing across the bow. Eddy tried to fly away, but his feet felt as if they were bolted to the boat. He grabbed the railing on the port side to keep from falling overboard. He glanced toward the bow. Nonna was gone. Lightning lit up the dark clouds. A clap of thunder rattled the boat. Eddy sprung up from the couch, gasping in silent terror.

Another thunderous boom shook the walls of the living room. Eddy lay back down, his hands clasped behind his head. What did the dream mean? Follow the rules?

"Sheesh," Eddy mumbled. *Even in my dreams people tell me what to do.* The dream seemed real: Nonna sitting on the boat, her head tilted sideways, a faint curve in her lips and the creases around her large brown eyes folded into warm wrinkles. He remembered how they would sit together on the front stoop eating her homemade popsicles on hot summer days. She would smile at him the same way and say, "Eddy you're such a sweet little boy." He didn't run off and play. He'd sit with her and watch Cub fans stroll by. She tamed his restless energy, comforted him with her sweet smile and soft soothing voice. She had found a home in his heart, and he didn't even know it until it was too late.

His nonna was really gone, and so was Lockerbie, Eddy realized. It was as if they went on a long trip and were never coming back. Whenever the family went on vacation, Nonna would say "unni pessi scamp u signuri." She'd laugh and explain, "We're going where Jesus lost his sandals."

Eddy stared at the ceiling. Jagged lines of cracked plaster like lightning bolts zigzagged in no meaningful direction. Did Nonna and Lockerbie find Jesus's sandals, he wondered?

Eddy licked his lips, time for a cigarette. He bounced off the couch, ran through the kitchen, and raced down the backstairs to the tavern to steal another pack of Lucky Strikes.

He snuck through the back and was surprised to see most of the customers wore cowboy hats. A couple of cowboys sat in a booth playing Twenty-Six Dice. Kitty flirted with them, kissing one on the cheek. Her musty-scented perfume stunk up the place. Sinatra sang "They All Laughed" on the juke, his voice muffled against the noisy bar chatter. A few more cowboys circled around the front of the bar with Sailor, Walter, and Uncle Jimmy, yakking with his dad.

"Let me get this straight. If I ride that bull for ten seconds, I win one thousand dollars? Christopher Columbus, that's a lot of lettuce," Sailor said.

"Y'all ain't gonna ride it for that long. No one can," said one of the cowboys in a laconic drawl. "Big Sid is fulla try."

"Full of what?" Walter asked.

"Courage. Spunk," said the cowboy who spoke in a flinty manner. His neck was creased like leather in the back where the sun hit it below the brim, and he had a crouch with a sinewy build. "That damn Brahma bull is a bodacious bucker. Try as y'all may, Big Sid refuses to be ridden."

"I'll hang on to dat sweet bull like a flea on a rat's back for dat kind of money," Uncle Jimmy said. "For ten seconds, it's more'n pennies from heaven."

"Y'all don't know nothin about Big Sid," said another cowboy, his words spilled out with laughter. "A few years back, that damn bull tossed a rider and then smashed straight through the gate. It was at a Benny Goodman concert and rodeo in Cleveland. He lept over a rail and into the stands, kickin' and fussin' about. People were scramblin' around for their dear sweet lives. We all had a hell of time ropin' that damn Brahma."

"So what happened? Did anyone get hurt?" Ernie asked.

"A few people went to the hospital, but were okay." Then he winked so Eddy didn't know if he was telling the truth. "Big Sid butted one man and stomped on him. The police made us tie the damn bull to the seats in the stands until the show was over."

Uncle Jimmy took a long swig of beer and slammed the glass on the bar counter. "I don't give a rat's ass, I'm riding dat bull. Which one of youse is da timekeeper?""

The cowboys looked at each other in confusion. The leather-necked man said, "I think that'll be you, Larry."

Uncle Jimmy leaned over and whispered in Larry's ear. "See here, go in cahoots wid me and fudge da bull riding time. I'll split da winnin's wid ya, sixty-forty."

"What the Sam Helen are you talkin' about?" Larry bellowed. "Who are you?"

"Why do ya wanna know? You a cop?" Uncle Jimmy said.

Larry rolled his eyes. "We got into town a few hours ago and about one hundred people signed up to ride Big Sid. Y'all have to pay to ride the bull. And not everyone gets to ride him. Only the folks whose name was pulled out of a hat. And no one has ever ridden that damn bull for more than seven seconds. Not even the best bull riders."

Eddy tugged his dad's shirt sleeve. "What's going on, Dad?"

"The rodeo's in town. They're doing it at Wrigley Field. Some of these men are using our lot to park their trailers," he said, pointing toward the back. "Go back there and see. They have horses in them. And take the trash out while you're at it."

Eddy headed toward the back. A meaty and calloused hand hooked him by the shoulder and whisked him into the washroom. The door latch clicked and locked.

Uncle Jimmy grabbed and twisted Eddy's shirt, and shoved him against the wall. The knuckle-chinned bookie leaned in close and stared with an unblinking scowl.

"Uncle Jimmy. I got the money right here," Eddy said as he dug into his pocket for the seven dollars he owed the bookie.

"Dat's small potatoes compared to da problem ya got now," Uncle Jimmy said in hushed but a stern tone. "I'm gonna give it ta ya straight, Eddy. Barney lost and no surprise that flat-footed felon stiffed me. Congratulations, you're on da hook for seventy-five bucks. I can't have someone walking around not paying dat kinda moola. It sends a bad message to udder bettors."

Uncle Jimmy released his grip. He reached around his back and pulled out a handgun. He held it in his palm. "Now it's time for you to make your bones as a runner. You'se gonna take dis heater and shoot Barney. Don't have ta kill him. Just get 'im in da leg or arm. Then toss it in da lake."

Eddy stood in stunned silence.

"Come on, take it, big shot. I told you not ta take a bet from him. Doncha dink youse can walk straight down a crooked alley. Dis bookie busines ain't no walk in da park."

"I can't do it," Eddy said, his voice cracked. His legs shook so bad that he struggled to stand. His hands trembled as he raised them for mercy. "I'll get you the money. Promise. Let me do it my way."

Uncle Jimmy's narrowed eyes burned through Eddy. He shoved the gun in the back of his pants. "Ya got one week or I'll squeeze your ol' man for it. Ya wouldn't want dat, wouldja? Capisce?"

Eddy nodded.

Uncle Jimmy pranced out of the washroom and yelled for Kitty to give him the next game. Eddy gripped the sink and bent down, feeling as if he was going to throw up. The door was still open. The scuff of barstools dragged across the floor. A cacophony of laughter, belches, and bets pierced the smoky tavern. Eddy wanted to slink into the basement and hide. How was he going to get seventy-five dollars in a week? He closed his eyes and took a deep breath. He exhaled and looked into the mirror. He could handle Barney. Or could he? He raked his fingers through his hair and scrunched his face in a James Cagney wiseguy squint. "What's da matta with ya? Ya scared? You dirty, yellow-bellied rat."

Eddy grabbed the garbage and hurried out the back door.

A damp smell of lemon-scented rain bathed the city air. Eddy kicked the garbage can. Rats scratched and screeched at the bottom. He pulled the lid off the garbage can and held it like a shield. He dumped the garbage and slammed the lid. A horse whinnied. The sound came from the other side of a trailer parked in the back, next to the alley. Eddy walked around the trailer and saw a cowgirl hitching a team of horses to a stagecoach. She stroked the neck of a reddish-brown horse with a flaxen mane and tail. "Whoa, take her easy, boy. Stay still."

The horse whinnied again, shifted sideways, and pawed at the ground. Eddy stepped closer. A dirty blond ponytail poked out from the back of a black cowboy hat that hugged snugly around her head.

She swiveled around and her mouth opened with a broad smile. She had buck teeth, a pug nose, and one of her eyes was blue and the other brown. "Do you mind, sweetie, holdin' the reins? I'm fixin to put this here hitch on."

She handed Eddy the reins before he could answer. The cowgirl latched the hitches and pullstraps to the horses. She turned and said, "Thanks, sweetie."

She was of medium build and wore a short-sleeved white shirt and blue jeans that fit tightly around her stout legs. She was probably a freshmen or sophomore in high school.

"You must be one of the bad guys," Eddy said with a smile.

"I ain't no guy, but I can be bad," she said with a giggle as if she knew something no one else did. "What makes you say that anyway?"

"Because you're wearing a black hat. The bad guys always wear black hats."

"You been watchin too many movies. My name's Shirley. What's yours?" Shirley's lips tightened for a moment, but her mouth broke open, spit oozing between the gap of her front teeth.

"Eddy Pareti. Pleased to meet your acquaintance. Where are you all from all?" said Eddy in an attempt to sound like a cowpoke that fell flat.

"Are you making fun of me?"

"I would never make fun of a pretty girl like you," Eddy lied. "Whaddya you think I am. Stupid?"

Shirley examined Eddy's green softball jersey. "Is that the name of your team, the Savinas?"

"Yeah, we're the Junior Savinas. The captain of the senior Savinas came back from the war and started this softball team he named after an orphaned girl in Italy. We got rained out today."

"Well, Eddy Spaghetti, ya wanna ride with me? I need some company and someone to show me how to get downtown in this here stagecoach."

He studied the stagecoach. Posters were plastered all over it, advertising the rodeo at Wrigley Field. The only stagecoach Eddy had ever seen was in the Field Museum. "You gonna take this on the road, with *horses*?"

"Yeppers. That's my job today," Shirley said brightly. "Ride around town and tell folks about the rodeo."

Eddy turned to look at the tavern. Uncle Jimmy was in there having a good time, waiting for his seventy-five bucks. What did Uncle Jimmy mean when he said he would squeeze the money from his dad?

"You comin' with me, Eddy Spaghetti?"

Eddy rubbed his peach-fuzzed chin. "I heard the rodeo is offering a prize if you can ride a bull for ten seconds. Is it really one thousand dollars?"

"You ain't got no cockamamie idea of riding Big Sid, do ya?"

"For that, money? You bet."

"Come with me and I'll tell ya all about it."

"What ya waiting for? Hop on," Eddy said as he clasped his hands to give Shirley a boost. She giggled and climbed onto the driver's box in two moves.

Eddy placed his left foot on a brake shoe, hoisted himself up, and grabbed the door handle with his left hand. He stretched his right arm across the door, grasping for something to hold. His hand found the side lamp. He stepped on the leather thoroughbrace with his right foot and swung around, both hands holding onto the side lamp. Standing on his toes, his right arm strained upward for the driver's seat but he couldn't reach it. Instead, his hand found Shirley's outstretched arm. She pulled him onto the driver's box of the stagecoach. She was strong for a girl, Eddy thought.

"Hyah!" Shirley whipped the reins, and the horses pulled the stagecoach out of the alley and turned east on Waveland toward the lake.

The stagecoach rocked back and forth as the horse's hooves clip-clopped on the wet pavement, splashing sprays of water.

Eddy spotted Gerace, Elmore, Warman, and Hootie loafing on a corner at the schoolyard. He rose to his feet and whistled. Shirley pulled on the reins and stopped the horses.

"Look at this ritzy deal," said Gerace. "Where you goin'?"

Eddy smiled and crowed, "Downtown."

"Who's the dame?" Hootie asked.

"Her name is Shirley and keep your mitts and peepers off her."

Shirley smiled and waved. "Y'all can get in if you like."

Warman was the first to climb aboard. The others followed. They stuck their heads out of the window as the stagecoach lumbered forward.

"We're going to the rodeo. How about you?" Elmore screamed at a blue Ford Deluxe Coupe stopped at a red light. The driver, an old man in a fedora, studied the posters on the stagecoach, smiled, and turned away.

The stagecoach turned south onto the Outer Drive and veered on the right side of the road. The horses wore leather square blinders on the sides of their eyes. Passing cars didn't spook them as they plodded along, snorting and bobbing their heads, seeming to know where they were going.

There was an occasional clink of the harness. Shirley kept her eyes on the road, a half smile creased around her thin lips. Eddy felt like smoking a cigarette, but he didn't have any and Shirley didn't seem the type that smoked.

"So, tell me about this bull. Did anyone ever come close to ten seconds?" Eddy asked.

Shirley giggled. "No, sir. No one can stay on him for that long. It's kinda funny how hundreds of you city folks pay to ride Big Sid, but only a handful actually get to do it. That's probably a good thing too."

Eddy cocked his head to the side. "Only a handful? Who's been riding the bull all this time?"

Shirley sighed and turned away. Moments later, she looked at Eddy. "Promise you won't tell anyone?"

"Tell anyone what?"

"I'm gonna tell ya a secret, but ya gotta promise not to tell anyone."

"I promise."

"We tell 'em we pick names out of a hat, but we really call out folks that are part of the show. There are hundreds of us, so nobody can tell."

"So it's rigged!"

"No. Sometimes we'll call out a name of someone we think might not get hurt just so folks don't get to suspectin' nothin'."

"Can you rig it so I can ride the bull?"

"I dunno. You're kinda of a small fry." The cowgirl pursed her lips into a self-satisfied smirk. "Come by tomorrow afternoon, and I'll figure something out."

"It's a date. You ever ride him?"

"I tried a couple of times, but you never know what Big Sid's gonna do," Shirley said. "Sometimes he'll do a drop kick and then sidespin. Other times he'll just jackknife, twist, and do a belly roll. Sometimes, he'll do it all if he's in a real ornery mood."

Shirley gazed at the calm waters of Lake Michigan. "It's like an ocean. What's on the other side?"

"Michigan," Eddy said. "You're looking at Lake Michigan. Don't ask me why they don't call it Lake Illinois."

"Have you ever been to Michigan?" Shirley asked.

"No. Why would I go there?" Eddy asked.

"I've seen South America and been to every state except Michigan, Alaska, and Maine. Pretty soon we're gonna take the rodeo to Europe. The world is my home. How about you?"

The only state Eddy had ever visited was Wisconsin. "I've been around, kid. Let me tell ya. I've seen things you could only dream about."

Shirley laughed. "I reckon since you've been around you know how to drive this here stagecoach." Shirley didn't wait for a response. She handed

Eddy the reins. Eddy took them and acted as if he knew what he was doing. The horses didn't seem to notice who was driving them.

Gerace shouted, "Come on, can't ya go any faster?"

Eddy wasn't sure how to get the horses to speed up, but in the movies, the cowboys whip the reins. He didn't want to hurt the horses, so he lightly tapped the reins and barked, "Yow, giddyup." The horses trotted at the same pace. Shirley giggled.

Shirley folded her hands on her lap, her eyes surveyed the Chicago skyline, mountains of steel, concrete, and glass rose up in the distance. The Chicago Board of Trade Building towered over the other skyscrapers, capped with the three-story art deco statue of Ceres, the Greek goddess of agriculture. Ahead was the Drake Hotel.

"Do you ever let these horses run free without all that stuff on their backs and in their mouths?" Eddy asked.

"Why would we do that? The horses don't mind the bit and harness," Shirley said. "It's what they're meant to do."

"Would you like someone whipping the reins on your back and making you pull a stagecoach all the time?" Eddy asked, his tone playful and polite.

"I ain't a horse. And if anyone tries to whip me, I'll whoop them."

The stagecoach approached Wacker Drive. "We should turn here," Eddy said.

"Pull the reins to your right," Shirley said. Eddy did and the horses obediently turned onto Wacker Drive.

"You're a regular brother whip," she said. "That's what we call stagecoach drivers."

"When you drive the stagecoach, do they call you sister whip?"

Shirley stared straight into Eddy's eyes and smiled in a flirty way. "Are you spoken for?"

"What are you talking about? Spoken for?"

"Do you have a girlfriend?"

"I have lot of friends who are girls. Why? Who wants to know?"

Shirley's eyes widened, and she slightly lowered her head. "Have you ever kissed a girl?"

"You ask a lot of questions."

Shirley placed her hands around Eddy's cheeks and kissed him on the lips. Eddy pulled away for a second, but he remembered about the bull. He didn't want to upset the cowgirl. He leaned back in for a kiss.

This time Shirley pulled away. "Do you always kiss with your eyes open?"

"I can close them if you want," Eddy said. He leaned in for another kiss. Drool oozed down his chin.

Shirley pulled away again and wiped her mouth. "Slow down, cowboy, and don't be such a slobberin' puppy. This is how you kiss." She leaned in with softly parted lips and lightly nibbled Eddy's lower lip with her buck teeth. The pair locked lips, and Shirley slowly slid her tongue into Eddy's mouth. Eddy dropped the reins as his hands frantically moved up and down Shirley's back. His breathing grew heavier. He shifted his body forward, forcing Shirley backward. As he did, his right leg sprung out and accidentally kicked the rear end of one of the horses. The stagecoach jerked. The horses, their ears pricked, broke into a full gallop.

"Pull on the reins," Shirley yelled. Screams and shouts exploded from inside the stagecoach.

Eddy lunged for the reins dangling from the hitch, but he couldn't reach them. The stagecoach bounced and bucked and scraped the side of a milk truck as the horses galloped down Wacker Drive. The clippity-clop pounding of hoofbeats on pavement sounded like a drummer with sticks banging a tin can in four-four time.

Shirley slid off the driver's box and stepped onto the hitch, gripping the side of the carriage. She jumped on the back of one of the horses and splayed across its back. The cowgirl slid down the side of the horse and stretched out her left arm. The moment her hand clutched the reins, she dropped them when the runaway carriage made a sharp turn on State Street and careened into a lamp post. The left axle broke off. The horses dragged the stagecoach, leaning on its side, sparks flying like it was the Fourth of July.

"What the hell is going on? Get us outta here!" Gerace screamed.

Shirley grabbed the reins and pulled hard. "Whoa!" The stagecoach came to a stop.

Gerace, Warman, Hootie, and Elmore climbed out.

"I guess we gotta take the bus back home," Gerace said. "Uh-oh, here comes a cop. Let's beat it."

The boys bolted south on State Street. Elmore turned around and yelled, "Come on, Eddy."

"Go on, I'll catch up later," Eddy said. Elmore waved and ran toward the others.

Shirley stood over the rear left wheel that lay horizontal and spun counterclockwise on concrete. "My dad is gonna make mincemeat outta of me."

"Quiet, here he comes," Eddy said, his head nudged in the direction of a short pudgy beat cop. "Let me talk."

The policeman removed his blue cap and scratched his head as he surveyed the damage. "Which one of youse was driving this?"

"Me," Eddy said. "See, the wheel fell off. It's kinda like a flat tire. No big deal. We'll snap it back on and be on our way."

The cop sneered. "Oh yeah? How do you explain that bent lamppost and the scrape on the side of this stagecoach?"

"I dunno. A milk truck sideswiped us back there," Eddy said, pointing east on Wacker.

"Huh-uh. You must be the clown in the rodeo." The cop reached into his side pocket and pulled out a pencil and ticketbook. "This thing ain't licensed to be on the road. Who owns this?"

Eddy and Shirley glanced at each other. "My father, sir," Shirley said.

The cop pointed to a payphone and told Eddy and Shirley to call their parents and come remove the stagecoach. He handed them the ticket.

"Don't worry. My dad has connections," Eddy said. "He'll know what to do. These cops are crooked. You just have to buy them off or pay them a favor."

— — —

Later that day, Eddy lounged on the couch, gazing out the front room window. Dust swirled in sunbeams. Why couldn't it have been like this in the morning. He'd get to pitch in the game and try out his new moves. But then he would never have met Shirley. His father didn't sound angry about the stagecoach crash. Eddy had told him Shirley accidentally dropped the reins but saved them with one of her rodeo tricks. By midday, Ernie fixed the problem, someone from the rodeo paid off the cops, and the ticket disappeared.

Margaret stormed into the front room, hands on hips. Her jaws clenched and unclenched. "The principal called today."

Eddy bowed, his shoulders slumped.

There was a faint tapping. Two flies spun around and whizzed against the window, trying to break through the glass.

"She tells me you been skipping summer school. She tells me you're failing, and you might have to repeat seventh grade!" Her voice rose after each word.

"I'm sorry, Ma. What do ya want me to do? I hate school."

"I'll tell ya what you're gonna do, mister," she shrieked. "I'm gonna walk you to school and walk you home every day like I did when you were six. You're gonna stay in the house until summer school ends. No baseball. No softball. No friends."

"What about the weekends, Ma? There's no school on the weekends. Can I go out then?"

"You're gonna use that time to catch up on the work you didn't do."

"Ma, ya gotta let me go out. I gotta paper route and stuff."

"You can forget about that. The only places you will be is at school and here with us."

For a split second, Eddy wanted to tell his mother about Uncle Jimmy and the money he owed just to get it off his chest. But he held back. This wasn't like jail. They couldn't be with him all the time.

— — —

The next day, Margaret escorted Eddy to school and later walked him home. On the way back, they ran into Uncle Jimmy on Sheffield.

"Hello, Margaret. Where you goin?" Uncle Jimmy asked.

"What do ya mean where am I goin'? It's none of your business, Jimmy. You notice I didn't ask you where you're goin'."

Eddy's lips cracked a half smile. His mother was giving Uncle Jimmy the business. She never liked him and treated him the worst of all the regulars

"Take it easy. I was just bein' friendly. Dat's all." He looked at Eddy holding his school books. "How's summer school treatin' ya?" Uncle Jimmy said, grinning as if it was someone's death sentence.

Eddy's shoulders and legs tensed. He could barely breathe. "It's fine."

"Come on, Eddy. We' don't have time to stand around and chat. We'll see you around, Jimmy."

"You can bet on dat."

Once they got home, Eddy was told to sit at the dining room table and do his math homework. Hours passed and Eddy had hardly made a dent in his homework. He sat there worrying how he was going to pay Uncle Jimmy. He whispered figures he had earned from his paper route and bets, writing them down, adding, subtracting. It would take years to pay off his debt. The pencil occasionally slipped out of his sweaty palm. He had the shakes. Eddy rubbed his scalp. Every monotonous tick tock of the grandfather's clock rang out from the front room. Uncle Jimmy wasn't a top-drawer bookie, but he wasn't a shortstop either. He had a pretty good-size operation, and he knew people who knew people that could get things done.

His mother stomped into the dining room and stood over Eddy, arms folded. It was something his summer school nun would do before barking out an order or an announcement. "Eddy, I have to go downstairs and help your father. Florence is at the movies. She'll be home any minute. So don't get any funny ideas."

The second his mother walked out the door, Eddy ran to the back door and flew down the stairs. He rushed up to the trailer parked in the alley and knocked on the door. A scruffy cowboy wearing jeans and no shirt opened the door. "Whaddya want?"

"Is Shirley here?"

"No. She's at the rodeo."

"Thanks." Eddy raced to Wrigley Field. He saw an opening and, running full speed, jumped the turnstiles and got lost in the crowd.

The smell of cow manure mixed with stale beer filled the cramped spaces under the bleachers. It smelled like a farm Eddy and his family had visited in Wisconsin. Rodeo cowhands had built makeshift wooden pens that held bulls, horses, and sheep. People strolled around as if they were at the Lincoln Park Zoo.

A crowd had circled around a pen, built behind the center field wall. Eddy elbowed his way through and leaned against the four-foot-high fence. A bull that resembled a black fist with horns stretched and strained to browse hay in front of it. A black-and-white rope was tied around a ring in the bull's nose. The taut rope extended in two directions, each end fastened to steel girders under the bleachers.

Was this Big Sid? Eddy leaned into the pen and grabbed some hay. He threw it at the bull, strands landing in front of it. The bull snorted and grunted, lowered its thick head and ate the hay. Eddy reached in to pet the beast. "Don't touch it, spaghetti." In the corner of his eyes, he saw something loop over his head and around his body. The rope tightened, Eddy couldn't move his arms. He squirmed and twisted as he was being pulled backward.

"Well, lookey here. I just lassoed me some Eddy Spaghetti," Shirley said with a giggle. "Where've you been? I thought you'd come see me do my trick ridin'."

"I was back at the ranch makin' chitlins and all for them good ole folks down at the roe-day-yo."

"You're makin' fun of me again," Shirley said. She loosened the rope.

Eddy let it drop and stepped over it. "No, ma'am, just tryin' to fit in is all. I aim ta please."

"Well, you're getting better with that accent, if you can call it that. Pretty soon, you'll be talkin' like us. You can even come join the 'roe-day-yo.'"

"Yeah, and I can learn how to ride that bull you call Sid."

Shirley laughed. "You were just feedin' him." She pointed to the bull browsing hay in the pen behind Eddy.

"No kidding. Why is he tied up?"

"Cuz Big Sid hates to be in small spaces. He could probably break through this fence or even jump it."

"He probably thinks he's being led to slaughter," Eddy said as he studied the bull, a ball of black muscle. "Maybe that's why in baseball they call it a bullpen. The relief pitchers are like bulls being led to the slaughter."

"You got it backward. It's the bull riders who are being led to slaughter."

Eddy straightened. "Hey, I can handle that bull. And that ain't no bull."

"Sure, you can," Shirley said, laughing. "I betcha Big Sid'd go easy on ya on the account of feeding him some hay."

"Are you gonna fix it so I can ride him?"

"Tell ya what, Eddy Spaghetti, meet me at the corral in fifteen minutes, and I'll set you up."

"You gotta deal, sweetheart."

Shirley coiled the rope, hooked it onto her belt loop, and moseyed into the outfield.

Eddy turned to look at Big Sid. All he had to do was stay on it for ten seconds. Ten seconds for one thousand dollars. He counted to ten. It was the answer to his Uncle Jimmy problem.

A sheep brayed near the entrance to right center field. Eddy followed the sound, petted the sheep as he passed its pen and entered Wrigley Field. The outfield grass was full of ruts. Spectators sat scattered above on the bleachers and along the bottom rows of the field seats. Some lined up along a rope that cordoned off right field and all of the infield. A large crowd had gathered around a corral with a chute and podium built on a wooden scaffold in left field. There were about five thousand people in the stadium, Eddy figured.

A rider dashed out of the elephant gate in a full gallop, swinging a rope. He stopped near the pitcher's mound, stood up on his horse, and lassoed the rope around the horse's head and then himself, jumping over it. He sat on the saddle, still whirling the rope around his head as his horse spun in circles. The sparse crowd applauded.

Eddy walked to the corral, built with a flimsy four-foot wire fence. He placed his hands on the wire and watched a calf run out into the middle of the corral. Seconds later, a cowboy on horseback shot out of the chute and, in one motion, lassoed the calf, dismounted in a full run, picked up the calf, flipped it on its side, and tied the animal's legs. An announcer with a mic on the podium, said in a Southern drawl, "Nine point nine seconds." The calf bellowed in protest. The cowboy bounced back on his feet and clapped, dust spraying off his leather gloves.

It looked violent and cruel. Why did they think that was a sport? Eddy wondered. But what's the difference from that and riding on the back of a bull. The bull can take it and gets its revenge now and then, he concluded.

A hand the size of a baseball mitt grabbed Eddy's shoulder and turned him around.

"Hello, Eddy. Whaddya doin' here? Shouldn't you be at home reading books?" Uncle Jimmy said with a sly menacing smile.

Eddy swallowed his stomach. He cleared his throat. "I'm gonna ride that bull and win the money and pay you back. Okay?"

"How you gonna do dat? You gotta pay em under da table just to get ta ride da damn bull. I had to spot 'em three sawbucks ta get my chance. You ain't got dat kinda money."

"I got my ways," Eddy said with a bit of confidence.

Uncle Jimmy stared at Eddy with unblinking eyes. "I'm not gonna wait around too long for you to do what ya gatta do." He lifted his shirt and pointed to a reddish scar on the side of his stomach. "In this business, ya gotta earn your name sometimes, pay with your flesh sometimes too."

Eddy pursed his lips and looked away. He liked the money, but he didn't want to shoot anybody.

"Better get me dat money or take care of Barney," Uncle Jimmy said. "Or youse da one gettin' shot." He turned and walked toward the chute.

A speaker crackled with a whistle. "Folks, it's that time we all been waitin' fer. A thousand dollars goes ta anyone who can stay on top of this ol' wild Brahma fer ten seconds," said a cowboy, a beat-up old man who seemed he like he'd seen better days before bullriding busted him up good. "Our first rider on ol' Big Sid is Jimmy Ginnochio."

The bookie climbed a short flight of stairs to the chute entrance and listened as two cowboys gave him instructions. When he mounted the bull, a familiar voice shouted, "Ride 'em cowboy!" Eddy's father stood on the other side of the corral, his hands cupped over his mouth. "You better hold on for dear life, Jimmy. I don't want anything to happen to ya. You still owe me ten bucks."

Eddy ducked out of sight and slinked away from the chute entrance.

The chute opened and Big Sid shot out like a bullet, bucking and twisting. Uncle Jimmy flew off in two seconds and landed on his back, but his feet got caught in the bull rope. The bull dragged him around the corral for a few long seconds. Uncle Jimmy looked like tin cans bouncing around a car's bumper. He freed himself and scrambled to the fence as three rodeo clowns lured the bull in the other direction and back into the chute. There was muted applause.

Eddy couldn't believe his bad luck. If he rode the bull, there would be hell to pay with his father. He could go back home and maybe not get caught sneaking out. A big maybe. His sister could be looking for him right now. But he'd lose the chance to win a thousand dollars. As Eddy mulled over what to do, the announcer said, "The next rider is Eddy."

There was a long pause. The announcer whispered to another cowboy and Shirley. He shrugged his shoulders and said, "The next rider is Eddy Spah-ghetti."

Too late. He learned right then that if you don't decide fast, sometimes things choose for you. Eddy hustled to the chute and climbed the stairs before his dad had a chance to yank him away. Shirley and a chute man were there, smiling. Eddy shifted his feet back and forth as if he had to use the washroom.

"Okay, Eddy Spaghetti. This is your big moment," Shirley said in a serious tone of voice that was not followed by her usual girly giggle. "Hold on to this rope with your left hand. Big Sid is gonna fly out of this chute, and you're gonna find yourself in the ride of your life. You still wanna do this?"

Eddy nodded, but his eyes shifted to his dad who was laughing with Uncle Jimmy. It's not too late to bail, he thought. But if he could stay on Big Sid for ten seconds to win a thousand bucks, he could pay off Jimmy and start his own bookie business. Bobby would be jealous and maybe his dad might forget all about him ditching summer school.

"Eddy Spaghetti is ready, y'all," Eddy said.

Shirley plunked her Stetson hat on Eddy's head. "Wear this. You're about to become a real cowboy," she said as she chewed on her chapped lips. The chute man next to her told Eddy to gently sit on the bull's back. Big Sid was surprisingly calm as Eddy mounted him. He petted the bull's back. It was hard as concrete.

"When this chute opens, Big Sid is gonna jerk forward and buck side to side," the chute man said. "You're gonna lose yer balance fast like. The trick is to hold tight with your feet and lean high over the bull's shoulder. Loosen your hips and roll with every pitch and yaw. Any questions, Spaghetti?"

"What's a yaw?"

The gate opened, and the chute man poked Big Sid with a cattle prod. The bull blasted out of the gate, its hind bucking, twisting, and turning, its back legs kicking straight into the air. Eddy flew with every buck. His hands gripped the bull rope as his body slid sideways on the bull's back. Big Sid made a surprising twist and roll, and Eddy flew off and landed face first on the rutted outfield grass. He jumped to his feet and limped to the fence. He saw a pair of shoes and recognized them from the tavern. His eyes went up to the pants and then all the way up to his father's sour face.

"What am I gonna do with you?" Ernie barked. He grabbed Eddy's collar and led him to the outfield gate and back home.

Ernie tossed his son into his bedroom and slammed the door. Eddy heard his father mumble some words in the front room.

"He did what!" Margaret screamed. Footsteps stormed down the hall.

"He coulda killed himself," his mother howled. "That's it, Ernie. I'm at the end of my rope. He's not leaving our sight. For now on, he'll be in the tavern when we're working. And he'll be at home when we're at home. One of us will walk him to and from school. Where we go, he goes."

Eddy swung open his bedroom door. "Come on, Ma, I was trying win a thousand dollars to help pay for school."

"You snuck out of the house and rode a bull, Eddy," Ernie said. "Look at you—you're limping. And you're failing seventh grade. You bring shame to this family."

Eddy limped into his bedroom and slammed the door shut. He lay in bed and stared at the ceiling. He stayed there without moving until day turned into dusk that faded into night. This is what prison must feel like, Eddy thought. You can't do what you want to do. Everybody else's running the show. Locking you in. Telling you what to do.

Eddy rose out of bed and walked to the window. He opened it, sat on the ledge, and lit a cigarette. The windless night air was stale and smelled of soot and car exhaust. An ambulance wailed in the distance. How was he going to get out of the mess with Uncle Jimmy?

He could run off with the rodeo. But it wouldn't last. He was no good at bull riding, and he didn't like the way the animals were treated. Who could blame Big Sid for being mean?

Elmore had complained about city life and bullies, and talked about moving to his grandmother's house in Michigan. He could do a disappearing act with Elmore.

Eddy took a drag and blew a perfect smoke ring that soared skyward and dissolved into the murk of the city night. Dull light trickled through the window and etched a shadow of Eddy's head on the opposite wall. The silhouette slanted sideways, crooked and faded.

It was time to take a powder. How else could he be free?

BOTTOM OF THE FIFTH

Eddy rubbed his eyes under a grim sooty sunrise. A thin film of smog and smut blanketed the morning sky that peaked above rows of brick buildings east down Addison Avenue.

A slight breeze blew in from the lake. Eddy and his father stood at the doors of the Addison El stop, which was bustling with morning commuters rushing to work. Many of them were factory workers, some coming home after a long night and others leaving for a hard day's work to win the war against Japan. Streaks of faded sunlight streamed through the railroad ties above and lit up the El station and sidewalks in unfamiliar patterns. Eddy couldn't remember the last time he was outside so early. It had been dark when his father rustled him out of bed to help his campaign for alderman.

Eddy dropped two boxes of pamphlets next to the station door and stuck his hands in his pockets as he watched his father canvas the crowd.

Ernie stepped in front of a tall man with uncombed hair and an unbuttoned shirt. "Excuse me, sir. My name's Ernest Pareti, and I'm running for alderman for the Forty-Fifth Ward. Do you mind signing this petition?"

The man leaned down and glanced at the clipboard in Ernie's hand. He shook his head and grabbed the pen tied to the clipboard.

"Don't forget to write your address and your full name," Ernie said politely. The man scribbled his name, opened the door and hurried into the station.

"Eddy, don't just stand there with your hands in your pocket. Hand out those pamphlets," Ernie scolded with a gritted smile. He didn't want anyone to see him yelling at his son in public.

A portly man in blue overalls and work boots approached the station doors. Eddy yawned, stepped forward, and handed him a pamphlet. He said meekly, "Vote for Pareti, Forty-Fifth Ward alderman." His father made him say it twenty times before he handed him the fliers. The man brushed past Eddy without taking the pamphlet.

With a slight shake of his son's shoulder, Ernie snarled with a smile, showing his cigar-stained teeth. "Eddy, you gotta say it like you mean it. And don't forget to smile. You gotta sell it."

"Dad, why don't you put these pamphlets on the booth counter inside. People can grab them as they go through the turnstiles."

"Do as you're told," Ernie said.

A man in a green seersucker suit stopped in front of Ernie. "Why are you running for alderman? What's your platform?"

Eddy was confused by the question. The platform was upstairs inside the train station.

"If I'm elected, I will work to consolidate our trains and buses into one operation, and I will fight crime and corruption in our great city," Ernie said brightly. It was a line Eddy heard his father recite over and over in the bathroom.

"What would you do about the OPA?" the old man said in a suspicious tone of voice. "I own the Poodle Dog Lounge on Broadway. The OPA took me to court because they said I charged too much for a steak sandwich. How can I run a business when the OPA fines me for selling a product they say is priced too high? If someone is willing to pay my price, why can't I charge it?"

"I own a bar too, and I don't like the Office of Price Administration one bit," Ernie replied. He was smiling so big it looked like his chompers were going to fly out of his mouth. "Vote for me, and I'll fight the OPA with everything I've got."

The old man smiled and seemed satisfied with Ernie's answer. He grabbed the pen and wrote his name and address.

"Thank you for your support and don't forget to vote," Ernie said. The men shook hands.

The boxes painted by the sun shining through the El tracks had shifted east and slanted a little less as the morning sun slowly slid across the sky. The smog had lifted. Most of the commuters had refused to take a pamphlet from Eddy, even when he planted a fake smile on his face. His dad told him to place the pamphlets in their hands before they could say no. Eddy tried, but most of them would either pull away or just drop it on the ground.

Eddy shoved a pamphlet into a baby stroller when the mom wasn't looking. He snuck one in a woman's purse, but she pulled way and yelled, "He's a thief!" Ernie apologized and told her his son was a well-meaning, hardworking Eagle Scout who got carried away, passing out campaign fliers. His dad's charm calmed her, and she signed the petition, laughing as she did it.

A plump gray-haired woman in a mustard-colored summer dress dotted with pink flowers stepped within inches of Ernie's face. "You politicians are all crooks. You don't care about the little people."

Ernie's smile grew wider. "Sure, I do. That's why I'm running for alderman."

"Oh yeah? What are you gonna do?"

"If I'm elected, I will work to consolidate our trains and buses into one operation, and I will fight crime and corruption in our great city."

The woman stepped back and laughed. "Do you know where I'm going right now?" Before Ernie could answer, she said, "I'm on my way to court. Do you know why?"

Ernie shook his head, a smile still plastered across his round face.

"I evicted my tenants on the first floor so I could move in. The OPA says I can't do that. Now I have to beg a judge to let me move into my own apartment. What right has the OPA or anyone got to tell me what to do with my home?"

"I'm a flat owner too, and I don't like the idea of getting a certificate of eviction from the OPA or their permission to raise rent," Ernie replied. "If you vote for me, I'll fight the OPA."

The woman sighed and signed her name on the petition. She sauntered into the station.

"Dad, when are you gonna take me to school?" Eddy asked. The last time he had asked to go to school was in kindergarten. He had so much fun playing kickball back then that when it was time to go home, he cried. The next day, he ran to school. His brother and sister couldn't keep up. Eddy smiled thinking about it. Then his parents sent him to St. Mary's of the Lake. The nuns were mean. All day long, they yelled. He couldn't talk or get out of his seat. They would ask, "Why can't you be like your older brother or sister?" Today would be no different. The nuns took no summer break from yelling, even in a hot, stuffy classroom.

"Wait. I need to do something first," Ernie said. "Follow me."

His Dad led Eddy deep into the underbelly of the El and stopped next to a rusty trash can. He handed Eddy a clipboard with a blank petition and a list of names. "I want you to write the names from this list exactly as they are on the petition. Use your left hand."

"Who are these people?" Eddy asked as he awkwardly wrote with his left hand.

"Never mind who they are," his father said in a deadpan tone of voice.

Eddy stopped writing when he recognized one of the names on the list. It was Walter Lockerbie Jr. "Dad, this guy's dead."

"Just keep writing."

Eddy studied the names, mostly men, and saw the name of another neighborhood kid killed in the war. His eyes almost popped out of the sockets when he saw his nonna's name.

"You gotta be kidding, Nonna? I'm not writing down her name."

"Then don't." Ernie wouldn't look at his son.

After about three dozen names, Eddy's left hand throbbed, and he switched hands.

"Left hand, Eddy," Ernie barked.

"What should I tell Ma when she yells at me for being late to school? 'Sorry, Ma, but Dad made me write dead people's names on a petition with my left hand, and one of them was Nonna.' Whaddya think she'd say to that?"

Ernie mumbled sheesh and grabbed the clipboard and the list and headed in the direction of St. Mary's of the Lake. Eddy followed as they stepped out of the sun-striped shadowy alley and onto Addison, heading east.

Along the way, Ernie stopped strangers and asked them to sign the petition. He didn't ask them to write with their left hand. Eddy didn't mind all the wasted time. Any minute outside of school was like a day at the ball game. But eventually, they made their way to St. Mary of the Lake, and Eddy slouched into the prisonlike edifice like a criminal beginning his sentence. And he felt like one too.

Hours later, Bobby met Eddy at the front door of the school, and the pair walked toward home. Halfway there, Eddy stopped, his shoulders slumped as he sulked in silence standing on the edge of the sidewalk. Uncle Jimmy's deadline was up, and he didn't have the money.

"Eddy, what's eatin ya?"

Eddy wanted a smoke but didn't have one, so he chewed on his pencil until he tasted lead. He sighed and shook his head as if he dropped a routine fly ball. "I'm in big trouble, Bobby. I don't know what to do."

After Eddy explained his Uncle Jimmy problem, Bobby said, "Sheesh. Why didn't you just listen to Uncle Jimmy? You are so bullheaded. You know that?"

"That's not much help. What else ya got?"

Bobby laughed. "I got an idea. That's what I got. Follow me."

They walked to Uncle Laury's gas station on Addison and Sheffield and stepped inside. Laury and two men were playing cards.

"Uncle Laury, can we talk to ya for minute?" Bobby asked.

Laury laid down his cards face down and rose. He turned to the other men and said, "Don't you steal my two aces." He led Bobby and Eddy outside. "What's the matter, Bobby?"

Bobby scratched his head. "Eddy's been runnin bets for Uncle Jimmy, and he took one he wasn't supposed ta. Now he's on the hook for seventy-five."

Laury laughed as he scoured the intersection of Waveland and Addison with his watchful, twitchy eyes. "Who's the sour bettor?

"Some guy named Barney. He's a Wrigley man."

"You must be talking about that skinny guy who works the gate. He's no good. All washed up. He's not worth da trouble," Laury said. "Does your father know?"

Bobby shook his head.

"Yeah, he's too busy running for alderman to notice. I can't figure out his angle. If you ask me, he's kicking up dirt dat doesn't need to be kicked up."

Laury took a deep breath and said, "I'll take care of your problem. But listen, stay away from Jimmy. He's in hot water himself. Understand? Now beat it, will ya? I got two fish in there waiting to be hooked."

"Thanks, Laury," Bobby said.

They headed north on Sheffield on the way to the tavern. Bobby said, "You know there's a game today. Dad wants you to help run the grill while the game's on. I'll park the cars."

Eddy grumbled, "Why do you get to park the cars?"

"I don't care either way. But that's what Dad wants," Bobby said. "Hey, I just saved your ass. Why don't you pay me?"

Everywhere Eddy went, there was someone telling him what to do and where to go. He hadn't seen his friends in almost a week. He wondered if anyone had told Maria about Shirley. He wouldn't be surprised if Maria had dumped him by now. Eddy felt like he was behind in the count with a bum for an ump calling the game. All he could do was swing away and hope for the best.

The tavern was busy all morning and even during the game. Most were regulars, but a lot of them were servicemen too. Sailors right off the train still wore their blue-and-white. Marines and regular army and even a few army-air force still in their crisp uniforms.

Beads of sweat dripped from Eddy's cheeks as he flipped patties on the grill, the red meat sizzling to dark, the hiss of the grease drowning out the bar chatter. The orders just kept coming. They ran out of buns in the seventh inning. Ernie had to make an emergency call to his bread vendor, who ten minutes later delivered another batch. But it was enough time to put Eddy behind the orders.

After the game, more fans poured into the bar. It was standing room only. The radio was on. It was news about the war, but the announcer's voice blended in with the bar chatter, and Eddy couldn't make out most of the words. A stocky moon-faced man with big shoulders stepped into the tavern with his arms raised. He knocked Eddy's apron loose as he snuck himself a half glass from the tap.

"Christopher Columbus, it's the Mad Russian!" Sailor shouted.

"The Clouting Cossack," added Walter.

"The Moscow Mauler," yelled Uncle Jimmy. Eddy shot a sidelong glance toward the bookie, afraid of making eye contact.

"The Suave Slav," Kitty said.

"Lou Novikoff, the Soviet Slugger," Ernie yelled as he scurried around the bar to shake hands with the husky man. "What are you doing here? Did the Cubs call you back to the majors?"

Novikoff's big head rolled backward, and he belted out a laugh. "Not yet. I'm on my way to do a hitch in the army. Thought I'd stop in Chicago to say hello to everybody."

Sailor shouted, "Well, Ernie, whaddya waitin' for? Lou came all this way to see us. Pour this thirsty man a beer. Will ya?"

The men crowded around the middle of the bar and raised their glasses. "Here's a toast to the Mad Russian. May he survive his stint in the army and make his way back to the Cubs and Ernie's Bleachers," Sailor said. After the sound of beer glasses clinking, Novikoff chugged down his beer in less than five seconds. He slammed his glass on the bar and yelled in a baritone voice, "Pour me another, Ernie."

Novikoff noticed Ernie hadn't finished his beer. "Ernie, there's still beer in your glass."

Ernie laughed. "I like to savor the taste, Lou. What's wrong with that?"

"You must be a half-glass-full kinda guy," Novikoff joked.

"And you must be a half-glass-empty kinda guy," Ernie shot back.

"No, Ernie. I'm the kinda guy that says, 'If you don't hurry and drink that half glass of beer I will.'" Novikoff reached over and chugged the rest of Ernie's beer. The men laughed as Ernie poured another round.

Margaret entered behind the bar from the back door and walked over to her husband. "Are you buying the house a round?"

"Margaret, I forgot how beautiful you are. It's nice to see you again," Novikoff said. He leaned over the bar and tried to kiss her cheek.

She pulled away. "What are you doing here, Novikoff?" she asked. "I thought they sent you down to the minors?"

"You're about as subtle as a loud belch," Novikoff said, and then he burped. Everyone roared. "I come back just to see if ya was still married so I could propose t'ya."

Margaret's face turned red. Eddy wasn't sure if she was blushing or angry. Probably angry, he thought.

"Nah, I come back because how can I say no to all the free beer?"

Margaret's frown lines carved deeper into her thin petulant face, her widely spaced eyes narrowed, and her dimples disappeared in her clenched jaw. "You can afford to pay for your drinks."

"Say, Margaret, you're short a bartender. Why don'tcha let Lou work for his drinks?" Sailor joked.

"Oh no, we can handle the work back here," Margaret said as she drilled a hard stare through Sailor's skull. Then, a stiff silence.

Novikoff looked over toward the grill and spotted Eddy. "Eddy Pareti! Now there's a ball player." Novikoff placed his left arm on the bar and vaulted over it as if he were leapfrogging a turnstile. He picked up Eddy and threw him over his broad shoulders. He then grabbed Eddy's ankles and lifted him upside down, playfully shaking the thirteen-year-old as if he were trying to jiggle loose any change in the teen's pockets.

Eddy and everyone in the bar laughed.

"Put him down!" Margaret shrieked.

Novikoff gently lowered Eddy, who stood up. He was amazed that Novikoff could lift him by his ankles. The former Cub was strong, with a hard head, Eddy thought, remembering a few years back when he saw Novikoff get beaned in the head by a fastball. A fleshy thumping sound filled the stadium as Novikoff's wool cap flew off. The ball bounced off his head and into the seats behind the dugout. The Mad Russian fell to the ground but quickly got up and jogged to first base as if nothing had happened.

Novikoff wrapped his arm around Eddy. "Why aren't you outside playing ball?"

Before Eddy could answer, his mother barked, "I don't want you behind my bar."

"Come on, Marge," Ernie pleaded.

Margaret tugged her husband's sleeve and tried to pull him off to the side, but he resisted. "Ernie, I know what he's gonna do, and I don't like it, and I never did. We've got a business to run."

"He's just here for one day, Marge. Let us have some fun. Everybody likes him, and you know business was always good when he came here after the games."

"He's a cheapskate, Ernie. He drinks us dry and hands out free beer to the house. We paid for that. Why are you defending him?"

Sailor, Walter, Kitty, and Uncle Jimmy sat quietly and watched the argument.

Novikoff had wandered to the opposite side of the bar, taking orders and pouring beer for customers. The Mad Russian glanced at Eddy and winked. He turned off the radio and reached into his pocket and pulled out a harmonica. He blew a note and hummed. Then he sang as he turned toward Margaret.

"My wild Irish rose, the sweetest flower that grows, you can search everywhere but none can compare with my wild Irish rose. My wild Irish rose, the dearest flower that grows, and some day for my sake, she may let me take, the bloom from my wild Irish rose."

Sailor and the other regulars sang along. They'd learned the song from the numerous times Novikoff would sing it during the four years he'd played for the Cubs. Novikoff's baritone voice boomed over the crowd, his heavy arms swaying back and forth. Afterward, the crowd applauded. Novikoff bowed and slugged down another beer.

For almost two hours, Novikoff drank, joked, kissed women, poured beer, and told stories about his time with the Cubs until he slurred his beer-soaked syllables and wobbled when he tried to show them all what it was like in the batter's box.

Patrons shifted in and out, and eventually, only the regulars remained at Ernie's Bleachers, except a young couple smooching and whispering at the end of the bar. The woman sipped on a martini, talking quietly to the man next to her. He wore sailor blues. The woman plucked an olive from the martini and was about to eat it when Novikoff said, "Excuse me, miss, but I wouldn't eat that if I was you."

She looked at the olive. "It looks fine to me."

Novikoff turned and snuck a glance to see if Ernie and Margaret were watching, which they were not. He reached under the bar and pulled out a jar full of olives. "You see this label on the jar? It's a jar for tomatoes," Novikoff said, his words slurred. "The owner reuses olives that customers don't eat." He put his fingers to his lips and said, "Shhh, but you didn't hear it from me," and winked.

The woman dropped the olive on the bar. "So, you're the famous Lou Novikoff," the woman said with a scent of sarcasm. "I heard about you. You're afraid of the ivy."

"You ever run full speed into a brick wall, lady?"

The sailor said to the woman, "I read that Coach Wilson rubbed ivy on his face and hands to show Novikoff here it wasn't poison ivy. Then he says, 'Can you smoke the ivy?'" The sailor and his beau laughed.

"It was a joke! He was rubbin' that crap in his face, so I says, 'Why don'tcha just smoke it.' That ivy story you read in the papers is all made up. They write whatever they want." Novikoff clenched his hands. His face was red, and he was breathing heavily, almost snorting like a bull.

The uniformed man said, "So I guess the reporter who wrote that you tried to steal third base with the bases loaded made that up too?"

Novikoff bowed his head and smiled as he poured himself another beer. He took a deep breath and leaned on the bar, his head inches away from the sailor. "Are you lookin' for trouble?"

The sailor shrugged and, in a shaky voice, said, "Just asking. That's all."

"The man on third was s'pose to steal home, but he stopped and ran back just as I got to third. Coach Wilson told the papers it was my fault. He never liked me or anyone on the team. He rode all of us every day. The poor guy was angry that we got to play baseball while his son fought in the war. None of the players liked him, and that's why he was fired the first week of the season. Poor Coach Wilson, his kid didn't make it." The Mad Russian pounded the bar. "There, you heard it from the horse's mouth."

Novikoff picked up the olive the woman dropped and threw it at Eddy, who was cooking hamburgers on the grill. Eddy turned around, and Novikoff bellowed, "Eddy, come over here."

Eddy walked over, and Novikoff gave him a side hug. He said to the couple, "See this kid? He's a great ball player. He's gonna make it someday. And you better not make funna him cuz he won't take it all nice and lyin' down the way I'm doin'. He may just decide to come over and throw you both out on yer asses."

A wave of excitement surged through Eddy's body. The couple smiled politely and continued their private conversation.

"Ah, who cares about them," Novikoff said, his meaty hand brushing back their disinterest. Novikoff squeezed Eddy's bicep and said loudly, "You're getting stronger."

"Eddy, get back to the grill," Margaret barked. Novikoff playfully punched Eddy's cheek and said, "See ya around, kid."

Novikoff walked around the other side of the bar. He slugged down another glass of beer and wrapped his arm around Sailor, who was perched on the middle stool like his ass was glued to it. "It's good to see you guys again. I should go. I don't want to wear out my welcome." Novikoff turned and glared at the sailor and his girl. "But don't worry. I'll be back with the Cubs once I'm out of the army. Hell, I'd a probably been with them this year if my number hadn't got called."

Ernie reached over the bar and shook Novikoff's hand. "Say, Lou, why don't you have dinner with us tonight? You know how you love Margaret's gravy."

Margaret kicked him in the leg.

"Ow," Ernie said, scowling at her.

Novikoff beamed. "How can I say no?"

— — —

"Where the hell is he?" Margaret snapped.

"Don't worry, Marge. He'll be here," Ernie said.

Eddy had on his Savina's softball jersey. He and Bobby sat on the couch with their dad, waiting. Florence and Margaret scurried in and out of the kitchen. They had set the table an hour earlier and were trying to keep the food warm.

"How long do you expect us to wait, Ernie?"

He counted the signatures on a petition and matched them with the obits.

"We never wait this long when Eddy's late for dinner. What makes this guy so special?" Margaret shrieked.

Ernie picked up a newspaper, shook it, and read.

"Hey Ma, you don't have to wait when I'm late for dinner," Eddy said. "You can eat without me. I don't care."

"Stay out of this, Eddy," Margaret scolded. She marched over to her husband and stood over him with her hands on her hips. "Why did you invite him anyway, Ernie? You think you're somebody if you got a friend who's a ball player? He isn't a ball player for the Cubs anyway. They sent him down because he's a bum. You know how that man drinks. He's probably passed out in his hotel room right now. That makes him twice the bum."

Ernie sighed and rustled the paper to page two of the sports section.

"The newspapers said Lou Novikoff is the next Babe Ruth," Margaret laughed. "He's a bum, and no one on the team liked him. You know that, Ernie. He's a bum." Ernie winced when she said *bum*, as if the word was somehow meant for him.

Margaret waited for a reply, but the buzzer rescued his dad, Eddy thought.

Novikoff stumbled through the front door, his arms raised, ready to hug anyone in his path. He held something in his hand.

"Eddy, I got somethin' for ya," the Russian shouted. His eyes were red, and he was squinting. Novikoff put the object behind his back and told Eddy to close his eyes and hold out his hands. Eddy did. Novikoff dropped the gift in his hands. It felt leathery. Eddy opened his eyes and saw it was an outfielder's glove.

Eddy's eyes danced with excitement as he stuck his left hand in the glove. He pounded it with his throwing hand. The mitt was big, but he was able to open and close it with ease—it was already broken in.

"Whaddya say, Eddy," Ernie said.

"Thanks, Mr. Novikoff," Eddy said, surprised he addressed the Mad Russian by his last name.

"I used that mitt when I was with the Cubs and made some great plays with it," Novikoff said.

Novikoff stuck his nose in the air. "Somethin' smells tasty." He walked over and sat at the head of the table.

The family followed him. Eddy sat on Novikoff's right, with the glove still on. Margaret took a seat at the opposite side. Ernie sat to Novikoff's left and didn't seem bothered that the Russian was sitting at the head.

The Russian poured himself a glass of wine, filling it to the brim. He drank, downing half the glass in one swig and then wiping his mouth with his meaty forearm.

"Take it easy there, Novikoff," Margaret said, her voice dripping with disgust. Eddy recognized her contempt. But Novikoff didn't seem to notice. "We may own a tavern, but we don't have an endless supply of wine, ya know."

"Don't worry, Marge. When you run out of wine, I'll be happy to drink your beer," Novikoff said as he turned to Ernie, expecting him to laugh, which he did.

Margaret sighed. Her pouty lips curled around the rim of her wine glass and took a slow sip.

As Novikoff piled his plate with spaghetti, he read Eddy's jersey. "The Savinas," he said loudly. "That a baseball team?"

Eddy explained it was a team that played sixteen-inch softball.

"You know, before I broke into the minors, I was quite a softball player. I played professional softball under the name Lou Nova in high school." The Russian paused as if he'd lost his train of thought. "You probably want to know why I played under that name. It's cuz I woulda been kicked out of high school prep sports if I earned money playing professional ball. Guess what? They caught me and kicked me out of the program anyway."

Novikoff laughed. "That didn't stop me. I pitch 'em lights out, hit like DiMaggio. I once fanned twenty-two batters in eight innings of fast-pitch softball. And whaddya know, a scout for the Cubs saw me, and we signed a contract, just like that."

Eddy turned to his dad. "See, Dad, softball ain't a waste of time."

"That's right. If you're good at something, don't let anyone stop you from doing it," Novikoff said as he stuffed his mouth with spaghetti. "Ya gotta be your own man. When I held out three years ago for more money, a reporter asked how come. I said, 'Cuz I'm my own man.'"

"I hit a grand slam last week in a softball game," Florence said with a cheerful tone.

"Ya don't say," Novikoff boomed. He made a loud smacking sound as he chewed with his mouth open. He swallowed and shoveled another fork full of spaghetti, slurping several errant noodles that hung from his pasta-covered mouth. "Some of you gals can really play ball. I threw practice with a bunch of them gals trying out for that new league Wrigley started a few years ago. They're not too bad."

Novikoff packed his mouth with more spaghetti and then washed it down with a long swig of wine. He clumsily fumbled the wine glass as he set it down. "I know some people in that league. If you want a tryout, I can get you in."

Florence laughed. "No, thanks, Lou. I'm not that good."

"She doesn't even know what a grand slam is," Eddy said.

"Oh, be quiet, Eddy. I do too."

"Oh yeah? Then how did you hit your grand slam," Eddy asked. He leaned into the table as if he was interrogating Florence.

"I hit the ball with the bases loaded and scored," Florence responded.

"When you hit the ball, did you run around the bases without stopping?"

"No, I stopped. But then I scored."

"Did you score when somebody else hit the ball."

"I don't know. Yes, Eddy, we all touched home base."

Eddy shot a playful look at Novikoff, who belted out a laugh that shook the walls.

"Lay off your sis, will ya? Whether it was a grand slam or not, she hit the ball. Got on base and scored," Bobby said laughing, which ended with a hissing sound as if he was taking in a deep breath.

"You're the smart one," Novikoff asked Bobby. "How many grand slams have you hit?"

"None this year. I've got better things to do."

"What could be better than playing ball?" Novikoff asked, his mouth full and crammed with spaghetti.

"For starters, earning a buck, studying," Bobby said.

"I guess but you'll end up workin' for someone in a nine-to-five job. Might as well have fun now while you can," Novikoff said.

"Whatever my kids do it will be honest work," Margaret howled, stabbing the overfed Russian with a sneering stare.

"I plan to work for myself someday. Ya know, be my own man," Bobby laughed.

Ernie tapped Novikoff's arm that was holding his wine glass and asked, "How's your wife, Esther and the twins?"

"They're fine. They like L.A. but miss Chicago."

"Does she still taunt you at games?"

"Uh-huh." Novikoff grunted as he slurped his spaghetti. Pasta sauce dripped from his chin, and bits of it flew out of his mouth when he talked and landed on the white tablecloth. "I get mad when she screams, 'Strike the bum out.' But it works. I was batting three hundred until I got inducted by Uncle Sammy."

"You know, Dad, you'd be the batting champion the way Ma taunts you," Eddy said.

"My batting average would be even better if Margaret were in the box seats taunting me," Novikoff added. The big Russian went in for seconds. "I heard you're running for alderman."

"Yes, if I'm elected, I will work to consolidate our trains and buses into one operation, and I will fight crime and corruption in our great city," Ernie said.

"When I'm back with the Cubs, I'll endorse you and even help you if you want," Novikoff offered.

"Oh brother. I've had enough of this," Margaret grumbled. She stood up and walked out of the dining room. Florence followed her to the kitchen.

Eddy, Bobby, Ernie, and the Mad Russian sat at the table, talking for hours. After the men emptied two bottles of wine, Novikoff stumbled to his feet and said goodbye.

"This is a short goodbye," Novikoff said as he placed his giant arms around Ernie. His words were slowed and slurred. "I'll see ya next year. The Cubs will come calling again because I'm hittin 'em like mad in the minors."

"We'll be waiting for ya," Ernie replied, louder than usual. He was tipsy.

"Thanks for the mitt, Lou. When you come back, maybe we can throw around," Eddy said.

"You bet. Live it up, kid."

Ernie opened the front door, and Novikoff stumbled out and down the stairs. Margaret instantly breezed into the room as soon as Novikoff left. "Thank God he's *gone.* I thought he'd never leave."

"Marge, why are you like that?"

"I know why you invited him. You think it will help with your campaign for alderman. Knowing a professional ball player. Don'tcha. Well, I've got news for you, buster. I'm not going to do everything around here while you run around asking people to vote for you. Do you hear me!"

Ernie listed into the living room and plopped on the leather lounge chair. He turned on the lamp, picked up his newspaper, and read about the war.

"You are impossible!" Margaret screamed as she slammed the door on her way out.

Eddy went back to his room. He couldn't wait to show his friends his new mitt.

TOP OF THE SIXTH

Eddy leaned against the wall next to the grill and gazed out the takeout window. Cub fans lingered outside, drifting toward the bleacher gate. A street vendor screamed, "Get your Cubs souvenirs!" Car horns beeped as drivers circled the stadium in search of parking. A slight breeze filled with car fumes blew through the open window but offered little relief from the heat. Eddy tossed a rubber ball in the air and caught it with his new mitt, waiting for customers.

"Eddy put down that mitt and get to work," Margaret yelled.

Eddy laid his glove and ball on the takeout counter, grabbed the spatula, and flipped two patties. Beads of sweat rolled off his cheek and hissed on the grill. A few drops landed on the burgers.

A little salty sweat on a burger won't hurt anyone, Eddy thought as he wiped his brow with his forearm.

A loud cry rose above the din of bar noise. Eddy turned and saw a woman wearing a white blouse with a ruffled collar stooped at the end of the bar, sobbing. "He's gone. Killed in the war. For what? I'll never see him again. I'm all alone."

Sailor, Kitty, his dad and Dean Steiner, the new bartender, crowded around her.

Eddy had figured she'd lost a son or husband in the war. It wasn't uncommon to see women in the bar crying over a loved one, either lost in a breakup or worse, from the war, which always let loose rivers of tears and sometimes, though rarely, guttural moans and wails. It was more difficult to spot a man grieving. Sometimes they got drunk and belligerent; other times they acted as if they had won a big bet at the Bleacher's, spending recklessly. The woman seemed too young to have a military-aged son. Eddy swiped sweat off his cheek and stepped closer.

"I'm sorry. I miss him so much is all," she said. She took a deep breath and exhaled. "I'm okay now." But seconds later, her lips crumbled into another sob. Tears bubbled out of her bloodshot eyes and flowed down her red mottled cheeks, soaking the ruffled neck of her blouse. Her thick eyelashes clung together as if she'd been swimming in Lake Michigan. She blew her nose in a drenched white handkerchief clutched in her fist.

Kitty, reeking of perfume, gently rubbed the woman's back. Sailor offered to buy her another drink, but Ernie was quick on the draw and gave her one on the house. Steiner placed both hands on the bar and turned toward her, his glass eye rolling lazily in place.

"I can't imagine what you're going through," he said. "Tell us about him."

The woman sniffed and wiped her eyes. "Ray 'n' me, we'd only been married a couple of months. His name was Ray Giorgi. He was my husband. He was kind, loving, handsome. Wait." She reached into her purse and pulled out a nicely folded piece of paper. She opened it with care. "He wrote this poem after he saw me and other women crying when they said goodbye to their men at the induction."

She read it:

The Felt- Hat Soldier

You saw me in a picture and
You felt you'd like to cry
I stood in line
Your man, "all mine"
A tall felt-hatted guy,
I hurried to the call, Felt hat and all,
I hurried to the cry

For I love America well enough to die
Other fellows in my line had come
Too, on the fly
Put aside toys
Brave American boys.
I guess it strikes a chill somewhere,
The bravest won't deny.
All that I love,
Away to shove,
And set my teeth to die
But better dead,
When all is said,
Than wrapped in peace to lie—
For we love America well enough to die.

The men looked down at their drinks. Sailor picked up his, took a long swig, and set it on a soggy napkin. Kitty wiped her eyes. No one seemed to know what to say. Meaningless bar chatter from customers filled the vacuum of the long pause.

"He sounds like a swell guy. Someday you'll be talking about him, and a smile will come to your face before a tear," Steiner said. "Then, you know you've moved on, but you'll never forget him."

The woman smiled. "Thanks. You guys are too nice."

"That a girl. You'll be fine," Sailor said. "How've you been, Dean?"

"Good, thanks. I got my good days and bad days," Steiner said. Ernie had set him up with an eye doctor, free of charge, and then hired the one-eyed war vet as his campaign manager and bartender.

Sailor leaned over the bar and took a closer look at Steiner. "Which eye is the bad one?" Steiner pointed to his left eye. Eddy figured Sailor was just being polite. It was easy to see the glass eye.

"How's your boy?" Steiner asked.

"He's still in the Pacific on the *Indianapolis*. I gotta a letter from him a few weeks ago. He said he won't be writing letters for a while. They're on some kind of mission."

"Tell him I said hello and we gotta softball team needing his services." Steiner's good eye shifted to the front door.

A few customers slid off their stools and sidled to the end of the bar near the front door. Eddy's eyes widened and then squinted. He tugged hard at his dad's sleeve. "Dad. Dad. You're not going to believe this." Eddy pointed.

A white duck waddled back and forth on the bar counter. A small red blanket draped over its back read The Billy Goat Inn

A mob swarmed around the animal, hands reaching out like fans begging for autographs. Margaret stood guard, her disapproving eyes glued to the duck. A man with a goatee unlatched the leash off the duck's collar.

"Go ahead and pet her. She don't bite," he said in a heavy Greek accent. "Her name is Suzy Q."

"Yeah, well, Suzy Q better not crap on my bar," Margaret snapped.

"Don't worry. She's trained," the man responded with a smile.

"Hey, Billy, I've got your goat," Ernie shouted.

"Which one? I have lot of goats," said Billy Sianis, who on occasion would bar hop with one of his pets, advertising his own tavern, the Billy Goat Inn. The previous year he walked a goat into Ernie's Bleachers.

Margaret ordered him to leave. "That thing belongs in a zoo not a tavern," she said. But a half smile broke across her face as she watched Suzy Q.

Ernie and Sianis shook hands. "Look like business is good," Sianis said as he scanned the tavern.

"Yeah. The Cubs are in first place, and soldiers are coming home," Ernie said. "How about you?"

Sianis laughed. "Don't you hear? The Republicans have their convention at Chicago Stadium, across from my place. The first night I only get twenty dollars in business. That make me mad. So, next day I put a sign in the window that say, 'No Republicans served here.' That make *them* mad. They say they demand service. Next day, my place is packed. Business is never better."

"We just had the rodeo here. You would've loved it. I never saw so many animals."

"Yeah, I hear. Nobody ride the big bull long enough to win the thousand bucks. Too bad. We have our circuses and rodeos at Chicago Stadium. Lots of reporters and politicians come in too. I hear you running for alderman."

"Yeah. You gonna endorse me?"

"Sure. You can put your name on my duck. It say, 'Vote for Ernie—he quack you up.'"

As the men talked, the grieving woman, her sobs muffled, gently stroked the duck's back and then its head. The duck wagged its tail and rubbed its beak on her arm. Her lips trembled and then parted into a smile.

Eddy reached in and petted Suzy Q, its feather's soft and white as snow. The duck wasn't the first animal he had seen in the bar. A man in overalls once came in the bar with a white cat that looked like Hitler. A splotch of black fur under the cat's nose resembled a toothbrush mustache. The man named the cat the *Furr Reich*. He wasn't advertising anything. He just wanted free drinks. It worked.

Suzy Q turned and walked across the bar toward the door. It dipped its beak into a drink but quickly pulled back and shook off the liquor. A man gripped his hands around the duck and was about to pick it up when Sianis yelled, "Don't hold the duck. She don't like it. Would you like it if a strange giant pick you up?"

Sianis latched the leash around the duck's collar and picked it up, holding it under his armpit like a football. "I gotta to go to the next bar. Thank you very much. Hey, Ernie, come see me. I'll introduce you to my politician friends."

"You got it."

A few customers pleaded with Sianis to stay and offered to buy him drinks. But he just waved and walked out the front door. Margaret wiped the bar counter with a clean washcloth where the duck had walked.

"I'm goin' to the washroom, Ma," Eddy said.

He closed the door and lit a cigarette. The washroom smelled of urine, and beer bottles overflowed in the trash can. Grime and rust lined the sink. The washroom needed cleaning, but Eddy ignored it. He inhaled and let out a perfect smoke ring. He studied himself in the mirror, his head cocked sideways and a cigarette hanging loosely on his lips. He clenched his right fist, bent his elbow, and flexed his biceps.

"Live it up, kid. I'm my own man," he said to the dirty mirror.

The door flew open. It was his dad.

"Son of a pup," Ernie said. He held out his hand, palms up. "Give 'em here."

Eddy reached into his apron pocket and dropped a pack of Lucky Strikes in his father's hand. Ernie snatched the cigarette from Eddy's mouth, stubbed it out on the sink, and tossed it in the toilet.

"How many times have I told you you're too young to smoke? Please stop stealing from the bar."

Eddy bowed his head and slumped his shoulders.

"It's all right, son. Just go outside and help your brother in the parking lot." Eddy expected to hear something such as "I oughtta crack ya." It was strange to hear his father say please, and his tone of voice was different. It was calm and good-natured, not angry or frustrated.

Eddy sauntered out to the parking lot and searched for his brother. He was happy to get away from the hot grill and the noisy bar. Bobby sat in a Hudson Commodore, facing Sheffield. He was smoking a cigarette and reading the paper.

How does he always get away with everything? Eddy wondered as he tapped on the window.

Bobby rolled it down. "What took ya so long? Take the back. I parked a convertible along the alley, just for you," he said with a hint of sarcasm.

"What a guy," Eddy fired back.

Bobby jingled the keys out the window. "It's the mayor's car, so don't muck it up."

Eddy snatched the keys and ran toward the back of the lot. Sure enough, a blue Lincoln Continental convertible was parked along the alley next to Waveland, a perfect spot to watch cars and pretty girls. Eddy leapfrogged into the driver's seat. He set both hands on the steering wheel and turned it.

What could be better, he thought. *I'm sitting in a convertible and it's the mayor's car.* A blonde about thirty years old in a red dress dashed by in a fast pace toward Wrigley. Eddy cupped his hand over his eyes to block the sun and whistled.

"Hey doll face, wanna go for a ride?"

The woman turned and smiled, but hurried on her way.

Eddy opened the glove box and rifled through paper, an unopened owner's manual, and a glass case. He pulled out a booklet of gas ration stamps. There must have been fifty stamps in it. They were Class X rations, reserved for politicians. *Figured the mayor would have this many*, Eddy thought. He stuffed the booklet back in the glove box and keyed the ignition, turning it slightly so he could hear the radio. He shifted the dial to the ball game.

Bert Wilson announced the score: "Cubs nothing, and the Reds nothing as we go to the top of the sixth inning here at beautiful Wrigley Field." Eddy didn't want to hear the commercials. He turned down the volume. As he did, an arm wrapped around his neck. Maria reached in to kiss his cheek.

"Where have you been, Eddy? I missed you." Their foreheads touched, and Maria's dark hair blanketed his face. She smelled of lavender soap and just a whiff of vanilla-scented perfume. Her smell was delicious, warm, and sweet like baked cookies fresh out of the oven. He remembered once he had tried to tell her how he felt about her, and in a loss for words, he blurted out that she made him feel like he was at home. She thought it was a compliment. It was at the time, but home wasn't where he wanted to be. Not anymore.

"I missed you too, doll face. I was gonna come by, but they got me going to summer school and working."

A voice behind Maria startled Eddy. "All right, break it up, you lovebirds," Gerace said.

Gerace and Elmore stood behind Maria, smirks plastered across their mugs. Before Eddy could respond, Gerace hopped in the back seat. Elmore followed. Maria ran around and opened the passenger door and got inside.

"Okay guys, take it easy, will ya? This is the mayor's car, and I don't want more problems with the old man. Got it?" Eddy said. "Hey, Gerace, got a smoke?"

Gerace pulled out a pack of Lucky Strikes and handed a cigarette to Eddy. He offered cigarettes to Elmore and Maria, but they shook their heads. Gerace leaned over the front seat and lit Eddy's cigarette and then his. He took a drag as he gazed at the control panel.

"How fast you think she can go?" Gerace asked.

"I don't know, and we ain't gonna find out," Eddy shot back.

"Oh, I forgot. You're a chicken," Gerace said. He leaned back, placed his hands under his arm pits and started flapping, "Buck, buck, buck, buck." The cigarette in his mouth swung vertically up and down in rhythm with each word.

Eddy shook his head. "Did you miss the part about this being the mayor's car? Huh?"

"He won't know. Look at the odometer. There ain't even five thousand miles on it, and this car's gotta be at least five years old. He drives it like an ol' lady."

Eddy checked the miles, and Gerace was right. The game came back on, and Eddy turned up the volume. It was the top of the sixth inning and still goose eggs across the board. There was enough time to take it for a spin, put gas in it, and get it back before the game was over. Bobby wouldn't notice. Eddy turned the ignition all the way to the right, and the big Lincoln roared to life. The convertible shook and shimmied.

Gerace yelped, "Whew! It purrs like a pussycat."

Maria clapped. Elmore crossed his arms and smiled.

Eddy had learned how to drive parking cars in the lot, starting at age ten. It didn't take him long to skillfully back the cars into tight spaces, though he scratched a few in the beginning. Three years later, he thought of himself as a pro, like Novikoff.

Eddy shifted the gears and drove out of the alley and down Waveland. He steered the convertible with his right hand, and his left arm lazily massaged the driver's door. Gerace and Elmore sat on top of the seats as if they were riding in a parade. Their shirts fluttered in the wind as the mayor's car rolled north and turned on the Outer Drive.

The headwind lifted Maria's hair in all directions, and shadows flickered across her grinning face as they passed under a row of maple trees. She could have been riding on the roller coaster, the Bobs, at Riverview, anticipating a dip and a sharp turn. There was no destination in Eddy's mind. He was just driving. Time stood still.

The wind's blast drowned out the game on the radio. A whistling cackle in the sky caught Eddy's attention. He craned his head skyward. A squad of spitfires screamed past, flying just above the tree line. A flash lit up Foster Beach, and then an explosion.

"Did you see that?" Maria yelled. "Something's going on over there. Look at all those boats."

Eddy turned down the radio. Sounds of *ack-ack-ack* filled the air, punctuated by thunderous booms. Flares lit up the afternoon sky over Lake Michigan where sun glint bounced off whitecaps beyond the break water. Eddy took the Foster exit and parked the mayor's car on the side of the street. They jumped out and ran toward a large crowd gathered on a ridge above the beach. Eddy tapped the shoulder of a middle-aged man and asked what was happening.

"The Marines are invading Chicago," he said with a laugh. He was tall and built like a linebacker. A scar ripped across his right cheek. He wore black trousers and a white short-sleeved shirt. He was holding a tan felt hat. The man pointed to one of the dozens of landing crafts slowly heading toward the beach. "Look. They're about to jump out and storm the beach."

The back door of one of the landing crafts lowered like the Wells Street bridge, and a dozen marines leaped into the lake. The sound of sporadic gunfire saturated the beach. The first wave of marines reached the beachhead and hit the ground. More boats opened and soon Foster Beach was crawling with jarheads.

"They can't be firing real bullets, right?" Elmore asked. The man turned and shot Elmore a good up and down stare for several seconds as if that was the dumbest question he'd ever heard. He shook his head and said sternly, "Whaddya think? You think they'd be shootin' live rounds with all these people around and on their own men?"

Embarrassed, Elmore shrugged and studied the sand.

The man softened his tone and said some of the explosions were real but adequately marked. He said the mock invasion was preparing marines for the inevitable assault on mainland Japan. Elmore asked the man if he was in the military.

"Yes, son. I served with Patton's third army." His eyes shifted toward the beach. He was about to say something, but paused as if he were remembering. Then he turned back toward Elmore. "All I can say is I sure hope we win this war soon. Too many good men are gone, and you boys are the next batch."

"I'm not afraid of those Japs," Elmore said. His voice cracked, surrendering a hint of false bravado. "Five more years and I'm joining the army."

Eddy shifted his feet nervously and looked away from the beach. He calculated that in four years he'd be old enough for the draft. He smirked and bummed another cigarette from Gerace. "With your eyesight, Elmore, you'd be four F'd the second you walk in the door."

"There *are* soldiers who wear glasses," Elmore said. "Heck, General Eisenhower wears glasses."

"He's an old man, fathead," Gerace said.

The words *old man* set Eddy in a panic. "What time is it? We gotta get back."

Eddy sprinted toward the convertible and hopped in. He started the engine and turned on the radio. The Cubs game was still going, but how much time did he have? The others jumped in, and Maria asked, "What would happen if the mayor caught us in his car?"

"I'm not about to find out," Eddy said. He ordered Maria to grab the gas ration booklet in the glove box and take out a stamp from the back. The car skidded into reverse and then jerked forward as he headed back onto the Outer Drive. He turned up the radio. It was the bottom of the ninth, and the Cubs were ahead, 1–0. It was a pitcher's duel, and the game would be over soon. Eddy sped up and took the Irving Park exit. He stopped at a Texaco station and sunk eight gallons in the car, more than enough to make up for the used gas. He accelerated down Sheridan, turned on Fremont and finally onto Waveland. He screeched to a halt a block away and ordered everyone to get out.

"See you around, Mister Mayor," Maria said as she climbed out of the car and ran around to the driver's side. When she leaned over to peck Eddy on the cheek, he held her close and gently nibbled her lower lip. Their lips locked. Eddy slid his tongue into Maria's mouth, and they slowly kissed for what seemed an eternity. It was their first real kiss, and Eddy didn't slobber like a puppy.

"Look at those lovebirds go," Gerace said.

Maria pulled away, blushing. Eddy for a moment wasn't sure where he was.

"Oh, I almost forgot." Maria handed Eddy the ration book. He stuffed it into his pocket, never taking his eyes off of her. Maria stood next to the car, and they smiled at each other.

"Eddy, snap out of it," Gerace said. "You're driving the mayor's car. Remember?"

Eddy waved and then clumsily shifted the clutch, causing the car to screech forward. As he pulled into the alley, Eddy's chest heaved, and his heart raced. Blood pounded in his ears, *thump*, *thump*, *thump*. His breaths were sharp and shallow. Was it the kiss or the consequence of taking the mayor's car out for a joyride?

There, by the back door of Ernie's Bleachers, stood his father and Mayor Ed Kelly, two bespectacled middle-aged men, one a bar owner and precinct captain with ambitions to be an alderman, and the other a wealthy, well-connected, and crooked mayor, sporting a striped blue tie and a straw hat. They were laughing.

The men saw Eddy drive in and walked over. "Thanks, Eddy. I was getting worried. You got it here in one piece," Ernie said in a fake high-pitched voice as he looked over the mayor's convertible.

Eddy stepped out, his legs shaking. He left the driver's door open, walked around the back of the convertible, and stood next to his brother.

"I really appreciate the extra service, Ernie. What's the charge?" Mayor Kelly asked as he pulled out his wallet.

"It's on the house," Ernie said spryly. "Just think of me when you're ready to make an endorsement for this ward." The mayor pursed his lips and nodded. The men shook hands, and the mayor stepped into his car and drove away.

Ernie draped his arm around Eddy and told him to come inside for an early dinner after his work was done in the parking lot. The old man smiled and walked back into the tavern.

Bobby playfully punched Eddy in the arm and said, "You owe me."

"How'd you do it?"

"I told him we parked his car in a garage a block away on account he's a special customer. He bought it."

Bobby usually had his back, but he'd taken a big gamble, lying for his brother, and it surprised Eddy. "Come on, you did it for Dad, right?"

"What does it matter anyhow. Nobody knows nothing," Bobby said. "It's good that way."

Eddy pulled out the ration book from his pocket and handed it to Bobby. "You could use this more than me. I got it from the mayor's car. Don't worry—he hardly drives that car. He won't notice it missing."

Bobby opened the booklet. A folded piece of paper popped out. Bobby unfolded it and read it.

"What's it say?" Eddy asked.

"It's a list of names for the sewer department. Look at this one. James Adduci equals James Addison, and there's an R next to Adduci. He's a sewer inspector. Addison must be a phony name. Why is there an R next to this guy's name?" Bobby's eyes gazed up at the sky. His eyes widened. "James Adduci. He's a Republican congressman! Kelly's a Democrat. Eddy, this is a list of names on a ghost payroll the mayor is sponsoring. Dad would go apeshit if he saw this. This'll give him some leverage."

Eddy nodded. He wasn't sure what his brother was talking about. "Whaddya think would've happened if Dad knew I went for a joyride in the mayor's car?" Eddy asked.

Bobby hesitated, and then said with a smirk, "Nothing that hasn't already happened. You might be surprised."

BOTTOM OF THE SIXTH

Eddy scrambled down the stairs two at a time and tore out onto Sheffield. A blast of heat hit him square in the face. Heat haze shimmered off cracked sidewalks and streets under the blazing August sun.

He wiped his brow and squinted, holding the mitt Novikoff had given him and a rubber ball. Today was Sunday, and there was no school. The Cubs were out of town and business was slow, so his mom and dad let him go outside as long as he stayed within "eyeshot," as his father put it, and be home for lunch. There were guests coming over.

Eddy stood in the middle of Sheffield and threw the ball high and hard against Wrigley's Field's redbrick wall. The ball thumped against the wall, and the impact kicked up a cloud of dust that lazily trailed off into the windless summer sky. The ball bounced back in the air, and Eddy caught it over his back. He reared back and hurled the ball as hard as he could in the middle of the wall. The ball zipped back, and Eddy grabbed it on a one-hopper. He threw it again. Shifting his feet in front of the ball, he scooped it up with his mitt and quickly fired it back at the wall.

Eddy stopped. He gave a sidelong glance at a short man of about thirty watching him from the sidewalk. He was pleased he had an audience. It was time to show off. He whipped the ball as hard as he could against the top of the wall and caught it behind his back. The next throw, he caught the ball between his legs. He turned to look at the man as if to say, "I got more of this, just watch." The man smiled and walked over.

"You're a regular crackerjack, aren't ya?" the man said brightly. He wore a straw hat and a blue suit and solid red tie. "What's your name?"

"Who are *you*?" Eddy said as he threw the ball against the wall.

"I'm Tony Lucadello. Ever hear of me?"

Eddy brushed him off and kept flinging the ball hard against the wall.

"I'm a scout for the Cubs, and I'm on my way to see the big man up there," Lucadello said, pointing in the direction of the front office at Wrigley Field. "I think you got talent, kid. Why don'tcha come with me, and I'll introduce you to the general manager."

Eddy stopped throwing and sized up Lucadello. "Is this some kind of joke?"

"No." Lucadello laughed. "We're always looking for new talent, and there's plenty of room in the minors and the majors what with the war 'n' all. Whaddya gotta lose?"

Eddy shrugged and followed Lucadello, who unlocked a gate just north of the elephant gate. They walked under the bleachers and onto right field. Lucadello walked a few steps, turned left, and entered through an open gate below the right field lower terrace section. He stopped at an elevator and rolled back a brass gate. The cage rattled as he did it.

"I never knew there was an elevator here," Eddy said.

"It's a secret elevator," Lucadello said.

The elevator took them to an area above the upper terrace section. They stepped off the elevator and walked past the Pink Poodle Lounge. They strolled a catwalk that stretched the length of the right field line. It led them to a series of office doors.

Lucadello knocked on a door with a placard that read "James Gallagher, General Manager."

"Come in," a voice shouted from inside.

"Hello, Mr. Gallagher. Sorry to barge in, but I brought you the next Peanuts Lowrey," Lucadello announced. He waved Eddy inside.

The office was stuffy and stunk like bad cigars. A man with a pencil mustache wearing a dark wool suit and a red-striped bowtie sat behind a wooden desk crammed with paper, books, and a black rotary telephone.

Behind the desk was a window that overlooked Clark and Addison. Salt-and-pepper hair slicked back neatly on his head, and bushy eyebrows clung to his round wired-framed glasses like ivy around the outfield wall. The ridge of his nose hung down like a bird's beak. He swiveled around in his leather chair, clasped his hefty hands behind his head, and puffed on his cigar. Smoke swirled around his head.

"The next Peanuts Lowrey, huh? More peanuts than Lowrey, by the looks of him. Where'd ya find this peanut?"

Lucadello pointed toward the bleachers and raised his voice for effect. "Right outside the ballpark. He was throwing the ball against the right field wall. Should've seen him catch. I'm tellin ya, Jimmy, this kid's got great footwork and attitude. He's agile and has great hands. Believe me. Look at his eyes. It's all in the eyes."

"I see," Gallagher said. He leaned forward and tapped his fat fingers on the desk. He eyed Eddy up and down. "This guy is really big on players throwing balls against the wall, ya know? What ya call it, Tony? The Lucadello Plan? Say, where'd ya get that mitt?"

Eddy glanced at the mitt and said, "Lou Novikoff gave it to me."

Lucadello and Gallagher brushed back as if someone had hit a hard liner straight for their heads. "Lou Novikoff!" Gallagher roared. "Why, you know how many balls he probably dropped with that mitt? He didn't catch balls—he wrestled them to the ground. The big lug. Good riddance. How did you manage to get one of his mitts anyway?"

Eddy shifted and fidgeted his mitt. "He came over for dinner a couple of weeks ago and gave it to me. He's friends with my dad."

"Well, it's gonna be a long-distance friendship cuz he ain't comin back to the Cubs," Gallagher said. "Novikoff wasn't one of your guys, was he, Tony?"

"Oh, hell, no," Lucadello said.

Gallagher smiled at Eddy, his thin lips closed. "Well, if Tony says you're good, then that's good by me. How old are ya, kid?"

"I'm, uh, fifteen," Eddy lied, adding two years to his life.

"Come back next year when you're sixteen, and we'll take a look. Hell, Joe Nuxhall was fifteen last year when the Reds brought him up. Gotta say that didn't work out well."

Gallagher stood up and shook Eddy's hand. Lucadello walked him to the door. He patted Eddy's back. "Keep throwin' against the wall. See ya next year, kid."

Eddy raced down the ramp and shot out of Wrigley Field like a Hank Bowery fastball. He couldn't wait to tell his dad that the Cubs were interested in him. He ran full speed down Sheffield and jumped the steps two at a time up to his flat. He burst through the front door, breathless and excited.

His parents sat on the living room couch. Ernie smiled, but Margaret frowned with her arms crossed. A man in a military uniform quickly stood up from the lounge chair his dad usually sat in, and held out his hand. "You must be Eddy. I've heard a lot about you."

The color drained from Eddy's face. He sneered at his parents. His mother folded her hands on her lap. "Eddy, we enrolled you at Roosevelt Military Academy. We think it's what you need. You're going to fail seventh grade. This is best for you. I want you to listen to what Col. Kincaide has to say." It sounded rehearsed.

A shock shuddered through Eddy's body. His knees buckled, and his heart pounded. He glanced at his dad, hoping he would slap his knee and laugh, saying it was all a joke.

"I hear you're a good ball player. We're always looking for good athletes," Col. Kincaide said. His stout frame towered over Eddy. He was smiling, holding his military hat in both hands. "Our academy is one of the best in the nation, and we have a great athletic program. You like football, Eddy?"

There was a long pause. Eddy thought, *If only I were sixteen*. He clenched his right hand and gritted his teeth. His jowls rippled with rage.

"Eddy, this is for the best," Ernie said as he stood up, his arms crossed. "We gave you a wide strike zone but you threw it away."

"I'm not going to your crap-ass school," Eddy shouted and stormed down the hallway toward his bedroom. Margaret jumped off the couch and hurried after him. She caught him in the kitchen and grabbed his arm. "You sure as hell are going, buster," she screamed.

Eddy twisted free from her grip and fell to his knees. Margaret whirled and slapped him with an open hand hard across the face. The blow snapped Eddy's head back. He froze and stared at his mother, wide-eyed, his left hand over his reddened cheek. His mouth opened, but no words came out. He stumbled around his mother and lunged into his bedroom, slamming the door behind him

Footsteps marched down the hallway at a fast pace. Eddy's booming heartbeat pounded with the cadence of the steps. His skin tingled, and his breathing labored. He was trapped in his bedroom like a condemned prisoner awaiting execution but hoping for a pardon.

"Let him alone for now," Ernie said. Footsteps faded back into the front room. Eddy placed a glass against the wall, trying to hear what they were saying, but he couldn't make out the words. For the next hour, his parents and the colonel talked, the voices muffled and relaxed.

Eddy laid in his bed, rubbing his cheek and staring at the ceiling. He took a deep breath and slowly exhaled. He owed money to Uncle Jimmy he couldn't pay back. His parents stuck him in solitary confinement and were about to ship him off to military school. He had no choice. There was only one thing he could do.

— — —

"It's after eleven, Ernie. Where is he?" Margaret groaned. "Something's wrong. I just know it."

"He'll show up, Marge. He always does."

Florence was washing dishes in the kitchen. Ernie and Bobby sat on the dining room table, reading the paper. They had finished dinner hours ago. Margaret paced back and forth in the front room.

"He won't be doing this at military school. That's for sure," Margaret said. "They'll put him in his place, teach him discipline."

"I don't know about that," Bobby said. "Eddy's a wild horse with a hard head. There's no tellin' what he's gonna do next."

Margaret fidgeted with her dress, straightening it. She peered out the front window. It was dark and quiet outside on Sheffield. "Should we call the police?" she asked.

The phone rang. "I'll get it," Florence screamed from the kitchen. "I bet it's Eddy." She picked up the receiver and, seconds later, yelled, "Dad, turn on the radio. Something really big happened." Florence hung up and hurried to the front room.

Margaret raced to the Stratosphere and turned it on. An announcer introduced a presidential address from President Harry Truman. The radio hissed and crackled. Static filled a long pause. Then Truman spoke.

"Sixteen hours ago, an American airplane dropped one bomb on Hiroshima, an important Japanese army base. That bomb had more power than twenty thousand tons of TNT. It had more than two thousand times the blast power of the British 'Grand Slam,' which is the largest bomb ever yet used in the history of warfare."

The phone rang again. Florence ran to the phone and answered. "Yes, Aunt Millie, we're listening. Have you seen Eddy?"

Florence ran back to the front room. "No one's seen Eddy."

Ernie set his forefinger over his lips and turned up the volume.

"We are now prepared to obliterate more rapidly and completely every productive enterprise the Japanese have above ground in any city. We shall destroy their docks, their factories, and their communications. Let there be no mistake: we shall completely destroy Japan's power to make war."

Ernie grabbed Bobby's shoulder and shook it. "Do you know what this means?"

"Yeah, Dad, we're gonna win the war," Bobby shouted.

Ernie squeezed Bobby's shoulder a little harder. "Yeah, and I bet they'll surrender. We won't have to invade!"

"Ernie, quiet," Margaret scolded. "He's still talking."

"The fact that we can release atomic energy ushers in a new era in man's understanding of nature's forces. Atomic energy may in the future supplement the power that now comes from coal, oil, and falling water, but at present it cannot be produced on a basis to compete with them commercially..."

The phone rang again. Florence ran to the kitchen. "Dad, it's Dean, the bartender. He wants to know if you're going to come down and help close."

"Tell him we'll be down in a minute," Ernie said.

After Truman's speech, Ernie, Bobby, and Margaret went downstairs to close the tavern.

"Ernie, it's past midnight. He's not in the bar. He's not home. He could be in trouble. If you don't call the police, I will."

"I already did, Marge. We have to wait twenty hours before we can file a missing person's report."

Bobby rubbed his hands and cleared his throat. "I'm gonna go and check the pool rooms. Maybe's he's hanging out there."

Ernie nodded.

"Don't be out too late. I don't wanna have to go looking for you too," Margaret said.

Bobby ran to Uncle Jimmy's house. The lights were on, but once Bobby knocked on the door, the house went dark. Bobby pounded on the door and screamed, "Open up, Uncle Jimmy. It's me, Bobby. I really need to talk to you."

The door squeaked and inched open. "Who else is wid ya?"

"Just me."

The door opened wider, and Bobby squeezed inside. Uncle Jimmy turned on a lamp. Clothes were stuffed inside two opened suitcases on the couch. The living room looked as if a bomb had exploded. The chalkboard was on the ground, and the desk was upended. Folding chairs, smashed phones, and horse racing handbooks littered the floor.

"Eddy's missing. Have you seen him?"

"Why ya askin me dat? I ain't his mudder."

"Come on, Uncle Jimmy. He told me everything. You showed him a gun and told him to shoot some guy who owes you a lot of money."

"Whaddya sayin, Bobby? That I have some din ta do wid Eddy missing? I got no beef wid him. It's all square now. And for da record, dat heater was a phony. I was just scaring da boy."

"You know where he might be?"

"Haven't a clue. I got bigger problems ta worry about if ya haven't noticed. Got pinched today. Somebody ratted me out. Da crummy flat-footed coppers busted in here and slapped da braces on. Dey gave me a free ride downtown. I had ta pay a pile of wad ta get outta dere."

Uncle Jimmy clamped his hand on Bobby's shoulder and led him to the door, stepping around the mess on the floor. "I won't be needin' ya, Bobby. Ain't gonna play da ponies for a while. My racket's gone flooey. I'm layin' low. Leavin' town. Turns out I played on da wrong team, and I don't wanna wear a Chicago overcoat, if ya know wad I mean." He shoved him out the door.

Bobby hurried down the steps and stopped on the sidewalk. He lit a cigarette and surveyed Wilton Street in both directions. He exhaled and walked south to Addison, searching every pool room, back alley and gambling joint on the near north side, no sign of Eddy.

At three in the morning, Bobby walked into the front room and saw his mother sleeping in his father's arms on the couch. Ernie locked eyes with Bobby who shook his head.

Eddy never came home.

— — —

Eddy slid into the window seat of a Greyhound bus. He gazed out the window, the country landscape flowed past as the bus rolled east toward Michigan, passing steel mills and oil refineries. A stench of rotten eggs filled the bus. Eddy held his nose.

He wondered what his parents would do once they found out he had run away. Would they cry? Would they say, "Good riddance"? They wanted to send him off to military school, so what difference did it make if he ran away. He'd be gone, out of their hair. What would they say if, after military school, he joined the army and was killed in the war? He'd never written a poem, so there was nothing they could read at his funeral. Maybe they'd say, "He was a good ballplayer who could have played for the Cubs, but the war got him first." But it might not have gotten him if they wouldn't've sent him to military school and made him join the army. Would they hang a gold star on the front room window and drive his body around the tavern a few times like they did for Nonna? Would they make Bobby kiss his face at the funeral? That thought made Eddy laugh.

"What's so funny?" Elmore asked.

Eddy shook his head as he peered out the window. He had been on the bus for less than an hour, but it seemed like an eternity. The bus driver said the ride to Grand Rapids would take about three hours with a few stops in between. Eddy figured they'd arrive at Elmore's grandmother's house around six o'clock, about the same time Eddy's family ate dinner.

Elmore had already planned to visit his grandmother and invited Eddy to come along. It was perfect timing. Eddy stuffed a pair of overalls, a flannel shirt, a sweatshirt, and two pair of underwear in a knapsack and ran out the back door and to Elmore's. When Elmore realized Eddy was running away from home, he said they could live with his grandmother and get a job cutting down trees. It was a plan, Elmore told Eddy. "Every good general has a plan and a back-up plan." Elmore didn't provide details of his back-up plan, but Eddy didn't care.

"You sure your grandmother won't turn me in?" Eddy asked.

"No, she's a recluse. She's off the cob," Elmore said. "If she does get a funny feelin', she can't call anyone. She lives outside of town and doesn't have a phone or a car or anything."

Eddy and Elmore played war, the dog-eared playing cards slip slapping on the leather bus seat between them, the cards shaking and sliding down the seats with the movement of the bus. After a few rounds, Eddy got bored and looked out the window, watching the world of Indiana and Michigan pass by. The land was flat and open. Eddy didn't see buildings for long stretches of the bus ride, and when he did, they were white tumbledown wooden shacks. He wondered how people living out here could walk around at night. There were no streetlights, and where would they go anyway? The sense of home was fading. He had been to the country before on family trips to Wisconsin. But now he was on his own and could go anywhere and do anything he wanted. He was going where Jesus left his sandals.

Who needs school, anyway? Eddy thought. His dad never went to high school, and once his brother and sister graduated high school, they'd have to find jobs. He was lousy at school, and it made perfect sense to skip it altogether and work. "You're gonna do it sooner or later, might as well do it now," he mumbled.

The bus slowed and took an exit down a dirt path. It rolled to a stop, next to a white sign with black letters and an arrow that read "Benton Harbor, 1 mile." The bus turned right and drove down a gravel road, kicking up dust along the way. A few minutes later, the driver announced, "Next stop, the House of David Amusement Park, also known as Eden Springs."

The bus pulled into a circular stone driveway and stopped. A few grownups and their kids stood up and shuffled toward the front of the bus. A line of people outside waited to board.

Eddy jumped out of his seat, his knapsack strapped around his shoulder, and headed down the aisle. "Come on, Elmore. Let's check this place out. Go on a few rides. I'm loaded." He had six dollars and fifty cents in his pocket. He had stolen it from his parents' dresser.

The bus driver told Eddy the next bus going to Grand Rapids would arrive in the next hour, and it was the last bus for the day. Elmore and Eddy hopped off the bus and followed the crowd into the park's north train depot. It was a hot and humid late afternoon, and Eddy was relieved to be in the shade inside the depot.

There was a ticket booth inside, and Eddy paid the ticket taker two nickels to ride the train.

"This way," Eddy said, running to a windowless miniature steam engine train, jumping into the first passenger car behind the locomotive. Elmore trailed behind and slid in next to Eddy.

They sat in leather-cushioned seats behind the train's engineer, who had long thick brown hair. At first, Eddy thought the driver was a woman. But when the driver turned sideways Eddy saw that he had a full bushy beard. He nudged Elmore and pointed at the driver.

"They're Jesus boys," Elmore said. "The people who run this place are in a goofy religion. They never shave or cut their hair because Jesus didn't."

The engineer shouted, "All aboard." Seconds later, the train whistle screamed and steam sprayed out of the engine's front exhaust port as the minitrain slowly chugged its way out of the depot and into the park. Its smokestack belched out coal fumes, a smoky odor that reminded Eddy of Chicago.

The train shook and shimmied as it rounded a bend in the tracks heading for a trestle bridge. Eddy closed his eyes and clung onto the backside of the engineer's seat, unaware it was caked with soot. His heart pounded, and his stomach churned when the train chuffed-chuffed onto the bridge that stood forty feet above a creek.

"Elmore, tell me when we're off this damn bridge."

"Oh, you'll know when it crashes. Look, the track is broken ahead. We're gonna die!" Elmore joked.

Eddy giggled. He couldn't help himself. "Shut up, Elmore. I mean it."

At any time, it felt like a gust of wind could tip the train off the bridge. When the train veered left, Eddy's hands squeezed the seat as if he were strangling it.

"You can open your eyes now. We're on ground level."

Eddy opened his eyes and saw a stone lighthouse about ten feet high sprouting up from the middle of a pond, surrounded by large white stones. He saw in the distance an empty amphitheater with about two hundred seats in front of it. At the opposite end of the theater were more buildings and a stone-terraced hillside with a fountain in its center. People strolled around the park while others sat along the terrace, eating and drinking.

"Where are the rides?" Eddy asked.

"You mean like carnival rides? I don't think there are any."

"Then what's there to do here?"

"I've only been here once when I was like six or seven. They have a zoo and a racetrack."

A bell rang, and the train's whistle blew again. Steam hissed out of its engine as it rumbled into the park's south depot and stopped.

"Welcome to Springs of Eden Park, paradise on Earth. Praise be the Lord,"' said the bearded engineer, his voice echoing off the depot's stucco walls and high ceiling like the words of a priest reverberating in a church.

Eddy jumped off the tiny train and ran toward the exit. He stopped under the depot's archway and surveyed the buildings around it. Across a dirt road stood a one-story feedstore, and kitty-corner from it was a two-story hotel with a wooden exterior that reminded Eddy of a frontier hotel in the Old West. There was an ice cream shop on the first floor. Eddy ran to it. Elmore trailed behind.

The screen door screeched open, and the wood floors creaked as they entered. Several customers sat on old rickety chairs lapping ice cream, above them a tin-plated ceiling about fifteen feet high. There was no line when they walked to a wooden counter and ordered chocolate ice cream cones. An old man with a gray scraggly beard and horn-rimmed glasses gave no expression as he scooped ice cream into a waffle cone and handed one each to Eddy and Elmore, taking two nickels in return.

"Let's walk around. See what's goin' on," Eddy said. The floorboards beneath their feet creaked as they strolled along the side of the hotel, passing a souvenir shop, a jewelry store, and a restaurant.

"Where's the racetrack?" Eddy asked.

"I think it's that way, just past the zoo," Elmore pointed east.

They found a stone trail behind the feedstore and followed it around a row of white orchards and sycamore trees. Lining the trail were neat columns of daisies, lilies, peonies, and purple poppies. After walking for about five minutes, the stone trail gave way to sprig stunted grass, weeds, and shrubbery. They walked past dilapidated pens with broken or missing rails. If animals were kept here, they'd escaped, Eddy figured.

"There's the lion house," Elmore shouted. He stuffed his mouth with the tip end of the waffle cone and walked toward it.

It was a white stucco building with four iron cages jutting out. Three finials shot up on the top of the roof like spears. Three of the cages were empty. A leopard in the middle cage laid on its back, against a tree stump, probably asleep. Elmore ran to the cage and poked his hand through a four-inch gap under the fence and petted the animal.

"Are you crazy?" Eddy said. "It's gonna bite."

"No, he won't. He's friendly. See?"

The leopard laid on its back and playfully pawed Elmore's hand. "It doesn't have any claws. Go ahead pet him."

Eddy inched closer to the cage and slowly reached under the fence with his left hand while his right hand held his nearly finished ice cream cone. He petted the leopard's head. Its fur was soft and thick. It was like a petting a cat. He could never have done this at the Lincoln Park Zoo. The leopard spotted the cone and suddenly rolled to its feet and lunged at Eddy's left hand with both paws. Eddy pulled back.

"Come on, Elmore. Take me to the racetrack."

They wandered through the zoo gardens along a path that wound around a fieldstone-lined creek bed. A long row of blue moon wisteria flowers drooped from a gateway trellis. The sweet scent reminded Eddy of Maria. Did she miss him? If he called her, would she rat on him? There was a whirring sound of engines in the distance. They followed the sound that led them to a circular dirt track. About a half-dozen red miniature autos roared around it. They looked like Duesenberg, or Duesie, race cars, about six feet long, with a front grill and cowl lights. The Jesus boys constructed the cars' chassis and front bumpers using old metal bed frames, and built the engines with washing machine gas-powered motors.

Eddy ran to the line, behind three boys, and shifted back and forth in excitement as if he had to use the washroom. He had dropped his cone on his run to the line but never broke stride. Elmore was several paces behind and caught up.

They watched the cars zoom around the track. Each were numbered with a flag on the hood. The driver in car three was winning, and Eddy figured that was the fastest car.

After ten minutes, a Jesus boy wearing a frayed seersucker flat cap and a yellow flannel shirt walked on the track and waved a white flag. One lap later, the drivers pulled into spaces near the track gate and climbed out. Eddy and Elmore and the others handed the Jesus boy a nickel and raced to their cars. Eddy squeezed into the cockpit of car three and waited. He grabbed the four-spoke steering wheel with both hands and set his foot gently on the gas pedal, waiting for the signal to go.

The Jesus boy stepped onto the track, still slipping nickels into a coin changer hung on his belt and said, "When I wave this red flag, then you go. When I wave the white flag, that means you have one lap left. You come in and park along the fence here by the gate." He looked at Elmore. "Does everyone know how to drive?"

Elmore and Eddy nodded.

The man tilted his head slightly and smiled. He stepped backward and waved the red flag.

Eddy gunned it, and a cloud of white fumes rose around his car. He didn't mind the acrid smell.

The car's steering was sturdy and smooth, and the engine grumbled with an occasional sputter. The cockpit vibrated like Eddy's bed when an El train passed.

The wind slapped Eddy's face and ruffled through his hair. His jaws clenched and eyes bulged as he steered the car around the corners at full speed, passing other drivers. *No need to use the brakes*, Eddy thought as he bumped the back of Elmore's car and then sped around him for a second time. When the Jesus boy waved the white flag, Eddy, his hair sticking up in every direction, parked his car, jumped out, and bolted to the line to race again.

Eddy hopped into car three again and won. After several go-arounds, Eddy chose another car, and Elmore hurtled into car three and won. They lost track of time as they sped around the track for hours with only getting back in line serving as a punctuation between their races. Hunger ended their racing.

It was early evening, and shadows blanketed Eden Springs. The sun had dropped behind the amphitheater, west of the park. Eddy and Elmore walked to a concession stand in the beer garden and bought hots dogs and pop. Eddy ordered beer, but the Jesus boy smirked and handed him a Coke instead. They sat down on the stone terrace that looked like something out of ancient Rome.

"Damn, that was great!" Eddy said.

"Yeah, it sure was," Elmore replied and then bit into his hot dog.

"We passed through Indiana. Where's the Indy 500?" Eddy asked with a mouthful of bun while chewing his food.

"I don't know. I'm from Michigan. Remember?" Elmore said as he took a swig of his pop, then stuffed his mouth with another bite of his hot dog. "Did you know that racecar spelled backward is racecar?"

"Uh-huh," Eddy grunted.

A Jesus boy with long hair reaching to his butt sat down next to them and took a big bite out of a green apple. Sweat poured down his face and drenched his long sleeve corduroy shirt. He reeked of body odor, a familiar smell that reminded Eddy of the Cubs locker room. Eddy could hear the apple crunching in his mouth.

The man stopped chewing and said, "If you were to die right now, do ya think you'd go to heaven?"

Eddy slewed his eyes without moving his head. He could run, but to where?

"You mean this isn't heaven?" Eddy said with a half laugh. "Say, I need a haircut. Is there a barber shop around here?"

The Jesus boy cracked a crooked smile and asked, "Where ya boys from?"

"Chicago. We're on our way to Grand Rapids to live with my grandmother," Elmore said. Eddy set his hand on his forehead and looked down, shaking his head in disbelief. You never tell strangers where you're going or where you live, he thought.

The man's eyes shifted to the bulging knapsack fastened across Eddy's shoulder and said, "What's the matter? Did your friend tell me too much?" The man laughed and inched forward. "I was about your age when I ran away. Came here and joined the House of David. This been my home for thirty years or so. Joined the baseball team and barnstormed around the country. Played against Babe Ruth, Satchel Page, Grover Cleveland, Dizzy Dean. Now I just play ball here at our stadium. You like baseball?"

"You're looking at Eddy Pareti, a prospect for the Chicago Cubs," Elmore said, pointing to Eddy.

Eddy smiled and shrugged. "What can I say?"

The man laughed. "You ever hear of Paul Mooney?"

Eddy and Elmore shook their heads.

"That's me. In year nineteen hundred and twenty-two, the Cubs offered me twenty thousand dollars to pitch for them. Ya know what I said?"

"You asked for more money," Eddy said.

Mooney smiled and gazed off in the distance. "I turned them down. They wanted me to cut my beard. I didn't want to do that. I didn't want to leave my home and be away from my brothers and sisters."

The corners of Mooney's mouth tightened. He looked straight at Eddy. "Being on your own away from home is like being on base and taking a big lead. There's danger. Risk. You could get picked off, or you could run into a double play. The only place you're really safe is when you're at home base. It's the only base in the ground like a foundation, that's shaped like a house. Funny, in baseball, you start at home, and you journey across the sacks trying to get back. Home is where all the action is. You defend it, clean it, run to it, throw at it, step on it. Some try and steal it. All the important stuff happens at home."

The man paused in thought and then said, "The House of David is my home, and soon Benjamin Purnell will resurrect and return on his white horse and lead the twelve tribes of Israel into the millennium where we will inherit the earth."

Eddy shot Elmore a look of "let's get outta here." But Elmore asked, "Benjamin who? And what do you mean he will resurrect?"

"Benjamin Purnell is God's seventh angelic messenger sent down to earth to teach about the coming thousand years in paradise. He founded this colony years ago. He died in the year nineteen hundred and twenty-seven and is now sealed in a glass coffin up there in the Diamond House." The man pointed toward a building about two football fields north. It was a Greystone mansion set on a hill, and partially hidden behind a batch of maple, oak, and tamarack trees.

"Come on, we got a bus to catch," Eddy said.

The man laughed. "I'm afraid you boys are stranded here tonight. The last bus left three hours ago."

"What!" Elmore screamed.

"Don't worry," the man said. "There's plenty of room here. You can sleep in one of the cabins by the ballpark. It won't cost ya much. The next bus to Grand Rapids comes in tomorrow at one o'clock. You'll have time to watch a ball game here in the morning, right behind the cabins. We still have a good team, ya know. And there's gonna be a special player pitching for our team."

"You?" Eddy asked.

"Not me. Can't tell ya. You'll have to find out yourselves. It's a surprise to our fans." Mooney raised his head and studied the sky. "It's gonna get dark soon, and the park will close. Follow me. I'll show you where you can sleep tonight."

Mooney led Eddy and Elmore southwest on the main trail in the park. They walked past clusters of orchids and roses surrounding Japanese bonsais. Birds tweeted, and a strong honeysuckle scent saturated the air. A Jesus boy watering a pink hibiscus in bloom turned the hose away as they walked by.

They came across about a dozen rustic log cabins neatly lined on each side of the road. Rows of maples towered over the cabins, providing shade. It was almost dusk and the road had ominously darkened under the trees. Several families lolled outside, the men sitting on log benches, smoking cigarettes. Children played tag or kickball. Mooney stopped at the last cabin on the trail. It was smaller and set back about fifty feet from the other cabins.

"This'll do. That'll be two dollars."

Eddy pulled two dollars from his pocket and handed it to Mooney.

"The park's closing soon, so stay inside. Remember: the bus to Grand Rapids leaves tomorrow at one."

Eddy thanked him, and he and Elmore stepped inside their home away from home. It was a one-room cabin without a washroom. The wood floors creaked, and a musty smell bathed the cramped cabin. There was a stone fireplace on one wall and two single beds lined up against the opposite end. A rickety rocking chair sat next to the cabin's only window, near the front door. The log cabin could have been the birth home of Abe Lincoln, Eddy thought.

"Where we gonna pee?" Eddy asked.

"Outside. Mother nature's one big giant toilet," Elmore said, laughing.

The two of them spent the rest of the evening in the cabin playing cards under candlelight. They played gin, but Elmore lost every hand. After Eddy barked, "Gin!" yet one more time, Elmore accused, "You cheatin'?"

"The hell with this. I'm goin' to bed," Eddy muttered, and he slumped onto the rickety metal frame, sending up a cloud of dust that made Elmore sneeze as he walked over and vaulted on his own skinny mattress, the kind with stripes that Eddy thought they had in prisons.

After about ten minutes of Elmore's restless tossing on the squeaky old springs, Elmore asked, "You awake?"

"Yeah."

"You think that Purnell guy will resurrect?"

"Are you kidding? No way."

"There's a lot them Jesus boys here. Maybe they know something we don't."

"Then let's go find that coffin and wake him up," Eddy quipped.

Elmore jumped out of his bed. "Great idea!" He put on his shoes.

"I was kidding. I'm not going in that house."

"I forgot. You're a chicken."

Eddy sat up and put on his shoes. The cabin door squeaked as they opened it and stepped outside in the cool cloudless night. A full moon gave them enough light to see the trail.

"Which way is it?" Eddy asked.

"If we know which way the lake is, then we know where east is. Right, Eddy?"

"Don't be cute. We came from that way," Eddy said, pointing south. "So, I think we need to go in the opposite direction."

Eddy and Elmore hiked north down the main trail. They passed the beer garden and amphitheater, now empty and dark, and continued north. "How big is this park?" Eddy asked.

"I think about five hundred acres."

"How big is an acre?"

"How should I know. A half a mile?"

"You're crazy. That would make this place two hundred and fifty miles wide."

"Ssshhh, I heard something in the bushes," Elmore said.

Eddy shook his head and kept walking. Seconds later, he stopped. "That's it. Up there."

The gothic mansion loomed on a hill, only its hulking silhouette showing in the moonlight. A gravel road led to the house that Eddy figured to be about a half block away. Pallid moonlight crept through twisted branches of swamp oak trees. Gravel and dead leaves crunched under their gym shoes as they slowly made their way to the mansion. They reached a stone path that was narrower. It curved around a swooping line of boxwoods, and a four-foot statue of an angel, leading to the mansion's front porch steps, which were wide and made of concrete. They walked past the statue to the front stairs. There were no lights. Tree branches swayed, and leaves trembled in the whistling wind. Crickets chirped from mysterious places in the dark giant toilet.

"I gotta pee," Eddy said. He hurried behind a bush near the statue, unbuttoned his pants, and relieved himself. He pulled up his pants, buttoned them, and reached in his pocket for a cigarette and Zippo lighter he had taken from his family's tavern. Some GI was too busy with a dame and must have forgotten about it. There was still fluid inside. The black crackle that coated it was peeling. He stuck the cigarette in his mouth and flipped open the lighter. He flicked the flint wheel several times with his thumb. Sparks flickered until he got a flame. He lit the cigarette and took a drag.

"Now what?" Elmore asked.

"This was your idea. You tell me."

"You're chicken. You almost peed in your pants."

Eddy took another drag, the tip flaring an orange glow. He exhaled, the smoke floating in the cool moonlight like a ghost. "Okay. We walk up these stairs and check it out."

Something fluttered past his face. Eddy flinched and ducked. "What was that?"

"It was a bat. Or was it a vampire?" Elmore joked.

"You really crack me up," Eddy said.

The wind whipped up leaves in a whirl in front of them and blew down the stone path like a minitornado, disappearing into the darkness. Eddy gulped. He turned to look at the house. One of the window shutters on the second floor hung crooked off a hinge. The moonglow lit up the stairs, but it was too dark to see the front door.

Eddy took a deep breath and treaded up the stone-cold steps toward the porch. He could make out the pillars at the top of the stairs, but the front door was dark, brooding. He reached the top and turned around. Elmore bumped into him.

"Will you cut it out? Give me some room."

Eddy plodded to the front door. He waited a few moments for his eyes to adjust and then held up his cigarette to the door for more light. It was a solid-oak double door with a dark-stained varnish. There were two gold knobs and a gremlin door knocker just above his head but within reach. Eddy grabbed the door knob and turned it. The door was locked.

Something touched the back of his shirt. He jumped and wheeled around. It was Elmore clinging to him. "Get off of me, will ya!"

Behind Elmore, Eddy noticed a faint flicker of light coming from a window at the end of the porch. He walked to it, a stained glass window, and peaked inside.

"Look at that!" Eddy said in a choked hush. "It's real."

A glass-cased coffin that looked like something Eddy had seen at the Chicago Field Museum sat in the middle of a parlor room. A lit candle flickered on a table next to the coffin that was mounted on a wooden platform. There was enough light to see who was lying in the coffin. The candlelight, stirred with the full moon, lit up the corpse of one Benjamin Purnell, God's seventh angelic messenger. Purnell wore a white suit and shoes. Long silver hair flowed around his head and a gray scraggly beard draped across his chest. A ruby locket hung around his neck. Long yellow fingernails curved inward from his pallid fingers, one of which adorned a diamond ring.

Cast by the candlelight, shadows danced across the old man's bony face.

A white orchid lay on top of the glass coffin. The faint scent of burning incense drifted through the cracks of the old window frame. The fragrance reminded Eddy of a funeral Mass.

Eddy gently tapped on the window. "Wake up! Wake up!"

"Be quiet. Somebody might hear," Elmore whispered.

Eddy glanced away for a moment to take another drag from his cigarette. When he turned back to look at Purnell, there was a thump and then the guttering candle went out. Eddy's cigarette fell out of his mouth as he and Elmore dashed down the porch stairs. Elmore tripped and fell. He picked himself up and ran down the trail, trying to keep up with Eddy.

Eddy reached the cabin first. He waited at the door when Elmore came racing down the trail.

"In here!"

Elmore rushed in, and Eddy slammed the door, barricading it with the rocking chair. Elmore fell to his knees, gasping for air.

The wind wailed through the cracks in the dark cabin walls. It sounded like the high-pitched cries of a gold-star mother back home moaning in grief after learning her son had been killed in the war. The sound chilled Eddy down to his thudding heart.

Hours passed until Eddy and Elmore, hearts bumping and lungs bellowing, finally fell asleep, their first night away from home.

TOP OF THE SEVENTH

Sunlight streamed through the cabin's shutter slats and lit up Eddy's face as if he were under interrogation. He opened his eyes and rolled to the side. Elmore lay curled up in his bed, hugging a pillow, his glasses crooked on his face and his mouth agape.

Eddy reached for the walking stick Elmore had found on the hike to the mansion and poked Elmore's nose. The big little general rubbed his nose, but his eyes didn't open. Eddy lowered the stick into Elmore's wide-open mouth and twirled it, accidentally touching his top front teeth. Elmore rose out of bed.

"What was that?"

"Wake up, chucklehead. Time to go."

Eddy jumped to his feet, walked to the window, and peered outside. People strolled past the cabin, all traveling in the same direction. How long had they slept? What if they missed the bus again? Eddy didn't want to spend another night stuck in a spooky cabin surrounded by a weird religion.

Eddy slipped on his shoes, pulled the knapsack over his shoulders, and walked outside, covering his eyes in the bright sunlight. It was a hot muggy morning. A couple with young kids hurried by the cabin. An old man straggled behind them.

"Excuse me, what time is it?" Eddy asked.

The old man stopped and twisted his arm to read his watch. "It's noon. You better hurry. The ball game started." He then continued on, following the others as they made their way to the stadium.

"Thanks," Eddy yelled. He turned to find Elmore practically glued to his back. "Will you give me some room? What's wrong with you?"

"You're always running everywhere. I don't wanna lose you."

"Come on, this way." Eddy followed the crowd down the dirt path that led to a small stadium. "Let's see how these men in beards play ball. We got time."

Elmore shrugged. "I'm out of money."

"Don't worry. I gotcha covered, kid." Eddy handed eighty cents to a man with braids and a bushy beard and wandered inside the two-story wooden stadium with Elmore following like a scared puppy.

They walked up a ramp that led to an upper and lower section on each side of home base. Everything was constructed of wood. Eddy figured the stadium could hold about five thousand fans, but it seemed only half full. The crowd was sparse and spread out.

Eddy and Elmore chose the lower section behind first base and plopped down on a bench just above the home team's dugout. It was as if they were sitting in the bleachers at Wrigley. An overweight, older couple sat to their right, and a Jesus boy rested one row behind them.

"I can't believe Jackie Mitchell is pitching today. This is so exciting," the older woman boomed. Her flaccid arm flapped as she pointed at the pitcher. She wore large- framed glasses with a beaded chain that hung from the handles. A worn-out Detroit Tigers hat barely fit her head, squashing thick sweeping curls of gray hair tufted underneath.

Eddy stuck a cigarette in his mouth and flipped open his Zippo lighter to light it. He took a drag, his eyes glued to the bearded pitcher warming up on the mound. The pitcher was short and skinny and had an awkward side-armed delivery. His hat tilted slightly to the right.

"Excuse me, but is that Jackie Mitchell pitching?" Eddy asked the old woman.

"Oh, yes, it is, young man."

"I don't see anything great about his pitching," Eddy said.

"You mean *her* pitching."

Eddy stared in disbelief. "You're joking. Right? Did you notice he's got a beard, lady?"

"It's a fake beard. To play for the House of David, players have to wear fake beards if they don't have one," said the old man. He was balding and wore thick-framed glasses. Suspenders held his trousers tightly over his round belly.

"Verne, these boys are too young to remember Jackie Mitchell," the woman said. She leaned forward as if she were about to reveal a juicy secret. "Jackie Mitchell struck out Babe Ruth and Lou Gehrig. Back-to-back!"

"Oh, come on, Mildred. It was a gimmick," shouted the old man. "Ruth and Gehrig played along in a scheme to attract attention during an exhibition that would have been on April first if it hadn't've rained. That game was set up by Joe Engel, ya know. He did everything to bring in fans. He once staged an elephant hunt, raffled off a house."

"Aw, you're nuts, all right," Mildred said. "No way would Ruth or Gehrig let a seventeen-year-old girl strike them out even in an exhibition game. Hell's bells, neither of them ever said otherwise. And right after that, she signed a major league contract."

"They pulled that quick," the old man quipped.

Mildred rose to her feet. "Pulled because Ruth said girls can't handle a man's game. He was embarrassed and didn't want to face female pitchers. And he never did again. Did he? They were all afraid of her, and that's why she was banned from baseball."

"Oh, why don't ya sit down already. You can believe whatever you want."

Sulking, Mildred obeyed, and they turned their attention to the game. A batter hit a ground ball to short and was thrown out.

"They wouldn't sign Babe Didrikson to a minor league contract either. She struck out Joe DiMaggio when she played for the House of David," Mildred muttered.

"Oh, you just can't let it go, can you?" Verne shook his head. "All a publicity stunt."

Mildred stood again and shouted, "She holds the record for the longest baseball thrown by a woman. She threw it two hundred and fifty-nine feet, Verne. Farther than a lot of major leaguers can. And she can run faster than a lot of them. She won a gold medal in the Olympics, and this year, she won the Western Open golf tournament for the third time! She's a better athlete than most men!"

The crowd cheered after a batter hit a lazy pop-up to first for the third out.

Elmore elbowed Eddy. "Maybe we should go."

"Where ya going, young man?" the Jesus boy said. "You're gonna miss them playing baseball on donkeys."

"What are ya talking about?" Eddy asked in a tone as if the man was nuts.

"It's true. They play an inning on donkeys," Mildred said. "It pulls the game down. It's undignified."

"Another gimmick," Verne added.

"Why would they play on donkeys?" Eddy asked.

"Zechariah chapter nine, verse nine. 'Lo, your king comes to you, triumphant and victorious is he, humble and riding on a donkey,'" said the Jesus boy. "And we all know Jesus entered Jerusalem on a donkey."

Eddy shook his head and sat down. He took a drag and waited for the donkeys.

The next inning, all of the House of David players sat on donkeys in the field. All except the pitcher and catcher. The batter let two pitches go before he hit the third one for a base hit in left field. The batter ran and hopped on the back of a donkey that stood next to home plate, but the animal refused to move.

Meanwhile, the left fielder jumped off his donkey and caught the ball. He mounted the beast and threw it to the second baseman who also sat on his own mount. The batter leaned forward and repeatedly kicked his donkey's side. No matter how hard he tried, it just stood there. The second baseman tossed the ball to first for the out.

"Most of these other teams can't never ride a donkey," said the Jesus boy. "They're lost. We're all lost." He locked eyes with Eddy. "Are you ready for the Second Coming? It will happen in a gradual way. When it comes, it will be the windup of evil."

Eddy gave a half laugh. He wanted to tell the man to get lost but instead said, "Would I be saved if I grew a beard and long hair like you?"

Elmore elbowed Eddy hard in the ribs, but he brushed it off. Eddy had watched and listened to his dad and friends' banter with each other while sitting in the bleachers at Cubs Park. It was all fun and meaningless talk.

The Jesus boy showed no expression as he said, "Leviticus, chapter nineteen, verse twenty-seven, 'You shall not round off the hair on your temples or mar the edges of your beard.'"

"Uh-huh, I betcha a quarter this next batter gets on base," Eddy taunted.

The man rose and shouted, "Proverbs, chapter twenty-eight, verse twenty-two, 'He that hasteth to be rich hath an evil eye, and considereth not that poverty shall come upon him.'"

Verne leaned over and whispered, "You got him all riled up. They're nice folks and all, but they can get *real* preachy at times. Just ignore him."

"What time is it, mister?" Elmore asked Verne.

Verne looked at his watch. "It's almost one o'clock."

"We've gotta go, Eddy. Our bus leaves at one!" Elmore shouted. The boys jumped out of their seats and bolted out of the stadium, heading north toward the train depot and bus station. Once they arrived, the ticket taker told them the bus going to Grand Rapids picked up at the south entrance, so they ran the other direction

Elmore stopped halfway there, gasping for air. "I…have…to…rest."

"Come on, Elmore. We're almost there. I don't want to stay here another night."

"Go without me. Tell them to wait." Elmore panted with his hands on his knees. He handed Eddy his bus ticket from yesterday.

Eddy sprinted down the path to the south entrance. He saw the bus and ran to it, boarding just as the doors closed. He stood on the first step, showing the driver their tickets.

"Where's the other passenger?" the driver asked.

"He's coming. He walks slow."

"I can't wait. I have a schedule. He can catch the next bus in two hours," the driver said flatly.

Eddy pointed to the trail. "Come on. He's almost here. He has a bad heart."

The driver shook his head. "Either get in or step off."

Eddy folded his arms and stood on the first step. Just as the driver rose out of his seat, Eddy shouted, "There he is. Come on, Elmore. Hurry!"

Elmore picked up his pace and pounded on the bus. The driver opened the door, and Elmore, huffing and puffing, boarded. Eddy smirked at the driver as they walked past him and toward the back. The driver rolled his eyes, pulled a lever, and the doors banged shut. The bus roared out of the park grounds and toward Grand Rapids.

Eddy let out a whew as he and Elmore dropped onto a couple of open seats in the back of the bus, drawing the eyes of other passengers.

— — —

Ernie and Bobby searched Eddy's room for clues. They rummaged through his dresser drawers and nightstand. They even looked under the mattress. Nothing seemed out of the ordinary.

"He took his knapsack, but I don't think he took many clothes with him," Bobby said. "I don't see the mitt Novikoff gave him. He probably took that."

The roar of an El train rolled past the window. "If he took the train, Bobby, where would he go?"

Bobby looked out the window. "He could be anywhere, Dad. He has lots of friends. We should write a list of people who might know something and split up to talk to them."

Bobby and Ernie walked into the dining room. It was packed with aunts, uncles and cousins, along with Sailor, Kitty, Steiner, and Walter. Their murmurs wound down as Ernie stood at the head of the table, and raised his arms to quiet them.

"Listen up. I'm going to write a list of people we need to find and ask if they've seen Eddy or know someone who might know something."

"Did you call the cops?" Berk said. Berk was Margaret's older brother.

"They know. But we can do more," Ernie said. "We're going to hand out pictures of Eddy. You can hand them out to taxi drivers or store clerks and anyone you can think of."

"Are ya gonna tell us what he was wearing?" Berk asked.

"A white long-sleeved shirt and blue pants," Margaret said. "Enough with the questions. Let's go out and find him."

Bobby wrote down a list of names and places to search.

Margaret and Florence would go to Eddy's school and friend's houses. Berk and his sisters would hunt the neighborhood pool halls, grocery stores, soda shops, gas stations and train stations. Sailor, Walter, Steiner and Kitty would scour the alleys and streets. Ernie and Bobby planned to canvass Lemoyne School's playlot and the softball fields on the Outer Drive.

— — —

Gerace, Warman, and a few other boys stopped playing fast-pitch as Ernie and Bobby approached. "You still looking for Eddy, ain'tcha?" Gerace said.

"Have you seen him, Phil?" Bobby asked.

"No. I haven't seen him for almost two weeks. He didn't come out much after he took the mayor's car out. Um, I mean after he got to park the mayor's car and meet him. The mayor, wow. I hear you're running for alderman, Mr. Pareti. Ya got my vote."

Bobby rolled his eyes. Ernie sighed, pursed his lips and said, "Does *anyone* know where Eddy is or might be?" Everyone shook their heads.

"If you knew where Eddy is, would ya tell us? Honest now," Bobby asked.

One of the boys shrugged. "We don't rat on our friends, but we really don't know where he went. Honest. Like I said, we haven't seen him around much," Gerace said, pointing to a gaggle of girls sitting on a slatted wooden bench. "You could ask her." He looked down and said, "Uh, that's Eddy's gal. Maria."

Bobby and his dad strolled over to the bench.

"I didn't know he was sweet on anyone," Ernie said. He looked at Bobby. "Did you?"

Bobby shrugged.

The girls, five of them, stopped talking when Ernie and Bobby approached. "Which one of youse is Maria?" Bobby asked.

"I am," said a scrawny brunette sitting in the middle of the bunch. "Are you Eddy's big brother?"

"Yeah. We're lookin' for Eddy. Seen him around?"

"No. I don't know where he is, and he hasn't called me in a long time," Maria said in a disappointed tone.

Bobby handed her a matchbook with Ernie's Bleacher's number on it. "If you see him or know where he is, call us," Bobby said.

Maria blushed and forced a smile, as did her friends. They seemed anxious to get back to their conversation and were politely waiting for the men to leave.

Bobby and Ernie walked to Waveland Park and asked around. Eddy's softball team wasn't there, but other players said they hadn't seen Eddy for weeks.

The afternoon sun beat down on them as they spent hours pounding the pavement. They hit all of Eddy's usual haunts. Bobby knew every one of them.

"I don't get it, Bobby. I know every hustler, drunk, taxi driver, barmaid, greasy-joint waitress, newsie, store clerk, and goon on the north side, and nobody knows nothing," Ernie said. "It doesn't make sense. He's gotta be somewhere." Ernie swiped sweat off his brow. "Let's go back. Maybe he showed up at home."

They walked a few blocks back to Southport Avenue, where Bobby told his father Eddy pitched pennies with the older kids.

"You're kiddin' me?" Ernie said.

"Ya, and that joint there is where Eddy would hustle pool." Bobby pointed to a pool hall that, years ago, Ernie would go to before he had kids.

Bobby grew quiet when they walked past Uncle Jimmy's house.

Ernie was finding out how much Eddy got around. It seemed like miles.

Ernie stared at his wife when he walked into his establishment, and they both shook their heads at the same time. His eyes scanned the smoke-filled tavern for his son as he shuffled behind the bar and hugged his wife.

"What are we gonna do, Ernie?" Margaret sobbed. "What if something happened to him? Oh, I can't take this."

"We'll find him," Ernie promised. "He doesn't have much money. He'll come back when he runs out. He's a smart kid."

"He failed seventh grade!" Margaret said.

"He has street smarts. That's more important than books," Ernie said. He clipped a Tommy Palmer cigar, stuck it into his mouth, and lit it. His eyes hissed like the glowing embers of his cigar when he spotted Frank Young, the alderman, enter. Young took a seat at a round table in the middle of the tavern. He eyed Ernie, and waved him over. He wore a dark-blue wool suit with a vest and a red-and-yellow-striped tie. His hair was slicked back, and his wire-rimmed glasses perched neatly on a pointy schnozzle

Ernie slow-walked to Young's table, smoke billowing out of his mouth. He hovered over the alderman. "Hello, Frank. It's been a while. How ya doin'?"

"Been doing good, thanks. I see your business has picked up," Young said, his eyes wandering around the tavern. "Ernie, why don'tcha get me a beer and join me. I'd like to have a word with you."

Ernie strolled back to the bar and poured a draft beer, Fox Deluxe. He brought it to the table, and sat across from Young. The alderman took a long swig and gently set his drink on the table. His green eyes, the color of dollar bills, were fixed on the slot machine in the corner. Kitty sat on a stool, mindlessly feeding it nickels and pulling the lever.

The alderman's lips curved into a smile. "I see you have a one-armed bandit gracing your place."

"It was a gift from Guzik," Ernie said, hiding his contempt behind his poker puss.

"Is that right? That's the kind of thing that can get a place shut down."

"All right, Frank. I don't have all day. I gotta place to run. Whaddya driving at."

Young crossed his arms. "Why are you running against me? We're friends. We go back a long way. I rub your back; you rub mine. That's the arrangement we have. To be frank, you're rubbing me the wrong way, Ernie."

"You've been alderman for almost fifteen years. I think it's time somebody else gives it a try."

"Do you know what it's like dealing with everybody screaming at you with their hands out? It took me years to get a system in place to get the wheels running in a way that works for everybody. That includes you. I pulled strings so you could open this tavern without a hitch. With my help, you got through the worst of the Depression okay with that hot dog stand, didncha? I let ya have that too. Why do you wanna ruin everything we worked for all these years?"

"Whaddya want me to say, Frank? Want me to send you flowers with a note thanking you for all the memories? I put money in that brown paper bag for this bar and that hot dog stand, way I remember it. I helped get you elected and reelected over the years. Made sure your posters were planted in here and your little campaign buttons. I registered more voters for you than most precinct captains. I think it's my turn. You got your place on Sheridan. Why don't you retire and endorse me? We'll do the ole switcharoo."

Young pointed his index finger at Ernie. "Now look here, you son of a bitch. I..." He closed his eyes and inhaled. His fingers formed a steeple. He cleared his throat and in a soft tone said, "You're an honest hardworking family man, Ernie." Young leaned forward. "I'll give it to ya straight. Politicians mix truth and lies as easily as a card shark shuffles clubs and spades. Politics ain't your kinda business."

"I didn't just jump off a turnip truck. I know the score."

"I guess we're at sixes and sevens then. Look, you can't be that naive, Ernie. You know how it works. Voters don't elect us. You know who does, and they're all backing me. That includes Guzik's people and the mayor himself."

"We'll see about that."

"I can make one call to the mayor or anyone else that matters informing them that you have a slot in your place and that you hold fifty-cent card games in here after hours. They could close your joint faster than downing a shot of whiskey."

"I can get the mayor on my side."

"Oh really? You think you can change the mayor's mind. He and I go back a long way. You have nothing to offer him."

Ernie shot a lopsided grin and loomed closer. "I don't think he'd like it if the newspapers or anyone else that matters knew that he put a Republican congressman on the ghost payroll in the city sewer department."

"What are you talking about, Ernie?"

"Just what I told ya. It's true, and I can prove it."

"Ernie, you don't want to blackmail anyone in politics, especially the mayor. You're outta your league."

"I know, and I don't plan to. It's insurance, just in case." Ernie rose to his feet. "See ya on the campaign trail."

"You're mistaken if you think we'll let you stay on the ballot and split the vote. You're gonna drop out one way or the other."

— — —

Eddy sat next to the window and gazed out as the bus rolled northeast. The landscape, lush with maple and oak trees and grass, looked as if it were a never-ending movie looping around to the beginning. Everything appeared the same, shacks, trees and a patchwork of small farms. The barns were all painted red, and the grain silos were white, they reminded Eddy of the coal silos on Clark and Waveland. Maybe the world outside was moving and the bus was still, Eddy thought. He lit a cigarette and wondered about the Jesus boy who'd run away as a teenager and stayed at the House of David. Did he ever see his family again? Did he miss them? Was it worth it? Eddy might have stayed longer and maybe even tried out for their travel baseball team if he didn't have to wear a fake beard and recite Bible verses all the time. They never ate meat and were not allowed to have girlfriends. Who could accept that?

A few passengers in the front of the bus were talking loudly and seemed excited about something. They passed around a newspaper. Eddy could make out a few words of the headline, something about the war. Elmore nudged Eddy and showed him a deck of cards.

"Let's go. Me and you. It's war!" he said, trying to be funny.

"I'm not in the mood," Eddy said.

"What's the matter? You miss those Jesus boys?"

Eddy reached into his pocket to count his money. He only had two dollars and seventy-five cents left.

"Damn it. I've already spent almost five bucks. You sure there's work cutting down trees?"

"Yep, my grandfather was a foreman for the company, and they always needed help. Don't worry. It's in the bag."

"Okay, let's go. A nickel a game," Eddy said.

"I don't have any money."

"I take IOUs."

They played for an hour, with Elmore ending up twenty-five cents in the hole. The bus finally rolled into the Grand Rapids depot. The brakes squealed, and the bus stopped. Eddy and Elmore ran down the aisle, Eddy grabbed a newspaper from the front seat, and they jumped off the bus.

The town was quiet and the buildings spread out. The air was still with a scent of freshly cut grass, a smell familiar to Eddy when standing on the grass in Wrigley Field. The sun beat down on the cement platform of the depot as beads of sweat began to roll down Eddy's cheeks. Elmore led Eddy down a one-lane gravel road that was shaded mostly by mature white ashes, pines, and red cedars. Eddy thought it'd be blocks, but they walked for miles, passing one-story wooden shacks that were spread out in large lots. A rusted car on wooden blocks sat in the front lawn of one home. Another house next door tilted to one side, its porch partially collapsed. Eddy wondered what Elmore's neighbors were like. Did they have guns? Did they hunt for food? There were no beat cops walking around here.

Elmore stopped and pointed to another wooden shack with peeling white paint and furniture in the front lawn. Weeds sprouted around the perimeter of the home. "This is it. Home, sweet home."

"So, this is where you grew up," Eddy said as he looked around. It was a new world and he was on his own, out in the country. There was no one to boss him around. He could do whatever he wanted. "What did you do out here?"

"All kindsa stuff."

"What stuff?"

"You know, hiking, playing army, fishing in the creek." Elmore walked toward the house up a dirt path lined with weeds and grass. Eddy followed. Elmore opened the creaky screen door and yelled, "Grandma, it's me. I'm home," as if he'd been gone for the afternoon.

They stepped inside. A rusted metal table and chairs sat in a kitchen that smelled like stale cigarettes, rotting meat, and sweaty armpits. Patches of the linoleum floor were gouged, dirt filling the cracks. Dishes were piled up in a sink lined with grime. Portions of the worn flowery wallpaper peeled, and dark stains decorated the wall as if someone had spit tobacco on it. An old woman wearing a yellowish frayed gown slowly shimmied barefoot into the kitchen. She smiled, showing several missing front teeth.

"Well, hello, honey bunch. It's good to see you," she said in a gravelly voice. She hugged Elmore, squeezed hard, and rocked back and forth. She opened her eyes and flashed a toothless smile at Eddy. "Who's this handsome young man?"

"Eddy. He's my best friend."

Eddy feigned a smile and said, "Hi, how are you." Eddy realized he didn't know Elmore's last name.

"Such a nice lookin' boy," Elmore's grandmother said. "You make yourself at home. Are you boys hungry?"

"We're famished, Grandma," Elmore said.

"Well, then sit down and make yourselves at home," said Elmore's grandmother.

She made bologna sandwiches and placed two glasses and a water pitcher on the table. The bread was stale, and there was only one slice of bologna in Eddy's sandwich. There were lipstick smudges around the lip of his glass. Eddy ate half of his sandwich but didn't drink from the glass. After lunch, Elmore showed Eddy the rest of the house. Piles of clothes were scattered around his grandma's bedroom. An ashtray served as a soap holder in the bathroom. A black rim of algae lined the toilet bowl, and grime circled the tub and sink.

If his mother had seen this house, she would have a heart attack, Eddy thought, holding back a smile.

"Elmore, I only have one bed, sweetie. You two can sleep on it, and I'll take the couch."

"No, Grandma. We're gonna sleep in the tent."

Elmore seemed happy despite his family's poverty. His grandmother appeared in good spirits as well. Eddy remembered what his Nonna would say about the poor: "Blessed are the meek for they shall inherit the earth." Eddy and his friends at school would joke about that Bible verse—the meek were too poor to inherit anything. Would Elmore inherit this shack and the land it sat on? Would he want it? It didn't seem like much, but it was Elmore's childhood home. The only home he'd ever known, dirty, smelly and small.

Eddy snuck a glance in the living room and saw that it was just as messy as the kitchen. He had never slept in a tent, but it sounded better than the couch.

"Okay, do what you want, sweetie. Just don't drink from the faucet."

"Why, Grandma?"

"The city put a new chemical in it, something called fluoride. You can get water from the well."

"Okay, Grandma," Elmore said as he bolted through the screen door. Eddy followed.

Elmore walked around the rear of his grandmother's shack through foot-high weeds and entered a dilapidated wood shed that was leaning ominously to the side. Inside was a rusted push lawnmower, a metal gas can, a rake, and an old tire sitting on a wood box. Elmore rolled the tire off the box and opened it. He pulled out a neatly folded, dusty cloth tent.

"It's just dirty on the outside. The inside is clean," he said as he hoisted the tent over his shoulder. "Follow me."

Elmore led Eddy down a path that wound through a row of mature pines, oaks, and maples and opened into a clearing. He walked to the middle of the meadow and tossed the tent to the ground that made a clanging noise.

"What's in there?" Eddy asked, hoping it was money.

"The stakes and poles," Elmore said, as if that was the dumbest question he had ever heard.

Elmore told Eddy to hold up the middle of the tent as he slid the poles through the slats. He tied four ropes at the top of the tent and secured the ends on each side with the stakes.

"Let's hike around," Elmore said brightly. He was in his element, Eddy realized. It was as if their roles had shifted, Elmore was now the top dog.

Elmore picked up a pine tree branch, swiped off the leaves, and led Eddy into the woods, slashing through brush and Indian grass. They tramped about a half mile and reached the banks of a shallow creek, hidden under a scrubby mix of pines, oaks, maples, and white ashes.

The creek's lazy current bubbled and gurgled around a bend, flowing into some lake or river. Eddy picked up a pebble and skipped it along the surface of the water. Two bounces, not bad. He searched the moss-covered ground for a thinner rock. He found a shale and flung it sideways. Three skips. Not bad. He kept at it until he got five skips. Thin pebbles produced better results.

Elmore shook off his shoes and socks and waded into the creek, striking the stick at insects or anything that moved. Tired of skimming rocks, Eddy sat on a rock at the edge of the creek and pulled out his Zippo lighter and a cigarette. Sparks flickered but no flame. The lighter was out of fluid. He stuck the lighter back in his pocket and grabbed a book of matches he'd snagged from the tavern. Ernie's Bleachers was advertised on the front of the matchbook. He struck the match and lit his cigarette. The match fizzled and flared in the woods: no one was around to hear it except Elmore, who was now holding the stick like a gun and shooting an imaginary enemy.

Eddy's eyes scanned the openings of the tree branches. He wondered which way was west. "What time is it, Elmore?"

The big little general aimed his stick in the direction of a bright orange house finch, perched on an upper branch of a white ash. "I dunno. It's gonna get dark soon. Pow pow." The bird fluttered in the breeze and flew away.

Eddy flicked his half- smoked cigarette in the creek. It spun as it floated downstream. "It's getting dark. Let's go back."

Elmore splashed his way to the bank and slapped on his socks and shoes. "Follow me, soldier." He hiked up the path hunched over, holding his stick like a rifle.

"What are you doing, Elmore? That's a stick not a gun."

Elmore crept forward. "There's a Nazi prison camp around here. One of them escaped. An SS captain."

"And you're gonna shoot him with your stick?"

Elmore halted, his right hand raised and his eyes scouring the shadowy forest on his left. "I heard something."

"Stop clownin' around." Eddy passed Elmore and jogged through the murky woods. He came to a clearing and stopped, his mouth agape in amazement.

Thousands of lights sparkled in the meadow. The glow of countless fireflies floating in the fading sun flashed like yellow traffic lights on a lonesome country road in a shadowless world.

Eddy gently swiped one in midair and cupped it into his hands. The firefly illuminated on and off and tickled his fingers as it tried to escape the makeshift cage.

"Let's go, Eddy," Elmore shouted. He was halfway across the meadow.

Eddy opened his hands. The firefly flickered, raised its wings, and lifted off into the air.

"I'll race ya to the tent," Eddy yelled and broke into a full sprint. Elmore dropped his stick, wheeled around, and ran. They dashed through the field of Indian grass, cowbane, spiderworts, butterfly weeds, and creeping foxtail. Whirring dragonflies and bumblebees buzzed off in the ruckus.

The race was a tie. Elmore bent down, grabbed his knees, and gasped for air. Eddy gazed into the darkening sky, his lips parted in wonder. Sun streaks swept across the edge of the western horizon, an orange blaze smothered beneath a slumbering purple haze. How many times did he curse the sunset that ended ball games due to darkness? Here he was, standing free in front of his new home, a tent, its sides rippling in the wind, silhouetted in the dew-soaked dusk. True, there were no ball games to play, but there was nobody to boss him around. A summer smile beamed across his face. He welcomed the night.

Eddy and Elmore crawled into their new home. Two bedsheets, two flashlights, and a stained pillow without a pillowcase were neatly placed in the middle of the tent. Elmore's grandma must have placed them there. Eddy handed the pillow to Elmore. They both unfurled the bedsheets and laid down.

Eddy fished out the newspaper from his knapsack and then tucked the knapsack under his head for a pillow. He turned on his flashlight and read.

"Son of a bitch! We dropped a bomb that blew up a whole city!" Eddy yelled. The front-page picture showed concrete rubble that had once been Hiroshima.

Elmore turned on his flashlight and shined it on the newspaper. He read the headline out loud. "Holy mackerel! Sixty percent of the city was wiped out with one bomb. The blast rocks ten miles away, Four square miles destroyed!"

"Listen to this," Eddy said. "'Hiroshima was wiped out with such awful tho…ro…ness as if some giant bulldozer had swept across the buildings and houses. Hiroshima is a city of three hundred and forty-three thousand.' I wonder if they all died?"

"I don't know, but I'm glad the Japs didn't have a bomb like that," Elmore said.

They read the entire front section of the paper, each taking turns announcing the news. They even read the obituaries.

Elmore turned off his flashlight and lay down. Eddy turned to the sports section. The newspaper rustled in the still night. Eddy stopped reading and listened to the crickets chirping outside. There must have been a million of them, they were so loud. As a child, he once poked through bushes in his neighbor's front yard searching for crickets. He could hear them but could never find them.

"Hey, Eddy, if you could be any animal, what would you be?" Elmore asked from the dark corner of the tent.

"I dunno. What kinda question is that?" Eddy replied, thinking maybe a cricket, they're so hard to find.

"I'd want to be a lion, the king of the jungle," Elmore said, his arms outstretched for effect. "No one would bother me."

"People might," Eddy said. "I think I'd want to be a bird. I'd be free. I could fly anywhere I want and see everything below."

"Yeah, that's a good animal to be."

"You know, I could go for a Coke right now," Eddy said. "Does your grandma have any?"

"No. All she drinks is well water. Tomorrow you could buy some Coke at the grocery store. It opens in the morning."

"Good. I'm running low on cigarettes. Ya know, I love pouring Coke on ice and drinking it when it sizzles."

"Me too."

"What's your last name?" Eddy said.

"It's Morton. Elmore Morton."

"What is that, Irish?"

"No, Scottish and Jewish. My grandfather was Jewish. He died."

"Jewish? I would never have guessed that."

"Why, because I don't have a big nose?"

"No, it's us Italians that have big noses. Look at my nose," Eddy said as shined the flashlight on it. "Just go to sleep. I want to read my paper."

Eddy opened the newspaper and read the box scores. Cavarretta and Don Johnson each had four hits, and Bill Nicholson hit a homer with three hits. Ray Prim pitched a five hitter as the Cubs beat the Boston Braves 5–2 in the first game of a doubleheader.

A shadow darted across the top of the tent. Eddy jerked up. An insect, about a half a foot, scurried along the ridge of the tent, its antennas twitching in the twilight.

"Elmore, Elmore, wake up!"

"What's wrong?"

"Look," Eddy said, pointing to the top of the tent. The bug crawled back and forth across the tent as if it were looking for a way to get inside. "What the hell is that?"

"I don't know. I've never seen a bug that big out here."

Eddy poked at it, and the bug disappeared. "I think it flew away."

They waited, their eyes glued to the tent's crest. Seconds turned into long minutes. Crickets chirped, and leaves rustled in the forest wind. The bug was gone.

Elmore and Eddy laid back down. Eddy pointed the flashlight at the newspaper and read. The Cubs won the second game of the doubleheader in twelve innings. "Yes! Cubs are in first place," Eddy mumbled.

Something moved out of the corner of his eyes. "It's back, Elmore. Look at that. Does it bite?"

"Turn off the flashlight. It's attracted to the light."

Eddy turned it off. They strained their eyes searching for the bug on the tent's peak under faint moonlight. It had vanished again.

They waited in the dark. Nothing. Eddy turned on the flashlight to read. Busher had won the Kentucky Derby. The insect returned, creeping back and forth on the tent.

"Oh, for Pete's sake, it came back," Eddy grumbled.

Elmore took off his glasses and nudged his nose against the tent roof to get a closer look. "It's as big as my hand. Look at those antennas. It looks like a giant roach, and it keeps going round in circles."

"Why is it doing that?" Eddy asked. "Wait." He looked at the flashlight lens. There it was. A gnat crawling around the edges of the lens. Eddy burst into laughter.

"We were afraid of a tiny bug on the flashlight," Eddy cried out, barely able to get the words out.

They laughed so hard and for so long that Elmore's grandma came out.

"Is everything okay in there?" she asked.

"It's all right, Grandma. Eddy told a funny joke."

"Eddy, darling, tell me that joke in the morning. Good night, young men."

The laughter wore them out, and they fell asleep with the flashlight still on, and bugs crawling around the lens made giants by the light.

BOTTOM OF THE SEVENTH

Eddy crawled out of the tent, stood up, and stretched his arms, reaching for the misty morning sky. He looked around for Elmore, but all he saw were trees and brush. The scent of cedar and pine flooded the cool air. Eddy walked to Elmore's grandmother's house and peered through the screen door. A foul musty smell emerged from inside. Elmore and his grandmother sat at the kitchen table.

"You're up. Come in and have breakfast," said Elmore's grandmother.

Eddy opened the screen door, the hinges screeching, and slowly walked inside. He took a seat across from Elmore, who was chewing on Wheaties cereal. It sounded like footsteps on gravel.

"I woke up in the middle of the night, and you were gone. Where'd you go?" Eddy asked.

"Ground was too hard. I slept in my grandmother's bed. We can sleep there tonight if you want," Elmore said.

Eddy felt a slight pain in his lower back, but the thought of sleeping in the old lady's bed disgusted him. "I don't know. We'll see. I had a crazy dream last night. I hit a duck fart in right field, and then I was running to first base in slow motion, like I had lead feet."

"What's a duck fart?" Elmore asked.

"A blooper. A ball hit just over the heads of infielders. Anyway, the right fielder overthrows to first, and the next thing I know, I'm standing on second base. The next batter hits another duck fart in center field, and I take a few steps off second base, waiting to see if the center fielder catches the ball. Turns out the center fielder is a girl, and she slides and catches the ball. When I turn to go back to second, it's about twenty yards away, and I'm running in slow motion again. I keep running as fast as I can, but it's like running in quicksand. Just as I was about to slide, the ball rolled to the second baseman, and I woke up."

"How do you like your eggs, Eddy? Scrambled? Over easy?"

"Over here," Eddy joked.

"Your friend's a funny a guy, Elmore. He reminds me a little of your grandfather, rest his soul. So, Eddy, how do you like your eggs?"

Eddy wanted to ask for a frittata, but he figured she could never make one like his mother. "Scrambled, nice and easy."

"Grandma, do you remember what Grandpa used to say about people and how they liked their eggs?"

Elmore's grandmother smiled and looked out the window as if she were having a pleasant thought. "Let's see. If you like scrambled eggs, then you're disorganized and impulsive. Over easy, you're easygoing, and over hard, you're grumpy and moody. Hard-boiled, you're just plain mean. If you like your eggs sunny-side up, then you're happy-go-lucky, and if you like them poached, you're a bookworm."

Elmore laughed. "I like 'em raw, Grandma."

"Well, then you've got a lot of growing up to do, young man," Elmore's grandmother said tenderly as she placed a plate of runny scrambled eggs next to Eddy.

"I should have asked for poached eggs," Eddy joked again.

Eddy picked up a pitcher on the table and poured water into his smudgy glass. He took a sip. It tasted like rotten eggs. He held his fork and studied it. A crusty egg remnant was stuck in one of the tines. Eddy removed it and stabbed at his scrambled eggs. He was starving but sickened by the dirty house, unclean silverware and glasses, and who knew what was in the eggs. He took a few bites and forced himself to finish the plate.

Elmore wolfed down his plate of runny, over easy eggs, some of the yolk dripping from the corner of his tiny mouth.

Eddy finished what he could and slowly pushed his plate to the middle of the table, eyeing Elmore's grandmother, who was brewing another pot of coffee.

"Let's get out of here and explore the town," Eddy said.

The boys jumped out of their seats and rushed through the front door. They hiked along a dirt path for about a mile until they reached a grocery store. Eddy bought a Coke and cupcakes. He also paid for Elmore's snacks. He drank his Coke in one gulp. The boys strolled around the town center. They walked past a shoe store, a gas station, and a furniture store until they reached a small dilapidated bar set back about one hundred feet from the dusty road they were walking on. Eddy peered through a dirty window and saw two men playing pool. His eyes lit up. He plucked his money out of his pocket and counted. He had one dollar and thirty cents left. "I can turn this into a sawbuck, and we need it. Bad."

The rickety screen door slammed as Eddy sauntered in with Elmore behind him. Cigarette and cigar smoke floated like a hazy fog in the small dark and decrepit bar. Eddy yanked a pack of cigarettes out of his pocket, tapped it, and out popped a cigarette he had flipped. It was his lucky cigarette. He picked up on the idea from two GIs he had overheard in his family's tavern talking about flipping a cigarette for luck. The GI explained that if he survived in combat long enough to smoke his last cigarette—the one he flipped in the pack—he was lucky. Eddy had a half pack left, so he placed the lucky cigarette he had flipped back in the pack and pulled out another and lit it.

Two men stopped playing pool and glared at the boys. There was only one pool table in the place, and they were on it. Eddy reached into his pocket and pulled out a quarter. He shuffled toward the men, the floors creaking loudly, and dropped a quarter on the edge of the pool table. One of the men responded with a crooked half smile. He was overweight and bald, with a grubby stubbled face. He wore blue jean overalls without a shirt, showing excess fat from his chest and bushy thick tufts of gray hair. He quickly defeated his younger opponent and waited for Eddy to rack.

"Let's bet fifty cents," Eddy said.

The man shot Eddy the fish eye. "You ain't no pool hustler, son. Now are ya?"

Eddy held out his arms and said, "Look at us. We're just kids. We just wanna have a little fun. That's all."

"All right then, let's have fun and raise it to a dollar."

Eddy glanced around. A slowly moving ceiling fan squeaked above and looked as if it was going to fall on them at any moment. A bartender and the man who lost the pool game sat a bar in the corner of the room. These hicks can't be that good, Eddy thought. He had hustled good players at the Screwball Club.

"I don't know," Eddy said, with a tight smile and wide-open eyes. "I'm not that good a player."

The man shrugged and said, "A dollar or nuthin'."

Eddy plopped four quarters on the table and racked the balls. The old man cued his stick and said, "No same last and no slop." He bent over the table and broke. The room cracked with the clack of the balls crashing into each other. Three stripes went in, and the man shot in two more before missing. It had been a while since Eddy played pool, but once you know how to play, it comes easy. Eddy had watched Bobby hustle good players in the city, so why couldn't he hustle some country bumpkin?

Eddy lined up his first shot with the reflection of the light on the ball, a trick his father had taught him. Eddy shot, driving the solid ball into a side pocket like a bullet. He circled around the table and effortlessly made his shots. Only the eight ball was left, hugging the rail between two corner pockets. The cue ball ended up trapped in the jaws of one of those corner pockets.

"Gotta call it. What pocket?" the man asked.

Eddy studied the table. He'd beat this guy but good, make him come back for more. "A quarter says I make the shot in this corner pocket," he said, tapping it with his stick.

"You got it, kid."

Eddy bent down and shot the cue ball on the corner point of the pocket, sending it in the opposite direction. It hit the eight ball on the way, delivering it neatly into the corner pocket just like Eddy said he would. It was the pocket-point kick shot his brother had taught him.

"Well, I'll be damned," the man shouted as he handed Eddy five quarters. "Nice run, son. Hey, Mitchell, watch out for this one. He's a hustler all right."

Mitchell turned around and shouted back, "I'm feelin' lucky. Let me have a go at 'em."

He chugged his beer and drifted toward the pool stick rack. He was skinny, with greasy dark hair and a cigarette behind his ear. He wore a short-sleeved white shirt with a pack of cigarettes rolled up into his right sleeve. The muscles on his arms were long and tight like steel cable. He was drinking beer, but he looked younger than twenty-one.

Mitchell grabbed a stick and held it horizontally as if he were aiming a gun. He put it back, took another one off the rack, studied it, and placed it back on the rack. He repeated the routine several times until he found the right stick. "This'll do," he said as he chalked it furiously. "How much you got in your pocket, boy?"

"A half a fin."

"That all you got?" Mitchell laughed said in a disappointed tone. "Then let's bet that."

This kid wasn't much older than him, and his arrogance pissed Eddy off. "You got it," Eddy said quickly.

Mitchell racked. Eddy drew his stick in a back-and-forth motion three times like a pendulum, lining up his shot. He reared back with his shoulder and broke, the balls smashing into each other and spreading across the table like mercury from a broken thermometer. Eddy chose solids again and danced around the table in a rhythm that possessed every good shooter he'd ever seen play the game when they played it well.

The last solid, the red seven ball, was frozen behind two stripes near a side pocket. Eddy didn't have a shot, so he played it safe. He shot the cue against a stripe, sending the gleaming white ball bouncing off the rail where it snookered against the eight ball.

"Oh, you play like that. Around here that's called dirty ball. It don't matter," Mitchell said with a mischievous grin.

As Mitchell leaned onto the table and under the light, Eddy could clearly see his grizzled features. A sunken scar sliced across the side of the man's left eye and a tattoo of a tiger roared down his bulging right forearm. Suddenly, he was a lot older than Eddy had first estimated. And he seemed a lot smarter too. Eddy had a bad feeling in his gut. The man's knuckles had whorls like gnarled spots on a wood bat, and were caked with dirt. *Or was it dried blood?* Eddy wondered.

Mitchell cricked his neck, raised his pool stick high, and shot the cue ball in the air, over the eight ball where it bounced off the railing and turned sideways, striking a stripe, sending it straight into a side pocket. He then cracked his blackened knuckles by making a fist.

"Whoa," Elmore said slowly. Eddy scratched his head as his eyes glimpsed the front door. He could make a break for it, but he didn't want to leave Elmore behind. Maybe Mitchell would slip up. Eddy needed just one more turn at the table.

Mitchell struck the cue ball hard and downward, curving it around a solid, knocking the striped nine ball into the corner pocket. The cue ball bounced off the nine ball and rolled back to the middle of the table, lining up perfectly with the last solid, the fifteen ball. He hit the cue ball with a backspin shot, sending the nine ball squarely into the side pocket. The cue ball bounced backward, ending up where Mitchell had struck it. The eight ball sat pretty in front of a side pocket. It was an easy shot, but Mitchell called the far corner pocket instead.

"Let's make it interesting," he said. "Ya wanna raise the stakes?"

Eddy shook his head and turned away. He couldn't look.

The cue ball slammed against the rail and raced across the table, striking the eight ball and sending it into the corner pocket Mitchell had called.

"Pay up, boy. *You* just got hustled," Mitchell said.

Eddy reached into his pocket like he was reaching into his own stomach and planted ten quarters on the table with a look of agony pinched in his brow. He had one nickel left.

The screen door slammed behind them as Eddy and Elmore stepped outside into the hot August sun. Eddy dug into his pocket and pulled out his half pack of Lucky Strikes, grabbed his lucky cigarette with his lips, flipped it over, and lit it. How did he get suckered? Some small-town hick hustled him, and now he was broke, living in a tent in the backyard of some old, smelly woman who didn't know how to cook eggs. He could see his brother laughing and saying, "You moron, now you went and did it."

Eddy glanced at Elmore and realized he didn't have a care in the world and had no idea things were looking so bad. Eddy took another drag and surveyed the town, tears welling in his eyes. He needed money, and right now.

"I think it's time we go get ourselves a job," Eddy said. "Where's that tree place?"

Elmore led Eddy down several streets and took a gravel road. They walked past factories, warehouses and silos. They crossed a railroad track and headed toward a dilapidated two-story building with a crooked sign hanging from the porch that read Gabe's Tree Service. Several boards wobbled as the boys stepped on the porch stairs and made their way to the front door. Elmore opened it and walked in. Eddy followed.

A platinum blonde, the kind that ran with Edward G. Robinson in gangster films, sat at a desk kitty-corner from the door. "How may I help you?" she said in a friendly tone.

"Hello, Cindy, remember me?"

Cindy studied Elmore. Seconds later, her face lit up. "Why, Elmore, how are you? You have grown up. I thought you and your mom moved to Chicago?"

"We did. I came back to visit my grandma."

"How is she? We haven't seen her around lately."

"She's fine, thank you. This is my best friend, Eddy. We need a job."

"Oh, well, let me get Gabe for ya. He's in the back. Make yourselves comfortable." Cindy swiveled her hips down a hallway and out the back door. Eddy's eyes followed.

"Don't worry, Eddy. We're in like Flynn. My grandpa was a foreman here."

Eddy nodded and examined the office, a small room with a desk and two chairs. There was an earthy smell like trees. Piles of papers were strewn about Cindy's desk. The hardwood floor was worn from constant foot traffic and dusted with pulp. Small tree samples cluttered the corners of the room. A dusty picture of a redwood tree hung on the wood-paneled wall with two men with a giant two-handled saw on each side about to cut it down.

A short stocky man, balding, with a thin ring of blond hair, briskly entered the room. He seemed as if he were in a hurry.

"Elmore. It's good to see ya. How's your mom?"

"Hi, Mr. Moore. She's fine."

Gabe sighed and studied Eddy. He turned to Elmore. "So, you two want to work for us, huh? How's your asthma, Elmore? You know it's rough work, cutting down trees."

"I can hold the ropes and carry equipment like I did for my grandpa."

"Follow me," Gabe said. He led the boys out the back door. Once outside, Gabe pointed to a tree that was about eighty feet high. "We need men that can climb to the top of trees like this one, tie a rope around branches, and cut them with a saw. You think you can do that?"

Elmore shook his head. Eddy cupped his hands over his eyes as he surveyed the tree's height. There was no way he could climb that high. He'd freeze halfway up.

"Is there any other kind of work you can give us?" Eddy asked.

"Nope," Gabe said, his arms crossed. "Sorry, boys, you're too young. Come back in a few years, and we might have something for ya. Say hello to your mom, Elmore." Gabe hustled to his green Ford pickup truck and drove away.

The two of them wandered listlessly back home, their hands in empty pockets. Elmore's grandmother made them bologna sandwiches for dinner. Eddy's mother always told him he'd eat what was put in front of him if he was hungry enough. He finally knew what she meant. As he slowly chewed the sandwich, he thought about his mother's cooking. What he would do for a plate of her homemade spaghetti. The thought made him hungrier.

After dinner, they helped clean up and then hiked around the woods, looking for frogs until darkness. They both settled into the tent. Elmore was holding a flashlight and reading a book about the Civil War his grandmother had given him. Eddy lay on his back, reading the same newspaper he had taken from the bus. He shined his flashlight on the sports section. The Cubs were in first place, five and a half games ahead of Brooklyn. They had a seven-game winning streak. If only he was back home, he'd be there to watch the Cubs win. The crack of the bats, the roar of the crowd, he could hear it all from his bedroom. He closed his eyes and wondered what his family was doing. What was the take on the bar? What were the receipts and how much cash could they not declare? His dad was always worried about that. Did Bobby and Florence miss him? Were Sailor and the rest looking for him? How was his softball team doing? Who took his place as the pitcher? Thoughts of home hummed in his head for hours as the crickets chirped endlessly in the night.

Eventually, Eddy fell asleep. He dreamed he was running from a tornado at night. It was chasing him as it blew away cars and a newsstand. Street lights gave form to the giant swirling cloud that touched the stars, and it was gaining on him. He ducked inside a gas station made of glass. As the tornado surged closer, the glass walls shook, and the roof bent upward. Eddy scurried back and forth, frantically searching for something to hide under, but there was nothing—the gas station was empty. He felt like the bug on the flashlight crawling around in circles. Suddenly, in an earsplitting roar like the El trains that thundered past his bedroom window, the tornado shattered the glass, and the roof collapsed. Eddy screamed as he was sucked into the swirling mass. He awoke, crying out in the darkness. He sat up and fumbled around for his flashlight. He turned it on. Elmore was gone. He laid back down and watched the morning light slowly flood the tent.

— — —

Ernie quietly rose out of bed and dressed. He stretched the suspenders over his shoulders and clasped them to his trousers. It was early morning. He didn't want to wake Margaret, so he tiptoed out of the bedroom and the front door. He ate breakfast at a neighborhood diner and then walked the streets, searching for his son, his figlio, Eddy. It had been four days, and no one had turned up a clue.

For hours, he stopped at gas stations, stores, pool halls, diners, and friends' apartments, asking about Eddy. And while he did, he never missed a chance to campaign, getting more signatures for his ballot petition.

At noon, Ernie ate lunch at a restaurant on Clark and continued pounding the pavement. On a hunch, he made his way to Waveland Park, hoping to find Eddy's softball team. There they were, the Junior Savinas, in the field warming up for a game. Ernie recognized a few of the players and walked to the pitcher's mound. The players stopped throwing and came over, huddling around the mound.

Ernie studied their faces. "Has anyone seen Eddy?"

One of the players, the tallest of the bunch, said, "No, Mr. Pareti. We're hoping you might know where he is. We sure could use him today."

Other players either shook their heads or shrugged, except a pimply-faced boy who stood off to the side. "What about you, Warren. You know where Eddy is?" Warren attended the same school as Eddy, and they hung out sometimes at the LeMoyne lot.

Warren scratched his head and said no in a hushed tone.

"What? Speak up."

Warren hesitated for a moment as if he had something else to say, but then shook his head.

"I don't believe you. Now come out with it," Ernie demanded. "Where's Eddy?"

Warren just stood there.

"He could be in trouble, Warren," Ernie coaxed. His tone softened. Anyone could tell Warren wanted to tell him, but that he was sworn to secrecy. "Tell ya what: you tell me where Eddy is, and you can eat free at my tavern for the rest of the month."

"I don't know where he is, but if I tell you who he's with, do I still get to eat for free?" Warren asked.

Ernie nodded.

"He told me he was going to Michigan with some skinny kid with glasses. His name started with an *E*—Elijah, Elliot...Elmore! That's it."

"Son of pup!" Ernie cried.

As Ernie hustled off the field, he heard another player yell at Warren. "Why did ya go and squawk?" Ernie turned around and saw two players wrestling. He didn't have time to break it up. He hurried home.

— — —

It was late morning or maybe early afternoon when Elmore's grandmother asked Eddy to buy milk from the store. He wasn't sure what time it was. There was no clock in the house. He knew he had been away from home for almost a week, but the days had become blurred. He was constantly hungry and out of cigarettes. He stole cigarette squares, two at a time, from Elmore's grandmother's purse. The old lady wised up and hid her cigarettes somewhere in her messy house. Eddy was forced to go into town and snipe cigarette butts from restaurant and bar ashtrays or from sidewalks. His diet consisted of runny eggs, bologna sandwiches, and bananas. Things got so bad that Eddy stole grapes and apricots from Elmore's neighbor. He found the food in a paper bag sitting on a fence railing of a run-down barn. They were meant for the neighbor's pigs. He'd climbed a fence and trudged through the pigpen to get the bag.

He had one nickel to his name. He could use it to call his parents. But then he would have to go to military school.

Eddy meandered alone to the store, his eyes canvassing the ground for cigarette butts. Along the way he picked up rocks and threw them as far as he could. He wondered if he could throw a rock further than Babe Didrikson could throw a baseball. Eddy was about to fling another rock when he spotted a man walking at a fast pace toward him.

The man wore glasses and a brown fedora. Suspenders held up his slacks, and his black dress shoes crunched against the gravel as he hurried down the road. The man's gait was vaguely familiar, but it was his smile that gave him away.

"Where do you think you're going?" the man said from a short distance. He stopped in front of Eddy and placed his hand on his shoulder and squeezed.

Eddy averted his gaze from his dad and lowered his head, searching the gravel road for an answer. His father's lip curled upward in a friendly smile, but his large brown eyes smoldered through Eddy's soul. Ernie stiffened and rubbed the back of his neck as his eyes flitted over Eddy's head, surveying the woods like a manager sizing up an opponent's defense in the outfield. After a long pause, Ernie pulled Eddy in closer and said, "It's time to go home, son. Whaddya say?"

Eddy smiled and breathed a deep sigh as if the weight of the world was off his shoulders. It was no use to run away—he couldn't make it on his own. He rubbed his eyes, holding back tears.

"Do you know how much of a headache you gave us? We went all over hell and back looking for you. Your mother almost had a heart attack."

"I'm sorry, Dad." The words came out slowly.

"Don't tell us you're sorry, Eddy. Show it. You can't always do what you want. You're smart. You should know that. It's a cold, cruel world out there. It can suck you in and spit you right out if you're not ready for it."

Eddy nodded. After another long pause, he said, "I was on my way to the store to call home. How did you find me?"

Ernie smiled. "A little birdie told me. Let's go and say goodbye to Elmore and his grandmother and catch the next bus." Ernie squeezed Eddy's shoulder a little harder as they walked to Elmore's grandmother's house.

Eddy peeked a look so his father couldn't see him watching, and saw his father's glimmering eyes. But he didn't want his dad to know that he saw. He didn't want his dad to lose his pride, and he didn't want to lose any more of his own. He wanted his dad to see that he was a man now. All right, he'd proven it, in a way, by being on his own. He felt ashamed that he'd lost all his money. That he couldn't find work and support himself. That he'd been hustled and that he had to admit to his dad he was just about to call him, as if he were eight years old. He'd wanted to show them. He hadn't realized it up till now, but he'd wanted to show all of them: his dad, his mom, Bobby, Florence, Nonno, his friends, that he didn't need them. That he could do it. That he didn't need any Roosevelt Military Academy.

But now he'd lost. It was the same feeling he had when he'd blown a pitch or lost a game. It was feeling like a little boy. It was feeling ashamed and frustrated at the same time. His dad was right. He wasn't ready for the cold, cruel world. It was funny, but here he was, from the city, and it took the country to swallow him up and teach him that. When all the older boys like Lockerbie were getting drafted or volunteering and shipping off to war, he always envied them and wished he could fight alongside them. But now he knew he wasn't ready for that. Maybe that's what his dad meant by what he'd said. And maybe his dad was right about a lot of things. Maybe he needed to go to military school so they could make a man, a real man, out of him.

Ernie cringed when he walked into the house but managed to keep a smile as he thanked Elmore's grandmother. He threw a twenty-dollar bill on the table when she wasn't looking. Eddy shook Elmore's hand and said, "See ya back in the city, kid."

Eddy slithered into the window seat of the Greyhound bus. He expected his dad to yell at any moment. Instead, Ernie pulled out a pack of Lucky Strikes and handed them to Eddy.

"Go ahead. Take it. Have a smoke. It's okay."

Eddy lit up a cigarette and turned to his dad to see if he was joking. Ernie smiled and put his arm around Eddy.

Eddy gazed out the window. He thought maybe military school was like the shadow of that tiny bug on the flashlight, nothing to worry about. Didn't President Roosevelt say, "There's nothing to fear but fear itself?"

It was a strange feeling to sit next to his dad and not talk. Eddy took a drag from his cigarette and blew the smoke low, against the window. He couldn't tell if his dad was happy or mad. Maybe it was both. He blew a smoke ring that floated over the empty seat in front of him.

"Where did you learn to do that?" Ernie asked.

"A Negro ball player taught me."

Ernie smiled. Eddy figured his dad didn't hear him. The grinding hum of the bus made it hard for him to hear. Eddy didn't feel like repeating himself. He just smiled back, wondering how his dad was able to handle customers in a noisy tavern. After a while, Eddy finished his cigarette and dozed off.

It was late afternoon when Ernie and Eddy walked into Ernie's Bleachers. Frank Sinatra crooned out "Somebody Loves Me" on the juke. The tavern smelled like a mix of beer, hot dogs, and beef sandwiches, a scent Eddy had grown to love. Ernie shouted, "Look who I found."

Kitty and Walter turned around from the bar to see. "Welcome home, Eddy. Where the hell did you go?" Walter said.

Before Eddy could answer, Kitty kissed him, leaving a lipstick smudge on his cheek. *Great*, Eddy thought, *now the scent of her perfume would stick on him.*

A teary-eyed Margaret hurried around the bar and hugged Eddy. It was a long hug, and she squeezed hard. Finally, she released him and cried, "Do you know what kind of hell you put us through? What were you thinking?"

Eddy stood in front of her like a statute and shrugged as he surveyed the worn wooden floors he had swept and mopped a million times.

The bartender, Dean Steiner, entered the tavern. He was an hour late for the afternoon shift. He rushed past Eddy as he hustled to his post behind the bar.

"You're late, Dean. What happened?" Ernie said.

"I guess you didn't hear. I've got really bad news."

"Bad news? What can be so bad. Eddy's back," Ernie said.

Dean forced a smile and looked away.

"Well. What is it? Out with it," Margaret said.

Walter and Kitty froze as they waited on his words.

"I don't know how to say this. Sailor's gone."

"What do you mean gone? Where did he go?" Margaret asked.

"He's dead. He shot himself in the head today."

Ernie cupped his ear and moved in closer to Dean, almost touching his face.

"What did you say?"

"I'm sorry, Ernie," Dean spoke louder. "He shot himself. His son was killed on the *Indianapolis*. Ya know that cruiser in the Philippines the Japs sunk. Hundreds of men died. Some, the sharks got 'em. Sailor, the poor guy, just couldn't take it. Johnny was his only child and my friend."

"Are you sure? How do you know?" Margaret asked. Her tone, though, suggested she knew the answer.

"His wife said he left a note. All it said was, 'Forgive me.' They never found his son's body. I read the *Indianapolis* delivered atomic material that was used to bomb those Japanese cities. It was a secret mission."

There was a long pause. Kitty sniffled. Margaret and Ernie stood like statues next to each other with frozen stares. Walter unplugged the juke, and Sinatra's crooning stopped as if he had heard the bad news too.

Then Ernie spoke. "What a tough break. He told me he couldn't wait to take his boy to a ball game. Johnny was a big Cubs fan, and Sailor bragged that he took him to watch the Cubs play in the last three World Series they were in."

Ernie's bald head slowly swayed back and forth as if he was shaking the cobwebs out of it. He pounded the bar with his fist and stormed into the bathroom. The others left the bar.

Sailor must have really loved his son to kill himself, Eddy thought. Some parents would do anything for their kids, even take their own lives. He wondered if his dad would have committed suicide if he had died or never come back home. He wasn't an only child, though. There was Bobby, the straight A student, and Florence, the sweet daughter who never did anything wrong.

"Eddy, go upstairs and get ready for dinner. We have company coming over," Margaret said, her voice somber and soft.

That night, the Pareti apartment was packed with relatives who came to welcome Eddy back. He sat at the head of the table, devouring his mother's spaghetti as aunts kissed him and uncles affectionately patted him on the back. His parents sat on each side of him.

In the middle of dinner, between his mother's smiles and thank-yous and "please pass the bread," she addressed her number two son. "What the hell were you thinking, Eddy? Did you really think you'd make it on your own? You've got a lot of growing up to do, kiddo. And don't think you're gonna get out from going to military school."

Eddy stared at his plate, twirling spaghetti pasta with his fork. He wanted to ask his parents what difference would it make if he ran away to Michigan or was shipped off to military school. Either way, he wouldn't be home. He surveyed the room and wondered if any of his relatives opposed the idea of military school, but no one seemed to object."

"Don't worry, Eddy. Military school will make you a man," said his uncle Laury, as he took a drag from his cigarette and then raised his head and blew smoke toward the dining room ceiling.

"That's right, Eddy. You get to shoot guns, real guns," added his uncle Berk. Eddy guessed they'd all heard, and he was embarrassed.

Eddy forced a smile. He wanted a cigarette, but that was out of the question.

"One thing's for sure—he won't ever be late for dinner again," Margaret said. That drew laughter.

"Now, Marge, take it easy, will ya? He's learned his lesson," Ernie said as he playfully squeezed Eddy's right shoulder. "Right, Eddy?"

Eddy nodded and took another bite of spaghetti.

"Did he? He didn't come back on his own. We had to go get him. Who knows how much longer he'd have stayed out there in the boondocks of wherever the hell he was?"

"All right, Marge, you made your point," Ernie said with a smile. "We're glad he's back in one piece." He turned to Eddy. "Your mother thought you went to the rocks and drowned in the lake."

"Oh, Ernie, don't you start with that. You know he likes to jump off the rocks. It could have happened."

"Your mother was so worried I thought she was going to jump in the lake and either swim until she found you or drowned herself," Ernie said. The room erupted in laughter.

Margaret pursed her lips and blushed but with an icy glare that Eddy had seen before, one that meant his dad was really going to get it once the last dish was washed and put away.

"You know how much time we spent looking for your ass?" Bobby interrupted. "We searched hell and back to find you."

"Next time, I'll leave ya note," Eddy joked.

"Eddy, tell us about your adventures in Michigan," Aunt Theresa asked as she tousled his hair.

Eddy chewed excitedly as he talked about the House of David baseball team and how they played baseball on donkeys.

"Oh, what kind of crackbrained idea is that?" Aunt Theresa said.

"What a bunch of jackasses," Uncle Berk quipped.

Aunt Sadie reached over the table and handed Eddy a wrapped gift. "Go ahead Eddy. Open it, sweetheart."

Eddy slowly unwrapped the gift box and pulled out a new pair of overalls. "What do ya say, Eddy?" Ernie said.

"Thanks, Aunt Sadie."

Nonno reached over and placed a five-dollar bill in front of Eddy. "Don't spend it all in one place."

Bobby threw up his hands and said in a sarcastic tone, "It's Christmas in August. If I ever need new clothes, I'll remember to run away from home."

"Where ya gonna run to, Bobby?" Uncle Berk asked.

"I dunno. Maybe I'll disappear at your place," Bobby said, sucking in air and ending his sentence with a snort.

"All you'll get from me is one big headache," Uncle Berk replied.

Ernie tapped on the table with his knuckles. "We're glad Eddy's safely back home, Bobby. That's all. He's home. We're all home. One big happy, lucky family," Ernie shouted, his voice cracked as if he were about to cry. "Together. We're all together. In our safe home."

TOP OF THE EIGHTH

Although it was a cloudy day, sunlight beamed through a barrel-vaulted skylight and lit up the white marble floor of Chicago's Union Station. A bevy of commuters busily buzzed by in every direction, rushing to and from their train platforms. The din of murmurs, shouts, small talk, and high heels banging the floor echoed in the large chamber as Eddy and his family forged a path through the crowd. Eddy carried his trunk in both arms with his chin resting on the top of it. He had been to Union Station before, but as he followed his parents, he noticed small details such as the brass lamps, limestone walls, and large Corinthian columns that to Eddy made the place look like an oversized funeral parlor.

"We want platform thirteen," Ernie shouted. He led the family to the train that was to take Eddy to Roosevelt Military Academy in Aledo, Illinois.

Ernie stopped and glanced around the station.

"Ernie, are you lost?" Margaret shrieked.

"Hold on, Marge. It's one of these," Ernie said. He shuffled down a corridor, his family in tow behind him.

Eddy adjusted his hold on the trunk and straggled back, trying to keep up. Maybe the train had already left. There was still time to talk his way out of military school.

"Oh, for Pete's sake. You don't know where you're going," Margaret said. "Why don't we ask someone at the information booth?"

"Cut it out, Marge. I'll find it."

Bobby spotted a train engineer lounging on a bench. "Excuse me, where's platform thirteen?"

The man wore blue-and-white-denim overalls with a matching shop-cap hat. He bit into an apple and swallowed. "It's on the other side of the hall. You see that concourse next to the stairs? It's in there."

"Dad, it's on the other side," Bobby yelled.

The family cut through the crowd and found the platform. The stench of diesel wafted in the stale air of the cavernous station. They stopped in front of a silver train, its steely sheen shimmered off Eddy's watery eyes and its engines hummed in steady rhythm to his trembling body. He struggled to swallow down the hot tears that bubbled inside. *Hold it in. Hold it in.* He set his trunk on the vibrating concrete floor and swiped his nose with his forearm.

"This is it," Ernie yelled above the train's drone. "Eddy, they've got a car just for Roosevelt students. I don't know which one. You'll have to ask the conductor."

Eddy gulped and nodded with a blank stare. His shoulders slouched.

"Eddy, I packed a half-dozen shirts and pants and your winter boots," Margaret said, her voice hoarse. "That should be enough for now, but if you need something else, anything, just let us know, and we'll send it."

Eddy rolled his shoulders, hung his head low, and nodded again.

"Don't look so sad. You'll get to come home on weekend furloughs," Ernie said, fidgeting his fedora with one hand while his other hand jingled the loose change in his pocket. Ernie gave Eddy a quick sideways hug and then pulled his hand out of his pocket and extended it to Eddy. They shook hands. Why was his dad's handshake limp?

"Be good, Eddy. We'll see ya before you know it," Florence said and then kissed his cheek.

Bobby handed Eddy a five-dollar bill. "There's more where that came from. Don't forget to write."

A tear rolled down Margaret's button nose. She hugged Eddy and squeezed. She let go and pinched his cheek. "You're still my baby, and we love you so much, Eddy. Don't you forget that. Right?"

"Yeah, Ma, I love you too," Eddy said as he rubbed his eyes and sniffled. He loaded his trunk in the undercarriage baggage compartment and turned to step onto the train. He slow-walked up the steps as if in a trance and disappeared inside. He never looked back.

A train conductor in a three-piece navy-blue suit with brass buttons and a pillbox hat smiled. "I betcha you're looking for this guy." He pointed to a man in a forest-green service uniform with a matching garrison cap standing behind him. Eddy nodded.

The military man motioned Eddy to follow him. They walked through two cabins and reached the last train car. The man opened the door, pointed inside, and said in a sarcastic tone, "Make yourself at home."

Eddy entered and searched for an open seat. The cabin was packed with cadets. Quiet chatter filled the room. Eddy shuffled down the aisle. He sensed a lot of eyes were on him.

You can't show weakness," he thought. He returned eye contact with anyone who stared at him. There was an even mixture of ages, some clearly older while others were about his age. The older ones were doing most of the talking and seemed confident and animated. Most of the younger cadets sat quietly in their seats. Eddy spotted an aisle seat in the back and slumped on it. A boy with a crew cut sitting next to him nodded as he smacked on gum and maintained eye contact with Eddy as if he were waiting for a hello.

"What ya looking at?" Eddy barked.

"The name's Sammy Wyatt. Cadet Wyatt. You're a Johnny-come-lately, I bet."

Eddy figured he was about his age, maybe a year older. "What are ya talkin' about?"

"This is your first time at military school. I can tell."

"Good for you. Don't bug me, and I won't bug you, and we'll get along just fine. All right?"

Wyatt laughed and smacked harder on his gum. "What's eating you?"

Eddy clasped his hands, slumped back in his chair, and closed his eyes. He hadn't slept the previous night and was exhausted. The train rolled out of the station.

Minutes passed, and Wyatt finally spoke. "There are two kinds of cadets. Either you want to come to Roosevelt, or your parents force you. You didn't want to come. Am I right, Johnny?"

Eddy leaned forward and slowly turned his head toward Wyatt. "You call me Johnny again, and I'll give ya a knuckle sandwich. Understand?"

"Jesus mageezus, a real tough guy. Take it easy already. I'm just trying to be friendly. What's your name?"

"Eddy Pareti. No more questions."

Eddy leaned back again and tried to sleep. He nodded off for a few seconds but woke each time the train jerked. He wanted to gaze out the window but that would risk eye contact with his seat mate and trigger a conversation.

Eddy's eyes focused on the aisle floor as his body swayed to the rhythm of the train. He glowered at every cadet who smiled or laughed. He wanted to scream at them, *What's so funny? Your parents didn't send you off to some prison because you didn't make good grades or come home in time for dinner. Mom and dad must be relieved to finally get rid of him. One less mouth to feed. Bobby's gotta to be happy. He has the whole bedroom to himself.*

Eddy closed his eyes again. He had a lump in his throat. His friends were probably playing fast-pitch right now. *Gerace and Hootie are by now best friends. Why does Hootie cut the arm sleeves off his shirts? And he never buttons them. Will he make a move on Maria? Naw, she won't go for it. He's too much a hothead. The Savinas are likely in last place. Who's going to be their pitcher?*

Nobody on the team can throw an accurate high-arced pitch like me, he thought. *Where did Uncle Jimmy go? Not a bad guy, really. His tough-guy act is all show. He took time to teach me the bookie racket. I shouldn't have taken Barney's bet. I mean, sure, he was gonna make me shoot Barney, but here, they'll teach me to shoot anybody! Will Mom and Dad give away my bed now that I'm gone? Bobby'll put his stuff in my dresser, take over the whole room. It'd be funny to watch him go to military school. Love to see the look on his face when some jarhead screams at him.*

Eddy yawned, and a minute later, he dozed off.

— — —

He felt a tug on his shirt.

"Wake up. We're here," Wyatt said.

Eddy leaned forward and looked out the window. "Where are we?"

"Galesburg. We catch a bus from here, and it takes us to Roosevelt," Wyatt said.

The man in the military uniform yelled for the cadets to hustle off the train, get their luggage and load it onto the bus undercarriage. They snapped to and did it PDQ.

Eddy and Wyatt took a seat in the back of the bus. Wyatt nudged Eddy and offered him a piece of gum. Eddy took it and thanked him.

"It's not so bad if you just follow the rules," Wyatt said. "It takes a while for plebes to get used to the place. Most of them get really homesick. There's a lot of crying."

Wyatt wrinkled his eyes and said, "Boo hoo hoo."

"What's a plebe?" Eddy asked.

"A new recruit. Until you earn cadet, you're a plebe. Most plebes become cadets at homecoming. They march through the ceremonial gate."

Eddy sighed. He really wanted a cigarette. "Do they let you smoke?"

"You have to get smoking privileges from your parents. If they catch you smoking without permission, you get five demerits."

"What's a demerit?"

"It's a mark against you. You can get demerits in a lot of ways, like if your shoes aren't shined or you're late for class. You have to walk the slab for a half hour to work off each demerit. If you have too many demerits, you could lose weekend furlough privileges."

Eddy shook his head. What kind of nightmare was he walking into, he wondered. "Today is September 11, 1945, the worst day of my life," he mumbled.

Eddy closed his eyes and tried to sleep. But all he could think about was marching on some slab, whatever that was, wearing shiny shoes. He sensed he was going to deal with a lot of formalities. He hated wearing monkey suits to church. Now, he might have to wear some goofy military uniform with a stupid hat every day. His thoughts switched to the Cubs. Maybe they'd win the pennant. If they did, would he be able to go home and see a World Series game? What if they didn't let him go home? As the bus rolled faster toward his doom, foreboding thoughts filled his mind.

He imagined marching in a column of soldiers going off to war. He spotted his family in a crowd of onlookers. Tears rolled down the cheeks of his mother and sister as they waved white hankies in grief. His father's arms were crossed, and a proud smile spread across his face, exposing those bottle openers, varnished by White Owl cigars. He could hear Bobby's catcalls, clapping, whistling, and hoots and howls of laughter over the steady thud of marching feet as Eddy marched off to certain death.

Eddy marched through cities, the countryside, over bridges, sledged across creeks and rivers and finally onto a slab made of white sludge in the shape of home base. He marched in place on the slab and sank into it like it was quicksand, deeper and deeper until he fell asleep.

Not long after, the bus stopped, and Eddy awoke. It was late afternoon. He looked out the window and saw trees as high as the Wrigley Field scoreboard. Behind the trees stood a three-story yellow brick building with two Corinthian columns on each side of wide stone steps, leading up to wooden doors. The building was set back off the road about a city block, flanked by two redbrick buildings. The cadets on the bus snapped to and filed off in order. Three men in uniforms stood outside screamed at cadets to fetch their luggage and stand in formation.

A tall muscular man with a granite face and jutting jowls introduced himself as Col. Melvin Mulligan. He was at least six foot five inches tall and built like a tank. A sword hung from his belt, and his starched uniform was decorated with stripes. He rattled off names and told the cadets which company they belonged to.

Eddy nudged a cadet next to him. "Did he say Company G?"

The cadet didn't move or say anything.

"You! Step forward! What's your name?" screamed Col. Mulligan, pointing at Eddy.

Eddy casually stepped forward. "Eddy Pareti."

The pigeon-chested colonel ran up to Eddy and leaned down in his face and yelled at the top of his lungs. "Attenshun! You miserable plebe, you will address me as sir. Hands to the side, feet together, chin up, chest out, shoulders back, stomach in!"

Eddy did as he was told.

"There is no talking unless we say you can talk. There is no running unless we tell you to run. You can't turn your head unless we tell you to turn your head. You will not dream unless we tell you to dream."

"Yes, sir," Eddy said.

"Did I say you could talk?" Mulligan screamed.

Eddy hesitated. He wasn't sure he should answer. "Um, no sir."

"Congratulations, plebe, you have your first demerit. Get back in line."

Eddy quickly got back in line. Another uniformed man wearing glasses screamed that he was Lt. Phillip Andrews, and he was commandant of Company G. He ordered everyone from Company G to march behind him. A bugle blared, and Company G cadets grabbed their luggage and followed Lt. Andrews toward one of the buildings. They stopped on what appeared to be a concrete patio in front of a redbrick building.

"This is Niles Hall, your home for the next nine months," Lt. Andrews shouted. "And you're standing on the slab. You will spend a lot of time marching here."

The lieutenant pointed to a swamp oak adjacent the slab. "See this tree? It was once a sapling. Edith Roosevelt sent it here in honor of Teddy Roosevelt, after whom this military academy is named. It is a symbol of what we stand for at Roosevelt Military Academy." The lieutenant ordered the cadets to look up their room numbers posted on the entrance door of Niles Hall. Cadets crowded around the door. Eddy lingered behind them, and was the last one to read his room number.

Eddy gripped his trunk and slow-walked up three flights of marble stairs to the third floor. He ambled down the hallway and entered Room 35. He dropped his strongbox next to a bunk bed on the left side of the only window in the room, which overlooked the entrance side of the campus. The room was small. It held two bunk beds on opposite sides, flanked by an armoire and a wooden desk. The room smelled like soap. The wood floors glowed, and the blankets on the beds were perfectly folded. His mother would be delighted, Eddy thought.

Eddy was alone in the room. He collapsed into the lower bunk and clasped his hands behind his head. It had been a while since he'd felt a bit relaxed. *A cigarette would be nice about now.* He'd hidden a pack inside a pair of overalls folded at the bottom of the trunk. Maybe a few quick puffs and blow the smoke out the window. He leaned upright, his eyes fixed on his luggage.

A cadet with a hangdog face straggled into the room. He was shorter than Eddy and looked younger. He dragged his feet to the other bunk bed and dumped his trunk on the floor with a bang. He plopped down in the lower bunk and stared at the top bunk.

Eddy thought he might be in the wrong room.

"I'm Eddy. What's your name?"

"Julius Logan."

Julius spoke softly, and Eddy cupped his ear to hear him. "How old are you, Julius?"

"I'm ten. I skipped two grades."

Eddy figured Julius was a Johnny-come-lately.

Two more cadets burst into the room.

"Well, speak of the devil, I'm taking the top bunk over you," said Wyatt.

"Be my guest," Eddy said. "If you fall off, I'm not gonna catch ya."

Wyatt snickered. "Remember, ladies, I'm the floor captain, and I won't go easy on ya. Chow in nineteen hundred hours."

The other cadet, tall and lanky, climbed the bunkbed that Julius chose. He sat up with his legs hanging down. "Hey, Wyatt, looks like we're roomin' with two plebes."

"Watch out, Rosengarten. The one bunkin' below me is trouble," Wyatt replied.

Rosengarten let out a tommy-gun laugh, "Eh, eh, eh, eh, eh. You show him the ropes. I'll help this one below me. Remember one thing, plebes: we're a unit. You get out of line, we all suffer."

A bugle blared in the hallway. A voice in the hallway screamed, "Line up, ladies. Single file."

Wyatt jumped off his bed and made it to the door first. Rosengarten was right behind him. Eddy followed, and Julius tagged along in the rear. The boys marched single file down the stairs and out the barracks and headed toward a single-story building.

Long wooden tables stood in neat rows in the mess hall. Cadets lined up in the chow line and then took their seats in orderly fashion. Eddy grabbed a plate and slowly made his way to the cook, who plopped a scoop of mashed potatoes and meatloaf on his plate. He followed Wyatt to a table and sat down. No one talked.

Eddy stabbed his undercooked meatloaf with a fork. "I think it's still alive."

A uniformed cadet who was standing at the end of the table rushed over to Eddy and yelled, “Stand up and state your name.” He couldn’t have been older than fourteen.

Eddy lazily stood up from his seat and said, “Eddy Pareti.”

“One demerit for talking,” the uniformed cadet shouted.

Eddy sighed and sat down. After dinner, the cadets marched into a large auditorium and took their seats. Col. Mulligan walked on the stage and welcomed the cadets.

“So begins a new year at Roosevelt Military Academy. This will be your home for the next nine months,” Mulligan said. “Roosevelt Military Academy cadets are held to the highest ethical and moral standards. A cadet treats all individuals with courtesy and respect, stands up for those who cannot defend themselves, solves problems rather than creates them, believes in himself, and never stops trying. Throughout your journey here, you will take ownership of your lives and develop the tools needed to succeed in life. You will treat every cadet here as your brother and face adversity together as brothers. To quote Teddy Roosevelt, for whom this academy was named, ‘Character in the long run is the decisive factor in the life of an individual and of nations alike.’ Character is shaped by our example and by good daily work. Rough Riders, bold and strong, building men all life long. So, with that said, first call will be at 0630 hours. You will have ten minutes in the morning to wash and dress before you go to the slab for reveille. Your floor captain will explain the rest. Now go back to your barracks and get a good night’s rest.”

A bugle blared, and the cadets filed out of their seats and walked back to their barracks. Eddy flopped down in his bed and curled up in a fetal position, hugging his pillow as if it were his teddy bear. His dad told him years before that teddy bears were named after Teddy Roosevelt. Regret filled his mind. If only he hadn’t skipped summer school, snuck out, been late to dinner, or stolen cigarettes from the tavern, he wouldn’t be in this mess. He hadn’t seen this coming, and now he was stuck in this prison for who knew how long.

A cadet in the hallway played taps on his bugle.

“Why’s he playing the bugle?” Julius asked.

“It means it’s time to hit the rack, ladies,” Wyatt said. He closed the door, turned off the lights, and climbed on the top bunk. “The first verse goes like this:" He sang. "The day is done, gone the sun, from the lake. From the hill, from the sky, all is well, safety rest, God is nigh. Good night, Rosengarten. Good night, plebes."

Tears welled in Eddy's eyes. He rolled over on his stomach and rocked his right leg back and forth, trying to fall asleep.

"What's that noise?" Wyatt asked.

"It's Pareti. What are you doing?" Rosengarten said.

"Leave me alone," Eddy said, his words muffled in his pillow.

Wyatt leaned his head down over Eddy's bed and shined a flashlight. "Oh, brother, he's got the jimmy legs. Cut it out, will ya? We're trying to sleep."

Eddy ignored him. He shook his leg, but he couldn't fall asleep. Everything was quiet except for occasional shuffling from his roommates. His mind raced. How could he convince his parents to bring him back home? Apologize? Promise he would be home on time for dinner every night? He would work two jobs to pay them back for the money they had already given to this hellhole. He wanted to write a letter, but he would have to wait until morning.

Eddy laid in bed for what seemed like hours. His roommates were asleep. The steam radiator, every now and then, clanked. Tree branches outside rustled in the wind. The room was pitch-black except for a sliver of light from the hallway that leached through the cracks of the door.

The soft tread of boots echoed in the hallway. The measured footsteps grew louder and halted outside the door. Eddy rose and whispered, "Anyone awake? Who's there?" No answer.

Eddy pulled the covers over his head and curled into a fetal position. The footsteps retreated down the hollow corridor. Not long after, Eddy fell asleep.

He dreamed he was lost, running east on Waveland. He crawled up a flight of stairs he thought was his flat and fumbled around in the darkness for the door knob. He opened the door and walked inside a quiet and dark apartment. "Ma! Dad! Where are you?" No answer. He blindly stumbled into the hallway. The floors sloped downward like the bleachers ramp at Wrigley. The floor grew steeper with each step, and soon Eddy was racing down the hallway that twisted and shrank. His descent turned into a slide and he was in a free fall. "Help!"

There was an explosion.

Eddy jerked up. Wyatt and Rosengarten jumped out of their beds and dressed. A bugle blared reveille.

"What just blew up?" Eddy shouted.

"That was the cannon outside. They fire it every morning," Wyatt said.

"Let's go, ladies. Up and at 'em," yelled someone in the hallway.

The entire third floor had rumbled to life. Shuffling feet pitter-pattered on the polished linoleum floor toward the bathroom.

Julius sat up, tears welling in his eyes. He had slept in his clothes.

Eddy refused to move. He lay back down, facing the wall. He started sobbing.

"He's crying," Wyatt said as he sat on Eddy's bed. "Come on, Pareti. Pull yourself together. You've got to get ready, or you'll get another demerit."

"I'm not going anywhere," Eddy cried.

"What did the hat say to the necktie?" Rosengarten said. Eddy didn't respond. "You hang around, and I'll go on ahead." Out came his annoying laugh, "Eh eh, eh, eh, eh."

Eddy stayed in his bed and cried.

"It's okay if you cry, but you have to come downstairs," Wyatt pleaded. "I'll bet you five dollars there will be at least a half-dozen other cadets crying. It happens."

"I'm not going anywhere. Leave me alone," Eddy cried, his face in the pillow again.

"Aren't we supposed to go downstairs in our uniforms?" Julius asked.

"We don't have uniforms yet," Wyatt said. "We get them tomorrow from the quartermaster. So just wear your civies and follow me."

Eddy's roommates dressed and left the room. About twenty minutes later, Lt. Andrews marched into the room. "Get up!"

"I'm not going anywhere until my mother comes and gets me," Eddy insisted. Tears streamed down his face.

"Your parents are not coming to get you," Lt. Andrews said in a stern voice. "We are your new parents, and this is your new home. You had better get used to it, or you'll be walking that slab for so long you'll be sleeping on it. Now get up out of that bed and get dressed. You've already missed the exercises, so I'll walk you to the mess hall for breakfast."

Eddy slowly rolled out of his bed and pulled the covers over the pillow in a vain attempt to make his bed.

"That's not how you do it at Roosevelt Military Academy, plebe," Lt. Andrews said. "One of the most important things you will learn at this academy is how to properly make your bed. Do you know why it's so important?"

Eddy shook his head.

"Making your bed in the morning is the first task you will do for that day. If you do it right, you will start off the day right. After that day ends with many failures, and you will have them, plebe, you will come back at night and see the first success you had that day. It will encourage you to try again the next day. Do you understand me?"

Eddy nodded, noticing the glint on the lieutenant's shiny black shoes.

"Listen to me and do exactly what I tell you. First, tuck the sheet tightly and lay it flat on the rack."

Eddy tucked the sheet and swept it with the back of his hand, smoothing the creases.

"Lay the top sheet nice and flat and evenly spaced," Lt. Andrews said. "Make sure the sides of the sheet hang evenly over the sides of the bed. Then you're gonna fold it over and make sure it's nice and pinched. You're gonna get a forty-five-degree angle."

Eddy tried it, but the sides were at a ninety-degree angle.

Lt. Andrews yelled, "Fail. Fold it up!"

Eddy folded the side, but he wasn't sure what a forty-five-degree angle was.

"Fail. You don't know what you're doing. Watch closely, plebe. I'm only gonna do this one time."

The lieutenant folded the sides. He lifted the top sheet about a foot away from the foot of the bed on the bedside. He pulled the sheet straight up to form a diagonal fold and laid the fold flat on the top of the bed. He tucked the piece hanging in the corner under the mattress. He smoothed the diagonal fold down over the side of the bed and tightly tucked it under the mattress. He tucked the side of the top sheet under the bed and did the same on the other side of the bed. He centered the pillow at the head of the bed.

"That's how you do it, plebe. Get dressed! Let's move it!"

Eddy's face was red and his legs were shaking as he put on his socks and pants. He got his buttons wrong on his shirt and the lieutenant barked.

— — —

The Cubs game blared on the radio as Ernie poured Walter another beer. It was the end of the seventh inning and the Cubs were ahead 4–0 against the Phillies. Cub's ace, Hank Wyse, had a shutout going as the Cubs tried to hold onto a two-game lead over the World Series champs, the Cardinals.

"I have a good feelin' about the Cubs, Ernie," Walter said. "They're playing like champs and that trade for Hank Bowery put 'em over the top."

The tavern was crowded and noisy. Ernie thought Walter said stop, so he stopped pouring.

"You runnin' out of beer, Ernie?" Walter said, pointing to his half-full glass. "Come on, fill her up, my friend."

Ernie laughed and poured. "I guess you're not a half glass kind of guy. I thought you wanted me to stop."

"You didn't hear me. I said the Bowery trade put the Cubs over the top," Walter shouted.

Bobby, who was making change at the register, said, "If ya think about it, the glass is never half full. Half of it's air, and the other half is liquid."

"Well, ya can't drink air, now can ya?" Kitty said, pinching Bobby's cheek. She slapped a dollar bill on the bar and asked for twenty nickels. She rarely ran her dice games but instead spent most of her time pulling the one-arm bandit.

"Ernie, guess where I just found my lucky coin? It was wedged in between the seat at that booth," Kitty said, pointing to a corner booth where she once held her dice games. "You have no idea how hard I looked for it. It's a sure bet the Cubs will win the World Series this year." She held up the coin, kissed it, and placed it carefully in her purse.

Margaret burst through the front door and held up a postcard. "Ernie, we got this from Eddy."

She gave it to Ernie, and he read it out loud.

Dear family,

I just arrive in school. Our rooms are nice. I just made two beds. I getting along find. Well, inspecting is going to start. Goodbye. Might see you in the World Series.

Your son,
Eddy Pareti

"He must have been in a hurry," Margaret said. "He didn't say too much, and there's some grammatical errors."

Ernie sighed. "I told ya, Marge. He's getting along fine. We made the right decision to send him there."

"What are you talking about? We? You didn't think it was a good idea. I had to fight you tooth and nail."

"Aw, cut it out, Marge, will ya?"

— — —

After Eddy dressed, Lt. Andrews escorted him to the mess hall. Eddy sat between Wyatt and Rosengarten, who had saved him a seat. Julius sat across from them, whimpering and holding back tears. Eddy scanned the mess hall. There were several plebes with mottled faces and teary eyes. It was the first day, and all Eddy wanted was to leave this rathole and smoke a cigarette.

He looked at his plate. "What's this?"

"Biscuits and gravy à la carte. Enjoy," Wyatt said in a sarcastic, gleeful tone. "Tonight, the chef will make us gourmet bologna sandwiches."

BOTTOM OF THE EIGHTH

Eddy stared at the top of his bunk bed. He couldn't sleep. The room was dark, but there was just enough moonlight for him to make out faded objects in the room. Wyatt shifted. The top bunk creaked and bent slightly downward. It had been about two weeks, and Eddy still could not get a good night's sleep. Every night, he heard the dull echo of footsteps walking up the stairs and down the hallway. It was a different sound than the one made by cadets in the middle of the night shuffling half asleep toward the latrine. A few high school cadets joked that it was the ghost of a Company G cadet who'd collapsed and died on the parade grounds a decade earlier. Eddy laughed it off, but it scared the hell out of poor Julius.

One night, Julius rose up and yelled, "Get me out of here!" then lay back down and fell asleep. He didn't remember saying it.

There were no footsteps tonight. The entire third floor was dead silent. Eddy's thoughts wandered. Most of them were somber, but one kept him hopeful. Lt. Andrews had told Company G cadets they could have a weekend furlough in October if the Cubs won the pennant. Wyatt warned Eddy that he had too many demerits, low grades, and poor inspections, and that Lt. Andrews could change his mind. Eddy walked the slab every day, made Cs and Fs on daily tests, and earned low marks on every barrack and personal inspection. He was batting a thousand, and it didn't look good.

So what? Eddy thought. He'd run away again and watch the World Series at Wrigley no matter what.

Eddy cracked a defiant smile and closed his eyes. He was relaxed and drifting into sleep. The cannon exploded. Seconds later, the bugle blared reveille, and cadets stormed out of their beds, dressed, and hurried to the latrine. Eddy slowly rolled out of bed and dressed. It was another day of drudgery: marching, military drills, yelling, studying, and eating crappy food.

As Eddy stepped into the hallway, a hopeful thought popped into his head. Maybe today he could ride the horses. He felt at home at the school's horse barn, a wooden building that stood about two hundred feet from the slab, surrounded by a wood-board fence and set on about five acres of pasture. He knew the name of all fourteen geldings and two colts and visited the horse barn every chance he could get to clean, brush and feed the horses. The horse trainer, Lachlan Addair, a crusty old Scottish man with graying red hair and a beard, had grown fond of Eddy, especially after the plebe washed his car. He told Eddy he was a natural with the horses and could ride the horses once he earned riding privileges, which was up to Lt. Andrews.

Each day Eddy walked the slab, he jealously watched other cadets ride them out onto an open field and disappear into a path that wound around ten acres of woods. If he didn't earn riding privileges soon, he would sneak into the barn and ride them himself.

Cadets raced by as Eddy lumbered to the latrine. He peed and washed his hands. He cupped his hands under the faucet and splashed his face with cold water. He looked into the mirror and saw dark circles under his eyes. He lurched into the empty hallway and stumbled his way downstairs, his footsteps echoed in the dank stairway.

It was the crack of dawn. A pine-scented mist filled the cold air after an early morning rain. Cadets had already lined up in a V-formation on the slab and begun routine jumping jacks when Eddy appeared, his black hair mussed and shirt untucked. First Sergeant Cadet George Wilbur, who was leading the calisthenics, bawled, "Another demerit for Pareti!" Cadet Wilbur picked up the demerit sheet and placed another checkmark next to Eddy's name.

Eddy shrugged as he stepped into the formation and half-heartedly did his jumping jacks. Julius stood next to him, tears rolling down his chubby cheeks. He could barely keep up. The cadets were in the middle of pushups when Lt. Andrews arrived. "Attenshun!"

The cadets rose, saluted, and stood at parade rest.

"It has come to my attention that Company G has lost all barrack inspections and has not won points in any academic competition," Lt. Andrews said. "We can do better, and you *will* do better. There are a few here who are dragging this company down. We all know who you are."

Lt. Andrews eyes shifted to Eddy. "This ain't no damn holiday. If things do not change, I will withdraw recreation privileges for the entire company. Remember, cadets: Good, better, best. Never let it rest. Until your good is better and your better is best. That is all. At ease."

Lt. Andrews turned on his heels and headed to the administrative building to teach a class. A few cadets spun around and glared at Eddy. Cadet Wilbur barked out an order, and the cadets filed into pairs and marched to the mess hall for breakfast.

Eddy stabbed at his biscuits and gravy. He was hoping for pancakes, the only breakfast food that was half decent. Two weeks ago, he had cried at breakfast. He was over that now. He just went through the motions.

"Hurry up and eat, Pareti. We have to get back to our room and prep for inspection," Wyatt said. "I'm the CO today. I don't want to give you another demerit. The rate you're going, you'll be walking the slab for life."

"I can't eat this mush," Eddy said as he chugged down his milk. He stood up and hustled back to his room. He had about twenty minutes for a quick catnap before barrack inspection.

Eddy jumped into his bed and fell asleep.

▬ ▬ ▬

"Come on, Pareti. Get up," Wyatt said. He poked Eddy. "You've got five minutes for inspection."

Rosengarten and Julius were dressing and making their beds.

"All right. Hold your horses," Eddy said. He slowly got up and made his bed. He had done it so many times he could do it in his sleep. He had nightmares where he made his bed over and over.

"That's good, Pareti. You're getting it," Wyatt said as he swept his hand across the top sheet. "You know the drill. Open your towel and lay it on the bed with no creases."

Eddy did it and then placed his comb, toothbrush, and toothpaste on the towel. He dressed in his uniform.

Wyatt tugged at Eddy's sleeve and patted his shoulders.

Eddy stepped back in anger. "Don't touch me. You're not my mother."

"Sorry, just tryin' to help."

"You're not helping. You're annoying me," Eddy shouted.

Wyatt's body tensed. He stepped closer to Eddy. "I've about had it with you, Pareti. Let me tell ya something. I'm proud to be a cadet at Roosevelt Military School. I'm not some kinda Chicago thug like you. I wanted to come here. This is the best military school in the nation, and it's a privilege to be here."

Eddy smiled and moved in closer. They were face-to-face.

"If you wanna fight, let me tell ya, pretty boy, you're gonna lose."

"Cut it out, you two," Rosengarten said as he grabbed Wyatt's arm.

"We get our football pads and uniforms today. Did ya know that, Pareti?" Wyatt yelled. "That means tackling. I'm gonna knock you on your ass so many times you'll be crying for your mommy again."

"We'll see about that, tough guy," Eddy smirked.

Wyatt walked out of the room but, seconds later, popped his head back in and said, "One demerit for Pareti. You failed to shine the brass buttons on your coat."

"See you at practice, Wyatt Earp," Eddy promised. But the smirk fell from his face. He'd never played tackle football before.

Eddy shuffled to the administration building for class. It was only eight in the morning, and it felt as if half the day was over. Julius walked next to him, quizzing him for a spelling test. "Spell *humerus*."

Eddy blurted out the letters. "H-u-m-o-r-e-u-s."

Julius laughed. "We're studying bones in the body not comedy."

"That's what I think of this place. Gimme another one."

"Sphenoid."

"Forget it," Eddy said dejectedly. "I can't believe that you're the smartest guy in our company, and you're only ten."

Julius shrugged. "I can't make friends like you can."

Eddy smiled. "Friends? Whaddya talking about? Nobody likes me in Company G."

"They like you. Sometimes you do too much smoking and joking and get them in trouble. But they like you. You're probably the best athlete in junior high."

Eddy thought about Wyatt. Eddy knew he was faster, but would he be in football gear? Wyatt knew all the plays and seemed to be the coach's favorite player. A natural leader, the coach would say.

"You haven't walked the slab once since we've been here. You could light a candle, and people would think you're an altar boy. Why do you hate this place so much?"

"I dunno. I want to be with people my own age," Julius said. "I might be smart, but I'm not athletic or funny like you."

"Someone told me you faked an asthma attack to try and get outta comin" here."

Julius shrugged. "My father's a colonel in the army. My grandfathers served in the military. My parents expect me to join the military when I'm old enough. I guess they wanted me to get a head start."

The boys walked into the classroom and took their seats in the back next to a window. Eddy's desk wobbled, and the hardwood floors creaked, just as they did at his school back home. He realized on the first day of class that the teachers at Roosevelt were meaner, stricter, and a helluva lot stronger than any nun he had ever faced.

Lt. Johnny Seago strode into the classroom. The cadets snapped to and Lt. Seago growled, "At ease." He picked up a stick of chalk that was down to nearly a nub, and scraped it across the blackboard, making a continuous squeaking sound. The lieutenant drew a circle on the blackboard and then turned to face the cadets.

"Most of you had low scores in yesterday's spelling test. One of you failed. Pareti, come up here."

Eddy rose and walked to the front of the classroom. He stared up into the face of Gene Kelly and expected him to spring into a dance. He'd write his sister that Lt. Seago looked just like Gene Kelly.

"Place your nose in the circle," the lieutenant barked, pointing to the blackboard. "The rest of you open your books and place them on the floor. I want all of you to kneel and put your left hand behind your back. For the next thirty minutes, you will study for today's quiz. I catch anyone talking, they will join this plebe up here."

Eddy heard loud sighs as cadets shuffled out of their desks and onto the floor. After the lieutenant left the room, Eddy thought he heard somebody say they were going to take his head off during tackle drills.

After morning classes ended, cadets marched in pairs to the mess hall for lunch and then marched back to the slab for military drills. They lined up in formation and stood at parade rest. Lt. Andrews addressed the cadets.

"For the next five weeks or so, we will be practicing for the homecoming parade. Some of you are aware that homecoming is one of the biggest events of the year at Roosevelt. Your parents will travel from all over this great nation to watch barrack and personal inspections, homecoming football games, and parades. I've been company commandment of Company G for seven years and not *once* have we won parade honors. I aim to change that this year. I will personally supervise the drills. So make sure you have extra pairs of shoes, because you will be wearing them out. You will drill and drill and drill!"

Lt. Andrews pointed to the "gate," which stood next to the flagpole in front of the administration building. The gate was made of rustic wrought iron connected by two brick pillars. Above it was an arched metal work with the words *Roosevelt Military.* "Right, now, you plebes are the lowest of low. You know who you are," Lt. Andrews yelled, spittle flying into the frozen faces of the cadets. "But during homecoming, you may get the honor to march through the gate and become cadets."

Lt. Andrews stared at Eddy and added, "There are no guarantees."

For the next hour, cadets practiced marching to different cadences and drilled with wooden rifles. Eddy noticed Julius's eyes welling with tears. The little guy was exhausted, but he hung in there. After the drills, cadets marched to their barracks to change out of their uniforms and into gym clothes. They were given five minutes and ordered to report to the gym behind Niles Hall.

About two dozen Company G cadets put on their new orange-and-brown football uniforms, their gear, and lolled around the football field, waiting for their coach, Major Jim Hutson. Eddy's leather helmet shifted sideways on his head. It was too big, but it was the last one in the pile. He bent down to tie the shoelaces of his cleats, which clenched too tight around his feet. The laces were frayed and uneven. What else could go wrong?

He had blown off studying the plays Coach gave them, but he understood the game. He had watched the Chicago Bears at practices and during games at Wrigley Field numerous times. Once, he had wandered into a practice, and the Bears center, Forest Masterson, bet Head Coach Hunk Anderson that Eddy could throw with quarterback Sid Luckman if he picked Eddy up from his feet, starting in a squat position. Masterson, who weighed two hundred and fifty, won the bet, and Eddy got to throw with Luckman.

Coach Hutson burst onto the field, blowing his whistle and yelling for the cadets to line up single file. He split the players into two teams and assigned them positions on offense and defense. Eddy was assigned to receive the ball on kickoffs and play right half on offense and linebacker on defense. Coach Hutson growled in a Southern drawl, "Y'all gonna scrimmage today, boys."

As the players took their positions for the kickoff, Wyatt ran past Eddy and hollered, "We're kicking it to you, Pareti, and I'm comin' for ya. Gonna take your head off of your shoulders."

Before Eddy could threaten him back, Wyatt was already halfway downfield.

Blisters covered the bottom of Eddy's feet from all the marching and walking the slab. His tight shoes didn't help. Eddy hobbled to the ten-yard line for the return. "If you keep your head in the game, you can play through the pain," Cubs manager Charlie Grimm had once said.

The ball holder set the pigskin up on the twenty-yard line. To Eddy, the goalposts seemed a mile away. The placekicker ran up to the ball and Eddy heard the soft thud of the steel-toed kicker's cleat as it bit into the hide. Eddy watched the oblong ball spiral upward into the air and then peak midfield as it sailed downward in a line that seemed destined for him. He had shagged a million fly balls, but this was different. Eddy caught it on the run.

He sped past two defenders on his right and headed down the sideline, following his blockers. He spotted an opening and cut back to the inside and ran in a full sprint down midfield. Once he crossed the fifty-yard line, Eddy peeked behind him and saw one player in full pursuit about five yards behind. He snapped his head forward and dashed full speed as if he were trying to beat out a grounder to first base. As he crossed the goal line, he looked back and saw that Wyatt sputtered ten yards behind out of gas.

Coach Hutson blew his whistle as he ran down the field toward Eddy who was collapsed in the end zone, yanking off his cleats. "The wolf in heart rises in battle. Well done. You're a natural, son." The coach spotted the open blisters on Eddy's feet and added, "You got grit too. You're gonna make it, kid."

Eddy jammed his shoes back on and limped downfield, taking his place on the kickoff team for the kickoff. The kick was high, and the ball spun like a flywheel. Eddy never took his eye off the ball. Just like in baseball, that's where the action was. He was the first player downfield, dancing past all the blockers, who seemed to move in slow motion. He glanced at the uncertain eyes of the return man who took his eyes off the ball as he gave a fleeting look downfield to see if there was an opening. But he hadn't caught the ball yet. And when it did land square in his gut, it filtered through his hands like water and bounced on the cold late September ground. Eddy dove on it.

The next play in the huddle, quarterback Cadet Wilbur called a reverse pitch to Eddy.

"What's that?" Eddy asked.

"I pitch it to the left half, and you come around, and the left half pitches it to you and you run," Wilbur explained. "Got that?"

Eddy nodded.

"You didn't study your plays, did you?" Wilbur said.

Eddy remembered the words of Hack Wilson that Cubs Manager Grimm hung on the dugout door. It was something about kids who think, because they have talent, they have the world by the tail. It wasn't true. Don't be too big to accept advice.

"Sorry, it's my fault. I should've studied. I'll make it up to you guys. Promise."

They broke huddle and lined up, their breaths snorting out like stallions in the cold.

Wilbur took the snap and pitched the ball to the left half, who ran a few steps and turned to pitch the ball to the right half. Eddy had moved too quickly, and the ball was behind him. However, he reached out with his right hand and flicked the ball into his gut as he ran full speed around the end. He outflanked the entire defensive line, but there was one man to beat: Wyatt, who was gunning for him from the linebacker position. Just as Wyatt dove for his feet, Eddy, battling the pain in his soles, vaulted over him and his ham-hock fists for the touchdown.

Before the coach blew the final whistle on the meaningless scrimmage, Eddy had scored four more times and caught an interception for a touchdown. After the scrimmage, Coach Hutson asked the players to nominate four cadets and vote one of them as captain of the team. Eddy, Wyatt, Wilbur, and Cadet Tandon, whose mother was the school nurse, were nominated.

"All right, boys. Last year, Wyatt was your captain. How many of y'all want him captain this year? Raise your hand," Coach Hutson said.

Twenty hands went up.

"Well, looky there. Wyatt wins overwhelmingly. All right, Wyatt. Now ya gotta pick your cocaptain."

Wyatt smiled and said, "That's easy." He pointed to Eddy. "Him, hands down."

"I don't want to be cocaptain," Eddy said.

"Are you crazy? You're our best player. Ya gotta be our cocaptain," Wilbur said.

Wyatt walked over to Eddy and held out a piece of gum. "Here's a peace offering. If it were up to me, you'd be our captain. We're glad you're on our team. That's all. Come on, whaddya say?"

Eddy's shrugged, and his hands fidgeted. His eyes moved downward and then off to space as he tilted his head back and forth. After a whole half minute of cold silence, Eddy finally nodded. A few of the cadets cheered him. It felt like he was standing on the grass of Wrigley Field in the World Series, fans applauding him.

Cadets changed out of their football uniforms and walked back to the barracks for a two-hour recreation break. Eddy, on the other hand, had to walk the slab.

Eddy paced back and forth, occasionally shifting the rifle from one shoulder to the other. He knew every crack and scuff mark on the slab. His shoulders felt tender to the touch. Normally, he'd pass the time thinking about his mother's homemade ziti or drinking Coke on a hot day behind home plate for a game at Wrigley. On this occasion, his mind raced about football. He could have played all day. He was now cocaptain of the football team, but with no stripes or medals. It figured.

A light drizzle fell as Eddy marched up and down the slab. Julius stood watch on slab guard duty. He thought about stopping to rest, but Julius could get a demerit if some fathead fuddy-duddy reported it.

"Okay, Eddy, take five," Julius said in a high-pitched voice.

Eddy set his rifle against the wall and ran across the slab to the north barracks, adjacent to his barracks where the older kids bunked. He opened the door and raced downstairs to the recreation room, reserved only for upperclassmen.

"Hey, you're not 'pose to be in here. Beat it, buddy," said an older cadet, his voice deep. He was wearing a school sweater emblazoned with a red letter *R*, indicating he played on the varsity football team.

"I just wanna buy cigarettes," Eddy said.

"Well, why didn't you say so, plebe?" The older cadet reached into his jacket and pulled out a pack of Lucky Strikes. "How many you want?"

Eddy scanned the recreation room. It was nearly empty, and the cadets there didn't seem to notice the transaction. "I'll take five."

"That'll be twenty-five cents."

"You're kidding. I could buy a pack for that."

"Then go ahead," the varsity player said as he placed the cigarettes back into his jacket.

"Come on, gimme a break. Ten cents."

"Fifteen."

Eddy reached into his pocket, came out with some change, and counted it. He gave him the money, grabbed the cigarettes, and ran upstairs and outside. It was pouring rain. He pulled up his collars against the sidelong rain and scurried around the building and down the back-basement steps to smoke. He didn't have smoking privileges, and if they caught him, he'd be slapped with more demerits.

Eddy bent forward against the building, shielding the cigarette from the downpour, and puffed away. By the time he finished, he was drenched, his uniform clung to his skin like paint. He ran up the stairs toward the slab and decided to make a run for the horse barn. Julius's voice, muffled in the monsoon, pleaded for him to return to the barracks. Eddy ignored him and dashed for the barn.

When Eddy entered, a horse whinnied. Mists of rain sprayed into the barn through a half-open door. The wind whipped through the barn, giving it an odd scent of sweaty leather, moldy hay and a sweet earthy fragrance. A gelding stuck its head outside the stall that emitted a strong odor of ammonia. Eddy walked over and scratched its neck. The horse pawed at the ground.

"Ya like that? How are ya doin', Silver?" Eddy said, stroking the horse's nose. "You guys need a good cleaning, don'tcha?"

Julius tapped Eddy on the shoulder, and he flinched. Eddy didn't hear him walk in the barn.

"We have to get to the mess hall. Company G is already there," Julius said, in a pleading tone.

"You're not gonna get in trouble, Julius. See that black horse at the end? That's Morgan. He's the fastest horse."

Eddy grabbed a grooming brush and walked over to Morgan's stall. He gently stroked the horse between the eyes, all the way down to its snout. The horse's ears purged forward, and its tail swished gently back and forth.

"What are you cadets doin' in here?" snarled Addair, who entered through the back door.

Eddy jumped back and dropped the grooming brush. "Hi, Mr. Addair. It was raining on us, and we came in here," Eddy said in an enthusiastic tone, one that he used when taking customer orders at his father's tavern. "Hope that's okay. We can help ya clean the horses if you want."

"Why, Eddy, I didn't see it was you." Addair stroked Morgan on the nose. "I see you calmed Morgan. Some of the cadets, they try'n' feed 'em mallow or chew'n' tobacco, or they pull on the bit. But you're good with 'em. You're welcome here anytime."

"Can I ride 'em?"

"Not today, son. It's a monster rain out there. The ground is soaked."

"We have to get back, Eddy," Julius said nervously. "We can't be late for mess."

"And miss what?" Eddy sighed. "Okay, let's get outta here. Sorry, Mr. Addair, we can't stick around to help. Duty calls, ya know."

Julius and Eddy ran to the mess hall. Company G was already at the tables, sucking down their K-rations. Eddy and Julius got in the chow line. The lower classmen plopped food onto their heavy plates. They found their seats and sat. A cadet walked over and loomed over Eddy. "You guys are late."

Before Eddy could give a sarcastic answer, Col. Mulligan entered the mess hall. Someone yelled, "Attenshun!" All cadets rose and saluted.

"I have an announcement to make," Col. Mulligan shouted. "The Cubs today beat the Pirates to win the pennant!"

A large number of cadets roared, and some even jumped on the tables. A few cadets from Michigan booed. Col. Mulligan smiled and held up his hands to calm the cadets. "The game was tied in the ninth when Andy Pafko hit a sacrifice fly to score Stan Hack."

The majority of cadets broke into another roar. Shouts of "Go, Cubs" thundered throughout the chow hall, drowning out the boos.

Col. Mulligan quieted the crowd. There was silence, and he spoke again. "The first three games of the World Series will be played in Detroit. The remaining games will be played at Wrigley, starting October sixth. Cadets in good standing will be given furloughs to see the World Series. At ease."

— — —

Margaret set beef sandwiches on the dining room table along with the salad. They were leftovers from the bar. Ernie's Bleachers had been packed all week, and there was little time to cook. But she made sure the family sat each night at the dinner table.

Nonno chewed on garlic bread while Florence finished setting the table. Bobby read the paper on the couch. Ernie was missing in action.

"Where's your father?" Margaret yelled.

"He's coming, Ma," Bobby said. "He's showing the new bartender the ropes."

"Well, come on, Bobby. Sit at the table, will ya?" Margaret asked.

Bobby folded the paper and laid it on the couch. Just as he sat down at the table, Ernie barged in. "I know, Marge. Sorry, I'm late."

"Sit down and eat," she ordered. "We don't have much time. Boy, we're so busy we're gonna need to hire more people."

Ernie smiled and sat at the head of the table. After the prayer, the family dug in to homemade lasagna.

"Dad, I just read that today is Charlie Grimm's wedding anniversary," Bobby said, chewing with his mouth full. "The day the Cubs win the pennant in Pittsburgh is his anniversary. Not only that, they got married in Pittsburgh! What are the odds?"

Ernie turned to his wife and said, "Our anniversary is coming up. How long has it been, Marge? Almost twenty years. Twenty heavenly years."

"Oh sure, Ernie. We're in seventh heaven." She pulled out a letter from an envelope. "Just got a letter from Eddy. He still likes it there. And he's coming home for the World Series."

"What does it say, Ma?" Bobby asked.

Margaret cleared her throat and read the letter:

Dear Mom,

I'm feeling fine. How are you feeling? Well, I said I wanted to be a jockey, and I'm going to be one because the man who takes care of the horses said I can feed and ride them anytime I want, and I water them, and I brush them. Boy, do I have fun with the horses.

I got good news. I'm coming home Oct. 5–6–7. Meet me Oct. 5 at 8:50 p.m. at Union Station. Don't forget.

Mother send me my clarinet music, because I'm going to show these guys how to play. Say hello to everybody.

Good-by,
Your loving son, Eddy

P.S. Don't forget the candy.

"Oh brother, now he wants to be a jockey. First, a ball player and now a jockey," Margaret said. "Why doesn't he want to be a lawyer or a doctor or something like that?"

"You send him off to military school. and you expect him to want to be a doctor?" Florence said, laughing.

"He's gonna get the discipline he needs. And there's nothing wrong with wanting to be a doctor," Margaret said. "You have to dream big in this world. Right, Ernie?"

Ernie smiled.

"Oh, you're not listening. Are you?" Margaret said.

"When Eddy gets here, I'll stick him at the window. We could use the extra help," Ernie said. "Remember the 1938 World Series? They were lined up all night around Wrigley. We were so busy. I was up all night, countin' nickels and quarters."

"We didn't do too bad in the '32 and '35 World Series either," Margaret added.

"Say, Dad, you should raise your food and drink prices," Bobby said. "For that matter, you need to raise your parking rates. You could mark up your prices twenty-five percent and get a twenty percent profit margin."

"Bobby, your dad has a sixth-grade education. I finished high school, and I don't understand that math," Margaret said.

"It's simple, Ma. Let's say you do a fifty percent markup. Convert fifty percent to a fraction, a half. Add the numerator plus the denominator, which is three then divide the numerator, one, by three and you have thirty-three percent."

There was a long silence at the table. "That doesn't sound so simple, Bobby," Florence said.

"Well, Marge, there's your doctor," Ernie said.

— — —

The bugle blared taps, and the lights went out. The room was quiet for a few moments, then Eddy spoke. "The little umps did a wonderful job on the Cubs in the 1929 World Series against the Athletics. It happened in the crucial fourth game."

Wyatt leaned on his left elbow to listen. Rosengarten sat up and said, "Sounds like he's gonna tell us a bedtime story, eh, eh, eh, eh."

"You guys wanna hear this or what?" Eddy said.

"Yeah, we're all ears," said Wyatt.

"The Cubs went into the seventh inning leading eight ta nothing. The As came up, and here's what happened: Simmons homered, Foxx singled, Miller singled, Boley singled, Burns popped out, Bishop singled, Haas homered, Foxx singled, Miller was hit by the pitcher, Dykes doubled, and the next two batters fanned. The total was ten runs, ten hits, and the World Series. The Cubs haven't won a World Series in thirty-three years."

"Philadelphia scored ten runs in one inning? I didn't know that," Wyatt said in disbelief.

"They called it the Mack Attack. Mule Haas hit an inside-the-park homer because Hack Wilson dropped the ball in the sun. It was his second fly ball drop of the game," Eddy said.

"What did the umps have to do with all this?" Rosengarten asked.

"Everybody says Haas was out at the plate. Had he been called out, the Cubs would have won the game and tied the series. And get this: nobody ever hit an inside-the-park homer in a World Series."

"The Cubs will break that losing spell this year. I can just feel it in my bones," Wyatt said.

"I can't wait to see the games. I know a guy who'll sell me World Series tickets for cheap," Eddy said. "I'm gonna buy some and resell 'em for a profit. Just think how much money I can make."

"I'll buy a ticket from you," Julius said.

"Are you crazy, Julius? You never buy a ticket to get into a game. We sneak in. I'll sneak you in, okay. You can stay at my place, and we can go together."

"That would be swell!"

"Stick with me, kid. You'll go places."

TOP OF THE NINTH

A crashing boom shook the room and woke Eddy. Instinctively, he rolled out of bed, put on his neatly folded pants and shirt in the dark. Rain rattled the window. He hurried into the hallway half asleep, his feet slapped on the cold linoleum floor. He stopped. Something was odd. The lights in the latrine were off. There was no bugle blaring in the hallway. Eddy walked back into his room to see if anyone else was awake.

"Wyatt, you up?" Eddy whispered.

A flash of lightning lit up the room, followed by a clap of thunder.

A tiny voice whispered back, "Is that you Eddy?" It was Julius.

"Yeah, what time is it?" Eddy asked as he peered out the window.

Julius didn't answer.

Another flash lit up a large tree on the parade grounds below, its huge branches hauntingly swayed in the whipping wind. Eddy reached into his desk drawer and fumbled for his flashlight and watch. He had broken the band and couldn't wear the watch, so he kept it in his desk. It was three in the morning.

"We still got three hours. Don't get up, Julius."

Eddy climbed back into his rack in his uniform. Wyatt and Rosengarten never woke during the storm. Julius cried, his whimpers drowning in the chaos of thunder and rain. Eddy fell asleep.

It seemed, as soon as Eddy closed his eyes, the cannon exploded in its ritual morning blast. Seconds later the bugle blared. The hallway lit up, and Company G buzzed to life. Wyatt and Rosengarten jumped off their top bunks and landed on the floor with a thud. They quickly dressed. For a split second, Eddy thought it was another false alarm. It was still dark outside, but he didn't hear rain. He swung out of bed, rushed out of the room and raced down the hall past Wyatt and Rosengarten. He peed and washed and hustled downstairs. A half-dozen cadets were already lined up for exercises, but Eddy had beaten the majority of Company G to the slab, including his roomies.

"What in the hell," cried Wilbur. "What's got into you, Pareti?"

Eddy stood at attention, saluted, and said in a sarcastic tone, "Eddy Pareti, reporting for duty, sir."

Wyatt and Rosengarten hurried in formation, their mouths agape.

"Back of the line, boys," Eddy said with a smirk.

Wilbur yelled, "Right dress right," then "Ready front." After the singsong of roll call, cadets began their calisthenics with five sets of jumping jacks followed by five sets of thirty pushups.

After the exercises, Wilbur yelled, "Fall in. Right step, forward march!" Company G lined up in pairs and marched to the mess hall with Eddy first in line, high stepping in unintended exaggeration and shouting louder than the others, "Rough Riders bold and strong, making men all life long."

Eddy dug into his biscuits and gravy as if it were his mother's homemade mostaccioli. He finished and sped back to his room to prep for the dreaded white-glove inspection. Everything had to be spotless from ceiling to floor: chairs, desks, lamps, and beds wiped and dusted; windows cleaned; pens and pencils aligned; uniform brass buttons, belt buckles, and doorknobs polished. The sheen on the shoes had to sparkle like diamonds, and the beds had to be made tighter than two coats of paint. Each violation or gig could add up to a demerit, or worse, a week's confinement in the barracks.

Eddy never had to clean his room, pick up after himself, or make his bed at home.

"Okay, what happened to the real Pareti? Did you shoot him and bury him on the parade grounds?" Wyatt said, smiling.

Eddy sat on the bottom bunk, buffing his shoes. "I'm gonna see the World Series," Eddy promised as he blew on his right shoe, set it down, and picked up the left one to shine. "I'll sweep and dust behind the radiator. Wyatt, you sweep the floor, and, Rosengarten, you mop."

Wyatt looked at Rosengarten as if he had lost his hearing. "Who died and made you squad leader?"

Eddy glanced up and smiled. "Nobody. We're a team. If you have some ideas to pass inspection, let's hear them."

"Why didn't you give Julius something to do?" Rosengarten accused.

"Give him a break. He's having a tough go of it," Eddy said.

Wyatt looked down at a teary-eyed Julius, who was lying in his bed, sniffling. "What's the matter with you?"

"I just wanna go home."

Wyatt rubbed his forehead. "Oh brother. He's gonna drag us down. This *is* your home. So, buck it up, plebe. Straighten out the desk and clean it."

Julius started sobbing.

"Look what you did," Eddy said as he walked over and sat at the foot of Julius's bed. "Don't worry, Julius. In a couple of days, you'll get to go home and watch the Cubs win the World Series. You'll forget all about this place."

"Yeah, but then I have to come back to this slammer," Julius said, wiping his nose with his forearm.

Eddy scratched his head and sighed. He felt the same way. "But then summer'll come, and you'll get to play ball."

"I hate baseball," Julius cried.

"Or dissect frogs or whatever it is you like to do."

Julius sat up. "I'm like some old beaten-down stray dog with a stripe running down its nose, sent away from home to live with mean strangers who chain you up, spit on you, yell at you, and feed you table scraps. They call you plebe to make you feel worthless and dumb."

"You skipped two grades, and you have straight As. You're not dumb." Eddy laughed as if Julius told him a joke.

"I'm not good at sports, and kids my own age picked on me at school. My mom and dad said this place would make a man out of me. I don't see how marching everywhere with a wooden rifle on your shoulder makes you a man. Hell, I'm ten years old!"

Eddy turned around to look at Wyatt and Rosengarten, as if they might have something better to say. No one did.

"Tell you what. Don't worry about cleaning. Just get dressed. I'll even make your bed. All right?" Eddy said as he stood up. Julius nodded and put his pants on in bed.

"You can't baby him. He's gotta carry his weight," Wyatt demanded.

"He'll get over it, but for now, let's take it easy on him," Eddy shot back.

Cadet Wilbur stepped in the room. "Atten hut!"

Eddy, Wyatt, and Rosengarten snapped to. Julius bolted out of bed, his pants halfway on, and stood at attention.

Wilbur barked, "Pareti, you're calling balls and strikes. The officer of the day is out sick, and you're fillin' in. You get to prep the cadets today for inspection. Aren't we so lucky? Come with me, plebe. At ease."

Eddy brushed past Wyatt and winked. Wilbur sent Eddy to the lieutenant's office, who gave him instructions to visit each room on the floor and make sure the cadets were ready for the white-glove inspection.

The first room Eddy visited was his own. He strutted in and barked a little louder than necessary. "Attention!" Wyatt, Rosengarten, and a smiling Julius snapped to. As the cadets stood like statues, Eddy made Julius's bed and neatly placed the boy's comb, soap, and toothbrush on a towel in the center of the bed. He turned on his heels and walked up to Wyatt. He bent down to inspect Wyatt's black shoes, and then his eyes slowly rose in earnest, inspecting the socks, pants, buckles, shirt, coat and its buttons, and hat. Eddy shook his head as if to say, "Ya got it wrong." He squinted and then shouted, "Shine those buttons, Cadet! That's an order!"

Wyatt winced. Rosengarten and Julius giggled. Eddy turned around and gave them a playful frown. "At ease." Eddy marched out of the room.

A while later, Eddy returned with the lieutenant and three sergeants. They poked and prodded the beds, wiped their fingers along the windowsill and desk as the cadets stood motionless like toy soldiers.

"All good here. Well done, cadets. At ease," Lt. Andrews said.

The men left for the next inspection. Eddy followed behind, but after he stepped outside the room, he poked his head inside and said, "At ease, you miserable plebes." And he winked.

Eddy enjoyed helping the cadets prepare for the white-glove inspection. It was good to be on the same side as the sergeants and the lieutenant as they inspected every inch of the nervous cadets' uniforms and their rooms. If only his brother were here, standing like a statue in uniform.

I'd give him a million gigs, and he'd be walking the slab from sunset to sundown till the end of time, Eddy thought.

After inspection, cadets ate lunch and then attended classes. The first game of the World Series had started. Cadets restlessly shifted in physiology class, waiting for Lt. Seago, who was late. The lieutenant was never late. Eddy could hardly sit still. To pass the time, he wrote letters home.

"Anyone know the score?" a cadet near the front asked.

"I thought I heard cheers coming from the faculty lounge on my way to class," answered a cadet on the opposite side of the room.

About twenty minutes later, Lt. Seago marched in. He plunked a pile of books on his desk, folded his arms, and said with a smile, "How many Cubs fans we got in here?"

Almost the entire class raised their hands.

"I've got good news for you. The Cubs scored four runs in the first inning and are ahead five to nothing in the second inning."

"Yes!" Eddy shouted from the back of the classroom. No one turned around.

Lt. Seago stopped smiling and glared at Eddy. "You, attenshun!" Eddy rocketed up. "This is an order. Tell me the name of the bone that connects to the head of the femur and spell it."

Eddy's eyes gazed out the window as if the answer was outside. There was a long pause. Julius whispered the answer from the seat behind. Then Eddy said, "Antebellum. A-u-n…"

"If you were two times as smart as you think you are, Pareti, then you'd be four times as smart as you really are. Cadet Wyatt, what's the answer?"

Wyatt stood up. "Acetabulum. A-c-e-t-a-b-u-l-u-m."

"Correct. And congratulations, Cadet," he barked at Julius. "You just earned your first demerits. That's plural. Five demerits. I will not tolerate cheating in my classroom."

Lt. Seago ordered Eddy to sit, and he continued teaching physiology. An hour later, before it was time to switch to American history, Lt. Seago left the classroom for about fifteen minutes. He came back in with an update of the World Series. "The Cubs are ahead nine to nothing in the eighth inning." The class remained quiet. Eddy gritted his teeth and snorted. He'd bet a cadet from Detroit one dollar that the Cubs would win the series.

After classes, Company G was given special privileges to use the recreation room. When Eddy entered, he noticed that the upperclassmen were huddled around the radio, and they seemed to be in a good mood. Eddy listened. "The final score, Cubs nine, Detroit nothing."

"What a game. You plebes missed it," said an upperclassman in a mocking tone. He had sold Eddy cigarettes. He was holding a pool stick. "Cavaretta and Pafko got three hits each, and Borowy pitched a complete game."

He saw Eddy and said, "Hey, hot shot, I hear you're a football stud. Any good at eight ball?"

Eddy held back a smile. "I dunno. I'm okay, I guess. How much we bettin'?"

"Let's make it a buck."

Eddy nodded and racked. The upperclassman confidently bent over the table and, with the weight of his body, reached back and broke. The balls blasted into each other, and two stripes flew into opposite corner pockets. The cue ball, however, had curled next to the eight ball in the middle of the table. Because the upperclassman didn't have a shot, he played it safe and lightly struck the cue ball, which moved a few inches.

"So that's how you play it," Eddy said. He chalked his stick and lowered himself as if he were going to lay on the table. "Six ball, side pocket."

Eddy hit the cue ball low, and it bounced over the eight ball and gently nudged the side of the solid, sending it into the side pocket.

"Three, corner," he said lowly and knocked the red ball in. "Seven, kick into the corner." Eddy put a little English on, and the cue ball rebounded after the shot onto the far side of the table, where he had his pick of easy corner shots.

The room hushed while Eddy worked the table as he'd done it a hundred times at the Screwball Club on Clark Street. He remembered his dad once telling him he was in the catbird seat. He wondered what that'd meant, and his dad told him. Eddy felt like he was in the catbird seat now.

After it was over, the upperclassman swore, and he threw his stick across the room.

"You gotta learn how to lose before you can win," Eddy said, remembering what Walter Lockerbie had once told him. He wondered what Walter would think of him now that he was in military school, marching, drilling, scoring touchdowns, and beating an older kid in pool. The Cubs were in the World Series, and one of their scouts was interested in him. Lockerbie would be proud. But he was gone. Forever, with so many other men before him.

Eddy tapped his fingers on the edge of the table. He could play pool, football, softball anywhere, whether at Wrigley Field, the schoolyard, the Screwball Club or Roosevelt Military. It didn't matter. He was alive, competing and not buried six feet under.

A tear welled in Eddy's eyes as he muttered under his breath, "This one's for you, Lockerbie."

Another upperclassman challenged Eddy and racked. Eddy chalked his stick, inhaled, and broke, the balls crashing aimlessly into each other and caroming around the green table as if they were running scared from something. He ran the table for the next sixteen games, and won enough money in bets to buy cigarettes for the entire school year. The cadets called him king of the pool table. Eddy laughed at the compliment. With the money he had won, he felt like a king.

— — —

Bar chatter at Ernie's Bleachers had shifted to soft whispers as patrons listened to the radio, hoping for a Cubs two-out rally in the top of the ninth in game two of the World Series. Cigar and cigarette smoke floated in clouds, fouling the beer-soaked tavern air. Ernie nervously puffed on a White Owl cigar as the play-by-play man crackled over the radio, "And pinch hitter Heinz Becker walks to the plate."

"If it wasn't for that damn Greenberg hitting a three-run homer, we'd be in this game," shouted Walter, who was quickly shushed. "Don't shush me. Why da hell is Becker up to bat? He can't run. His feet are full of bunions."

"The windup, the delivery and strike two. Becker stood there like a tree on the side of the road, watching the ball go by. The count now is two strikes and no balls."

"Oh, for Pete's sake, Becker, swing at the damn thing, will ya?" Walter shouted.

"You think he can hear you?" screamed Kitty. "One thing's for sure, we can't hear the radio on account of your claptrap."

"Here's the pitch. Becker swings and misses. The ball game is over. The final score Tigers four, Cubs one."

The bar erupted in moans and groans.

"Aw hell, what I tell ya? Becker's got bunions in his brains," Walter said as he chugged his beer and then slammed it on the bar. "Gimme 'nother beer, Erns."

The bar quietly thinned. Bobby took a break from working the grill. He walked over to his dad, who was pouring a drink.

"I got a letter from Eddy today," Bobby said. "He sez his colonel was wondering if we're gonna get a lot of business this weekend."

Ernie laughed and said, "Write him back that half the neighborhood's made our place their living room." He glanced at the men's room and waved his nose. "And their bathroom. What else did he say?"

Bobby read the letter out loud:

Dear Bobby,

I just received your letter. Well, so far, the Cubs are winning five to zero in the second inning. Nicholson hit a three-base hit with bases loaded. I just heard that the Cubs are winning nine to zero in the eighth inning. The Col. just asked me if my mother and father are going to get any business Saturday, Sunday, and Monday. They will because I'll be home then.

Well, I hear that the Bears aren't doing so good this year. They lost their first game off Green Bay thirty-one to twenty-one. Tell Mother I got a B in spelling, C in arithmetic, D in physiology. Well, that's all I got to say.

Thanks for writing.
Your brother
Eddy
P.S. I just heard over the radio that the Cubs won nine to zero.

"Looks like he's failing physiology," Bobby said.

"What's that?"

"The study of organisms. Like the human anatomy, cells, body parts, and stuff like that."

Ernie took a puff on his cigar, exhaled, and said, "He failed that, huh. And your ma wants him to be a doctor?"

Ernie bit hard on his stogie when he saw Joe Gill walk into the bar. The man wore a three-piece dark suit, shiny black shoes and a striped-blue-and-yellow tie. He removed the fedora as his eyes scanned the tavern. He locked eyes with Ernie and smiled, strolling to the bar. He sat on a stool, and said in a pleasant tone, "You're just the man I'm looking for, Ernie. Give me a Manhattan."

Gill was the Democratic party's ward committeeman and the chief clerk of the city's municipal court. A former state congressman, Gill was a bigwig in politics and he did favors for anyone who mattered, including Ernie, a well-known and successful precinct captain.

Ernie's lips tightened when he set the drink in front of Gill. "On the house."

"Thanks," Gill said as he held up his drink in a salute and took a swig. "Gotta say, you make the best Manhattans. I should come here more often."

There was pause, and then Gill said, "Remember your friend, that eye doctor who needed help with a DUI? You came to me for a favor. Turns out that eye doctor returned *you* the favor, helping out your bartender." Gill laughed and took a sip of his drink. He set it down carefully, his hand cupped around the glass. "I've done you a lot of favors over the years, haven't I?"

Ernie nodded. "Why do I get the feeling you're gonna ask me for a favor?"

"You're a smart man, Ernie. I'd say you know more than most men, and I'm sure you know why I'm here," Gill said, his voice soft and smooth. He had a voice for radio. "Let me give it to ya straight. We can't have you on the ballot. Frank Young's gonna be our guy. I don't know why you decided you want to be the alderman. Maybe you're tired of being the precinct captain, I dunno. I do know, if you run, you'll split the ticket, and that might hurt Young's chances. We can't have that."

Gill paused, waiting for a response. There was none.

Gill took another swig, set the glass down, and rubbed the rough edges along the wood-top bar. "I like you, Ernie. Always have. You should know that there are powerful people unhappy with this situation. They're the kind that stalk and hover over politicians like a murder of crows. They want you to stop your campaign right now. They will do what it takes to do that. I told them I would handle it." Gill leaned forward, his eyes widened and the corner of lips inched up. "How would you like to be on the payroll in the municipal court's office? You won't have to do anything, really. It pays two hundred and fifty dollars a month. All you have to do is walk away from your campaign."

Ernie smiled and scratched his head. "I dunno know, Joe."

Gill smiled, his white teeth glistening in the smoky tavern. "You think about it." He downed his drink, scooted off the stool, and said, "But don't think about it too long. We need an answer by the end of the week. See ya around." Gill put his hat on and walked out the bar.

— — —

Eddy woke in the middle of the night. He lay on his stomach and wiggled his leg, which usually helped him fall back to sleep, but this time, it didn't work. Thoughts raced by like Hank Wyse fastballs. By this time tomorrow he'd be in his own bed at home. He would have three full days to catch up with friends and his girlfriend, whom he had written three letters to. Maybe some of the girls at home who'd been going with the guys who'd gone away to fight had problems. Did they get lonely? And the girls sometimes found other guys and they'd write what everybody called "Dear John" letters. Those girls double-crossed their guys. Ma said they broke the hearts of these men and were kinda like traitors. Eddy wondered if Maria was a traitor too. Did she double-cross him since he was away in military school? Tomorrow, he'd find out.

"Puttana," Nonna called those traitors. Ma would never say what that meant. His mouth watered just thinking about his mom's cooking, the scent of garlic and tomatoes swirling in the air as he shoved a forkful of her homemade spaghetti into his piehole, sauce spilling on his shirt. The Cubs would play at least two home games, maybe four if it went to seven games. How many World Series tickets could he buy and resell and how much would he make? How was he going to sneak into Cubs Park with Julius? Wrigley would probably hire an army of those goofy Andy Frain ushers in their dumb blue uniforms for the World Series. They had walkie talkies. What a bunch of morons, dressing in those stupid gold stripes like they were coppers and telling fans they can't sit in seats unless they have their tickets.

"Hey, Eddy, you awake?" Wyatt whispered.

"Yeah, I can't sleep."

"Me neither," Wyatt said as he leaned his head over his bed, looking upside down into Eddy's lower bunk. "My dad said he got me a job cleaning the stands at Cubs Park. He said I'll get to sit in the dugout before the game."

"Maybe I'll see ya there. I'm gonna sneak into one of the games with Julius. Come over to my dad's tavern, and I'll get you free hot dogs and drinks."

"Deal," Wyatt said as he extended his hand. Eddy shook it.

The cannon exploded, and the bugle blared. The cadets dropped down from their bunks like monkeys. They dressed and raced to the latrine, then down to the slab for calisthenics. They marched to breakfast, then dressed in uniform, and went to class. Same routine, every day.

After an hour enduring Lt. Seago's physiology class, the restless cadets strolled into Lt. Jim Martin's literature class. Just as the cadets took their seats, Lt. Martin stormed in. He was carrying a radio, one of those portable jobs. Everyone quieted and sat to attention. No one wanted a demerit now.

"Most of you cadets are from the Chicago area and are leaving later today," he said. "I know your minds are on the World Series. You can listen to the game in class, but you must stay in your seats and remain quiet."

Lt. Martin plugged in the radio and turned it on. Game two of the World Series was already underway.

"So, here's the situation," said the announcer. "In the top of the fourth inning, Peanuts Lowry grounded out. Cavarretta doubled off pitcher Virgil Trucks. Andy Pafko grounded out. The game is scoreless but the Cubs are threatening with two outs.

Several cadets forgot they were in class and yelled as if they were already at Wrigley Field. Lt. Martin turned down the volume. "This will be the last warning, cadets." The lieutenant turned the volume back up.

After the play, Lt. Martin turned down the volume. "This will be the last warning, cadets." The lieutenant turned the volume back up.

"Now here's big, bad Bill Nicholson, and he's got that great big chew of tabacca stored away in his jowl there, just as he usually does. And there's that wide stance and that chin stuck out at the pitcher and that menacing attitude as he switches his bat back and forth across the plate..."

"Pssst, Eddy. I'll bet you a nickel Nicholson gets on base," whispered Rosengarten, who sat across the aisle. Nicholson was Rosengarten's favorite player. Eddy nodded. The room was silent.

"The pitch is swung on. It's foul right outside of first base. Bill had a stellar Game 1, with three RBIs. Detroit fans are eerily quiet. Here's the pitch a little low again. Trucks trying to get that strike past big Bill Nicholson. He was trying for the outside corner, and he just missed it. That raises the count to one ball and one strike. Here's the big pitch. Nicholson swings. It's a solid hit straight up the middle to the center fielder. Doc Cramer has it. Cavarretta rounding third. Here comes Cramer's throw. He's got a good arm. It's gonna be close, but Cavarretta scores! Cubs draw first blood."

Rosengarten pounded his fist on the desk. Eddy sunk his head into his hands. A cadet entered the room and gave Lt. Martin a document. The lieutenant turned down the radio and announced, "Pareti, go see Lt. Andrews in his office. Now."

— — —

Sweat raced down the side of Ernie's cheeks. Every move he made mattered, the orders were coming in fast and furious, and he could hardly keep up, even with two bartenders and Bobby, who was working the grill. Margaret had gone upstairs to make more beef sandwiches. It seemed the entire city decided to drink and listen to game three of the World Series at Ernie's Bleachers. The last Tiger batter came to the plate in the bottom of the ninth with the Cubs ahead, three to nothing. The tavern became as quiet as church service during communion.

"Mayo, incidentally, is a Detroit boy. He's playing in his own back yard."

"Ernie, turn up the radio," Walter shouted.

Ernie turned the volume higher. Bar patrons listened as if the president was about to speak.

"Mayo is the last hope for Steve O'Neal and the Tigers in this third game, and Passeau, who has a beautiful one-hitter in the fire, is anxious to close it out. Here it comes. Mayo swings at it. Hits it foul on the ground down the third baseline. Two strikes. Passeau is one strike away from hanging a shutout over the Tigers. One man has pitched a one hit game in one series. He was with the Cubs. That was Reulbach back in nineteen hundred and six. Two strikes on Mayo. Here's the pitch. It's a little too high. Now the count is two balls, two strikes. Two outs, nobody on in the bottom half of the ninth inning. Chicago with the victory in their grasp and Passaeu working hard for it. Mayo fouls it off. The count remains two balls and two strikes."

Margaret roughly tapped Ernie's shoulder, holding what looked to be a letter. "I just got the mail," she yelled above the bar noise. "It's from Eddy. You've got to read this."

Ernie waved her off as he listened to the radio.

"Mayo swings on one. There's a high foul coming up in back. Back comes the catcher, Mickey Livingston. He's under it. He's got it. The ball game is over!"

The bar exploded in cheers. A patron tried to make an order, but Ernie couldn't hear it. He pointed at the beer taps until the patron nodded. After he poured the beer, Margaret handed him the letter and shouted as loud as she could, "Read it!"

Ernie opened it and read:

Dear parent,

I regret to inform you that your son failed to meet the minimum requirements for his weekend pass and will, therefore, not be home this weekend.

We require a cadet to be doing passing work in every subject he is taking. Your son has not met this requirement. We certainly do not wish you to feel that your son will not pass this year. We believe that, in depriving him of this weekend pass, he will realize the seriousness of a failing mark and will settle down to doing better work in the future. We appreciate the fact that it will be a disappointment to you as well as your son, but we know you will understand and will cooperate with us in remedying the situation.

There are fifteen cadets who failed to qualify for this weekend pass. We have, therefore, decided to permit these cadets to take a pass next weekend. They have the full week to make up their deficiencies, and all should be qualified by next Friday. The same train connections will be used as for this weekend.

I'm terribly sorry about this, but it is for the boys' own good.

Respectfully yours,
Col. M. Mulligan, Supt.

Ernie stood there shaking his head, ignoring the customers screaming for more beer.

— — —

Lt. Andrews sat at his desk and didn't look up when Eddy walked in and saluted. The lieutenant pointed to a chair.

Eddy slid into a wobbly metal chair that had foam peeling from a cut cushion and wiped his sweaty palms on his pants leg. He looked up at the lieutenant, who seemed to be sitting a couple of feet higher in a comfortable leather-bound chair. There were no windows and no pictures hanging from the battleship gray walls. The only light in his office came from a lamp placed near the cadets' chair as if it might, at any second, be pointed on the cadet for interrogation.

Seconds that seemed like hours passed. The lieutenant had his head down, calmly flipping pages in a gradebook. He clucked his tongue and cricked his neck. He finally looked up, clasped his hands together and leaned over them. He cleared his throat.

"The colonel tells me your parents own a bar across from Wrigley Field," the lieutenant asked in a soothing tone. "He says you told him they'll get a lot of business tomorrow when the Cubs play at Wrigley? You think they will?"

What a dumb question, Eddy thought. *He must be a momma's boy, living like he does in in an apartment on campus with his mother.*

"It'll be a record. They're gonna need me. That's for sure. Sir." He almost forgot to say sir. Or was it, lieutenant sir? Eddy had been at the school for almost a month, and he was still confused by all the ranks.

"Uh-huh. Are you aware of Roosevelt's furlough requirements?"

Eddy gulped. The question alarmed him. This can't be happening. "We were told we could go home this weekend."

The lieutenant sighed as he adjusted his specs. Eddy figured he'd never seen combat.

"Only cadets who meet the minimum academic requirements and have no outstanding demerits may be granted furlough. You have outstanding demerits, and you're failing," the lieutenant looked down at something on his desk, "Physiology and literature."

"I'm doing the best I can, sir." Eddy's body felt as if it were on fire.

The lieutenant cleared his throat again. "I've got good news and bad news. The bad news is I can't grant you furlough. I'm sorry. It's the rules. The good news is, if you get your grades up, you can have furlough next weekend, and I'm giving you riding privileges. I hear you're really good with the horses. You can start tomorrow. That's all. You're dismissed."

"But, sir, you gotta let me go. I've never been to the World Series." That was a lie. His father took him to see the Cubs play the Yankees in the 1938 series. He had been six, and the only thing he remembered was that DiMaggio hit a home run.

"That's the way the pickle squirts. You're dismissed," said lieutenant in a gruff tone.

Eddy's mind went numb. His legs grew weak, and for a second, he wasn't even sure how to get back to his barracks or whether he had the strength to walk. It must have been instinct, but Eddy, like a stray dog finding its way back home, found his barracks. He slammed the door behind him and nosedived into his rack. Wyatt and Rosengarten were packing.

"You're not gonna believe this, but our little genius, Julius, here can't go home. He has outstanding demerits," Wyatt said.

Julius was sobbing, his head buried in his pillow.

"He ain't alone. They won't let me leave this hellhole, either," Eddy said.

Wyatt shot a look at Eddy as if he was about to say, "I'd eat my shoe if you got furloughed." Instead, the captain of the football team held his tongue and said, "That's a tough break, boys. It's not fair. I'll bring ya back something. Promise."

Wyatt and Rosengarten then walked out the room and gently closed the door.

Eddy sat on the edge of his bed and rubbed Julius's back. "I'm sorry, Julius. This is all my fault. I got you in trouble. What can I do to make it up?"

Julius popped up, his face beet red and tears streaming down his face. "Run away with me."

Eddy stood up and scratched his head.

"I dunno, Julius. Where we gonna go?"

"To my uncle's house. He'll take us in. Come on. You hate this place, right? You owe me."

Eddy paced back and forth in the room. *What's the worst they can do*, Eddy thought. *Make ya walk the slab? Big deal.*

"There is a way to get outta here."

Julius sniffled and asked, "How?"

"You know the fire escape that looks like a slide behind the barracks? It goes all the way up to our floor and the escape door is in a room at the end of the hall. This place'll be a ghost town tomorrow, and chances are the two cadets in that room will be gone. When everyone's listening to the Cubs game, we go into that room and escape down the slide and sneak into the woods. No one'll see us, and we can hop on a train or a bus and get the hell outta here."

"That sounds swell," Julius shouted.

"Ssshhh, not too loud. But first, I wanna ride the horses."

BOTTOM OF THE NINTH

Eddy bolted out of bed, jumped into his clothes, and flew downstairs. He dashed out of the barracks and sped across the slab, racing to the barn as if he were rounding the bases toward home plate. The crisp, cool, early October air slapped his face. He hopped a white wood-board fence as easily as a turnstile at Cubs Park, and pushed open the stall door. He stepped inside the barn, his stomach growled. There was no time for breakfast.

"Eddy, ready for an early start, are ya?" Addair said while carrying a saddle. "Well, pick a horse and saddle up."

Eddy walked over to Chestnut's stall. He stroked the horse's neck. "I want Chestnut."

Addair dropped the saddle and scratched his head. "That's not a good idea. Chestnut's unpredictable. A little on the wild side. Does what he wants when he wants sometimes. He ain't a good horse to start off on. How 'bout Morgan?"

"No, Mr. Addair. I want Chestnut. I can handle him."

"All right then, Chestnut it'll be. Saddle 'em up."

In one motion, Eddy slid the halter over Chestnut's nose and flipped it behind the horse's ears. He ran his hand across Chestnut's back to check for sores or bumps. "Looks like you're ready to ride, Mr. Chestnut," Eddy said. Chestnut blinked and nickered.

Eddy placed a plaid blanket on the horse's shoulders and slid it to the center of its back. He lifted a saddle off the rack, and swung it over Chestnut's back. He walked around to the other side of the horse and buckled the girth as he had several times before. The image of Shirley sliding the halter over the team of horses behind his father's tavern flashed into his mind. She taught him how to drive a horse carriage and kiss. She's probably riding a horse in some rodeo right now.

Damn, she'd be proud of me now, he thought.

Several minutes later, Julius and another cadet, Nicky, strolled into the barn. They stood in the middle of the barn like the plebes that they were, unsure what to do next. Addair assigned them horses, and Eddy showed them how to saddle. The cadets walked the horses out of the barn, stepped on the stirrups and slid on top of their beasts.

"Remember, boys: hold onto the reins at all times," Addair said. "If ya wanna turn left pull the left rein and so on. An incorrect flick of the wrist can change the outcome of your direction like the difference between a foul ball and a home run."

Eddy wondered how the House of David players threw and caught a baseball on donkeys while holding the reins. He remembered that a few players on opposing teams fell off their donkeys as they tried to catch a ball. Maybe they flicked the reins in the wrong direction.

The cadets' horses trotted out of the corral and followed a marked trail that wound over several hills and into a wooded area. The slow staccato beat of the hooves pounding the dirt relaxed Eddy as he led the trio down the winding path. He felt taller, as if Chestnut's legs were his. A simple tug on the reins and the horse obeyed. It was different than riding in a horse carriage or on the bare back of a crazy-mean bull. Eddy had full control, and the horse under him was part of him.

Eddy began to sing. "Oh, give me land, lots of land, and the starry skies above. *Don't fence me in.* Let me ride through the wide-open country that I love..."

Eddy pointed to Julius, who sang, "Don't fence me in."

Eddy continued: "Let me be by myself in the evening breeze and listen to the murmur of the cottonwood trees, send me off forever but I ask you please..."

Eddy pointed to Nicky, who sang, "Don't fence me in."

As they sang, they ducked under low branches and crossed a creek, the horses' hooves splashed water, and climbed a steep embankment. Once they reached the top, the woods opened into a meadow the size of three football fields. Eddy pulled back the reins to stop Chestnut.

"You guys wait here. I'm gonna race Chestnut," Eddy said in an excited tone.

Eddy pressed his legs against Chestnut's side, and the horse started into a canter. He raised his body from the saddle, leaned forward, and pushed all of his weight on the stirrup and kicked again. The horse snorted and broke into a gallop.

Eddy yelled, "Charge!" His body rocked back and forth, and the wind whipped through his cowlicky hair. The reins jingled, and leather straps slapped across the saddle. Chestnut blazed straight ahead through tall grass, and his hooves like thunder beat against the ground in 4/4 time. Eddy reached a row of trees in no time and pulled the reins to the right turning the horse around and galloped across the meadow in the direction he came. Eddy pulled back on the reins, but Chestnut resisted with a buck. The horse relented as Eddy pulled harder and Chestnut slowed and then stopped in front of the cadets. It was exhilarating and better than any World Series.

Eddy's hair was mussed and eyes wide open. "That was aces!" he yelled, his voice hoarse from shouting.

"Let me try it," Julius roared. Before Eddy could say anything, Julius kicked his horse, Morgan, hard, and it bucked and bolted into a full gallop.

Julius panicked and dropped the reins. The boy hugged the horse's neck as it scampered into the meadow. Eddy chased after, shouting, "Julius, grab the reins!"

Julius cried out but wouldn't let go as his horse raced across the meadow. Eddy chased behind, screaming for Julius to take the reins. Julius slid off Morgan and fell to the ground. Chestnut, chasing behind, leaped over the boy. Eddy pulled the reins to the right, turned around, and headed toward Julius who was standing in the meadow, crying.

"Are you all right?"

Julius nodded. Julius's horse had turned around and headed back to the barn.

Nicky rode up. "Are you okay? What happened?"

"He dropped the reins when Morgan went into a full gallop," Eddy said.

"Dropped the reins? That doesn't make any horse sense," Nicky said with a laugh.

Julius squirmed. "The horse bucked me off."

"What? Yeah, sure," Eddy said as he dismounted. He bent over and cupped his hands. "Get on the back of my horse. I'll give ya a boost, cowboy."

Julius hesitantly placed his right foot into Eddy's hands and swung his left leg over Chestnut's back. Eddy mounted behind Julius and trotted back to the barn, with Nicky trailing behind.

The boys limped around the barn after dismounting.

"My ass is killing me," Eddy said, wincing in pain.

Nicky and Julius sat on a bale of hay, rubbing their legs.

"Ya boys have a bad case of saddle sores," Addair said, laughing. "I'll make men out of ya bug-eyed bastards."

Eddy had removed the saddle and halter from Chestnut and was feeding the horse hay when Nicky said, "Why did the traffic light turn red?"

"I dunno. Why?" Eddy responded.

"Because it had to change in front of people."

Eddy laughed, and Chestnut nipped his forefinger. "Ow! That hurt like a dog!"

Addair walked over and inspected Eddy's finger. It was red and swelling, but the skin was not broken.

"He just nipped ya. You're lucky man. The horse coulda chomped your whole finger off. It's gonna bruise real good. Go to the nurse and have her clean it and bandage it."

Eddy, Julius, and Nicky walked across the parade grounds to the nurse's station. On the way there, Eddy jokingly marched through the gate and declared himself a cadet. Julius and Nicky followed.

After the nurse cleaned and bandaged the wound, the boys ate lunch at the mess hall and hurried back to their barracks. It was study period, but Eddy had no plans to study. Game four was about to start.

Julius packed clothes inside his duffel bag. "Why aren't you packing? We're going soon."

Eddy stood at his desk, writing a letter. "Are you kidding? I can't go anywhere. My ass is killing me."

"Are you bailing on me?" Julius asked, his voice cracked.

Before Eddy could answer, two upperclassmen walked in. The taller one said, "Which one of you has a radio?"

"Who wants to know?" Eddy shot back.

"I wanna know. Someone took the radio in the rec room. We wanna hear the game," the taller cadet said, his eyes darting around the room in search of the radio. He saw it on the desk and placed his hands on it. "We'll take that, thank you."

Eddy grabbed it at the same time, and the two tussled for control. "Lay off, Henry. It's his radio," the shorter cadet said.

Henry let go.

"Tell ya what, boys. Let's listen to the game here," said the shorter cadet. "Whaddya think?"

Eddy ignored him, and continued writing a letter.

Henry grabbed the letter. He held it up and read it:

Dear Maria

Thanks for writing. Well, we lost are first football game last Saturday twenty to nothing, but we'll win the next one, I hope. Your my favor girlfriend, I hope, unless you didn't find another boyfriend while I was away. But I don't think you would double-cross me, I hope.

Today, we were riding the horses fast, we were galloping them. Boy, my ass is red, don't tell my mom I'm cursing in this letter. I'm standing up writing this letter, because my ass hurts. I won't be able to ride tomorrow because my ass will still hurt. School is getting harder every mineut. There is an asshole in my room right now, and he's getting me in trouble. He's a moron. Well good-by and write some more.

Your boyfriend
Eddy

"Asshole? John, this plebe called me an asshole, and he can't even spell."

"The game, Henry. We wanna hear the game," John said.

"We're supposed to be in study period. You can't be in here," Julius said.

"We won't tell anyone if you don't. All the bigwigs are listening to the game at the sergeant's quarters," John said.

"I'll betcha a dime the Cubs win this game," Eddy said.

"You're on," John said.

Eddy reached under his mattress and pulled out a pack of Lucky Strikes. "I've got five cigs left in here. Anyone wanna buy 'em?"

"How much?" Henry said.

Eddy shot a lopsided grin. "Thirty cents."

"Are you kidding? I could buy a whole pack for that. I'll give ya a dime."

"You know the supply store is closed this week. Twenty cents and that's my last offer."

Henry grimaced. He dug out two dimes and handed them to Eddy. He swiped the pack out of Eddy's hand.

Eddy turned on the radio and shifted the dial until he found the game. It was the fourth inning.

"Here's Eddy Mayo, bats left handed. The left-handed pitcher Prim delivers, fastball strike. Mayo's an interesting character. He's inventing sunglasses for infielders. He's also taking a correspondence law course. He's busy. Pitch is low and outside to him, ball two. Two balls, one strike. Prim working with considerable deliberation. He's taking his time, probably has a pattern in his mind on the kind of game he wants to weave. He's working hard on it. Now it occurs to him he wants the resin bag, so he turns around and picks that up, rubs his left pitching hand on it. Now, Mayo's a little tired of waiting, and he backs out of the batter's box, uses the bat to knock the mud out of his spikes, not too much mud because the infield is in good shape..."

Several cadets barged into the room and were greeted with an enthusiastic shush. "The game is on," said Henry.

A dozen cadets hunched over the radio, sopping up the sound. One of them stood by the door as a lookout.

Julius nudged Eddy and motioned for him to step outside the room. "Let's go. I'm ready to get outta of this hellhole."

Eddy smiled. "My ass is killing me, and my hand hurts." He held up his bandaged hand. "Not a good time."

"You promised."

Eddy took a drag from his cigarette, squinted his eyes, and said, "What's the hurry? We got two days."

▭ ▭ ▭

Game four blasted on the radio, drowning out the low chatter of patrons at Ernie's Bleachers. It was standing room only. The Cubs were losing four to nothing in the seventh inning and the crowd in the stadium and the tavern were growing restless. Ernie was working on two hours sleep. He had kept the tavern open all night, serving coffee, Danish and sandwiches to hundreds of people lined up around Wrigley Field who had waited all night for the ticket office to open. Margaret was upstairs napping. She was expected to come back down when the game ended.

Bobby took orders from the window and worked the grill. Like his dad, he had an eye for making a buck. He had stayed up all night selling blankets, old wooden crates he found in the basement, and playing cards with mismatched backs he fished out of a junk drawer to fans camped out around the ballpark, grumbling in the nighttime chill. He paid two neighborhood kids to stand in line and took their place to buy six tickets. He hawked them at a two hundred percent profit. Business was good.

A paunchy old man wearing a patch over his left eye stepped inside. He wore overalls and a wool Brixton hat crooked to the side. He sauntered up to the bar and yelled, "I'll take your coldest Fox Deluxe and bill it to Mr. Wrigley."

"Who are you?" Ernie shouted.

"One-Eye Connolly! You heard of me. I'm the world's greatest gate crasher."

"Sure, you are," Ernie said sarcastically as he handed the man a beer. "You're not a Wrigley man. That'll be a dime."

Connolly laughed. "I was a Wrigley man about a minute ago. Andy Frain hired me as a ticket taker. Then some Johnny-come-lately tried to crash the gate, sayin' he was Phil Wrigley, I own the joint. I said, 'Baloney,' and wouldn't let 'em through. Turns out, it was him, and he canned me right there. The men in blue whisked me out like yesterday's garbage. Don't matter. I'll crash their gates just like I done in the '29 series." The one-eyed braggard thrust his hands in his pocket and pulled out a dime. He handed it to Ernie, and took a long swig.

A short wiry man smoking a stogey and wearing a checkered suit and stained tie turned to Connolly and said, "Ain't that funny. Wrigley hired me just today."

"Doin' what? And why ain't you there?" Connolly replied.

"I just got into town. See, Wrigley's gonna pay me to give the Tiger's the evil eye. I'll put a hex on the bums just like I did to Hitler." The man washed his throat with gin and then squinted his left eye while his bloodshot right eye bulged.

"Hitler? Whaddya talking about?" Ernie said.

"I was in the army and they shipped me to Paris where I put the evil eye to work long distance on Hitler, and two weeks later, the bum blew his brains away."

A hush fell over the bar. The last batter for the Cubs in the bottom of the ninth was at the plate and the Cubs were down four to one.

"With two outs in the ninth folks are starting to go for the exit gates. It's Nicholson up there. He struck out twice, hit back to the pitcher in the seventh inning and was thrown out. Bill Nicholson is hitless for the afternoon. Dizzy Trout trying to wind this one up. Trout gets ready, flips it in there. Nicholson swings on it. There's a tremendously high foul ball up in back. Paul Richards comes back to the screen and has it for the out. That's all in the ninth inning. The ball game is all over."

A loud groan in the bar synchronized with the fans' groans in the stadium. Ernie shook his head and said to Connolly and the evil eye, "I wish my son was here. He'd love your stories. If I had a nickel every time he snuck into Cubs Park, I'd be a rich man. Get on his bad side he'd give you the evil eye."

"Did he sneak into the game today?" Connolly asked. "He certainly didn't get by me."

"No, we shipped him off to military school," said Ernie with a worried half smile.

"If the boy can sneak into Wrigley Field, I bet you a wooden nickel he can sneak out of that school," Connolly said and then took another long swig of his beer.

As Ernie poured another customer's beer, he replied, "Nah. I think Eddy's learned his lesson. You can't run from your troubles."

The next day, Eddy gulped down his oatmeal and eggs, rushed out of mess, ran across the slab, and saddled Chestnut. He rode his favorite horse all morning and afternoon. He had lost track of time, and by the time he limped back to his room, game five was over. A few cigarette butts littered the windowsill and paper cups were strewn about the floor. Only one cadet remained. It was Henry, who sat at the window, smoking a cigarette. Julius sat on his bunk, his duffel bag on his lap.

"There ya are, Puff Puff," Henry said as he was leaving the room. He gave Eddy the nickname on account of how he could blow smoke rings. "Cubs lost, eight to four. One more game and the Tigers take it. And by the way, I stopped the other cadets from taking your radio. You're welcome."

Eddy was too tired and sore to respond. He nosedived into his bed and closed his eyes. Julius walked over to Eddy's side of the room and flung a duffel bag on Eddy's bed.

"I packed for you, and I did a dry run. The room is empty, and the fire escape door is unlocked. We can slide down it tonight and get outta here," Julius said in a high-pitched whiny voice.

"Not tonight."

"Why not?"

"Cuz my ass is still sore. That's why."

Julius's stood there, down in the mouth, sniffling. Eddy sighed at the sound of his roommate's sniveling. He leaned up on his elbows and picked at a scab on his knee. He then threw Julius's duffel back off his bed.

Julius's chest heaved, and his lips crumpled into a sob. He ran to his bunk and collapsed into it, curling into a fetal position.

"All right," Eddy finally said. "Tomorrow. Wait until tomorrow during game six."

Julius sat up. He dried his eyes and managed a smile. Eddy smiled too.

═ ═ ═

Eddy woke early the next morning and hurried to the horse barn. When he reached the stable, he saw an upperclassman cadet leaning against the barn door.

"Where do ya think you're goin', Puff Puff?" the cadet said, smiling. "Get back to slab. Time to walk off your demerits."

"I'll do it later. Promise," Eddy pleaded.

"You got away with too much already. Go!" the cadet demanded, pointing to the slab behind them.

A guard on the slab watched with amusement as Eddy marched back and forth, muttering vulgarities under his breath. "What a shithole." Thoughts of running away filled his head. If he ran away from Roosevelt, where would he go? Not home. Why did he promise to take off with that crybaby? How could he make it out there with a ten-year- old at his side? Running away with Elmore didn't work out. He'd eaten crappy food in a messy house and had to sleep in a tent on the hard ground. After some redneck had hustled him in pool, Eddy'd had nothing left. He had been hungry back then and missed home.

He'd never forget the look on his dad's face when the two met on a dirt road somewhere near Grand Rapids. Surprise, relief, and mixed with anger. Even though his dad had been madder than he'd seen in a long time, the whole ride home on the bus with him felt like his dad really loved him.

The guard on concrete duty blew a whistle. It was time for grub and then study period.

═ ═ ═

The usual crowd loitered in Eddy's barracks, waiting for game six to start. Julius leaned into Eddy's ear and whispered, "I stashed our duffel bags in the room with the fire escape."

The plan was to sneak into the room during the game, slide down the escape hatch, and catch a bus to the train station.

During the bottom of the fifth inning, Julius nudged Eddy's elbow and motioned to the door. Eddy held up a forefinger as he listened to the game. Stan Hack had just singled, scoring two runs. The room erupted in cheers. Henry bought another cigarette off Eddy, who was making a killing, selling cigarettes. The Cubs were up four runs until the eighth inning when Cubs starting pitcher, Hank Wyse, fell apart. He walked Bobby Swift. Then Hub Walker doubled. Joe Hoover reached first on an error, scoring Swift. Mayo singled and was thrown out trying for two, but Walker scored. After Cubs manager pulled Wyse and replaced him with Ray Prim, Doc Cramer hit a sacrifice fly, scoring Hoover. Greenburg tied the game with a solo homer.

"Ah crap," Henry mumbled. The mood in the barracks grew grim. The game went into extra innings and it wasn't until the bottom of the twelfth inning that Eddy noticed Julius was gone.

Eddy rushed out of his barracks and down the hallway. He burst into the room with the fire escape and saw Julius climbing into the slide. He ran over and tried to grab Julius's shirt, but it was too late. The boy was on his way down.

"Julius. Are you down there?" Eddy's voice echoed inside the fire escape that wound around like a water slide. Eddy heard footsteps approaching and the sound of Lt. Andrews voice. The doorknob turned.

▬ ▬ ▬

All eyes hypnotically watched the radio perched on a shelf in the corner of Ernie's Bleachers, listening to the announcer's excited voice. The tavern was as quiet as Wrigley Field in the middle of the night. Hack came to bat with two outs in the bottom of the twelfth with a man on first. Ernie could hear the floor creak. Just then, the screen door squeaked open. Two burly men with hats crooked to the side burst in and, without breaking stride, stepped up to the bar and glowered at Ernie. They didn't seem to care about the game. The taller one leaned across the bar top and said, "Remember us?"

Ernie nodded.

The man riveted his head in the direction of the jukebox near the front door and said, "I'm glad you saw it our way and took our juke. Smart man. Everybody's happy, right?"

Ernie nodded again. There was a long pause as the men gazed at the radio that filled the vacuum.

"That's two outs and here comes Stanley Camfield Hack. Now, let's take a look at what Hack has done today. He's worked the pitcher for a walk three times. The other four times he's gotten a single. He's hit twice to center field and once to left field…"

The taller man nudged his partner and said, "Say, Nicky, looks like he ain't gonna flap his lips." They laughed, and then Nicky said, "I think he's got the jumps. You have any idea why we're here?"

Before Ernie could answer, Margaret hurried over. "What do you two want now? Can't you see we're busy."

"It's all right, Marge. Let me handle this," Ernie said, gently rubbing his wife's arm.

"It's you. What a mouth you got," Nicky said. "This doesn't concern you."

"It sure the hell does. I own this place too, and I have a say on what goes on here."

"Then you're gonna have to face the music along with him," Nicky said, stabbing Margaret with a sadistic stare.

"What do you guys want?" Ernie asked, his voice firm.

The men smiled at each other, and then Nicky said, "The Outfit sent us to give you a warning, and you had better listen."

— — —

As the door opened, Eddy jumped into the escape slide that was more like a tunnel.

"Hey, get back here," Lt. Andews shouted. He peered inside the tunnel and yelled again. Eddy slid down about twenty-five feet when he bumped into Julius. It was like finding a stray ball stuck in a factory gutter.

"Now we're in trouble," Julius moaned. His nervousness showed. There was too much white in his eyes.

"Don't worry about it. They don't know you're here," Eddy whispered. "I'll go up. Wait about twenty minutes and then you climb up and go to the room."

A cadet at the bottom yelled up through the tunnel, "Lt. Andrews, I think he's still in there."

"Eddy Pareti, is there a fire? Are you on furlough? You forgot your duffel bag. Come on up and get it," Lt. Andrews said in a gleeful tone.

As Eddy climbed the tunnel the thought of marching on the concrete didn't bother him. It was something that had become as natural as throwing a ball. Military school was like that bug crawling around the flashlight—things were not as scary as they appeared. You just have to learn to see things how they really are.

— — —

Nicky leaned in and said in a rigid tone, "We collect politicians like bananas, by the bunch. And you ain't one of them. Understand?"

"Whoever said I wanted to be connected with you?" Ernie said confidently.

"Don't get cute with me," Nicky snarled. "Do you know who you dealin' with?"

"Now you listen to me, buster. You aren't going to push us around anymore," Margaret howled.

"Get a load of this dame," Nicky laughed. "I don't know who's boss."

"Why are you keeping me in suspense? What is it you want?" Ernie demanded.

"Okay, I'll give it ya straight," Nicky said. "Drop out of the race. You ain't our guy."

"The hell he will. He's going to run for alderman, and I'll see to it that he wins," Margaret yelled.

"Did you read about John Hoellen?" Nicky asked.

Ernie and Margaret didn't respond. The bar grew quiet again.

"It's one and two on Stanley Camfield Hack, one of the greatest third baseman in the history of baseball. There's a throw to first and Shuster has to dive in on his stomach. He was traveling right there on the pit of his stomach, sliding and reaching for that bag."

"You ain't flapping your lips now, are ya?" Nicky said with a menacing grin. "We told Hoellen not to run, but he ignored us." He turned to his partner and said, "Can you believe a button on his coat saved him from that shotgun blast."

Nicky paused, and glanced up at the radio that blared from the top shelf above the grill.

"Here's the pitch to Hack. It's fouled off. Hack busted his bat on that. Hack goes trotting over to the Cubs dugout, which is just opposite third base, to get a new bat. He's gonna pick up the bat that he himself personally selects. Little Jimmy Shalick is the batboy for the Cubs, finds one for him. Hack looks at it, says it's all right. Now, he's beating the handle end of it on the ground just to make sure it rings true 'cause I doubt Hack has ever been up to bat in a more important spot than this one right here."

Nicky turned to his partner. "You remember what happened to Prignano a decade ago? He had the balls to defy Nitti's order to not run for ward committeeman. He got it just before New Year's Day." Nicky looked at the radio again.

"Now Shuster's breaking. Hack hits it out into left field, and it bounces over Greenberg's head, and it's rolling towards the wall, and Shuster's rounding third and Shuster comes into score, and the Cubs win with two outs in the bottom of the twelfth inning and a man on first."

The tavern broke into cheers. Walter, who was sitting next to Kitty at the bar, hollered, "It's that damn evil eye guy. He did it again!"

"What do you mean again?" Kitty yelled over the noise.

"Remember in the seventh inning, Chuck Hostetler rounded third and was going to score, but he fell flat on his face?" Walter screamed. "That kind of thing in baseball is unheard of. Had he scored, the Cubs would have lost the World Series. Hostetler got the evil eye. No doubt in my mind."

The bar noise drowned out the conversation between Ernie, Margaret, and the two goons. Nicky pointed to Ernie and then made a cut motion across his neck. Walter, the bar's anointed bouncer, was sitting within earshot of the conversation, but he and Kitty next to him were glued to the game and had no idea what was going on.

The roar of the crowd in the tavern and at Wrigley rang out across the whole north side of Chicago as Nicky and his partner left the bar. Nobody seemed to notice them or heard their threats. It was as if they were ghosts.

— — —

A gust of cold October air smacked Eddy's ruddy face as he paced the slab. Game seven of the World Series was underway, and he was stuck marching, the soles of his shoes slapping across the crumbling concrete. The guard on duty fidgeted, scanning the grounds as if he were ready to beat it.

Someone opened a third-floor window and shouted, "Eddy, the Tigers scored five runs in the first. They pulled Bowery." It was Henry, who gave him the lowdown. He was in Eddy's barracks with other cadets listening to the game. "Cubs are batting now."

Eddy and the guard looked up and heard a crackling sound. Henry placed the radio on the windowsill and turned the volume full blast. Other cadets poked their heads out to laugh at Eddy, who they dubbed the king of the slab.

"One ball, no strikes, Newhouser gets ready, throws a fast one in there. It's hit out into left center field. Cramer chases it, picks it up. Johnson's on his way to second. Here comes the throw. It's not in time, and Johnson slides, and he's safe at second with a double."

Eddy and the guard let out a whoop. But they quickly regained their composure as a lieutenant hurried past, most likely on his way to the superintendent's quarters to listen to the game. He didn't notice the radio.

"Newhouser throws at the plate. Peanuts Lowry bunts it back to the mound. It's picked up by Newhouser. He bobbles it for a moment, picks it up.

Throw not in time. Chicago now have runners on first and second. Here's Phil Caveratta batting left handed. An error is being charged to Newhouser. Down it comes. Phil swings on it. it's a base hit down right field. Johnson comes whistling by third and comes in to score and Lowry slides into third. Now, Chicago has runners on first and third. One out. Detroit ahead five to one."

Eddy kneeled down on one knee to listen. He squeezed his wooden rifle and mumbled, "Stay relaxed, Pafko. Keep the rally going."

"Now standing up at the plate is Andy Pafko, who's hitting two-oh-eight. He takes the first curve. It's in there for a strike. Pafko swings on the next pitch. There's a ball hit to short. It's played back to Mayo for one out. Throw to first for two outs. And that's all for Chicago in the bottom of the first."

Eddy threw up his arms and yelled, "Damn it to hell." Eddy and the guard slumped on the slab and smoked cigarettes, listening to the game. On occasion, someone important would walk by, and the guard would wave to the third floor to turn down the radio and hide their smoking. Eddy would march, and the guard would snap to and bark at Eddy's drilling. "Step to. Keep that back straight!"

Newhouser was dominating the Cubs. The Tigers scored a run in the second and seventh innings and two more runs in the top of the eighth. Eddy felt weak.

"Now here's the situation. There's two out in the eighth. Lowery's at third. Caveratta's at first base and the count on Bill Nicholson is one ball, two strikes. Now the left-handed batter, Nicholson, is in there and his jaw is stuck out at Newhouser. He pitches low and outside. Two balls. Two strikes, Two outs. Newhouser stretches, Nicholson swings on it. Foul down the first baseline. Detroit has a lead nine to two. This game like all baseball games, and that's one of thrilling aspects. This great American pastime is not over until the last man is out. No one is saying that to himself more sharply than Nicholson at the plate right now. Swings on one into center field for a hit. It goes to the right of Cramer. Lowery already scored. Caveratta is rounding third and holding up, and Nicholson's in second with a double."

Eddy and the guard popped up as if they had been doing jumping jacks. Cheers came from the third floor and even from the superintendent's quarters. Eddy swiped his sweaty palms on his uniform. His legs felt heavy, and his stomach was doing somersaults.

"The score is nine to three, and the batter is Mickey Livingston, batting right handed. He's one for three for today. He has driven in four runs in this series. He has eight hits on twenty-one times up. The pitch is good for a strike. So it's two strikes on Livingston. Runners on second and third. Two outs in the bottom of the eighth. The Cubs trying to rally."

Eddy kneeled and recited a couple of Hail Marys.

"Newhouser pitches high inside. The next pitch, Livingston swings. Strikes out. And Newhouser rips through his ninth strikeout of the ball game."

Eddy felt as if someone had punched him in the gut. Everything grew quiet and still. Even the wind stopped blowing. The Cubs were down six runs with one more inning to go.

"Close the window. We don't wanna hear the game," Eddy yelled.

Eddy marched. Maybe if he didn't hear the game, the Cubs would miraculously score six runs in the bottom of the ninth. The guard slumped against the wall.

After twenty more agonizing minutes of Eddy drilling, wondering about the game, because it did matter—win or lose—he knew it was over. Cadets, teachers, and staff slowly filed out of buildings. No one was smiling.

— — —

Eddy curled in his bunk and stared at the ceiling. When Wyatt and Rosengarten returned that night, they were all smiles.

"Did ya miss us?" Wyatt said. He set down a bat he was holding and reached into his duffel bag and pulled out a Cubs pennant. "This is for you, Julius. Straight from Wrigley Field."

Julius took it and held it up. "Thanks, Wyatt. I'll hang it on the wall."

"What about Eddy? Did you get him anything?" Rosengarten said.

"I sure did." He grabbed the bat, took a swing, and then handed it to Eddy, who sprung to his feet.

"For me? You should have."

Eddy moved to the corner of the room and took a few swings. He twirled the bat and swung it around his back to his left hand. The bat handle clipped the side of the desk but Eddy managed to hold on. He then balanced the bat handle with his forefinger for a few seconds, flung it up, and caught it. In one motion, he quickly swung the bat, let it go, and caught the handle after it made one rotation as if he were swinging through.

"Hey, Wyatt, you thinkin' what I'm thinkin'? Rosengarten said.

"Say, Eddy. Just spitballin' here, but you think you could do that with a rifle?" Wyatt asked.

Eddy laughed. "You kiddin?"

— — —

For weeks, cadets at Roosevelt prepared for homecoming. Faculty drilled the cadets ceaselessly in parade marches and maneuvers and inspections. Lt. Andrews must have had some kind of bet on the winner of the homecoming parade competition because he spent every possible waking moment working on Company G's parade routine. Eddy had hoped the lieutenant would order him to walk the slab. That way, his parents could see firsthand how they were getting their money's worth. But for some reason, the lieutenant had been easy on Eddy, who hadn't walked the slab since game seven of the series.

Shadows streamed across the parade grounds as the sun intermittently peaked through the clouds. Large oaks cast shadows around the perimeter of the field, and its bright yellow leaves rustled on branches that swayed lazily in a cool breeze as cadets in each company broke into groups, preparing to march in the homecoming parade. Company G was scheduled to go last.

"Attenshun!" Lt. Andrews barked. Company G cadets snapped to and quickly formed a line in pairs.

The lieutenant stood in front of Company G. His dour demeanor caused several cadets to freeze in fear. His starched uniform was neatly creased, and the bill of his white cap hung low, leaving shadows where his eyes should have been. "Weeks, we've been practicing for this moment. This is our chance to shine. We're the underdogs. So let's go, cadets. Show them what we're made of. Don't forget: the second you plebes walk through that gate, you will become honorary cadets."

Company G screamed in unison, "Rough Riders bold and strong, building men all life long."

As Company G cadets waited their turn, Eddy's eyes darted back and forth searching for his family. They were watching the parade along with hundreds of parents scattered on the opposite end of the field. Eddy had seen them the previous night.

His dad and brother had shaken his hand while his mother and sister hugged him for what seemed like eternity. They reeked of perfume, and the scent stayed on his football uniform during the game against the town's middle school team.

Company G had played twenty minutes during the halftime of the varsity game and scored every time they had the ball. It was such a rout that the coach stuck Julius in as halfback, and even he scored a touchdown.

Wyatt blew his whistle, and Company G marched onto the parade grounds. Eddy marched behind Wyatt. Julius was at the rear, banging on the drums, the sound crisp in 4/4 time.

As Company G turned to march through the gate, Wyatt blew the whistle again, and Eddy stepped in front, twirling his rifle around his back, over his head, and under his legs. Just before they entered the gate, Eddy tossed the rifle in the air, walked through the gate, and caught it. Company G won their parade stripes, and Eddy became a cadet.

Company G broke ranks, and the cadets met their families, posing for pictures. Eddy swaggered to his family. His mother and sister clapped. His Dad at short glance looked like Smilin' Stan Hack. His brother grinned and shook his head, his arms crossed.

Ernie wrapped his right arm around Eddy's shoulder. "Where'd ya learn how to spin a rifle like that?"

"I dunno, Dad. Around."

Lt. Andrews approached. "This young man was our secret weapon. Do you know Company G has never won the parade competition? I couldn't be prouder of Puff Puff. Um, I mean your son."

"Puff Puff? Why do they call you that, Eddy?" Margaret asked.

"I'll tell ya later, Ma. It's a long story."

Lt. Andrews clenched Eddy's shoulder and jokingly said, "At ease, Cadet," and walked away to mingle with other parents.

Margaret instructed Ernie and Eddy to pose next to the grounds' flagpole. As they did, Ernie squeezed Eddy's shoulder. "I'm so proud of you, Eddy, I think a few buttons just popped off my coat." There was a smile in his voice.

Eddy studied his dad as if he were conducting a white-glove inspection. His overcoat fit nicely around his slim build and it was not missing a button. His fedora sat evenly on his bald head, and his owl-like eyes smiled behind dark-framed glasses. He was almost as tall as his dad.

With a smile of recognition, Eddy realized how friendly his dad was to everyone around him, even to his wife. *How can he be so nice when he has to deal with drunks all day, fight with his wife, or put up with kids that don't listen?* Eddy wondered. *He runs a bar and somehow takes orders with his poor hearing. He only has a sixth-grade education but is a precinct captain, running for alderman. He's a somebody. Isn't that what everyone wants to be? A somebody?*

"Dad, are you hungry?" Eddy asked. "Let me take the family out to dinner. I know this nice place in town."

— — —

That night, the Pareti family ate a local diner called Ray's. They chose a table in front. Ernie sat at the head. Margaret and Florence sat on one side of the table, and Eddy and Bobby across from them. It was if they were at the dinner table at home. They gorged on greasy hamburgers and fries.

Bobby handed Eddy a ten-dollar bill. "You know I made one hundred and thirteen dollars during the World Series. Dad made a killin' too."

"Thanks, brother. Too bad I wasn't there. We could have made more dough."

Ernie placed his hand on Eddy's wrist. "Don't worry, Eddy. The Cubs will be back in the Series in three years. And you'll be there to see it."

"How do ya know that, Dad?" Eddy said.

"The Cubs were in the World Series in 1929, '32, '35, and '38, every three years," Ernie said, his voice raised in excitement as if he was revealing a big secret.

"How do ya explain '41 and '44 Dad?" Bobby asked.

"The war started in '41, so that threw off the pattern," Ernie said. "In '48 the Cubs will be back."

"Oh, Ernie, why do you have to be so silly?" Margaret said.

"But, Dad, all those times the Cubs were in the World Series, they never won," Eddy said. "When will they win?"

"Maybe in three years. Maybe in ten. Maybe next year. You'll see it in your lifetime. That's for sure."

EXTRA INNINGS

The sun beat down on Eddy as he leaned lazily against a Ford Packard, his legs sprawled on the parking lot gravel. He and Bobby had filled the parking lot in ten minutes.

It must be a record, Eddy thought. He guarded the front at the corner of Waveland and Sheffield while Bobby watched the alley. Horns blared intermittently as drivers circled Wrigley Field searching for a place to park. Car fumes choked the blossomed fragrance of a mid-May morning breeze. Oak and maples sprouted new leaves and dandelions littered rutted grass, some in a yellow blaze sprung through cracks in the sidewalk.

The stadium and scoreboard cast a shadow over parts of Sheffield, but sunlight streamed down Waveland under a baby-blue sky. Eddy blew smoke rings and squinted as he surveyed thousands of fans milling around the stadium, all of them trying to find a way to get in. The bleacher's gate had closed one hour before game time. It was standing room only.

Eddy shifted his legs and yawned. He had arrived home late last night from Roosevelt Military Academy and gone straight to bed. No matter how long he rocked his leg, he couldn't fall asleep. Wyatt wasn't above him, tossing and turning. He was kept awake by sounds he had forgotten. His bed squeaked, and the wooden floors in the hallway and dining room creaked. The bedroom window rattled each time the El train roared past: it was louder than the morning cannon.

His pillow and sheets smelled like soap. It had been nearly two years since he'd left home for military school. He came home on furloughs and holidays, but most of his time was spent at Roosevelt. It was an odd feeling, but he missed the academy he'd once called a hellhole. He was a star player on the basketball and football teams and earned respect from cadets, coaches, and even bullheaded Lt. Mulligan. He had just graduated eighth grade, and his parents had given him two choices, go back to Roosevelt for high school, or stay home and attend an all-boys Catholic School. He had to decide tonight.

Wyatt and Rosengarten had signed up for high school at Roosevelt. Julius, expected to become Company G team leader, had also enrolled for another year. They'd all begged Eddy to come back to Roosevelt.

Eddy scratched his forearm, the muscles more refined and noticeable. Hair sprouted all over his body, and he'd grown a half foot taller since he had been at the academy. His voice was deep. He rubbed his cheek and felt the stubbles on his face. He needed to shave.

Eddy turned to his right, and there was Gerace and Hootie Hale standing at attention with perfunctory salutes.

"What's buzzin', cousin? When did you get back?" Gerace said.

"Just got back yesterday. Hootie, you must have grown a half foot since the last time I seen ya."

Eddy slapped his pack of Lucky Strikes, and two cigarettes slid out. Without asking, he flipped one each to Hootie and Gerace and lit them with his Zippo lighter.

Gerace swung his arm around Hootie. "Hootie's a star on the baseball team. Crackin' home runs like Babe Ruth. He's a big shot. Even the Lakeview baseball coach went to his house and had dinner. Recruitin', they call it."

"Is that right?" Eddy said as he took a drag. "You threw like a broad last time we played."

"You still owe me a dime," Hootie said, smiling at Eddy's playful digs.

"You're not gonna start that again. It was two years ago, and you didn't strike me out."

"The bet was I'd get three strikes on ya," Hootie said.

"Yeah, yeah." Eddy took another puff off his cigarette. "Seen Warman around?"

Gerace brushed back his moppy hair. "You're not gonna believe this. Warman acts like he's king of the jungle, and he is." Gerace pointed down Sheffield. "He muscled his way under the El two blocks down and is parking cars right now. Some guy thought he was tough and challenged Warman for the spot. Warman hurt him bad. He's an animal, and everybody's afraid of him. Saw your girl Maria last week. She asked about you."

"Yeah, she ain't my girl no more. She stopped writing. Someone told me she's goin' with some guy from Lakeview."

"That's funny. She said you stopped writing her," Gerace said.

Eddy laughed and looked away. "There's more fish in the sea."

Gerace lightly jabbed Eddy. "Whaddya say we beat it and go to the ole hangout."

"Can't. I gotta watch these cars." Eddy took another drag, his eyes darting around the stadium.

There was a long pause in the conversation. Hootie and Gerace glanced around. "I've never seen so many colored people," Gerace said.

"Is there a Negro game today?" Hootie asked.

"They all look like they're going to church," Eddy remarked and then turned his attention across the street. His eyes locked on Clarence, who was wearing his signature overcoat and cowboy hat, waving off cars. Eddy placed his forefingers in his mouth and whistled. Clarence looked over, smiling.

Eddy hunched his shoulders, spread his arms, and shouted, "What's happening?"

Clarence's head bent back, and the big man burst into a bellow of laughter, his lips quivering like an opera singer belting out "The Star-Spangled Banner." He composed himself, cupped his hands over his mouth, and shouted, "Jackie Robinson's playin', the first Negro to play in the majors."

"All these people came to see one player, and he doesn't even play for the Cubs?" Gerace said. "He must be good."

"Why didn't we get him?" Hootie asked.

"The Cubs should get a guy named Buster Haywood," Eddy said. "He's a catcher. I've seen him throw out a runner stealing second, still squatting. He's a swell guy too."

As he puffed on his cigarette, Eddy realized he'd forgotten to give Clarence a ball that he got when he was the batboy for the Indianapolis Clowns. Haywood had autographed it. Where did he put it? Eddy wondered. Where did he put the mitt Novikoff had given him? Maybe they were buried in his closet somewhere or packed in a box in the basement. What did it matter? Clarence never asked for the ball. He probably forgot about it. What would he do with an autograph baseball, anyway? And what good is Novikoff's mitt? You don't need one to play softball or fast-pitch.

A boy dressed in a white suit ran up and waved a Cubs pennant. He jumped up and down and screamed, "Woo-woo!"

"Now that's a Cubs fan if ever I seen one," Eddy said.

"Does he know any words, or is he just gonna keep yellin' woo-woo?" Gerace asked.

A woman, dressed in a blue-and-red skirt and a white hat, ran over and grabbed the boy's hand and yanked him away. "I'm sorry about that. Come on, Ronnie, let's go see the game." As they walked away, the boy turned around and waved the pennant with his other hand and shouted, "Woo-woo!"

"Let's go see this Jackie Robinson guy," Hootie said.

"Who cares about the Cubs? They lost four in a row. They're not going anywhere. I'd rather play some pool," Gerace said.

"What about you, Eddy? You in?" Hootie asked.

Eddy exhaled a billow of smoke and shook his head. "I told you I gotta watch the lot."

"C'mon, Gerace'll watch it. Won't you?"

"If the pay is good, yeah," Gerace said.

"If you stay until we get back you can take half my cut," Eddy said.

Gerace shook Eddy's hand with a tight grip. "Come back when it's over. I don't wanna wait hours after the game for the last straggler to get his car."

"Don't worry 'bout it," Eddy said. "I can't last more than three innings."

"How we sneakin in, Eddy? Jump the turnstiles? Climb a fence?" Hootie asked.

"You kiddin me? What are we eleven? Follow me."

Eddy sauntered to the bleacher's gate. Hootie followed. A crowd of fans lingered around the entrance. An old man dressed in a red suit and blue-and-white tie limped over to Eddy and asked if he had tickets to sell. Eddy shook his head and walked up to an Andy Frain usher at the turnstile and whispered, "Hey, Mark, we need to see the boss."

"Hey, Eddy. Who sent ya?" Mark said, sporting a crooked mischievous smile.

"Ernie, and he's got what you need after the game, if you know what I mean."

Mark glanced over to Ernie's Bleachers and then looked at Eddy and said, "All right. Tell Ernie me and my pal are gonna see him after the game, if you know what I mean." Mark winked and stepped aside.

The turnstile clicked twice, and Eddy and Hootie raced up the ramp. The man in the suit and tie yelled at Mark. "Why you lettin' dem in? Dey didn't give you no tickets."

Eddy and Hootie weaved their way through the crowd and stopped behind two elderly Black women, who were sitting above the last row of the right field bleacher seats. They both wore white hats with wide brims and reeked of perfume. A white shawl was draped crooked over the shoulder of the shorter one.

Eddy fidgeted in his pocket for a smoke. Hootie wrung his hands as he nervously looked around the bleachers. The batter's box was empty.

Eddy craned his neck around the women. "Can you see who's batting next?"

"I dunno. Someone on the Dodgers," Hootie said.

"I know that. Who's up to bat?"

The woman wearing the crooked shawl turned, her forefinger over her lips. "Jackie Robinson."

Robinson's body rippled in sun and shade. He strutted to the plate, his steps brisk and purposeful and his head held high. He carried his bat in one hand as if it were an ax and stepped into the batter's box. He took big, level cuts. His eyes glared at the pitcher.

It seemed everyone in the stadium stood as if they were ready to sing the national anthem. The crowd was eerily quiet.

Robinson swung at the first pitch. A roar echoed in the stadium as he hit a high fly that landed foul in the upper box seats behind third base. There was a long applause after the hit. Robinson stepped back into the batter's box, facing lefty Johnny Schmitz. The stadium grew silent again. He took the next pitch for a strike, a fastball high and inside.

Eddy nudged Hootie and whispered, "Did ya know that Schmitz came up with the Cubs in '41 but missed the '45 World Series cuz he was in the navy? Can you imagine if the Cubs had him in the Series? They might've won. The manager calls him Bear Tracks cuz he has size fourteen feet."

The woman in the shawl swung around and scowled at Eddy, her forefinger over her lips.

"I read that Negro teams beat teams with Babe Ruth and other major leaguers in barnstorming games," Hootie said in a hushed tone.

The women turned again and, in unison, said, "Quiet, please." They swiveled back to watch the game, with hands over their mouths. Robinson was behind in the count with two strikes and no balls.

Schmitz delivered the next pitch. It was a curveball that dropped two feet. Robinson lunged at it and missed. A mix of jeers and groans filled the stadium. Robinson shot Schmitz a menacing stare and swaggered back to the Dodger's dugout.

A Black man wearing a straw hat and short-sleeved white shirt sitting in front of the women shouted, "Don't ya worry, people. He's anxious. He's a great player. He'll show 'em." He spoke in a raspy voice.

The next batter, Pete Reiser, grounded out, and the side was retired.

There was an eerie lull in the bleachers. Eddy looked around to see if anyone was making bets, but everyone seemed to keep to themselves.

Eddy smoked two squares in two innings. He tried to buy beer, but the beer vendor, Gravel Gertie, shook his head without a smile or funny remark.

Two innings passed, and there was no score.

"Someday, Eddy, I'm gonna be out there playin'," Hootie said.

"Is that right. Everybody says that, but you know how many actually make it?"

"You don't think I can?"

"I'm not saying that. Just sayin' the odds are against you. That's all."

Hootie took a puff off his cigarette, lifted his head, and exhaled. "What about you? I heard a scout had his eyes on you two years ago."

The old women jumped up and down, and the crowd roared to life. Robinson was at bat with a man on first. Schmitz threw two balls low on the outside. On the third pitch, Robinson hit a line drive straight to the center fielder that Pafko easily caught. More loud groans. The woman in the shawl grabbed her head as if she might pull out her hair.

Hootie turned to Eddy. "Are you gonna make tracks for that scout who wanted to talk to you?"

Eddy's shoulders jerked up. "I dunno. He said come back when I'm sixteen. That's next year. We'll see."

Hootie's eyes widened. "We'll see? You don't sound interested."

Eddy smiled and took a drag. He blew out a series of smoke rings, rings within rings. "I don't care where I play ball as long as I get to play. If it's at Wrigley, the park, or the schoolyard, it don't matter to me as long as I'm playing. You know I never played hardball. I only play softball."

"Softball's a waste of time," Hootie said.

"Yeah, maybe. But there's not a coach telling you what position to play or putting you on the bench so some crappy player can play instead of you," Eddy said.

Hootie shrugged and turned to watch the game. Eddy glanced around the bleachers and wondered which team the colored people were rooting for. They came to see Robinson, not the Dodgers. They lived on the South Side and were probably White Sox fans, he thought.

Gravel Gertie walked by screaming, "Beer! Get your ice-cold beer." It was always fun watching Gertie razz the fans, trying to sell beer or red hots. Eddy watched Gertie move up and down the aisle, yelling, "Beer!" but he wasn't joking with the fans today. He made no smart-aleck comments. He didn't smile at all. It was all business and out of the ordinary for the most popular vendor at Wrigley. Eddy wondered why.

— — —

In the bottom of the fourth, the Cubs were threatening, with men on first and second with one out. Lennie Merullo singled, scoring Bobby Scheffing from second. Don Johnson advanced to third on a throwing error. The next batter, Schmitz, hit a sacrifice to right, scoring Johnson.

Booming cheers erupted, and the stands rumbled. The old women and the man in the straw hat clapped and hooted.

The next batter was Stan Hack, and he walked, but the next batter, Eddy Waitkus, grounded out to short for the third out. Eddy nudged Hootie. "You ready to get outta here. I'm on my last cigarette."

"Naw, couple more innings," Hootie said.

The top of the next inning, Eddy knew who was coming to bat because there was a familiar hush in the stadium as if not to interrupt Robinson's concentration. It was as if he were taking a shot in a game of pool with everything on the line. There was one out, with a man on first. Robinson hit two foul balls, and all of a sudden the count was full. The old women were jumping up and down as if they had to use the restroom.

When Schmitz delivered, Eddy could hear the ball pop into the catcher's mitt low and outside for ball four. Fans politely applauded as Robinson jogged to first.

"He on base. He on base!" the old woman with the shawl shouted. "Y'all watch. He gonna steal second."

The man in the straw hat turned around and laughed. "He can't. They a man on second."

The next batter, Reiser, struck out in three pitches. The cheers from Cubs fans didn't seem as intense as they usually would be, especially at a sold-out game, Eddy thought. He nudged Hootie and said, "Seen enough?"

Hootie shook his head and gazed out into the field.

By the seventh inning, Eddy had smoked his last cigarette and was ready to leave without Hootie but the first three Dodgers reached base, and Robinson was at the plate. The stadium was so quiet he thought he heard players shouting from the dugout. A plane buzzed overhead. Schmitz worked a full count on Robinson. The old women shifted nervously, their hands covering their mouths. Everyone was standing. Schmitz threw, and the ball dropped two feet in front of Robinson as he lunged for it and missed for strike three.

A long rolling sound of ahs mixed with intermittent cheers soaked the stadium.

The cheers evaporated after the Dodgers scored four runs in the seventh.

"I'm thirsty. Let's get some pop," Eddy said.

This time, Hootie shrugged and made for the exits. They zigzagged through the crowd and made their way down the ramp and onto Sheffield. Back at the lot, Gerace leaned against the Packard. Eddy paid him his cut and then went inside the tavern to buy cigarettes.

It was crowded, but the usual loud chitter-chatter was restrained. Some patrons sat, and others stood, crammed together, watching the game. His dad had bought a Dumont Chatham television, nicknamed the Doghouse, because of its trapezoidal shape. The Doghouse was perched on a shelf, above the bar mirror. The player's uniforms glowed a fuzzy white, and the umpires looked like black bears. It was hard to see the ball on the twelve-inch screen. There were only a handful of channels the Doghouse would pick up, and sometimes there was interference that turned the sound into a blizzard of static. Ernie's Bleachers was the first bar in the neighborhood to have a television, and it was a hit.

"Eddy, come over here." It was Uncle Jimmy sitting at the booth with Kitty. Eddy walked over. "When you get back?"

Eddy studied Uncle Jimmy's haggard face. Fleshy pouches of skin sagged under his eyes like melted candlewax. He looked smaller, older and weak. When he talked from the side of his mouth his eyes narrowed as if he were angry. He never gave Eddy a kind word. Why was he even standing here talking to the washed-up bookie?

But Kitty was there, and she was nice, and what Bobby called "well endowed." "Got back yesterday," Eddy said. "Hello, Kitty, you're lookin' good."

"Aren't you a sweetheart. How come you don't say those nice things to me, Jimmy?" Kitty said.

"Ya wanna make some extra money, Eddy?" Uncle Jimmy said.

"Runnin' bets? Naw, I learned my lesson with that."

"Ahh, what between youse 'n' me is ancient history. I was just kiddin' around. I don't got your brudder working for me no more and now you? Wad am I gonna do?"

"I'm sure you'll figure it out."

Uncle Jimmy's eyes turned toward three Black men, standing at the corner of the bar near the door. "Who da dueces do dey dink dey are? Why'd your old man let dose jigs in here? Any ding for a buck, eh?"

Kitty nodded. "There are thousands of them roaming the park, and none of them came in here. Don't these guys know better?"

Eddy turned around to look at the men. They were set apart from everyone else, their eyes glued to the Doghouse.

"They're not bothering anyone," Eddy said.

"Are you gonna tell Ernie to make them leave?" Kitty asked Uncle Jimmy.

"Naw, it's not my place. Dey came here to watch dat Negro play. What's da big deal wid him. He don't seem so good to me. He struck out twice."

"I'll see ya around," Eddy said as he hustled to the bar to buy cigarettes from Dean Steiner, the head bartender.

"Eddy, good to see ya. All grown up. Look at you," Dean said, his bad eye rolling lazily into place. "What can I get ya?"

"A pack of Luckies," Eddy said, slapping down two quarters.

Steiner smiled and reached across the register for the pack and tossed them to Eddy. "Your old man's at the end of the bar. He's talkin' to the alderman. Why don't ya go and say hello."

Eddy nodded and strode to the end of the bar. His dad was all smiles, chomping on a cigar and yucking it up with the alderman he wanted to unseat.

"Eddy, come over here," Ernie said loud enough for everyone in the bar to hear. His dad reached up slightly and wrapped his arm around Eddy's shoulders. Eddy was taller than his dad now. Ernie turned to Alderman Frank Young, and said, "Eddy just graduated eighth grade."

"Is that right?" Young said. "Tell ya what: when you turn eighteen, I can arrange it where you work with your dad at the CTA."

"You gotta job, Dad?"

Ernie laughed and leaned in close. "It's nothin'. I go in the office once in a while, raise the flag, make coffee. And for that, I collect a weekly paycheck."

"Your father's one helluva deal maker," Frank Young said. "He's one smart dago."

Eddy smiled and nodded. "I gotta go, Dad. Got friends waitin' on me outside."

Ernie squeezed Eddy's shoulder. "You decided?"

Eddy held out hope that his parents would give him a third choice for school, Lakeview. But it wasn't the right time to talk about it. "Not yet."

"You have to decide by tonight. And don't be late for dinner."

"Okay." Eddy turned and walked toward the door. He glanced at the three Black men watching the game as he opened the door. One of them turned and smiled.

— — —

Eddy sat first at the dinner table. He clasped his hands in prayer and waited. The front door opened, and Nonno stepped inside. He squeezed Eddy's shoulder and sat next to him.

"You gettin' so big, Eddy. You bigger than your dad," Nonno said.

"And he's more handsome," Margaret said as she set a plate of eggplant parmesan on the table. She took a seat across from Eddy. Florence carried a pitcher of water and a bottle of Sandeman port wine from the kitchen and placed them next to the eggplant. She sat next to Margaret.

"Come to the table, Bobby," Margaret barked.

"Are we gonna eat without Dad?" said Bobby as he rose from the couch and walked to the table.

"He'll be here any minute," Margaret said.

Bobby sat and grabbed a slice of focaccia and stuffed his mouth.

"Bobby, wait for your father. You know we don't eat until your father sits down and we say the prayer," Margaret said.

"Did you wash your hands?" Eddy said.

"Yes, Eddy, I washed my hands," Bobby said, laughing and holding up his bony hands for everyone to see.

"Those fingernails don't look clean to me," Eddy said. "You're late to the table. You start eating before we say the prayer, and you didn't wash your hands." Eddy turned to his mom and said, "Looks like you're gonna have to send him to military school, Ma."

"Oh, don't be so silly," Margaret said.

The foyer door downstairs squeaked open and then banged closed. Eddy could always tell it was his dad coming up the steps by his heavy footfalls and the way the wood creaked. The front door swung open. Ernie walked inside, smiling. He put his hat on the lower peg of the coat rack like he always did and took a seat at the head of the table. "I'm hungry, Marge. Whaddya cook for me?"

"Eggplant and spaghetti. Ernie, you didn't wash your hands."

"I did, Marge, before I left the bar," Ernie said with a broad smile. And he held up his hands like Bobby had done. "Eddy, say the prayer."

Eddy bowed. "Dear God, thank you for this meat, good God—"

"That's enough of that Eddy," Margaret scolded. "I want to hear a proper prayer."

"Come on, Ma. We'll be here all night. He's just gonna goof off," Bobby said.

Eddy closed his eyes and bowed his head. "Bless us, oh Lord, for these your gifts which we are about to receive from your county. Through Christ our Lord and savior, we eat. Amen."

"It's *bounty*, not *county*," Florence said, laughing. "Geez-whiz, what did they teach you at that school?"

"I'll have you know we marched to church every Sunday. You ever march to church?"

Florence leaned forward, her elbows on the table, and said in an excited tone, "I have some news."

"You're pregnant?" Eddy said.

"Eddy, stop that kind of talk!" Margaret bellowed.

"I dropped out of DePaul."

There was a long silence.

Ernie's smile sunk into a frown. "You better get a job."

"I have a job," she said slowly, for effect. "I'm working for an insurance company. I'm the bookkeeper, and it's good pay."

"If that's what you want. You're an adult," Ernie said.

Eddy saw an opportunity. "Dad, let me drop out of school and get a full-time job. The alderman said he'd give me one. I can work with you."

"The hell you will," Margaret shrieked. "You're going to high school and that's that." Margaret's head swiveled in the direction of Ernie. "And what does Eddy mean the alderman offered him a job?"

"Aw Marge, I was gonna tell ya. Frank Young came into the tavern today and offered me a position with the city's new department that runs the buses and trains. I accepted."

"And who's gonna run the tavern? Me by myself? To hell with that."

"Nothing will change, Marge. I just go into the office for a couple of hours every week, and they pay me for full-time work."

Bobby snorted. "You're on the ghost payroll, aren't you, Dad? That's why you dropped out of the alderman race."

"He didn't drop out, Bobby. The Democrat Party challenged his petition in court, and the judges threw it out," Margaret said. "He didn't have enough valid signatures to qualify."

"That's right, Marge," Ernie said with a smile. "I could've fought it in court."

"It's a good thing you didn't," Marge said. "We don't have that kind of money to pay all them lawyers."

Ernie's elbows rested on the table, and he leaned forward. "I dropped out of the race, but I still won. All the things I ran on changed. The city's bus and train companies consolidated into the CTA, and the OPA offices are closing. Because I endorsed Frank Young, my voters voted for him, and he rewarded me with a job."

"What about crime and corruption? Did that change?" Bobby said.

Ernie laughed and said in a teasing tone, "This is Chicago. What do you think?"

"I think all politicians are crooks, and I was worried you might become one," Bobby said, ending his words with a snort.

Margaret sighed and then smiled. She reached across the table and gently stroked Eddy's cheek. "Look at you. You're about a half foot taller and thirty pounds heavier."

"Did you see Eddy's side of the room?" Bobby said. "He makes his bed every morning, hangs up his clothes, and puts his shoes together under his bed. He cleans up after himself. I don't even have to tell him to sweep under the bed."

"He's doing really good," Margaret said. "So have you decided which school you're going to?"

Eddy rubbed his hands. "I'd like to go to Lakeview, Ma."

"Well, you're not going to that public school. You're better than that," Margaret said in a stern tone.

"Eddy, Lt. Mulligan from Roosevelt called me today and offered half tuition if you'd go back there for high school," Ernie said. "The coaches want you to play football and basketball."

Eddy had made a lot of friends at Roosevelt. He was popular, even with some of the teachers and upperclassmen. But the idea of marching around all the time in uniform and carrying a wooden rifle was like eating stale bologna sandwiches, which he had done too many times at the military academy. On the other hand, an all-boy's Catholic School wasn't a bed of roses. "I dunno, Dad."

"They've got a good football team at St. George," Bobby said. "You'd be a lock to make the team. I'll show ya around and introduce you to anyone who matters."

Eddy shrugged. The idea of going to the same school as his older and smarter brother didn't sell him.

"Oh, by the way, I got into an argument with Brother Thomas today," Bobby said, chewing with his mouth open. "He says, 'God exists but is invisible because he's pure light.' I said, 'What are ya talking about it?' He says, 'Light is invisible in all spectrums: radio waves, gamma rays, X-rays.' He says, if we could see all light wavelengths at the same time, that we wouldn't see anything. I told him I don't believe in light I can't see on faith. I believe in light I can't see based on scientific evidence. I told him, 'Show me scientific evidence of God, and then we can talk.' Should've seen his reaction. He got quiet real quick."

Nonno banged on the table. "Whaddya mean, there ain't no God?"

"Oh, Bobby, don't start trouble at that school," Margaret said.

"That's what school is for: debate, think, argue," Bobby said.

Eddy remembered how a tiny bug crawling around a flashlight put the fear of God in him and Elmore. *Maybe Roosevelt or St. George are not a big deal after all.*

Margaret sipped her wine. She set the wineglass on the table and said, "Life's been really good in the past two years. We made enough to buy a Studebaker, this building, and the tavern."

"And I give you a good deal," Nonno said in a gruff tone.

Margaret's face tightened. She exhaled and took another sip.

"There were a couple of coloreds in your bar, today, Dad," Eddy said. "I could tell some people didn't like that."

"They followed Clarence in," Ernie said. "I'm surprised more didn't come in. We didn't have any problems. They drank pop and watched the television and left."

"I never seen so many coloreds," Bobby said. "The Cubs are gonna play Brooklyn again. Be careful, Dad. Some of the regulars might go somewhere else."

"The only color I care about is money," Ernie replied. "What was that player's name?"

"Jackie Robinson," Eddy said. "He didn't do much today, but he came off a fourteen-game hitting streak. A lot of those Negro players are good. I've seen them play. I think the Cubs will follow suit and sign some of those players."

Ernie tapped his fingers on the table. "I don't know if people around here are ready for that."

"They'll get over it. Fans will root for the Cubs no matter who plays for them as long as they're good," Bobby said. "Once a Cubs fan, always a Cubs fan. A player can have green skin and be from Mars, and it won't matter as long as he's good."

"I dunno. You could be right. If it brings in more fans, maybe the owners will sign some of them," Ernie said. "Wrigley made a fortune today."

"I think they will," Bobby said. "Baseball teams are like family, you care for them. You want them to win because they're part of you. A lot of people can't remember most of the players on the Cubs twenty or thirty years ago. But they remember if the Cubs had a good team."

"I think your father's been a Cubs fan ever since I can remember," Margaret said.

"Since nineteen eighteen," Ernie said. "They were in the World Series against the Red Sox. They switched the home games to Comiskey because there were more seats."

Ernie took a sip of wine, twirled his glass and said, "I remember they played all the World Series games in September."

"Why?" Eddy wondered.

"War was on," Ernie said. "I remember that's when they first played 'The Star-Spangled Banner.'" Ernie leaned forward and pointed his finger at Bobby. "Did ya know Babe Ruth pitched a shutout in the first game of that series? The Red Sox won it four games to two. Nobody homered in six games."

"Holy crap! They had Babe Ruth and no home runs? What are the odds of that?" Eddy said.

Margaret straightened. "Gee-whiz, Ernie. Do you know how many World Series we watched the Cubs lose? The year Bobby was born, they lost. Then the year Eddy was born, they lost. You'd think they'd win one of them."

"Yeah, Ma, and you're still a Cubs fan," Bobby said. "You don't care who plays for the Cubs as long as they're a good team. The owners know that, and I betcha they'll start signing the good Negro players."

"Just imagine, Ernie, if you were alderman right now, and you let them in the tavern," Margaret said. "All the trouble you'd get. Aye yie yie."

"We had worse troubles," Ernie said. "Remember those two gangsters?"

"Yes, I do. And you went right along with them. You did what they wanted you to do," Margaret said, her voice raised.

"You screamed and threw a fit when I said I was gonna run for alderman. Fought me like Jake LaMotta with his gloves off. Then you turn around and tell those hoodlums I was gonna run for alderman."

"Oh, cut the crap, Ernie. I said no such thing."

"Yes, you did as sure as I'm sitting here. You told them I wasn't going to drop out," Ernie said.

"What gangsters?" Bobby asked.

"Never mind, Bobby. Everybody's happy," Margaret said. "That's all that matters. The pursuit of happiness. Right?"

"Are you sure, Marge? I think deep down you're disappointed I dropped out. You said you'd do everything you could to get me elected. Did you forget that?" Ernie said.

"I did no such thing."

"Oh yes, you did when you mouthed off to those gangsters who came in the tavern."

"Why do you keep bringing that up!" Margaret yelled. She threw her fork across the table. It landed in the middle of the front room floor.

"Calm down, Marge," Ernie said in a warm pleasing tone.

Eddy scooched off his chair and went to pick up the fork. He placed it on the table and sat down.

"Eddy, have you made up your mind?" Ernie asked.

"I just got back. Can't it wait?"

"No. We have to know now in order to register you," Margaret said. "These are good schools. Everybody wants to get in. They're not going to wait around for *you* to decide."

Eddy looked out the living room window and stared at the brick wall of Wrigley Field. He must have thrown a ball against that wall a million times, and it always bounced back. But he didn't want to do it anymore. He wasn't sure what he wanted. That much he knew. He tried running away and living on his own but that didn't work out. He had gone where Jesus left his sandals.

He could pick Roosevelt where colonels and sergeants every day would shout out commands, ordering him what to eat and wear and when to march. Or St. George High School where, no doubt, brothers, priests, his parents, and every adult were going to tell him what to do. Eddy twirled his spaghetti, and came to accept the fact that there were always rules wherever you go.

There's nothing you can do about it. You just got to stay within the basepath when you run around the sacks and hope you can make it back home.

It's as simple as a bat and ball.

EPILOGUE

Eddy field stripped his cigarette and shoved the filter into his pocket. He swaggered inside Murphy's Bleachers and bent down to kiss his mother, who sat at a long table.

"Hey, Ma, want something to eat?"

"I'll have a beer."

"You're too young to drink," Eddy said with an impish smile.

"I'm ninety-five years old, kiddo. I think I've earned it."

"Ma, you sure you're not hungry?" Florence asked. "I can read you the menu."

"She said she's not hungry," Bobby said. "Eddy, get me a Manhattan on the rocks while you're up there."

"Oh, did you break your legs, Bobby? Flo, you want anything?" Eddy asked.

"Let the waitress take our order," Florence said.

"I don't wanna wait." Eddy bounced across the tavern and mounted his old bones on a stool. He leaned against the bar counter and shouted, "Hey, kid! Two Miller Lites and a Manhattan, rocks."

While he waited, Eddy stared at himself in the mirror on the back bar. His face sported a golden tan from the countless hours on the golf course. His gray hair was slicked back with gel, his eyes playful and a faint smile spread across his wrinkled mouth. He could see his father now staring back at him in the mirror, ready with a smile and a wisecrack. It was almost a decade ago that his father, old and frail on his death bed, smiled and shook Eddy's hand, father to son, man to man.

Ernie did all right for someone with a sixth-grade education, Eddy thought. He wished his father was around to see some of the things he had built were still there and that the tavern had become a local legend.

Much had changed, but much was the same.

The beveled-inset mirror he'd helped his dad hang was there. The old oak mahogany canopy with carved panels and columns was original. The ancient cash register that sounded like a typewriter with sleigh bells every time it was opened was still there but not in use. The carryout window, his mother's idea, remained.

A flat-screen TV beamed high on a wall, the same location the bar's first TV, the Doghouse, had been. Three other TVs were mounted around the bar. The grill in the corner where he had shed so much sweat was gone.

The new owners had expanded the tavern beyond what had once been the family's back porch and most of the lot where he used to jockey Packards and take joyrides in DeSotos.

The bartender, dressed in a purple Polo shirt and tan Khakis, set the drinks on the bar. He looked as if he had just turned twenty-one. "On the house, sir. Your family is royalty here."

"Thanks. You sure that's okay with the boss?" Eddy remembered how his dad would fire bartenders for giving away free drinks.

"Yep, orders from the boss. She said your family started this place."

"That's right. It was first a hot dog stand. My folks saved enough money and built the tavern in nineteen forty." Eddy swiveled around and pointed at Margaret. "The lady with the snow-white hair is my ma. They were married for sixty-seven years. Sixty-seven years. That's a long time, partner."

"Yep, sure is. Who are the other two?"

"My brother. He's a big shot businessman. And my sister. She's a school librarian at Gordon Tech."

The bartender nodded and wiped the counter.

"You know, I grew up next door. Your cook's slingin' hash browns right now where I used to sleep. Can you believe it?" Eddy said.

The bartender laughed. "Where'd ya go to school?"

Eddy drummed his fingers on the bar. He thought about Roosevelt. "They sent me to St. George in Evanston, but that didn't work out. So I went to Lakeview." Eddy glanced around. "So many memories. You know, I ran this place in the early sixties, but the neighborhood went to hell. We got burglarized about every month. The Cubs were terrible and drew about five thousand every game. You could count the fans coming out of that stadium." Eddy gazed out the window. He remembered better times, hopping the turnstiles, Jackie Robinson, driving a stagecoach down Lake Shore Drive and when he'd ridden Sid the bull.

"Cubs are drawing pretty good now," the bartender said.

"It's ridiculous. Everything's commercialized. Rooftop stands, cable games, sky boxes for CEO's and VIPS. It ain't a pastime. It's a racket. And the ball players make millions."

"I hear ya."

"You know, I traveled around Europe playing ball for the army in the early fifties. There were a few pro players in the league. Nobody you heard of." But Eddy needed to be sure. He wanted somebody to know. "Ever hear of Bob Hootie Hale?"

The bartender shook his head.

"He made it to the majors. Played for the Orioles, Indians, and Yankees. He grew up in this neighborhood. We played softball together."

"Is that right?"

"Yeah, but when they sent him down to the minors, he quit and became a school principal. Ball players didn't make the kind of money they make now, not even close."

"What did ya do after the tavern was sold?"

"I worked in Vegas as a pit boss. Mostly at the Bellagio and Golden Nugget. Did ya know the FBI blacklisted me in nineteen seventy-four cuz they thought I was involved with Tony Spilotro."

The bartender leaned forward. "Involved how?"

"You know, mobbed up." Eddy crooked his nose to one side with his finger and winked. "We're both Italian and from Chicago. We went to Vegas the same time. You ever hear of Tony Spilotro?"

The bartender shook his head.

"The Spilotro brothers? Tony? The Hole-in-the-Wall Gang? He and his brother were buried alive in a cornfield?"

The bartender shot a blank stare.

"Anyway, they thought I was an associate of his, and I couldn't work for a whole year."

"Hey, Eddy, get his phone number if you wanna date, and bring us our drinks," Bobby yelled.

Eddy thanked the bartender and tossed a twenty on the bar. He walked to the corner of the bar next to the front door and swung his head under the drip edge. There they were—the initials *EP* that he had carved when he was a child. He strolled back to the table with the drinks, and a smile on his face.

The Paretis talked and reminisced for about an hour. Then Eddy got the Cadillac, drove it to the front of the tavern, and waited. Bobby helped Margaret into the backseat and Florence sat in the back with her and held her hand. Bobby slid into the passenger seat. They sat in silence as Eddy drove north, beyond the shadows of skyscrapers, crowded apartment buildings and the El, and into the sprawling suburbs.

The wide-open spaces.

AUTHOR'S NOTE

After my father passed in 2014, we sifted through his belongings. I found a garbage bag filled with letters he'd written to his family during his time as a cadet at Roosevelt Military School in 1945 and 1946. I read them all and found that over time a very colorful and precocious boy had become a man.

The first batch of letters were filled with despair, a longing for home. But, gradually, the tone of the letters showed a grudging acceptance. His grades improved, and he was thriving in the school's sports programs. Incidentally, the letters in this book are authentic. I had always wondered why he was sent to military school. According to my relatives, he had failed seventh grade and played hooky in summer school. All he seemed interested in was playing softball at the schoolyard or sneaking into Wrigley Field, located across the street from the family bar, which my dad tended before he was old enough to get drafted.

When he learned his parents enrolled him in military school, he ran away with a friend to rural Michigan. He told me he lived in a tent in the backyard of his friend's grandmother's shanty. Soon, he'd run out of money, and his belly stretched empty like many other kings of the road back in the day. In the meantime, the Cubs made it to the World Series, and a pair of bombs nicknamed Fat Man and Little Boy ended World War II.

I'd heard stories from family about the characters that drank and gambled at Ernie's Bleachers, my grandparent's tavern: There was Cub's outfielder Lou Novikoff, known for an eccentric, larger than life personality. There were old school La Cosa Nostra. Everyone from bank robbers like John Dillinger to weaselly small-time bookies, from rodeo riders to and an African-American gas station mechanic known for wearing a trench coat and a cowboy hat, rubbed elbows in the tavern. My dad watched Jackie Robinson make his major league debut. He spoke fondly of kids he grew up with like Bob Hootie Hale who made it to the majors. He was best friends with Phil Gerace and Chuckie Warman, who would later become one of the most feared street fighters on Chicago's north side.

My father was a batboy for teams in the old Negro leagues. He ran numbers for bookies. He perfected a turnstile vault to get into Wrigley for games that made history. Or he'd simply walk in during practices for the Cubs, or the Bears. Cubs Manager Charlie Grimm and a few Cubs players were familiar faces in the tavern, drinking and playing five cent poker. Even Joltin' Joe DiMaggio didn't escape my father's gaze at a game. My dad was the kinda kid, though afraid of heights, who fell off a building in an attempt to sneak into a Jake LaMotta fight. He stood in pain while his mother argued with a cop about which hospital to send him to.

I sensed there was a story here. I spent countless hours combing though microfiche of local newspapers in order to get a better understanding of the times. Names of neighborhood soldiers killed in the war filled the pages of those newspapers.

In this work of historical fiction which brings in World War II, the Cubs voyage to the World Series, the beginnings of the integration of professional sports, the Mob, and Chicago politics, you'll read the poignant tale of Walter Lockerbie, a neighborhood "big brother" to my father who died in the war. The poem read by the war widow in this story was published in one of the local papers.

We read so much about ball players and baseball stadiums, but they've become impersonal corporations. Wrigley Field was like home, and this story is about one extended Italian family who ran a hot dog stand and then a tavern right across the street. It was called Ernie's Bleachers, and it eventually became Murphy's Bleachers, a famous bar that still stands today. Back then, Wrigleyville was truly a neighborhood where a local working stiff could meet in a corner tavern after a hard day's work. Where the crack of the bat and the roar of the crowd was and still is heard from blocks away.

Writing a work of historical fiction was the second hardest but most rewarding task I've ever set my purpose on (after having kids), and I learned so much in the process.

I'd like to thank my friend and fellow author, Mike Just, for providing incisive advice during the three years I pecked away on the computer. His fingerprints are all over the story.

A special thanks goes to the Wilmette Writer's Group for invaluable feedback on each chapter as I wrote them. Much gratitude also goes to Beth and Jim Murphy, owner of Murphy's Bleachers. The Murphy's have been gracious to the Pareti family over the years.

And none of this would have been possible without the patience and support from my wife, Donna, and two teenaged kids, George and Ella. They stood by me as I grumbled and griped and banged on the keyboard (the white letters on the keypads have disappeared).

Thanks goes to my aunt Florence, a character in the book, for her insights, understanding and support.

Finally, much love goes out to my grandparents, Ernie and Margaret, my dad and uncles, Bob and Emil, loyal Cub fans who did not live to see the Cubs finally win the World Series in the twenty-first century. But they lived colorful and meaningful lives that I believe hold greater weight than any world championship.

I hope you enjoyed these pages over which I've sweated and stewed.

If you ever get a chance, go to a game at Wrigley and see the sailboats on the lake, and the left and right field ivy waving like thousands of green flags in the warm breeze. If you listen hard enough, you might hear a boy about thirteen cheering for the home team he loved so much.